Praise for T

'*No one can mix a deliciously classy cocktail of intrigue, passion and glamour like Tasmina Perry.*' – Hello

'*Gripping from the off: sexy, scandalous brilliance, this book is a genuine must-read* *****' – Heat

'*Takes you to the most glamorous corners of the globe while keeping you on the edge of your seat*' – Glamour

'*A gripping, pacy read with a few dark twists I did not see coming. The perfect end-of-summer novel*' – Daily Mail

'*Excellent . . . A dark and devious thriller but with all the glamour you'd expect from Tasmina*' – Red

About The Author

Tasmina Perry is a *Sunday Times* bestselling novelist. Her books have been translated into twenty languages and have sold over two million copies worldwide.

A former lawyer and award-winning magazine journalist, she has edited several national titles, including InStyle UK and More.

She also writes psychological thrillers under the pseudonym JL Butler. JL Butler's debut thriller 'Mine' has been optioned by Sony Pictures for development with Original Film.

Tasmina is the founder of Sunflower & Co, a female-focused media company. The team plots escapist stories and creates content from their boathouse office by the River Thames.

This edition published by Sunflower & Co 2025

www.sunflowerandco.com

978-1-911297-55-0

* * *

If you'd like to be kept up to date with all the new releases from Tasmina Perry, why not join my VIP Book Club for news on books, giveaways, events and other book recommendations: www.tasminaperry.com/joinbookclub

* * *

This edition of The Malibu House is 'print on demand', meaning that only the books ordered will be produced, thus saving on paper and manufacturing and reducing waste. This book is also part of The Sunflower Seed Project. For every print book sold, Sunflower & Co will plant a tree in a part of the world with high levels of poverty, to restore the forests and create employment opportunities. The sale of this book means that a tree has been planted in Haiti.

The Malibu House

Tasmina Perry

Chapter 1

From the air, LA was dazzling. An endless plain of white roofs reflecting the relentless sun, ten thousand polished cars on a diamond-bright freeway streaming below the listing Hollywood sign. And as the aeroplane sank lower, Lara Stone could see the brighter sparkle of commerce: nail bars, bottomless cocktails and 24/7 valet services, all framed by palm trees and the glistening ocean far beyond. From her window seat, the City of Angels was mesmerising, but the moment the wheels scorched the runway, Lara was already moving, unclipping her seatbelt and shouldering her carry-on, a seasoned explorer ready for the concrete jungle.

LAX did feel like a forest, constantly alive, a tangle of legs and cases and beeping vehicles, the chatter and shouts in foreign tongues. As an investigative reporter, Lara Stone was used to being on the move, weaving through the vines and dodging the snakes – and normally, that was how Los Angeles felt to Lara, especially the airport: claustrophobic and hostile, all queues and questions. But today, she was excited. Today, she was here to see her boyfriend Alex. *Her boyfriend*; how strange that still sounded. For so long, Alex Ford had just been her friend and colleague. Handsome and funny, of course, but romance? No. Until six months before, when Lara had taken a visiting lecturer post at an Ivy College, and Alex had come out to see her.

Lara grinned to herself. *The best 'yes' I ever said.*

But it was just Lara's romantic luck that the moment they found each other, Alex was offered the editor-in-chief's job at the LA Globe. It was the job of his dreams, and who was she to stand in the way of that?

And now, here she was, not on a flying visit, like their previous snatched weekends, but a two-week *vay-cay* to spend quality time together. But first, Lara had to collect her case. She joined the stream of humanity following the signs for the baggage claim hall. This was an alien environment for Lara; she didn't usually check anything. As a reporter, Lara had perfected the art of travelling light – laptop, toothbrush, a change of clothes. But this was different, so she'd brought a bikini and an assortment of dresses– yes, she even had shoes, not just sneakers. Alex had also pestered her for Marmite and Jaffa Cakes, so Lara was standing by the baggage carousel, watching black cases drop onto the conveyor belt. She was wondering how people could tell one black case from another when her phone buzzed in her pocket.

'Hey, I've arrived,' she said with a smile.

'Glad to hear it, Darling!'

Darling? Alex was from Cumbria; 'darling' wasn't in his vocabulary.

Lara glanced at her phone screen. *Darius*. Her heart sank; it was too late to send the call to voicemail now. Darius was the flamboyant editor of the London Chronicle, where Lara worked as their investigative reporter-at-large. Darius was not a traditional newspaperman; he was a political animal, a sharp operator primarily focused on the bottom line. So, getting a phone call from Darius was never good news.

'Darius. How can I help?' Lara asked, as brightly as she could.

'I've been thinking,' he replied, 'We need to increase the paper's celebrity content.'

'Okay, said Lara. 'And you're telling me this why?'

'Because you're in Hollywood, Lara,' said Darius, as if it were obvious. 'And I had a brainwave: who better than the great Lara Stone to dig out a world-class scoop from the cesspit of La-La-Land?'

'You do know I'm on holiday, don't you?'

'Lara Darling,' he said. 'Reporters are *never* on holiday. So put on your party shoes and go out and find me some celebrity exclusives. Big ones. Tom Cruise shows you around his plane; Brad Pitt gives you a massage - that sort of thing.'

'I'm not sure Alex would be that pleased about the massage thing, Darius.'

Her boss snorted dismissively. 'I'm sure even Alex would give you a pass for Brad. Anyway, you get the idea: glitter, glamour – scandal!'

She fought down the urge to give him a piece of her mind. This was not the kind of thing she did. Tracking down crime lords or exposing high-level corruption at a government level - that was Lara Stone. Sharing a jacuzzi with the latest Spider-Man?

'Not really my kind of thing, Darius.'

'True, but the world is changing. If the readers want celebrity fluff, we have to give them celebrity fluff. All done in an intelligent and incisive Lara Stone way, obviously. Besides, it's has been quite a while since you came up with any of those world-shattering crime scoops, hasn't it?'

There was a pause. A pause Lara did not like.

'Not that I mind paying your retainer, and I understand how disruptive a long-distance relationship can be, but even so…'

But even so, do as you're told. Lara took a deep breath, squeezing her fingers around her phone, resisting the urge to smash it against the edge of the carousel.

Lara Stone wasn't short of money. Her uncle owned *The Chronicle*, and a series of trust funds meant she never needed to work. But that wasn't Lara's style. Journalism was her lifeblood, and she adored her job as an investigative reporter with the freedom to chase down stories, important stories that held people to account, not sensationalist fluff.

'Fine,' she said through gritted teeth. Her uncle might be the proprietor of the paper, but Darius was still her boss, and it would be just like Darius to terminate her contract just to prove the point.

'I'll keep my eyes open,' said Lara, 'And if I spot Serena Balcon smoking crack, you'll be the first to know.'

'Splendid, I knew you wouldn't let me down. Pip pip.'

And he was gone, just as Lara's silver suitcase thunked down in front of her.

'Dammit,' she muttered, wrestling it onto a trolley. Was this what she was reduced to? Recycling press releases and doing puff pieces designed to increase the box office of the latest superhero movie?

Cool your boots, she thought, steering the trolley towards customs.

Much as she hated to admit it, Darius had a point. Scoops won awards, and they kept newspapers relevant, but nobody bought a newspaper specifically for a Lara Stone expose. And such was the speed of international media that, even if she broke an exclusive story in the Chronicle, by the end of the day, every news outlet in the world would be recycling it as if it were their own. So she could see why

Darius and his paymasters were reluctant to invest in investigations when the readers were online gaping at cute cats and vacuous influencers. The truth was Lara Stone was an anachronism, and her deeply held conviction that a free press was vital to the effective functioning of a democracy was, well, just old-fashioned. God, *I need a holiday,* she thought as she pushed the trolley through the customs hall, hoping against hope that she would not get pulled over and have to explain Marmite to the stony-faced border agents.

Or maybe I just need a new career.

Lara had, of course, considered following Alex out here to LA. Even when they were 'just friends,' Lara and Alex had been inseparable. They had studied together at their post-graduate journalism college, both landing junior jobs on The Chronicle and coming up through a fast-moving newsroom. Alex had graduated to news editor via stints in the US and Far East bureaus, finally ascending to deputy editor, while Lara had won awards – and industry respect - for her world-class investigations.

But recently, the world of the media had changed radically. People absorbed news—if at all—through fast clips scrolling past their eyes in a small window. Lara doubted anyone younger than 25 had ever felt newsprint under their fingers.

It was one reason Alex had been so excited to take the editorship of the LA Globe. The paper's owner, Simon Desai, had given Alex carte blanche to change it, update it and make it as relevant as possible. Darius was clearly thinking along the same lines, so perhaps it was time for Lara to join them. Was there any point in clinging to your principles if no one was listening?

'Excuse me,' she muttered, sidestepping an overzealous tourist snapping selfies with his phone, but as she approached the arrival area, Lara's heart skipped a beat.

Alex Ford was waiting for her, a smile lighting up his handsome face.

'Hey,' he said, and she fell into his arms, squeezing and holding on.

'I've missed you,' she said into his shoulder. Alex had always been a rock on whom she could rely. Even as best friends, he was the person that she had always wanted to tell things first, and since they had got together, that feeling had only intensified; Lara realised how much she had felt lost without him over the past months.

'Missed you too,' said Alex, before fixing her with a mischievous grin. 'But you did bring the Frazzles, right?'

She swiped a playful swat at his shoulder. 'I thought you wanted Monster Munch.'

His face fell, and she snorted.

'Not a joking matter,' he said, taking her case and heading for the exit. 'Come on,' he said. 'I've got a surprise for you.'

'What is it?'

'It wouldn't be a surprise if I told you, would it?'

Chatting about flights and traffic, they quickly navigated through the tangle of high-rise parking, and then Alex stopped by a red convertible. Lara gave it a double-take.

'Wait. This is *yours*?'

'When in Rome...' he smiled. 'I did think about wearing a Hawaiian shirt for you, but I thought you might walk past me.'

'I've always liked the Magnum PI look. Maybe you could grow a moustache too?'

'If you say so,' grinned Alex, throwing her case in the back.

They drove out onto the freeway, Lara enjoying the rush of the warm air through her hair and the brush of sun on her skin. Back in London, spring had been trying to push through, but down on the Thames, where Lara lived on a Chelsea Harbour houseboat, it was more often drizzle and grey clouds. A giant fire truck ploughed past them in a flash of red and Lara laughed to herself; even after all these years working jobs in overseas locations, Lara still felt a rush of energy from arriving somewhere new. And she relished the idea of spending two weeks here really exploring; perhaps they could drive up the coast to visit the Bay Area - she had always wanted to see Carmel, Big Sur and Monterey. Steinbeck had been a lightning rod for Lara when she had been at university.

'So, how's the supplement coming along?'

'Slow.'

The moment Alex started at the LA Globe, he made a bold declaration: Los Angeles was a movie town, so its premier newspaper should reflect that. His flagship project was Limelight, a glossy 48-page Saturday supplement meant to rival the big trade papers of Variety and the Hollywood Reporter. It was due to launch at the end of the following week.

'I think I've finally got the advertising team on side, which is half the battle,' said Alex, with a sigh. 'But who knows? It's still down to whether the public buys into it. Sales of the paper were up last week– the changes we've made to the business pages have been popular, but we need to gauge what industry people think of Limelight.'

The Globe had planned a splashy party to present the magazine to players in the movie and TV worlds, and the demands of overseeing both the marketing and the editorial of Limelight alongside the main paper meant Alex had been working flat out.

'I know it's tough,' she said. 'So if you have to work late every night, I will totally understand.'

'You don't mind?'

'Mind? Alex, this is your big chance. I want you to

show the world how amazing you are. Besides, this is LA: I'm sure I can occupy myself. And I already know my way around Echo Park.' Alex had a beautiful duplex apartment in the hip LA enclave near the Globe's Downtown offices.

'On that subject,' said Alex with a smile, turning the wheel and taking an unfamiliar exit. Lara looked around, twisting in her seat.

'Where are we going?' Lara asked.

'I told you. I've got a surprise.'

'Are we checking in somewhere for a dirty weekend? Because FYI, it's a Sunday, which doesn't leave us much time...'

'Just sit back and enjoy the ride.'

Lara did as she was told, imagining herself as a character in a Kerouac novel, one hand waving in the slipstream, no particular place to be, just a crazy beatnik following her muse. Maybe it wasn't just a fantasy; maybe this was her future. Maybe it was time Lara Stone took her foot off the gas. Certainly, she wished Alex could join her. Even at the airport, she'd noticed how tired he was looking. Alex needed some serious R & R. Even in all this sunshine, his skin was pale, and Lara suspected he was spending far too much time in an air-conditioned bunker of an office. Newspapers were stressful environments at the best of times, but revamps and relaunches put the whole team under pressure, and right now he was being asked to compete with the immediacy and glitter of the Internet. It was an impossible task, yet Lara knew Alex Ford would try his best, even if it killed him.

She reached over to touch his knee, but suddenly, the windscreen was filled with sparkling blue.

'The ocean!' she cried, sitting up to drink in the sight of surfers, sunbathers, and swimmers silhouetted against a tan stripe of sand.

Alex glanced across, grinning. 'What's the point in

coming to the West Coast if you never see the sea? Especially when you love the water.'

Alex knew her so well. While Alex's new place was a practical choice that cut his commute to the bone, she yearned for the sea.

But where is he taking me? Lara wondered as they drove through Venice Beach towards the pier.

'Not Shutters then,' she said, as they sailed past Santa Monica's iconic white hotel out on the sand.

'Even better,' said Alex, driving down onto the Pacific Coast Highway.

Lara stopped trying to guess and just let herself enjoy the sight of the endless sea and the seagulls wheeling above. The bridge of her nose felt hot from the sun – already, she felt as if she was deep into her holiday.

'Nearly there,' said Alex, looking at the GPS on the dashboard. A sign reading 'Malibu City Limits' flashed past. To the right, the land rose to sun-scorched hills, while to the left was a long line of buildings squashed between road and sea, with barely a gap between them.

No great surprise, she supposed, given every square foot of real estate out here would be worth thousands of dollars each. Who wouldn't want this as their daily view?

'Hold on,' said Alex, as he clicked the indicator, steering the car off the highway into a narrow side road, pulling up next to a covered carport. Jumping out, he ran around and opened Lara's door.

'Alex, where are we?' Lara laughed, taking his hand.

'You'll see,' he said, trotting up a flight of steps to tap a code into an access panel. There was a low click, and a door opened. Lara followed him inside.

'O…M…G!' she gasped. The plain wood and brick box facing the highway had suggested a modest structure, but Lara could now see that was deliberate misdirection. The raised first floor was open plan, giving a perfect view through the floor-to-ceiling windows and onto the beach. It was a genuine Malibu beach house straight from a movie set.

'This place is incredible,' Lara whispered, eyes wide. It was furnished in a minimalist style, but Lara immediately saw an expert decorator had been at work; everything fit together perfectly. There was a vaguely Japanese theme, but it was sparingly used, letting the space breathe - and everything faced towards the sea, even the built-in slate-topped kitchen. It was smart; why wouldn't you make the most of the star of the show? Lara practically ran to the sliding doors and stepped out onto a private balcony with, yes, a little pool and a set of steps straight down onto the sand.

'Alex, it's just…wow! But why are we here?'

'Because it's home,' Alex laughed. 'For the next two weeks at least. It belongs to Simon.'

'Simon, your boss, Simon?'

He nodded.

'It's his car too. Simon has properties all over the world, and this is just one of them. So when he heard that you were coming over, he insisted we use it for the duration.'

'Now that's what I call an employee perk.'

'Well, Simon gets his pound of flesh from me,' said Alex. 'But it was bloody nice of him to offer. All he asked was that we water the plants.'

'Oh, I think I might be able to manage that.' Lara went from room to room, her excitement growing; each was more tastefully done than the next, with lots of cream and taupe furnishings and expensive-looking art on the walls.

Two bathrooms, a wet room and three bedrooms: one with a giant bed looking straight out onto the beach, the glittering ocean so close she could almost touch it.

'Alex, it's perfect!'

'Good, because I want you to have an amazing time,' said Alex, rummaging in the fridge and coming out with a bottle of champagne. 'I wish I could spend every minute with you, but with the launch, it will be sticky. I just hope this place will make up for the absence of my sparkling company.'

'I think that's a small price to pay,' she grinned, throwing her arms around his neck. 'Alex, this is amazing! Thank you so much.'

'Well, thank Simon,' he said, popping the champagne and pouring two flutes.

'To Simon,' said Lara, clinking her glass against his.

'To Malibu,' said Alex as he put his flute down, scooping his girlfriend up into his arms. Giggling, Lara let him carry her into the bedroom with the ocean view.

Chapter 2

Lara woke to the sound of the ocean.

Swoosh…pause… ahhh

Swoosh…pause… ahhh

It sounded like a dozing giant, breathing in and out, which Lara supposed it was. Opening one eye, she saw a chink of light between the curtains. A bright blue sky shouldn't be so exciting, but when you had spent the winter in overcast London, it felt like Dorothy waking up in Oz. Smiling to herself, Lara stretched lazily, listening to the waves. When she and Alex finally went to sleep – Lara's recollection was of a blissful tangle of limbs, skin, lips, and heat – the sea had been near-silent, the beach ghostly white in the moonlight beyond the balcony. But now, the water had crept closer, and the hiss of the Pacific felt familiar, like the river lapping against the sides of her houseboat on the Thames.

This is wonderful, she thought, sliding a hand towards Alex, but the other side of the bed was empty. She grabbed her watch; it was still early—a little after 6 a.m. Then she heard the clink of a knife against a plate.

Lara wrapped the sheet around herself and padded

down the hallway, following the aroma of fresh baking. Alex stood in the kitchen, looking crisp in a dark grey suit.

'I didn't mean to wake you,' he said, crossing to kiss her. 'But I've made breakfast.'

'Really?'

'Well, I heated some croissants Simon's housekeeper left for us. Want some?'

'God, yes,' she said, sliding onto a stool at the breakfast bar. 'Otherwise, I think I'll slip into a coma.'

'Feeling jet-lagged?' he asked sympathetically.

'My body clock's always thrown off when I fly east-to-west, but at least this time around, I'll have plenty of time to readjust,' she said.

She watched Alex work the dials and levers of the coffee machine; she loved to watch him move. Alex was wearing his customary work uniform of a tailored suit and open-necked white shirt – almost ready for the catwalk - and Lara felt another stab of desire rush through her. It was still a strange, almost forbidden sensation. For so long, she and Alex had been close friends – and when they became lovers, it had been wonderful, hot and unfettered, better than she had ever hoped; they fit together perfectly. But she still hadn't quite adjusted; she saw him new every time.

'Do you really have to go to work right now?' she said.

Alex grinned.

'Get thee behind me, Satan,' he said, bending over the counter and kissing her neck. She made a grab for the front of his shirt, but he managed to dance away.

'I've got a conference at 8AM.'

'Eight? That's two hours away.'

Alex groaned. 'I know, but I've got to get halfway across Los Angeles. I've never done Malibu to Downtown in rush hour traffic, and I'm not even sure I'll make it off the freeway in time.'

He looked at his watch and swore.

'I'm so sorry, I've got to go.'

He pulled a set of keys from his pocket and slid them across the slate top towards her.

'Keys to the car? Don't you need them?'

He raised his eyebrows.

'I have a driver.'

He'd mentioned that a personal driver was one of the job's perks, but Alex hadn't used it so far, insisting that a cab from Echo Park was quicker and easier on the Globe budget.

'I'm just using it whilst we're in Malibu; he's called Jake. He's like an extra from Goodfellas.'

'Get you, Mr Flash,' she said, laughing.

'Well, I thought it would make sense if you kept the convertible for the duration. I mean, I don't want you to feel as though you're stuck on this beautiful beach in this beautiful house...'

'That would be terrible, wouldn't it?'

Alex lingered by the door. 'Seriously though, I am sorry I have to go in today,' he said, but Lara waved it away.

'Alex, I knew that was the deal. I don't expect you to drop everything just because I've come to LA. Besides,' she gestured towards the picture window. 'I'm in Malibu. I'm going to channel my inner celebrity and hang out on the beach all day. Why don't I meet you at the office later? I want to see the Hauser and Wirth gallery; that's not too far from your office. And I'm sure there's somewhere close by we can have dinner?'

'Sure, that sounds great... Oh, damn it!' he said, palming his forehead. 'It's the deputy editor's birthday. There's a drinks thing: do you mind if we pop in first?'

Lara smiled.

'I'd love to,' she said.

Although Lara had been to LA three times since Alex

had relocated, he'd always managed to wrangle a few days off, so while Lara had heard all about the characters in the office, she'd never met his workmates properly. He came back across and put his arms around her, kissing her softly on the lips.

'I'm glad you're here.'

She wound herself around him, letting the sheet drop. Alex grinned through the kiss. 'You do know anyone on the beach can see straight in through the windows?' he whispered.

Lara gasped, scrabbling to cover herself, which gave Alex time to back away, chuckling. 'There's plenty of time for all that later,' he said.

'There had better be.'

* * *

After a long, lazy soak in the free-standing bath, Lara popped her case and chose a red cotton maxi dress. She wasn't usually a dress kind of girl – jeans and a white t-shirt were her usual style - but then she wasn't usually a Malibu beach kind of girl either. This was a chance to reinvent, wasn't it? Try on some new outfits, try out some new ideas – maybe even try those weird spirulina shakes or take up hot yoga. It was California, after all.

'*Definitely* time to hit the beach,' she said out loud. Taking a bag with a few essentials - sunblock, towel, dog-eared Jackie Collins novel - she walked onto the balcony and slid the door shut. There were steps straight down to the sand, and Lara's heart jumped at the prospect. The air out here was fresh, and the sky was baby blue, just brushed with a scud of clouds. The water had retreated now, and to her left, Lara could see the bright caps of open-water swimmers having an early morning dip, a couple of early riser dog walkers too. She smiled to herself, wondering if any of them were famous. It was that sort of place, wasn't it?

Lara walked towards the shoreline, tapping her toes against the wet sand, thrilling as the cold foam rushed over her feet. *The Pacific!* Yes, it was all sea, but there was something much more exotic about the west coast. She stretched her arms out and tipped her head back, feeling the sun on her face, still gentle at this early hour, and she let out a little laugh of pleasure. Lara had never particularly been a fan of LA before; she preferred the energy of New York, the laid-back vibe of Miami or the red-brick elegance of Boston. What did Dionne Warwick say about Los Angeles? *LA is a great big freeway?* She was also not keen on the city's obsession with good looks and status, but she had to admit that right now, she was beginning to see its appeal. *This* was why people flocked to California: sea birds squalling overhead, the fringed bluffs tumbling down to the shore, even the sand had a pink tinge at this time of the morning.

Lara turned back towards the house and stopped, suddenly feeling self-conscious. Someone was watching her. As she approached, she saw it was a woman sitting at an easel.

The woman smiled and waved her paintbrush. She was perhaps late seventies, with grey hair tied back beneath a wide straw hat, but she looked friendly.

'Are you painting the view?' said Lara, approaching. 'I hope I didn't get in the way.'

'No, no, I painted you in.'

'Really? Can I have a look?'

The old woman beckoned with a paint-smeared finger. The painting was a beautiful watercolour – simple but effective, just bold smears of colour bleeding into one another, blurring the line between sea and sky. And Lara had indeed been rendered as a few spare lines reflected in the wet sand.

'Your red dress pops,' the woman said by way of explanation. 'And it draws the eye, don't you think?'

Lara agreed. It did.

'Well, I'm honoured to be part of it,' she said. 'Are you a professional artist?'

The woman gave a wry smile.

'I only picked up a paintbrush about a year ago, but once I did, something just clicked. I'm Barbara, by the way. Barbara Bloom.'

'Lara.'

Barbara wiped off her fingers, and they shook hands.

'So you're in the Malibu House?' she said, nodding towards Simon's property.

'I wish; I'm just visiting. It belongs to my boyfriend's boss.'

'Mr Denai?'

'You know him?'

Barbara shook her head.

'Not really; he's hardly ever there, but he's a well-known guy. The beach grapevine is pretty efficient. You get to know who's moving out, who's moving in.'

'Well, Mr Denai was kind enough to lend his place to Alex,' said Lara.

'Alex being your boyfriend?'

She nodded. 'I live in London, but I'm here for a couple of weeks to see him.'

Barbara smiled wistfully.

'Ah, long-distance love. I know what that's like.'

'You do?' said Lara with surprise.

'Donny, my husband, was in the business,' she said. Lara guessed she meant the movie business. It was LA - the shorthand that everyone used.

'Don was away filming half the time, and I went with him when we first got married. But when we bought this place, I preferred to stay here rather than some Godawful hotel in Europe. Besides, I soon caught on that he didn't need the distraction when he was working 15-hour days.'

'Tell me about it,' said Lara, thinking of Alex's 8AM conference. Alex had been upfront about his work commitments, but even so, would she have preferred to have him drop everything, desperate to spend every moment with her? Of course she would. It was unreasonable, but whoever said love made perfect sense?

Lara looked at the row of beach houses behind them, squinting in the sun.

'You live here too?'

'That's my place just there,' said Barbara, using the paintbrush to point to a white three-story property two doors down from Simon's house. It was beautiful, with a wide white frontage facing straight onto the sand. Clearly, Donny had done well in 'the business'.

'No wonder you didn't want to leave.'

Barbara nodded.

'Waking up to this view takes some beating, I'll give you that. Hard to believe I didn't want to move out here - I always preferred the city. But Donny had an office on the Warner lot and wanted to escape the smog.'

Lara nodded as if she understood, but she had never experienced LA's famous pollution; the skies had always been bright blue whenever she had been here. A thought hit Lara.

'If you live here too, why did you call it 'The Malibu House'? Surely all the houses on this beach are the Malibu House?'

Barbara chuckled.

'It's what people of my generation call your place. Us oldies.'

'How come?'

Barbara pulled a slightly embarrassed expression.

'Well...did you know it used to belong to Verity Jones?'

Lara frowned. For a moment, she couldn't quite place the name.

'Wait. Isn't she the singer from the Sixties? She was in a band, wasn't she?'

'The Virginians. You're too young to remember them, but you might know their big hit, 'Flowers in the Wind'?'

Lara nodded. It was a stone-cold classic.

'Yes, Verity lived in Laurel Canyon,' said Barbara, 'But Simon's place was her weekend house. Everyone used to call it The Malibu House because that's where they all used to come to party.'

'Who's they?'

'Oh, the whole Laurel Canyon Set; a bunch of actors and musicians who lived up behind Sunset. So you'd get some pretty big names coming down here.'

Lara looked back to the house with fresh eyes. You'd never guess it had such a glittering history, but then she imagined it had been extensively remodelled over the years.

'Were you here then? Did you know Verity?'

Barbara shook her head.

'We didn't move to Malibu until '83 - she'd been gone a few years by then.'

Gone. The story shifted in Lara's brain.

'That's right. Verity died young, didn't she?' Verity Jones was on the long list of musical legends – Hendrix, Joplin, Morrison – whose mystique was only enhanced because they had passed in their prime.

'Verity was such a talent,' said Barbara. 'Even better than Joni Mitchell, if you ask me. That was such a tragic night.'

Lara looked up.

'What do you mean?'

She watched Barbara hesitate, circles of colour appearing on her cheeks.

'Are you sure you want to know?' she said, glancing back at the house.

'I'm a news journalist, Barbara. I've been shot at, intimidated, threatened - I don't scare easily.'

Barbara glanced around, then lowered her voice, even though they were the only two on the beach.

'Verity died in the house. Your house.'

She put a gentle hand on Lara's arm.

'I'm sorry, I shouldn't have said anything. You're on vacation in this beautiful place – I don't want to spoil it for you.'

'No, no, it's fine,' said Lara, curious now. 'So what happened? To Verity, I mean?'

She knew Alex would be intrigued, too—if he didn't already know. His appetite for stories was one of the things that made him a great journalist. Barbara looked out to sea.

'There was a party. Drink and drugs, I guess – it was the Seventies. Anyway, Verity was found dead in the bathtub: heart attack, they said.'

Barbara shivered. 'I try not to think about it too much.'

Lara suddenly wanted to hear every detail.

'Heart attack, *they said?* Were there doubts?'

'I'm not the person to ask,' said Barbara. 'My friend Martha would know. She was there that night.'

'Really?' said Lara, feeling a surge of excitement. 'Is Martha a musician as well?'

Barbara smiled to herself.

'She's a writer. Martha Riding.'

Lara felt her mouth drop open. Now *that* name she knew. Martha Riding was a literary legend, a Pulitzer Prize-winner, and an icon of the late sixties counter-culture and seventies disco decadence. Lara hadn't even been sure Martha Riding was still alive.

'You should meet her,' said Barbara. 'You both being in the business.'

'I'd love to,' said Lara, trying not to sound as excited as she felt.

'Well, she's coming for brunch tomorrow. You should join us.' Barbara paused. 'If you're not doing anything better, of course.'

What *could* be better than meeting Martha Riding? Thought Lara. 'Oh, I'd love to come. I'd be just waiting for my boyfriend to come home anyway.'

'Well, let us save you from that, at least. Around nine AM? Just come up the steps – it's very informal.'

'Thank you, I'll look forward to it.'

And Lara found she really, really was.

Chapter 3

Alex Ford sat hunched over his desk, poring over print-outs of that evening's front pages from newspapers around the world. This had been a ritual in the newsroom at the Chronicle back in London, and out here in LA, Alex couldn't quite shake the habit, even though American newspapers tended to be published for local markets. Today, there had been an earthquake in Sri Lanka and a plane crash in Turkey; the British press was focusing on an MP caught in a 'tryst' and an American rapper who had made inflammatory comments at a festival. It was all par for the course, but Alex's news instincts drew him to the crashed plane. Irish and French holidaymakers had been killed, and intelligence reports suggested a possible terror attack. If he'd still been at the Chronicle, Alex would have sent a team to investigate. But the Globe was in Los Angeles, seven thousand miles from Turkey. He doubted many Californians could find Turkey on a map, much less care about the political implications of a rogue missile strike. The foul-mouthed rapper, however, now *that* was a potential headline. He made a note on a Post-it, then leaned back in his chair, massaging the tension from his neck. It had been a long day at the newspaper. The lawyers had spiked a lead story, the sports editor had gone down with food poisoning before an interview with one of the Laker's newest signings, and Alex was butting heads with the art director over the paper's revamp. Most dispiriting had been a long meeting with the advertising team who were facing apathy across the board: 'No one wants to advertise in print anymore,' said one sales manager. 'They're throwing all their money at influencers.'

Alex spun his chair to face the window. It was a corner office on the tenth floor, which was high for downtown LA; he had a view all the way up Main Street. If you followed Main north, you'd pass through Chinatown and Little Tokyo before hitting Dodger Stadium. If you followed it south, you'd hit the beach.

He smiled, thinking of Lara sunbathing. No, Lara was never very good at sitting still. She'd probably already integrated with the surfer community and had mastered 'hanging ten' or whatever they did. The vision of Lara in a bikini led to thoughts of their frantic reunion yesterday; they'd barely made it into the bedroom. That, of course, was why he was having trouble keeping his eyes open right now.

Alex picked up the phone. 'Gina, can I get some coffee? Make it strong.'

He didn't like asking his assistant for coffee – to a reconstructed urbanite like Alex, it seemed a little demeaning for someone with a Master's in journalism like Gina - but when he'd suggested getting a machine in the office, Gina had gently explained, 'the coffee run' was part of LA culture; a chance to get out of the office, make personal calls, maybe flirt with the cute baristas. Just another of the cultural differences Alex was having to adjust to.

Right now, though, Alex just needed to stay awake.

After four months on the job, the 100-hour weeks were beginning to take their toll. When he took the job, he knew that the *LA Globe* was struggling - circulation and revenue all down - but finding out just how bad things were had been a real shock. 'Like a fire in a dumpster' was how one of the finance guys had put it. So Alex had hit the ground running and launched into an immediate revamp of the newspaper. A new masthead, new sections and an improved digital presence.

Most vitally, Alex had decided to create Limelight, a new 'film industry' section to compete with the heavy-weight Tinsel Town papers like *Variety*. LA was a town built on show business, and it seemed ridiculous that there was hardly any coverage of it in the LA Globe, especially since TV and film news and gossip was exactly the sort of thing their *real* competitors – the internet, social media – were doing so well. The increased coverage had been such a hit that they were spinning it off into a weekend supplement. The official launch of Limelight was less than two weeks away; invites to the party at one of the city's hottest roof-top bars had been sent out, but Alex wasn't entirely happy with the finished magazine. Not yet. It still needed work.

'Knock knock,' Gina stepped inside, bearing a paper cup. 'Rocket fuel for you.'

'That was quick.'

Gina flashed him a smile. 'I heard the desperation in your voice.'

Gina was young and switched on. She saw her PA role as a stepping stone to a management role and Alex didn't doubt she'd get there, and soon.

'There's also someone here to see you.'

He looked up in surprise as Simon Desai walked in. As always, his boss looked sharp in a light grey suit with a silver tie, his dark hair impeccable. Did Simon have his own hairdresser? Alex supposed anything was possible for a billionaire.

'Please, come in,' said Alex, standing.

'More coffee?' asked Gina.

'Nothing for me,' said Simon, raising a hand.

Uh-oh, thought Alex, catching the tone: Simon was all business. Alex gestured to a pair of sofas.

'I didn't think you were coming in until Friday.'

Simon wasn't a hands-on proprietor; he'd made his money in hotels and real estate and had no background in journalism, so Alex was left to run the Globe how he saw fit. Up until now, that was.

'I just met with Kenneth Michaels,' said Simon, sitting down without further preamble. Alex knew he was supposed to recognise the name, but if he was honest, he had neglected to familiarise himself with many of the LA powerbrokers; over the past few weeks, revamping the editorial had been his priority.

'Major tech investor. Very smart guy,' said Simon. 'Anyway, he told me about the newsletters he subscribes to.'

Ah, thought Alex. *That's where this is going.*

'Kenneth reads crypto newsletters and investment newsletters. Even Hollywood industry newsletters – and the last movie Ken saw was ET. He pays 15 bucks a month for some of these things, Alex – and it's just one guy writing them! We need to get in on this.'

Of course, Alex was aware of the trend—experts going directly to their audience through newsletter platforms. It was an interesting new business model—and, depressingly, just another one of the fields where the newspapers would struggle to compete. But Alex was experienced enough to know Simon wasn't interested in debating whether this fit with the Globe; he was interested in how Alex could make him more money.

'Funnily enough, I was going to talk to you about this,' said Alex smoothly.

'Because I think it cuts to the heart of what the Globe is and where it needs to be.'

Simon raised his eyebrows: *go on.*

'We have to ask ourselves: why do those newsletters work? It's because their writers are experts, right? Because they're insiders, because you don't want to miss what they're saying. These guys look at the world and go, 'Hey, this is what's happening', and people trust them.'

He looked at Simon.

'Which is why we need better journalists.'

He saw the surprise hit.

'Better? But the LA Globe has the best…'

Alex shook his head.

'Used to, Simon,' said Alex. 'The Globe used to have great writers, fantastic columnists – David Hersh on Sports, Cynthia Negras on politics, remember? But that was ten, fifteen years ago. Dave went to the Times and Cynthia has retired.'

'But I thought…'

Alex nodded. 'Yes, they've been replaced by a new generation who are young and energetic, but they don't have the gravitas to compete with the New York Times, the Wall Street Journal or experts going direct to reader.'

He saw Simon frown as he absorbed this.

'Why do I feel this is a shakedown?'

'Not a shakedown, a reality check,' said Alex. 'You just identified our new competitors – Kenneth's newsletters - and I agree we need to fight back, but to do that, we need the budget to attract the best writers.'

Simon adjusted his tie.

'That sounds expensive.'

Alex shrugged.

'I won't sugar-coat it; quality *is* expensive. But if you

want to bring authority to the Globe, a team of Zero-hour contract rookies just won't cut it.'

Alex's eyes met Simon's.

'But,' he said. 'If we can recruit some heavy hitters for the paper, we can also give them paid-for newsletters, generating more revenue and drawing people to the main newspaper while expanding our digital offering. It's a double-win strategy.'

Alex took a breath, his heart beating. He had created the whole pitch on the fly – he wasn't sure even if *he* was convinced. Still, he waited.

'That makes sense, said Simon, finally nodding. 'If we want the best, you've got to pay for the best, right? After all, that's why I recruited you, Alex. Okay, that's a green light, but make it worth my while.'

One thing Alex liked about Simon - he made a decision, and then they moved on.

There was a moment's silence.

'So how's the beach house?' asked Simon.

'Unbelievably beautiful,' said Alex. 'It's so awesome you're letting us use it. Thank you again.'

'And your girlfriend – Lara, isn't it? Is she enjoying herself?'

Alex couldn't wipe the smile off his face, remembering Lara's face when she had stepped inside it for the first time.

'She loves the Malibu house too.'

'Loves it enough to move to LA?'

Ah-ha, thought Alex. He had been naïve to believe Simon had loaned him the Malibu house to say 'thank you' for all the hours he had put in on the revamp. Clearly, there was another agenda.

'Perhaps,' he said diplomatically, 'But I can't persuade Lara to do anything she doesn't want to do.'

Simon steepled his fingers.

'Alex, turning this newspaper around is a big job.'

'I am aware,' said Alex, pointedly taking a sip of his coffee.

'So if I am going to invest further into it, as you request, I need to know that I have your full attention. I just don't know how easy that will be if you have a trans-Atlantic relationship.'

Alex bristled – his private life was none of Simon's damn business – but he knew he needed to be careful. No editor, however good they were, was indispensable. He let out a long breath.

'I would love her to move here,' he said honestly. 'Because I'm loving it – and not just Malibu either.'

Saying it out loud, Alex realised how true it was. When he'd left London, he'd rented out his high-end river view apartment – it had been a safety net in case LA had been a wash-out. But his tenant, a City banker, had fallen in love with the place and had offered to buy Alex's flat outright. It was one of those offers that was too good to refuse, and, to Alex, it felt like a sign that his future was in LA.

'So what's stopping Lara?' asked Simon. 'Is it her family connections? Presumably, she'd never leave the Chronicle.'

It was no surprise that Simon knew about Lara's family. Her uncle Nicholas owned the Chronicle, Alex's previous workplace, and was effectively Simon's counterpart in London.

'No, it's not that,' sighed Alex. 'Even though she worked for the Chronicle, Lara isn't close to her family. I think the truth is that Lara has never really warmed to LA, but perhaps two weeks in Malibu will convince her.'

'Let's hope so,' said Simon, rising and brushing imaginary lint from his immaculate suit. 'Because I need 100% from you, Alex.'

'Are you implying I'm not giving you that now?'

Simon laughed.

'No, no, quite the opposite. I've been impressed by your commitment, Alex - I didn't just lend you my beach house to impress your girlfriend. I need you to relax, too; I don't want you burning out because of this relaunch. The relaunch is just the start of it. Keep in mind this is a business. Your focus is on the editorial, which is entirely correct, but my focus is the future of this newspaper because I didn't buy it to watch it fail.'

Make damn sure it doubles my investment was what he really meant, thought Alex, watching his boss make for the door.

'Understood,' said Alex.

Simon gave him a polished smile, showing off his white teeth.

'Then keep up the good work. And cut yourself a little slack, too. That pool at the Malibu place is there for a reason, okay?'

He watched him open the door and disappear down the corridor, leaving Alex wondering if there had been more to this meeting than a casual check-in. Men like Simon Desai didn't do anything casually. Had Simon sensed something else in him, some hidden reticence? Alex hadn't been lying - he did love being in California – the weather, the service culture and, of course, Alex Ford was finally the editor of a respected newspaper. It would be churlish to complain about any of that. But he did miss London. Seeing friends, running along the Embankment, browsing bookshops along the King's Road. And most of all, spending time with Lara, sharing a bottle of wine on the deck of her houseboat, watching the swaying lights of the Albert Bridge. What would happen if she didn't want to move to LA full-time? If it came to a choice, what would Alex do? Honestly, he wasn't sure.

'You free now?' Gina was back at the office door.

'Sure. What's up?'

'Lara's waiting for you in reception.'

'Excellent,' said Alex, feeling his mood lift.

'Are you both coming to Brannigan's?'

Alex smiled at the prospect of showing Lara off to his team - and of a cold beer. He grabbed his jacket. He had achieved enough today. He had given Simon something to think about and increased the editorial budget. Now all he had to do was deliver on those huge promises.

'Yes, we're coming,' he said smoothly, 'we'll see you there. '

Chapter 4

Lara was feeling nervous, and Lara Stone didn't get nervous. *Come on, it's only a social thing.*

'So where are you taking me?' she asked, clutching Alex's hand as they stepped into the dark street from the Globe's reception.

'It's just a sports bar near the office,' said Alex. 'Basically, it's like The Anchor pub but with inferior beer and sports jerseys on the wall.'

'Sounds perfect,' said Lara, smiling with bittersweet nostalgia. The Anchor was the favoured drinking hole for the Chronicle's staff – Lara, Alex and their colleagues had spent many happy nights there after work. Suddenly, those days seemed a very long time ago indeed.

Alex glanced across.

'They're going to love you.'

No pressure then, thought Lara.

It was a little before 7PM and already it was starting to turn dark. In the daytime, the Downtown district was vibrant—the streets were thick with city slickers. Food courts like Grand Central Market, which sold pancakes, tacos, and egg sandwiches as thick as a fist, were hip, buzzy hubs. But certain areas of Downtown had a reputation for being sketchy, particularly after hours, so Lara didn't want to peer too hard into the shadows or linger near the alleyways.

She glanced at Alex, who looked tense. She knew he felt guilty about letting half the staff disappear for a drink.

'People are allowed to have fun, you know,' she said, squeezing his hand.

'But we're so busy,' he said, almost to himself. 'The night shift team won't be in for another half an hour.'

One of the things she loved most about Alex was his unflappability. He was the person she trusted most to get anything done, a natural leader, almost always the smartest person in the room, but tonight, he looked rattled and uncertain.

'Alex, the team have been working their socks off. They need to clock off a bit early and have a drink, now more than ever. Besides, you know a change of management makes people wobbly. Show them you're on-side and want them to have a life, and they'll work harder for you tomorrow.'

He nodded gratefully and quickened up his pace.

'Here we are,' said Alex, squeezing her hand as they entered the bar.

Alex's description had been spot on: Brannigan's was like a set from a sitcom set in a sports bar. Dark wood, concealed lighting, neon beer signs and squishy booths.

'Alex! Over here!'

The Globe gang was already in situ, gathered in a corner near the bar. Already people seemed to be in good spirits, clearly glad to be out of the office. Lara hovered awkwardly as Alex exchanged handshakes and shoulder clasps, and then he turned back to her.

'Everyone, this is…'

'Lara,' said a middle-aged man. He had a beard and

an LA FC hoodie. 'I'm Pete Barber, Alex's deputy. Glad to have you here.'

'It's Pete's birthday,' said Alex, although the oversized badge reading 'Kiss Me, I'm 50' had given Lara a clue.

'Can I buy you a drink, Pete?' she asked.

He laughed and shook his head. 'I'm barely standing as it is. These lunatics have been forcing booze into me since we left the office. Help yourself to one of the pitchers.'

Lara thanked him and poured some foamy lager from the giant jug on the bar. It was gassy and virtually tasteless, but Lara was still glad the tradition of post-work drinking was alive and well in California, a place with a reputation for pious abstinence.

'Hey there, I'm Natasha,' said a younger woman appearing at Lara's side. She had a sharp shoulder-length bob and a beauty mark above the corner of her lip, like a young Cindy Crawford. 'I work on the news desk. Well, news and features.'

'Lara,' she said extending a hand. 'I'm with Alex,' she said awkwardly. It still felt weird calling herself his girlfriend. Partner? That was even worse.

'I know. I've been looking forward to meeting you,' said Natasha. 'I enjoyed your piece about Kluven – the murder of that chef? I think it should be a movie.'

Lara was struck by the girl's confidence.

'Well, Spielberg hasn't made the call yet,' she laughed. 'But you never know what might happen while I'm in LA.'

'Hey, we've got a table,' said Pete, nodding towards the corner of the room. 'Let's make a night of it.'

Alex looked hesitant, but Lara grabbed his arm and pulled him over.

'If you're going to show your face, you might as well go all in,' she whispered into his ear.

The table was a wide corner booth that seated around

eight people. A waitress in a red checked apron thumped down another pitcher and a bowl of nachos.

Lara slid in after Alex and Natasha followed her.

Lara smiled to herself. As a junior reporter, Lara would never have dared to align herself with the senior editorial team at a social event. Natasha was obviously made of tougher stuff.

More introductions were made: to Ralph, the news editor, Steve Reynolds from sports, and Mischa Jenks from the picture desk.

'Alex tells me you've been at the Broad?' said Pete, sipping his beer. Lara was grateful to be included.

'Yes, it's pretty amazing – apart from it looks like a giant cheese grater.'

The achingly modern art gallery had long been on Lara's must-see list and, as it was just a 15-minute walk from the Globe office, she had arrived early to have a mooch about. It had Jeff Koons, Lichtenstein and Basquiat, the best display of Warhols she had seen in a long time, plus a Kusama infinity installation. Lara hadn't been disappointed.

'So, spill the beans. What's the boss's Malibu house like?' said Ralph with good humour. 'Us lesser mortals aren't even allowed to walk along the beach. There's a fifty-metre exclusion zone.'

'Snipers and mines,' laughed Steve.

'Did you know it used to belong to Verity Jones, the singer?' said Ralph, grabbing a handful of nachos.

'Who's Verity Jones?' asked Natasha.

'Only one of the greatest singers of the 1970s,' said Pete passionately.

'Pete thinks culture died when the Beatles split up,' laughed Steve.

'No, come on - Verity Jones, man!' Pete insisted. 'She had something. Plus that voice – it was the voice of her generation.'

'Tell that to Carole King,' smiled Alex.

'So how come I never heard her?' asked Natasha, taking a small bite from a single nacho. Pete's expression grew more serious.

'She died, Natasha. Drowned in the bath in Simon's house.'

'What?' said Alex, almost spitting out his beer. 'In Simon's house? When?'

'Don't worry, it was fifty years ago,' laughed Lara. 'The neighbour told me this morning.'

'Hey, Will's dad – Jack Anders – he worked on the story,' said Pete, lifting his arm and waving to a young man standing near the bar. 'Will, over here.'

Lara watched the reporter approach the table. He was around thirty, although his suit only made him look more baby-faced. Unlike Natasha, who seemed unfazed in the company of the senior editorial team, Will Anders looked apprehensive.

She didn't blame him. Countless times in The Anchor, she'd been called back to the newsroom for a breaking story. Pete beckoned Will into the booth, giving him a paternal pat as he sat down.

'Lara, this is Will Anders. His dad was a legend in the Globe newsroom back in the day and the apple doesn't fall far from the tree.'

She watched Will cringe at the drunken compliment.

'So your old man covered the Verity Jones story?' said Pete.

Will nodded.

'I think he'd only just started in the job,' he said. 'But he was definitely one of the first reporters on the scene.'

Everyone started talking over one another—conspiracy theories, speculations about whether Simon Desai had bought the house at a knock-down price and whether there might be *ghosts.*

'But what really happened? How did Verity die?' Alex asked Will.

Will looked embarrassed to be the centre of attention, but Ralph poured Will a beer, and the group bent to listen.

'As I understand it, the Malibu House was Verity's weekend place,' said Will. 'She threw a lot of parties out there, and they were pretty crazy, from what my dad told me. The night she died, there were about fifty people over, but for some reason, she threw everyone out at about 10.30pm. The next thing we know is early the following morning, someone found her dead in the bathtub.'

'Overdose?'

'It was a heart attack, wasn't it?' said Lara, repeating what Barbara had told her.

'That was the official line, yes,' said Will, nodding. 'But my dad always thought something was off about the whole story.'

'Off?' said Alex.

'There were a lot of rumours. About drugs mainly.'

'So it *was* an overdose?' asked Natasha.

'Some claimed it was deliberate. Others thought it was a terrible accident. Some said she wasn't alone in the house...'

'What does your dad think?'

'He thought there was more to it than a heart attack. A lot more.'

Chapter 5

Lara stopped at the bottom of the steps leading from the beach to Barbara's veranda. She was nervous; she could admit it. Lara didn't have many heroes, but she had loved Martha Riding ever since her college days when she had first read Martha's seminal collection of essays, 'New Girl in Town'. Martha's beautifully crafted words had conjured up visions of American boho cool: war photographers rubbing shoulders with heiresses, late-night dives and early-morning diners. Over the years, Lara had read everything Martha had ever written. Her series of dispatches from the war in El Salvador had earned her a Pulitzer for her clear-eyed view of bloody conflict. Her novels about life on the West Coast were sharp and observant, and her collections of essays on a host of subjects, from pop culture to political populism, were unmatched. And now Lara was going to meet her in the flesh.

'Lara, darling!'

She looked up to see Barbara waving a spatula at her from the top of the steps.

In a yellow shirt dress with the sleeves rolled up, her

grey hair tied back with a patterned scarf, she looked like a particularly benevolent grandma.

'I hope I'm not too early?'

'It's never too early at my age, honey,' she said, beckoning Lara up. 'I hope you're hungry.'

Lara stepped through wide glass doors into a warm open-plan living room filled with Moroccan rugs and African carvings. The sweet aroma of vanilla and brown sugar drifted through from the kitchen on the far side.

'I'm definitely feeling hungry now,' said Lara. 'It smells gorgeous.'

'You're too polite,' said Barbara, flipping golden-brown slices of French Toast from an iron skillet onto a plate. 'Wait until you've tasted it.'

Barbara directed her to a seat at the farmhouse table by the window while she fetched coffee. Lara took a moment to observe the space—the boho but expensive décor, the views of the beach, and the abstract art on the walls.

'Are these all your paintings?'

'Some are mine, but the good ones are by artist friends or relics from when Donny and I used to kid ourselves we were savvy art collectors.'

'Is that a Christopher Wool? And – that's not an original 'Love' graphic by Robert Indiana, is it?'

'You have a good eye,' smiled Barbara, placing a ceramic mug in front of Lara. 'Donny called them our pension, but I'm glad I haven't had to part with them yet. There are a lot of memories attached to them.'

Barbara poured her a cup of black coffee from a red pot.

'Don't worry, Martha is coming,' she said as if reading Lara's mind. 'She's always half an hour late for everything, so I told her to come at 8.30.'

The doorbell rang behind them.

'Ah, there we go,' smiled Barbara. Lara watched her open the door and tensed as the woman walked in. Martha Riding was taller than she imagined, wearing an olive green painter's smock, her salt and pepper hair cut into a bob. She looked more like an artist than a writer.

'What is that delicious smell?' Martha said in a clear voice as she walked Lara's way. 'Have I just walked into Ina Garton's place by mistake?'

Barbara waved the compliment away.

'Martha, this is Lara. She's a writer, too.'

Lara waited for a prickle of competitive hostility, but there was none.

'Good,' said Martha, giving Lara a firm handshake, the large tortoiseshell glasses hanging on a fine gold chain around her neck swinging from side to side. 'We need more creatives at the beach. These days, it's all private equity and media; awful people.'

Lara liked her immediately.

'Lara's boyfriend Alex works for Simon Desai,' said Barbara quickly. 'He was kind enough to lend them his place.'

Martha looked at Lara more closely.

'So you're at the Malibu House, hmm? Which means your boyfriend would be Alex Ford?'

Lara looked at Martha with surprise.

'You know him?

'I'm old, not dead,' said Martha, sitting at the table. 'I try to keep up with the papers, and I like what Alex is doing with the Globe. It's long overdue a shake-up. Newspapers are a tough gig right now, but if anyone can turn it around, he can.'

Lara suppressed a grin, imagining Alex's face when she told him, knowing he was also a Martha Riding fan. One of the first presents Lara had ever bought him was a battered copy of Martha's dispatches from Beirut, back when she and Alex were just friends at college, and Alex's big dream was to become a foreign correspondent.

'So he moved over from London and brought you too? How do you feel about that?' Martha's question was so blunt it made Lara smile.

'Actually, I still live in the UK. I work for the London Chronicle. This is just a holiday.'

'But they're tempting you out here with all this beach,' said Martha as Barbara put a pile of French toast dusted with powdered sugar in front of them. 'Well, it worked for me. I lived in New York with Griffin, my husband. He was a writer, too; then, he got a gig polishing scripts for the studios. I said I wouldn't leave Manhattan – no way - but then he brought me out here to see Malibu. And fifty years later…' she held up a hand.

'It's a magical place,' said Barbara, sitting down. The two older women pitched in, telling Lara about the treasures of Malibu. The El Matador State Park had rock formations 'just like Baja.' Also 'must see' were the natural pools and historic ruins in Solstice Canyon, the vineyards with ocean views and wine-tasting rooms just a few miles inland.

'The lagoon is worth an afternoon, too,' said Barbara, spearing a strawberry with her fork. 'And the beaches, of course. Broad Beach, Las Flores. Zuma and Point Dume are great for swimming.'

'Oh, but watch the water at Carbon,' said Martha. 'It gets deep very quickly. Are you a surfer? You look a surfer.'

'It's been a while,' Lara admitted. 'But I have a car, so I want to explore.'

'Well, you should check out the hillside communities,' said Barbara. 'I see a wonderful crystal therapist who lives in a trailer near the Serra Retreat if you want her number.'

'You're not still seeing the crystal woman, are you?' Martha said with clear disdain. But Barbara didn't seem bothered, and as the two friends fell to arguing about healers versus therapists, Lara smiled. She loved how familiar they were with each other and how their conversation had a rhythm. Lara's own best friend, Sandrine, had died two years earlier, and she missed having someone she was so close to.

'And, of course, there's the Getty Villa near Brentwood,' said Barbara. 'It looks like a Roman villa and has the most amazing collection of classical art. It reminds me of when I was living in Rome when Donny was shooting the 'Summer of Man' in Italy. I spent hours just wandering around the Forum and Palatine Hill.'

'You see? She *is* cultured,' said Martha in a theatrical whisper. 'She just won't join my book club.'

'The books Martha chooses are always far too highbrow for me,' said Barbara with an equally dramatic sigh.

'Barbara prefers crappy 80s TV detective shows,' said Martha. 'She's got the entire back catalogue of Kojak over there.' She pointed to a long shelf of DVDs.

'I prefer Hill Street Blues,' said Barbara defensively.

'Anyway, it's not exactly highbrow,' said Martha, 'Because tonight we're discussing Fifty Shades of Grey.'

Barbara tutted. 'Just old ladies trying to relive their delinquent pasts.'

'Past? You speak for yourself, Barbara Bloom.'

There was a wicked smile on Martha's mouth, but Lara was keen to head off what was obviously an old argument.

'Do you live in Malibu too, Martha?' Lara asked.

'Further North. I live on The Road.'

Martha caught Lara's blank expression.

'Malibu Road,' she explained. 'It's up near the Colony, where the big stars live now, but back in the late 60s, two writers could just about afford it.'

Lara saw she had an opening to ask the question that had been intriguing her.

'So Martha, Barbara said you were at The Malibu House the day Verity Jones died?'

The energy of their conversation dipped, and the veranda seemed to cool by a couple of degrees.

'Yes, I was,' said Martha, pushing her empty plate to one side. 'We weren't great friends, although she sometimes swapped books and records with my husband Griffin– they had similar tastes. But Verity's place was like an open house, especially at the weekend. Sometimes, it would just be a few friends for drinks; other times, you'd get half of Laurel Canyon descending on the beach.'

She paused.

'But that day was a Saturday, it was busy, but everyone seemed happy.'

Martha stopped, seemingly lost in the memory.

'One of the Globe team said Verity threw everyone out at 10.30?' Lara prompted.

Martha nodded. 'Apparently so, but I was long gone by then. Griff and I stopped at the house for an hour on our way to dinner with friends in Brentwood. So what happened later that night? No idea.'

'But why did Verity cut the party short? Did anyone know?'

Martha pouted.

'Afterwards, there were rumours that someone had called the cops, but I doubt that; they usually left us alone. Someone else said Verity felt sick; another thought she was upset because Eliot had shown up.'

'Eliot?'

'From the band - Verity's husband. Well, they'd separated the previous summer, around the same time The Virginians split up.'

'So what was Eliot doing at the party?

'Oh, they were still friends.' Martha gave a sad laugh. 'That was no surprise because Verity was the sweetest, most laid-back person. And I think they still loved each other.'

The older woman looked at Lara directly.

'Anyway, that was the last night. Verity was gone. You know how they say the Manson killings marked the end of the Sixties? Well, Verity's death was an end for the Malibu House.'

Lara's investigative mind began working, trying to see all the angles and imagine herself at the scene.

'The Globe reporter thought something felt *off* about what happened. What do you think?'

'Off? You sound like Griffin.'

Lara kept quiet, a classic journalistic tactic for getting a subject to talk. People, even other writers, needed to fill conversational gaps.

'Griffin started to write a story about Verity's death for Skim magazine.'

Skim magazine thought Lara with a thrill. Just the mention of it felt like falling back into a more glamorous time in publishing. The legendary underground magazine had made waves in the late sixties for its sharp blend of satire and scurrilous exposes. It had launched the careers of many big names in journalism, most notably its flamboyant publisher Harley Stuyvesant, who later became editor of high-end glossy magazine Prestige. Lara remembered her father kept a stash of the magazines in his study. Lara still had them somewhere; she had never been able to part with any of her parents' belongings.

'So what did Griffin write?'

Martha shrugged. 'Nothing. The story got spiked.'

It was one of the occupational hazards for a reporter.

You could spend days or weeks on a story, but if the editor had a change of heart or the lawyers thought it was contentious, it might never see the light of day.

'Griffin's investigation focused on the drugs.'

'Verity was on drugs?'

'Honey, *everyone* was on drugs back then,' Barbara laughed.

'Officially, Verity died of a heart attack,' continued Martha, taking another sip of coffee. 'But the autopsy found narcotics in her system.'

'I thought that Griffin was Verity's friend...' Lara said, unable to stop herself or hide her disapproval.

'You mean, why would he want to write a story that might show a seedier side of her death?' asked Martha bluntly. 'He wasn't trying to shame Verity, Lara. He was trying to hold people to account. You see, two other people had died of an overdose that month, and Griffin had a theory that there was a very bad, potent batch of something going around. His theory was that the dealer responsible was at Verity's that night.'

'Well, that sounds like a good story,' said Lara, putting herself in Griffin's shoes. 'So why spike it?'

'Griff was told that it would be hard to prove anything, and deep down, I think he agreed; better to let Verity rest in peace.'

Martha glanced at her watch, muttered a curse and pushed her chair back.

'That was delicious, Barbs,' she said briskly, 'But I've got to get over to the Polo Lounge to meet my agent.'

'You have a new book coming out?' asked Lara, impressed that a woman who must have been touching eighty was still blazing a trail.

'Not yet, but soon,' she said, smiling at Lara. 'I can tell you more if you come to my book club this evening. Say you'll come?'

'I will if Barbara will,' said Lara.
Martha grinned and pointed at her.
'I like your style, Lara Stone.'

Chapter 6

The entrance of the Beverly Hills Hotel still gave Martha a thrill. Passing that iconic swirling sign, then stepping onto the red carpet, everyone could be a star here, all it took was the price of a martini. Martha's heels swished as she strode through the grand lobby, past the oversized pillars and pot plants, and she was pleased to note it still had enough of that golden-era glamour to make you believe you might just bump into Frank and Sammy. Or maybe Rod and Britt. Martha didn't need to ask where the Polo Lounge was; she had been there many times. For decades, the restaurant had been one of the premier gathering spots in LA for entertainment industry power players, and a glance at today's diners told her it had lost none of its sheen. It was strange how a humble hotel terrace had survived in a town where a restaurant would only remain 'hot' for six months before the in-crowd moved on to the next fashion or fad. But over half a century from the days of Chaplin and Monroe, the Polo Lounge was still beloved by the Hollywood elite. Martha could see studio heads in wrap-around sunglasses hunched in conversation with actors glancing around furtively as if they were being watched on long lenses. This was why there was always an air of expectation for Martha whenever she came to meet her agent, especially at times like now, when she had a new book out on submission with publishers.

'Fade To Black' was her first collection in half a decade, but Martha felt it was one of her best. A series of essays and think pieces about the state of the nation, it was the voice of a battle-scarred revolutionary watching a new civil war unfold in her culture: at least, that was how she'd pitched it. Martha was proud of what she had written, and when her agent – the great Charles Harriman - had called her to arrange this meeting, she had heard the excitement in his voice, too.

'Miss Riding,' said the Maitre d', bowing his head deferentially. 'Your guest is already here.' Martha smiled as she followed him. Another of the reasons the Polo Lounge continued to be the place for power brunches; they knew how to make you feel special.

The maitre d' led Martha past table six, the tasteful green-striped booth supposedly preferred by Marilyn Monroe, and out onto the terrace, dappled under pergola and parasol. There was no need, of course, for Charles to meet her here. It would be quicker and easier to talk over Skype or Zoom. But they had been meeting at the Polo Lounge whenever Charles came to town, and after over 40 years of convivial lunches, why change now?

She waved to Charles as she crossed to their usual table. Like many literary agents, Charles was based in New York but came out to LA at least once a month. He was in his late 70s, but he still looked every inch the literary titan —silver-haired, impeccably dressed with a tuft of claret silk poking out of his top pocket; Charles still had a presence that commanded attention despite his advanced years.

Smiling, Charles rose slowly as he welcomed her with a warm air kiss.

'Martha, you're looking *splendid*,' he said, his voice gravelly; Martha had always felt that Charles should have been on the other side of the camera. Not Hollywood blockbusters, but maybe those soap operas that were so popular in the 80s – and Martha was pleased by the compliment. Her Ossie Clarke dress, bought on the King's Road in the Seventies, was still among her favourites. Martha had been considered something of a beauty in her day - that's what Griffin had maintained anyway, and that's all that mattered – but in a town where beauty was the currency, it became harder and harder to convince oneself that you were still desirable. Now, she would take the compliments wherever she could get them.

As she wafted a napkin into her lap, Martha looked around the terrace, casually scanning the tables for celebrities. Once upon a time, she'd know at least half a dozen people here, but today, there was no one she recognised; that was becoming all the more common. Martha tried to keep up, reading the dailies and the trade papers, but didn't everyone look all the same these days with those plump lips and talon eyelashes? Where was the new Bette Davis, the next Streisand? Women who looked like women, women who looked unique and interesting? The world was becoming bland and homogenised – or maybe she was just getting old. The waiter brought Martha an iced gimlet – no cilantro - he didn't need to be asked.

'I'll have the peach salad,' said Martha with a smile, handing the waiter the menu. She glanced over to Charles.

'I had a stack of pancakes this morning. Otherwise, I'd be joining you with the steak frites. Chin, chin,' she said, tapping her cocktail against Charles's sparkling water. He'd quit the booze at the end of the last century, part of the reason he was still going strong, she guessed. She put the glass down and aimed her full attention at her agent.

'So are we celebrating?' Martha asked. When she'd delivered the manuscript for Fade to Black six weeks earlier, Charles seemed as pleased with it as Martha was, which had been a relief, given that Martha had been working on the book for over three years. But now, as she watched Charles's expression, she caught the subtle lines of concern. *Uh-oh.*

'Charlie, what is it?'

'I'm afraid it's not good news from Francis Baker,' he said, his fingers tracing the rim of his water glass. Francis Baker had been Martha's publisher for the past twenty years. It had been nearly five years since they'd published her last book, and in the gap, her old editor Carolyn had retired. But still, Martha couldn't believe they wouldn't offer her a decent deal.

'What did they say? Is it a lowball offer?'

Martha wasn't expecting the stellar book advances of days gone by – Charles had already warned her that he'd seen advances down ten, twenty per cent across the board, but it wasn't just about the money for Martha. She had a decent nest egg, and the mortgage on her beach house had been paid off years before. There were no dependents to think of, and Martha had never had expensive tastes. All she wanted was a decent deal with an editor she respected and a team committed to getting her book out to people who might enjoy it.

'They think your new book is amazing, but it's not what they're looking for right now.'

For a moment, she thought she had misheard her agent.

'Not what they're looking for?' she said, registering the shock. Martha did not consider herself arrogant or entitled, but she was completely taken aback.

'As you know, they've got a new team of editors, a new generation, and they said they just can't make an offer.'

It felt like a sharp slap across the face.

'They don't want to make an offer *at all?*'

Charles shook his head. Martha took a moment to let it sink in, the humiliation and embarrassment, even in front of her old agent and friend, making her cheeks burn hot.

'What about other publishers? Simon and Schuster? William Morrow? I hear Jennifer Walsh at Random House is very good.'

'Martha, I've sent it out to everyone, and no one is biting.'

Charles slid his hand across the table and touched her fingers.

'Martha,' he said quietly. 'You know it's special. I know it's special, but…'

'But?'

For a moment, they didn't say anything.

'It doesn't matter how good your book is,' Charles continued, 'It doesn't matter how good *any* book is. It has to be the book they want to publish.'

'And 'they' are twenty-eight-year-old trust fund girls who have never heard of Roth, Bellow or Vonnegut?'

'Oh, they've heard of them,' said Charles. 'They've studied them in comparative lit classes at Dartmouth and Brown. They just don't *appreciate* them like we do.'

Usually, they both would have indulged in good-humoured cynicism, but not today. Martha was stunned. She knew she'd had a dream career and had never really experienced professional rejection since she won a Vogue New Talent award as a junior at Berkeley. But this still hurt.

'So what *do* they want, Charles?'

'More diversity?'

'I'm *old.* That makes me diverse,' said Martha, her

voice rising so much that someone on the next table glanced across.

'Martha, come on…'

She lowered her tone. 'Charles, I've seen what's getting commissioned, and it's a never-ending train of noisy thirty-somethings, activists with an axe to grind and big Instagram followings to help them grind it.'

Charles nodded in solidarity. 'Times are a-changing Marth. Young editors are looking for young writers. People they identify with, people with a ready-made following who can guarantee a return on their huge advances. I mean, are you even on TikTok?'

'Of course, I'm not on TikTok,' she huffed, fanning her face with her napkin.

'Have we fallen that far?' said Martha, trying to compose herself. 'Have we forgotten that great writing is what matters?'

The waiter arrived and placed the salad and steak frites before Martha and Charles.

'Perhaps we could go back to them with an introduction by someone...current?' Charles ventured with unusual hesitancy.

'Current?'

'An actress or singer? Someone like Selena Gomez or Taylor Swift?'

'Why on earth do we need them to write an introduction?'

'Well, they're *popular.* They speak to a different generation. Besides, they might quite like being aligned with someone of your literary pedigree.'

Martha squeezed her hands into a fist, regretting having gone to the trouble of painting her nails this morning. Regretting having come here at all. There was a time when writing was all about sharing ideas and expressing yourself in the clearest and most ringing way; people used to appreciate that; they used to appreciate the poetry of words. *Didn't they?*

Martha was no longer sure. Maybe it had always been about the surface; she was sitting in the Polo Lounge, a place that had always peddled the new and the most shiny. Perhaps Martha Riding was finally out of touch.

'Do *you* think my words need such endorsements, Charles?' Her question was calm, but beneath it lay a ripple of insecurity. She was, after all, a writer.

Charles's expression softened. 'Martha,' he began, his voice hesitant.

Martha looked up; Charles Harriman was a shark, a pit bull. He was never hesitant.

'There's something else I need to discuss with you,' he said.

She watched as Charles clasped his hands together on the table, a sure sign he was gearing up for difficult news.

'I'm retiring,' he said simply.

Martha tried to draw breath but could not. It was as if she had been plunged into a cold river.

'Retiring?' she repeated. It was inconceivable. Charles Harriman was a lion of the literary world, respected and feared in equal measure. There *was* no publishing industry without him. 'But you're an institution, Charles. You can't just—'

'It's time.' His voice was gentle but firm. 'I've been ignoring the signs for too long, and it wouldn't be fair to you or my other clients to continue half-heartedly. I've already told the team.'

'Is this because of my book?' asked Martha, forcing a smile, trying to lighten the tone to hide her disappointment. 'Is it me?'

Her agent smiled back. 'I believe this is where I say, 'it's not you, it's me'.

Martha felt a panic rising. Okay, she had been blindsided by her publishers not wanting her new book. But that would just be a setback with Charles Harriman in her corner. He had turned around the careers of countless authors over the years, pivoting bestselling airport novelists into Hollywood producers and literary lions to Tony-winning playwrights. He'd guided Martha's career from journalist to essayist to New York Times bestselling author. Even if those myopic New York editors didn't want Fade to Black, then screw them; they would find a heavy-hitter in London to publish her.

'Charles, people like us don't retire.'

Her agent chuckled. 'Martha, this can't be that much of a surprise; I'll be 80 this year. I've devoted nearly sixty years of my life to my job and loved every minute, but I want to travel a little, see the world. Judith is desperate to book this three-week cruise to the Galapagos. You know she only has fifty per cent vision in both eyes now, so we want to get there while we can.'

It was seventy degrees on the terrace, but Martha still felt cold all the way down. She liked Charlie's wife, Judith, and wanted her to see giant turtles and whatever else they had in the Galapagos Islands. But Martha also wanted an agent who could save her career. She pushed her plate away, her appetite gone.

'Martha,' said Charles gently, 'Maybe it's time for you too. Imagine no deadlines, no deals, no work. Just life, Martha. Pure, unadulterated life.'

'But writing is my life, Charles,' she said, ashamed to hear the quiver in her voice. 'I've always loved what I do. I've never found it a chore, never counted down the days to retirement because I don't want this to end. I'm Martha Riding. I write – and I write things people need to hear. If I ever stop, I will sink like a stone.'

Martha felt she was standing outside of herself, as if her words were being delivered by someone else. *I'm*

Martha Riding, she had said, but what did that even mean anymore? Nothing, apparently. She had become invisible, gagged, just an old lady in an ancient dress. She stood on unsteady feet, her big rousing speech fallen flat.

'Thanks for lunch, Charles,' she said, dropping her napkin into her empty seat. 'Thanks for *all* the lunches.'

'Martha…'

'Seriously, enjoy your retirement. And send my love to Judith.'

She headed back towards the exit, feeling crushed, consumed by sadness.

'Madame?' asked the Maitre d' as she passed. 'You are done already?'

'Seems that way,' said Martha. 'It really does.'

Chapter 7

Lara had been in such a good mood. The drive to Downtown from Malibu had been glorious. She had the top down on the convertible, the Mamas and Papas on the stereo, and the wind was in her hair as Lara sailed past Santa Monica Pier, past buildings decorated with murals, and shopfronts crowded with flowers or fruit. Then she had clicked on an incoming call over the car's audio system, thinking it was Alex.

'Darling!'

Lara came back down to earth with a bump.

'Hello Darius,' she said, trying not to grimace.

'So I had a features meeting with the entertainment team,' he said without preamble. 'We're planning our celebrity coverage for the next few months, so I thought I'd touch base. There's an LA junket with Ryan Reynolds tomorrow. I was thinking of a 'compare-and-contrast' piece about Ryan's UK life versus his US one: lots of colour about Wrexham. I mean, is he *trying* to learn Welsh?'

Lara groaned inwardly but knew the only way to deal with Darius was to appeal to his vanity.

'It's a great idea,' she said. 'But you know I'm just an investigator. A paper of the Chronicle's standard needs a celebrity specialist to draw the right details from Ryan.'

'Hmm…' She could almost hear him stroking his chin. 'Maybe you're right.

So what *have* you got? Correct me if I'm wrong Lara, but your contract says a story a month minimum—and I thought you'd promised me Cruise.'

Anger flaring, Lara mashed her foot onto the gas, darting past a Walgreens delivery truck and overtaking a lime green Porsche. Lara hated being put on the spot by Darius, especially since she had come here to escape work. Darius did, however, respect Lara's nose for a headline-grabbing story. Perhaps she could use that to her advantage.

'Actually, there *is* one thing,' she said.

'Go on.'

'Well, I'm staying in a house that used to belong to the singer Verity Jones. Lead singer of The Virginians? Sing Together?' she said, singing a bar of the band's most famous song.

'Yes. Remind me never to invite you on a karaoke night,' said Darius. 'But isn't Verity dead?'

'Long dead. Almost fifty years ago to the day.'

'Well, she's hardly Taylor Swift,' he sniffed. 'No one under 60 will have heard of her.'

'But Verity was the Taylor Swift of her day. She was a brilliant singer-songwriter, and she had tons of celebrity friends. She died the night of a big celebrity party. All the Laurel Canyon lot were there - Donna Phelps, Gene Henderson – and no one has ever investigated what happened. Hello? Darius?'

For a moment, Lara thought her boss had cut her off until she heard the faint tap-tap of computer keys. Darius was doing a search.

'Yes,' said Darius, with more interest. 'Verity *was* connected, wasn't she? And they found her floating in the bath. Very Ophelia.'

'And there are question marks over that,' said Lara eagerly. 'Was it a heart attack or...'

'Here's what we'll do,' said Darius, interrupting. 'Big centrespread about the 27 Club. You know, Joplin, Hendrix, Kurt Cobain, and Verity – they all died at 27. See what connects them. Drugs, childhood trauma, unsavoury associates. How does 1500 words by next Friday sound? Splendid, I look forward to it.'

Lara opened her mouth to respond, but Darius had already hung up. She jammed her hand on the horn and swerved around a taxi, narrowly missing its wing mirror. *Calm Lara*, she told herself. Getting T-Boned by a fire truck wouldn't help anyone. But it was hard to be calm. It was exactly as she had feared: even the Chronicle was dumbing down. Everything was becoming broad, splashy and light-weight, all the things Lara hated. And yet...this *was* a way to get Verity's story into the world.

She pulled into the Globe office car park next to the building. She was due to meet Alex for lunch, but before she could even get out of the car, the phone rang again.

'Look, Darius,' she sighed, 'I'm not sure this...' Lara stopped as she heard a laugh.

'Sorry, not Darius – you've got second best. It's me. Alex.'

Lara grinned into the phone.

'Oh. I've just been on the phone to our esteemed editor.'

'Former editor.'

'Lucky you,' said Lara, climbing out of the car. 'I'll fill you in when we meet. Where *are* we meeting, by the way? I've been reading about this place in the arts district which does these little milk doughnuts with sesame ice cream.'

'Oh Lar, that's why I'm ringing,' said Alex. 'Something has come up…'

Lara fought the disappointment. To be fair, Alex had warned her how busy he would be, and she'd suspected his suggestion of meeting for lunch might be optimistic.

'Alex, I'm already here,' she sighed. 'I'm practically in the building.'

'No, really?' he asked, sounding genuinely remorseful. 'I've just heard our cover star has dropped out for the Limelight launch edition. It's all hands on deck finding a replacement before we go to press.'

'…Which is in less than a week,' said Lara. 'Don't worry, I get it.'

'Lar, I'm sorry for wasting your time, dragging you in.'

Lara pouted, a thought popping up.

'Actually – it might not be a waste,' she said. 'Can you do me a favour?'

'Sure, what is it?'

'Darius wants me to write a feature about the 27 Club – you know the list of musicians who died early?'

'Hendrix, Morrison, yes, I know it.'

'Well, can I use the Globe archives? Lots of those deaths were in the Seventies and it would be nice to look at actual newspapers from the time rather than relying on a Google search. I was going to blow Darius out, but that might be quite interesting.'

'Of course – no problem,' said Alex. 'I'll call Stanley in the archives and tell him to expect you. And if I get a minute, I'll come and find you: those doughnuts sound good.'

* * *

The Globe was still in the same building it had been in since the 1920s—art nouveau with a Cali twist, marble and polished wood, but with a lot of gilt and brass, too. The lobby had been upgraded to give the newspaper a 21st-century media sheen, and the lifts - elevators, Lara corrected herself—needed a digital card pass Alex had left for her at reception. But down in the basement, the building showed its age. The walls needed painting, the floors were scuffed, and Lara's eye was drawn to the rows and rows of shelves stretching into the distance, each crammed with books, files and boxes. She felt a flare of excitement; this place had to be crammed with hundreds, thousands of headlines, past and future.

'Can I help?'

A man strode forward with silver hair and deep-set eyes framed by thin gold glasses. He was so tall and rangy that Lara immediately worried about him hitting his elbows on all those shelves.

'I'm looking for Stanley Butler?'

'That's me. And you'll be Lara Stone,' he said, offering an enthusiastic handshake. 'Mr Ford called me and said you were coming, but I would have recognised you anyway. I am a fan.'

He registered her surprise and chuckled.

'This is a newspaper archive, Lara,' he said, waving a big hand towards the depths of the basement. 'You don't come to work down here unless you're a committed news nerd. So yes, I'm an admirer.'

'Really?'

'The Pigeon Scoop, the Marboriogu investigation – and that thing at Kluven?' Stanley formed his mouth into an 'O'. 'Us mere mortals live vicariously through you, Lara.'

She couldn't help smiling. As an investigative journalist, Lara tried to avoid having her photograph in print because anonymity helped her job – but sometimes, it couldn't be avoided, and in this case, she was pleased with the recognition, especially by someone who knew his stuff.

‘Can I get you a coffee?’ asked Stanley. ‘Don’t ask for decaf or fancy milk because I’ll only disappoint you. We don’t get many visitors here, but we have a Mr Coffee.’

‘Actually, that sounds great; I’m still flailing from the jet lag.’

‘Then follow me.’

Stanley led her past rows of filing cabinets and metal shelves crammed with buff-coloured folders stuffed to the brim. The smell of old newsprint, aged paper, dust and ink and the muffled sound of her shoes on the concrete reminded Lara of the libraries at school and university, back when research was a new adventure. They stopped at a cluttered desk, where Stanley set about making the coffee.

‘So, how can I help you today, Lara?’

‘I’m writing a piece about Verity Jones, the singer? I heard one of your journalists was one of the first on the scene when she died.’

‘Jack Anders, yes he was.’

Lara looked at him. ‘You know that off-hand?’

Stanley shrugged.

‘Jack’s still a good friend. We started at the Globe around the same time. He was news; I was in features. And forty-odd years later – here I am still.’

Stanley gave her a self-deprecating smile.

‘I’m sure it’s given me a Vitamin D deficiency, but I love the archive. They have made noises about retirement, but not with much enthusiasm: I suspect it’d be hard to find a replacement.’

The coffee machine began to ‘shoosh’ and ‘phut’, and Stanley retrieved a mug from the shelf.

‘Anyway, Verity Jones,’ he said, pouring Lara a cup, then beckoning her to follow him. ‘This way.’

As he set off with long strides, Stanley explained the archive system. The Globe's newspaper content from the late 90s was stored digitally, but everything else was archived on microfiche film or in a sea of filing cabinets, each neatly labelled and colour-coded to make them easy to find.

'This aisle is sport,' said Stanley. 'LA Olympics from '84, Superbowl coverage, yada-yada. The next two aisles we've got crime – cold cases, major trials. Then here,' – he tapped a hand on the next stack. 'We've got files about various personalities: actors, politicians, mayors. It's all alphabetised. H, I, J....Here we go. Verity Jones,' he said, plucking out a file. 'That should get you started. You might need this too.' He handed Lara a thick, hardbacked book. 'I'll find the Globe editions from the week she died.'

As he disappeared into the next corridor, Lara sat on a chair wedged between two filing cabinets and started flicking through the file of newspaper cuttings. Lara had, of course, already scoured the internet for information about Verity, but it was something else seeing Verity's picture in grey, grainy newsprint – cuttings of Verity very much alive on stage at the Hollywood Bowl, a still from an appearance on The Tonight Show, even a snapshot of Verity standing in front of the Malibu House, with the date and a note 'Singer buys Malibu home', scribbled on the back. Flipping through the cuttings, Lara was surprised at how successful The Virginians had been – guest spots on national TV shows and playing prestigious festivals. Neither had she realised that Eliot Jones in the group was Verity's husband. Lara had, however, heard of Donna Phelps, who was now best known as a media-friendly wellness guru. There was also a fourth member of the group, Benny Dean, who seemed to have disappeared. Lara turned to Stanley's book: 'The Rolling Stone A-Z of Rock' and flicked to 'Verity Jones'.

'Ah, here we go.'

Skimming the entry, Lara learned that Verity had married Eliot at 20 and formed a folk duo named after their hometown of Virginia Beach, just down the coast from 'DC. Seeking the hippy dream, the newlyweds had decamped to LA where they had found that even Dylan had 'gone electric' and folk duos were old hat. So they teamed up with Donna and Benny and began pumping out catchy tunes with just the right hint of flower power. Reading between the lines, it seemed to Lara that the Virginians split at the same time Verity and Eliot went their separate ways, coinciding with 'Sunshine Smile', Verity's first solo hit. The Rolling Stone book also filled in another of the blanks: the fourth man, Benny Dean, had succumbed to another rock cliché: a drink-fuelled car crash in the late 70s.

Lara put down the book and turned to a copy of Verity's death certificate. A single sheet of faded paper that recorded the date, time and cause of death. Heart failure. Behind it was the more detailed autopsy, and Lara took photos of the pages to read in more depth later. She was just returning the files to the shelf when she heard Stanley calling her, his voice a soft echo through the aisles.

Lara found him standing at a Microfiche reader, another relic from her Uni days.

'Here's the Verity Jones story,' he said, gesturing towards the chair.

Lara sat forward to read the story.

'*Folk Singer Dies in Bath,*' she read out loud.

The body of pop singer Verity Jones was discovered at her home in Malibu in the early hours of Sunday. Law enforcement attending said Jones, 27, had been discovered in her bath and was taken to the Lutheran Medical Centre in Santa Monica, where she was declared deceased. Verity Jones rose to fame with folk quartet The Virginians, featuring her husband, Eliot Jones. The group topped the hit parade with their record 'Sing Together'. Recently, Jones has been working as a solo singer.

'Have you noticed: hidden away on page five,' said Stanley.

'Yes, I saw that,' said Lara. 'It's a very subdued tone too. If a pop star had died today, the press would have gone crazy.'

Stanley nodded his agreement.

'The Globe's editor back then was a guy named Harry Standish, and Harry hated pop music. He thought all the kids were commie beatniks smoking reefer and so on.'

Stanley quickly guided her through the files to the updates on Verity in later editions - *Singer's Death Tragic Natural Causes, say Police. Stars Attend Memorial Service. Heart Attack Cause of Death for Singer: Coroner.*

It was all matter-of-fact and perfunctory, as if the paper was somehow embarrassed by this grubby incident down by the beach. Perhaps they were.

'The journalist who wrote this story,' said Lara, reading the by-line on the first new report. 'Eddie Baxter. Is he still…?'

'Alive?' Stanley shook his head. 'Eddie was a big drinker. Passed away in '82, I think it was. Far too young, very sad. But you should speak to Jack Anders – he used to work with Eddie.'

'Jack's son Will works here, right?'

Stanley nodded.

'Will's a good kid, but his dad? There's a man who has newspaper ink running through his veins.'

'Do you think Jack would talk to me?'

Stanley gave Lara a wry smile.

'I think you'll find it hard to shut him up.'

He took a notebook and pencil from his back pocket and scribbled a number before giving it to Lara.

'I'll let him know you're calling.'

They both turned at the sound of footsteps. Lara immediately saw that it was the ambitious rookie from the bar the previous night.

'Ah Natasha,' said Stanley, pushing his glasses further up his nose. 'I don't see a soul all morning, then suddenly it's like Grand Central Station.'

'Lara?' said Natasha. 'What are you doing down here?'

'Just doing some research for a potential story,' said Lara, quickly getting up.

'Oh. Well, I hope you've cleared it with the boss!' Natasha said it light-heartedly, but she was letting Lara know this was her territory. Stanley picked up on the mood and stepped forward.

'What can I help you with, Miss King?'

It was Natasha's turn to look awkward, glancing towards Lara.

'Seagull poop,' she said with a sigh. 'Everyone is saying that the bird doo-doo situation on Santa Monica pier is worse than ever, so I wanted to see if it's always been a problem, maybe see if there have been any studies or…' she trailed off, embarrassed.

'No, that's good thinking,' said Lara, 'Seriously. If the problem grows, maybe you can turn it into a 'save our seaside' campaign. It's what I'd do: turn a shit story – literally, in this case – into something worthwhile.'

Natasha smiled gratefully.

'I'll try, although it won't win me a Pulitzer. I hope whatever story you're working on is more juicy.'

Lara shrugged modestly. 'Not really, my editor is twisting my arm over some celebrity story. Probably a dead end. Speaking of editors, do you know if Alex is still around? We were going to try and grab a coffee.'

Natasha pulled a regretful expression.

'Still busy, I think. I just saw him going into a meeting with the publisher, and then we've got a conference. Sorry.'

'Never mind. If you see him, tell him Daniel Craig called and said yes to lunch, okay?'

She walked off smiling, wondering if she'd dare tell him. Lara only hoped it happened in the boardroom.

Chapter 8

Natasha stepped off the elevator and let out a long breath, relief flooding through her. The fifth floor was where she belonged. Bright and modern: floor-to-ceiling windows, moulded modernist furniture, space - people! Natasha hated the Archive; all those creepy corridors were like walking onto the set of a teen slasher movie. She suppressed a shiver.

'Hey Dani,' she said, crossing to the desk of Danielle Diaz, the Globe's entertainment correspondent. 'Stanley said you asked for this.' Diaz barely looked up as she took the file, just a vague nod before she turned back to her screen. Natasha's smile didn't slip, but inside, she was snarling. *This* was why she hated going to the Archive: because the Archive represented failure. No – it represented Natasha King's failed career. Every time she was sent to the basement to fetch a file, Natasha was reminded of her low position on the totem pole. No one asked Danielle Diaz to 'swing by' the basement – certainly not since Alex had declared the Globe would cover more movie news. No one even asked Gina, Alex's jumped-up PA, to run around like a gofer. Natasha had majored in

Communications at Cal State. At school, she had been voted 'most likely to succeed, and yet here she was, almost 27, still running errands. *Well, all that's going to change.*

She strode down the open-plan passage to her desk, half the size of Danielle's and marooned on the edge of the features department. As a staff writer, Natasha straddled the news and features team. On the face of it, features were the sexy part of the newspaper, where you got to write long-form opinion pieces and interviews with cultural icons. In reality, they reported on the latest diet trends and covered the openings of new doggy-grooming parlours. The heart of any newspaper was the News Room, the furnace that drove the engine, fast-paced and high octane. In news media, nothing was better than breaking a story; getting a scoop could define your career. *There's little chance of that if you're stuck in the basement.* But when Alex had announced increasing the entertainment content of the Globe and the launch of the Limelight supplement, Natasha had suddenly seen a chink of light.

Natasha wasn't exactly sure what she wanted her future to look like. In college, she had dreamt of being the new Diane Sawyer, a glamorous broadcast journalist who could anchor her own show and interview the President of Russia or Brad Pitt with equal ease. Working for a hot entertainment industry-focused magazine like Limelight would increase Natasha's opportunities for networking with TV executives.

But first, she had to convince Alex she should be moved to the Limelight team – which meant she had to give him a reason why. Sighing, Natasha clicked on her screen and looked at the document she had left before going to the archive. *'Pizza parlour accused of feeding crusts to gulls: tourists complain of tsunami of bird-poop'.*

'Jesus,' she whispered. Was this why she'd racked up a crippling debt as a student? But then Natasha reminded herself she was lucky to have any kind of job in the media; most of her graduating class were unemployed. Natasha hated admitting it, but she had only landed this spot at the Globe because her parents had been lucky. They had gone to some swish resort in Hawaii and got talking to a guy at the swim-up bar. They happened to be boasting about their pretty, smart journalist daughter, and the guy with the frozen Margarita happened to be Jon Novoselic, editor at the LA Globe – Alex Ford's predecessor. When Jon had offered Natasha an internship, they had practically wept. Four years on, Natasha had worked her way up to a hybrid news/feature role and was waiting for someone to die so she could take their place; that seemed the only likely way Natasha would get promoted.

She looked up as two people walked past her, brushing against the back of her chair. Steve Reynolds, head of Sports and Mischa Jenks, picture editor.

'You not coming?' asked Mischa.

'Where to?'

Mischa gave a short shake of her head.

'Afternoon conference, Nat. It's almost three.'

Swearing silently, Natasha grabbed her laptop and notebook, scrabbling it all together and rushing towards the boardroom at the far end of the building. When Alex Ford took the reins as editor, he had started inviting junior staff members to conferences – the daily meetings when the team would discuss what would go in the following day's newspaper. It was a great way to get noticed, but she had spent so long wondering what Lara Stone was up to in the archives, the news conference had completely slipped her mind.

At the bar last night, Lara had said she was on vacation, but if that was the case, what the hell was she doing in the archives? She'd tried to be casual and pass it off as nothing special, but Natasha had seen the microfiche open on an old story about Verity Jones' death. Wasn't the singer's old house where Alex Ford and his girlfriend were staying? Could they be thinking of buying the property and wanted to know if the history was gory? If so, that wasn't good news. Lara Stone in LA was a threat. She was a top investigator; that was the last thing Natasha wanted at the Globe. Watergate, Blackwater, and Wikileaks were all long-term investigations that had brought glory to their writers. That was Natasha's goal, and she didn't need any competition.

Natasha tried to focus, knowing she needed to shine in this meeting. Everybody felt under pressure to deliver to the energetic new editor. When Alex asked, 'What have you got?', you wanted an answer. Trying not to look as flustered as she felt, Natasha took one of the last seats around the board table; at least Alex wasn't at his customary seat at the head of the table yet, so she was safe.

'Made it then?' said Mischa sarcastically, but Natasha ignored her.

The conversation died down as Alex strode in and sat down. There was no question that Alex Ford was hot - for an older guy, anyway. He obviously kept fit, and that dark hair flopped over his eyes. *Be professional,* she reminded herself - *for now, at least.*

'OK, what have we got on this plane crash story?' began Alex.

Ralph, the news editor, sat forward.

'Locally, they are saying the crash is down to a missile strike, but my contact in the Pentagon says definitely not. Sandy spoke to a guy she knows in the airline head office. Word is those liners were regularly grounded for maintenance.'

'Any Americans onboard?'

'No. We've just had confirmation: two passengers were

French, and the Irish woman they'd reported was a typo; she was from Iceland.'

Alex nodded.

'OK, not a priority for us, run it inside, half page max, but keep in touch with your aerospace connection; if there's a problem with BlueStar planes generally, that will impact domestic airlines.'

Natasha glanced around the table. She could guess what they were all thinking: what were they doing, wasting their time on an air crash in some distant country? Alex came from the UK, where the papers dealt with international news daily, but in the US, readers didn't care about the rest of the world, only what was happening in their home town or city: who cared about some dead French guy – I mean, where *was* France, anyway?

Alex tapped his pen on the table.

'I know many of you think this crash is irrelevant,' he said. 'But I'd argue we need more of this – big stories, stories that stir people up, things that anger and frighten them. Okay, this is happening in Europe, but engine failure could just as easily happen at LAX. What if it *is* terrorism? America knows better than anyone how important airline security is.'

No one spoke, so Alex continued.

'And let's keep upping the coverage of Hollywood – don't save it all for the Limelight supplement. We already know the readers have been responding to that. I want exclusives, big eye-catching headlines that speak to the readers emotionally. We want people to see the Globe as a force for good, the only thing standing between them and injustice – and their trusted guide to entertainment.'

They all nodded, but Natasha could see the dissent remained, especially among the older staffers. Most people had responded positively to Alex Ford's arrival. Okay, he was British and had never worked for a US paper before, but he was smart and dynamic and seemed keen to foster a keen team spirit – organising staff drinks and having an open door policy for whatever you wanted to talk about. But she had heard grumbles from some who didn't like Alex's changes to the paper - they didn't like *any* kind of change. And that meant opportunity for Natasha.

'Okay, here's a case in point,' said Alex. 'People are emailing in, complaining about the delays on the interstate because of those bridge works. It's having a knock-on effect, slowing traffic across the city.'

'You're telling me,' said Mischa. 'The junction with I5 has almost been at a standstill these last few weeks.'

'Yeah, how long does it take them to build a bridge?'

Alex raised a finger. 'Exactly. So let's find out why it is taking so long.'

Natasha nodded as if she was fully engaged but had already tuned out. This was the problem with working at a local newspaper; you had to deal with these boring local issues. Sure, Los Angeles was physically the fourth biggest city in the world, but that was mainly due to its urban sprawl—LA was dwarfed by New York in terms of population and by Washington in terms of cultural importance.

'Natasha, Will? I want you two on this one.'

Natasha looked up in alarm. She had been so preoccupied she hadn't heard the last minute's conversation.

'Sure,' said Will, looking over at Natasha. 'We'll get right on it.'

'Yeah,' said Natasha, trying not to look flustered. 'No problem.'

Had Alex just given them the freeway traffic story? Her stomach dropped. Her first proper assignment from the new editor, and it was some boring local planning bullshit. She glanced at Alex as he carried on with the meeting. Was this all he thought she was worth? Well, she wasn't going to take it lying down. She watched her boss's eyes. *Well, not unless he wanted her to.*

* * *

'Alex, could I have a word?'

Natasha had waited until the end of the meeting, shuffling papers and pretending to make notes while the others all filed out. Then she had walked straight to Alex's office, glad that Gina, his PA was still gossiping in the corridor.

'Sure,' said Alex, nodding to a chair opposite his desk. 'Close the door.'

Natasha sat, arranging her legs to best advantage, but kept her back straight. She was sexy but professional. That was the idea, anyway.

'So how can I help?'

'You may not know, but next month, I'll have been at the Globe for four years.'

'That's great; why don't we schedule a review?'

'Sure,' said Natasha. She had nothing to fear; she was writing pap, but she was churning out three times as much pap as anyone else on the Globe. No one could accuse Natasha King of not pulling her weight when it came to recipes, beauty products and open-air theatre. 'But ahead of that, I wanted to raise an issue.'

'What is it?' he asked, with a faint frown of concern. That was good. It meant he cared.

'I just wanted to tell you how excited I am about the launch of Limelight magazine, and I wanted to put myself forward. High-profile interviews are where I see my future, and it's where I feel I can offer the most value to the Globe…'

She trailed off as Alex held up a hand, his expression turning harder and more professional.

'Your enthusiasm is noted and valued, Natasha, but

unfortunately, the Limelight team is small and very experienced in that area. Matt has worked on Variety and Dani is the Globe's senior ents writer. That said, if Limelight is well received, we may look at expanding the team.'

Natasha knew all this. She'd already spoken with Neil, the executive editor, who had also tried to deflect her about future openings.

'If anything does open up, it will be a reporter's role,' continued Alex. 'And for that, we'll need someone who can generate news stories. Someone who can write about the business of showbusiness, the economy of Hollywood.'

She knew what he was saying. Natasha hadn't exactly scored any hot scoops for the newspaper. Then again, she had hardly been given the chance.

'I realise a lot of my experience is at the softer end of news,' she said, 'But I'm versatile.'

'Then the bridge story is a great opportunity to show that off. You'll be dealing with City Hall, industry, angry commuters....'

He made it sound like she had just been assigned to the Washington Bureau, and Natasha felt her resolve melt. Up close, he was so good-looking—those eyes, that square jaw, the hint of skin at the top of his shirt.

'Okay, I'll get on it,' she replied.

'Good,' said Alex more briskly. 'All good stories start with research, so I want comparison data: how much similar projects cost to build, how many quotes the City invited when they put it out to tender, and how much other cities pay for transport and construction costs. But most importantly, I want to know about the people. Who green-lit the project, who signed off on the budget? Any relationship between the contractor and City Hall? Good stories are always about relationships. Who can do what for whom.' He flashed a smile. 'Let me know how you get on.'

He opened the door, and Natasha stepped out in a

daze. She had come in hoping to sweet-talk Alex Ford into changing her assignment and he had somehow turned the tables on her, made her *want* to do this lame planning story. And what was all that stuff about relationships? Was he trying to tell her something? And that line 'Who can do what for whom?' Well, she was certainly prepared to do whatever he asked. Natasha grabbed her bag from her desk and strode over to Will Anders' cubby hole. 'Come on newshound,' she said, beckoning, 'We're going to the Archive.'

'The archive? What for?'

'Research, loser.' She said, turning on her heel, 'Don't you know that's where every story starts?'

Chapter 9

Lara loved Carla's Diner the moment she saw it. A classic eaterie in Pasadena's historic district, it had a space-age fifties logo lit up in neon, although it was hard to see the lights in the Californian sunshine. Inside were booths facing the street and a row of red vinyl stools along the counter. Best of all, the heady aroma of slightly burnt coffee mingled with bacon and grease. Carla's was as American as apple pie, which, according to a chalkboard next to the till, was 'Homemade and hot'.

Lara spotted Jack Anders immediately, sitting in the furthest booth, right next to an old wall-mounted phone, as if he was expecting an important incoming call. Even if she hadn't Googled him, Lara would have easily picked Jack from a line-up; grey hair slightly too long, wrinkled shirt with the sleeves rolled up, he certainly had the look of a newspaperman, but it was his eyes that gave it away: clear, sharp and watching everything in the room.

'Lara Stone, I presume,' he said, offering his hand. 'A real pleasure.'

'Likewise, Mr Anders.'

'Oh, Jack, please. I'm not that old,' he said, folding the

paper he had been reading. As Lara slid into the booth, he tapped a finger against it. 'Or perhaps I am. These days, when I read the papers, I just get angry.'

'Angry at the state of the world?'

Jack smiled, his eyes crinkling at the sides.

'Nah, the world's always been a mess. You think you've got it bad? Try having Nixon in the Big Chair.'

Lara took his point; it was easy to assume your problems were the biggest and most troubling the world had ever seen. You only had to look at a history book to see the folly of that thinking.

'No, I'm angry at the state of journalism,' said Jack, sliding the newspaper across. 'Take this story for example; 'Hernandez to sign for the Dodgers' – that's the headline, right?'

Jack turned the paper and read out loud:

'Jose Hernandez announced Thursday his intention to move from the Angels to rivals The Dodgers in a move that shocked fans. At a 1PM press conference, Hernandez said, 'It's always been my dream to play for such an iconic team. I look forward to helping them reach the playoffs.'

He dropped the newspaper and looked at Lara. 'Now, what's wrong with that?'

'They use the word 'move' twice in the first sentence.'

'Yeah, that annoyed me too,' said Jack. 'But really…?'

Lara didn't have to think too hard; this was second nature to her. She ticked off the points on her fingers.

'No mention of who Jose Hernandez is or his position. Where was the press conference? Was it the same day as the announcement? Why were fans shocked?' She craned her neck to look at the article. 'And actually…which sport is this? Baseball?'

Jack grinned, nodding.

'Well, you can't assume everyone reading the sports page knows that.'

'I'm with you, Lara. Whatever happened to teaching the news kids a bit of old-school journalism: who, what, where, why, how?'

Lara was glad she had passed Jack's test, because it would make the next part easier. A waitress with shiny red hair in a high ponytail came over to take their order.

'Twice in one day, Jack? You'll be moving in next.'

'Don't tempt me,' he grunted, although Lara could tell he was pleased with the attention. The waitress filled Lara's mug with hot coffee from a glass jug, and Lara ordered the peach pie.

'So you come here a lot?' Lara asked when the waitress had gone.

'Nearly every day since I retired a couple of years ago. I come, and I read all the papers, and I people-watch. My wife laughs at me and says I can't quite let the newsroom go - and I guess she's right. Retirement's not all it's cracked up to be. I miss the chase; I miss the thrill of the story. Even a local rag like the PE kept the old ticker going, but once you stop looking for the new thing, what's the point in life?'

'PE? You worked for the Pasadena Examiner?'

He nodded. 'For the last twenty years of my career. As you probably know, I was at the Globe before that, which I loved, but then I hit fifty, and I had to face up to the fact that I would never make editor or anything near it. Just wasn't *political* enough,' he smiled sadly. 'So I moved out here, thought I was giving up,' he said lowering his voice to a whisper. 'But you know what? I've loved it here, too. Never won any awards, never broke a news story that rang around the world. But this is what it's about. *Community.*'

He paused to sip his coffee.

'Your Felix Tait story was great, by the way.'

Lara gave a surprised chuckle.

'I got sued and almost suspended for that story.'

'Maybe, but it was good. When Stanley called me and said Lara Stone wanted to meet me, I had to cancel my Silver Surfer bowling afternoon and come meet you.'

Lara flushed at the compliment. She'd won awards for her work in the UK but hadn't expected her stories to be read and remembered by people in suburban LA – even if they were veteran newshounds like Jack Anders.

'So how can I help?' said Jack, as the waitress brought the pie. Steam rose from pale orange fruit peeping through a lattice of pastry.

'Stan said you wanted to talk about an old story?'

Lara looked at him in surprise.

'He didn't say which one?'

'Stan's a wily old goat. We play poker together; he literally plays his cards close to his chest.'

'Verity Jones.'

'Haven't heard that name in a while,' he said, looking up at her from under his bushy grey brows. 'Still, it must be coming up fifty years since she died. You doing an anniversary piece?'

'I'm staying at her old house in Malibu.'

Jack whistled through his teeth as he stuck his fork into the pie.

'Journalism's paying better than it did in my day.'

Lara gave a soft smile. 'Actually, it belongs to Simon Desai, owner of the Globe. He leant it to Alex Ford, my boyfriend.'

Jack raised a playful finger. 'Yes, that part, Stanley mentioned.'

Lara tucked into her dessert. It was hot and delicious – sweet and sharp in equal measure.

'So I met your son, Will, last night. Alex rates him.'

Alex hadn't exactly done a professional assessment on the Globe team but even at the bar, she had picked up that Will Anders was keen and well respected.

'Well, keep reminding Mr Ford of that. Obviously, I'm biased, but Will has good instincts and works hard – and that's all you can ask. I mean, I did try to talk him out of it; I saw the writing on the wall for the industry twenty years ago, but Will wouldn't be deterred.'

Lara raised her coffee cup in salute. 'Good for him,' she said. 'I'm glad young people still want in.'

She took a thoughtful bite of pie.

'So you covered Verity's death for the Globe. Do you remember much about it?

'Remember it?' said Jack, 'It happened my first month on the job – I can't forget it.'

He quickly told her how he had joined the Globe straight out of college and had been making coffee and opening envelopes for the first few weeks.

'They'd let me at a couple of stories. Interviewing witnesses to a traffic fatality, a dead whale washing up on the shore in Oxnard. But then I got the call about Verity.'

'Why you, if you were so junior?'

'The newsroom got the story at about 6.30am,' he said. 'The night-shift news editor remembered I lived in Santa Monica, not too far from Verity's place, so I got the call at home to head straight up to Malibu. I was supposed to get some early atmosphere at the scene until Eddie Baxter, the senior reporter I'd been shadowing, could get there.

'So, were you the first reporter there?' asked Lara. So much of this career was luck – being in the right place at the right time. Lara had got her own lucky break in a similar way, eating lunch on a bench in St James' Park when she had seen a senior politician in a clinch with a woman who was not his wife.

'No, there were a couple of reporters from the Metro and the News who were harassing the police for a quote. But everyone ignored me, this scrawny kid, just hanging around at the edges. So I took advantage of that.'

Lara nodded, imagining him hustling at the scene. The newsroom was no place for wallflowers.

'At this point, no one seemed to know what had happened. I was hearing different accounts – heart attack, drowned in the bath, maybe even an overdose: she was a pop singer, right? But no one seemed to know for sure and it, well, it didn't smell right. So I had to see for myself.'

'You got in?'

'I slipped twenty bucks to the guy taking the photos for the medical examiner. It was all the money I had in my wallet.'

Lara felt her excitement rise.

'What did you see?'

'Bottles and glasses everywhere– there'd been a party, remember? Although I did note that the ashtrays were all empty. And Hendrix on the turntable – I remember that. 'Scuse me while I kiss the sky.' He chuckled to himself.

'And did you see Verity?'

Jack shook his head.

'She was already gone, wheeled out by the medics. But I did peek into the bathroom. That's where they found her - in the tub, right next to the bedroom on the ground floor. There was nothing out of the ordinary. Just some soap in a dish near the faucet. No bottle of bourbon, no bottles of pills. But one thing was strange. I dipped my hand in the water; it was freezing cold.

'Why was that odd?'

He shrugged.

'Verity had kicked everyone out of the party a little before 11, right? So, say she had a hot bath straight away. The bath water would be cold by 7am but not ice cold. This is Malibu, remember? It had been a hot night, and this was before air-con. Plus, it was a cast iron tub. Those things retain heat for hours.'

Lara nodded, thinking it through.

'So what does it signify?'

'Maybe nothing. But I asked myself, 'Why would Verity get into a cold bath?' And I could only think of three things. One, she had a fever and needed to cool down. Two, she was in pain: that fits an interview she'd done a few months before she died. She said she'd back problems on tour, which was one of the reasons why The Virginians went on hiatus.'

'Did you mention this to the news team?'

'Sure, but they weren't particularly interested. Eddie spoke to the doctor at the Emergency Room, who said it was a heart attack: that was it.' He dusted his hands together.

'You said three reasons for the ice-cold water?'

'Well, drugs would be the other one. Classic way to revive someone on an overdose. And when the autopsy came back, there *were* drugs in her system, but the cause of death was still a heart attack, and everyone seemed to accept that.'

'Why?

By now, Jack had finished his pie. He pushed his plate to one side.

'Lara, this was the Seventies,' he said. 'No one was particularly surprised that another pop star had died from overindulgence. Hendrix choked to death, Brian Jones drowned. Janis Joplin, Gram Parsons, and Gene Henderson all overdosed. You fly high; you get burnt. Besides, there were bigger stories going on. Kids were getting flown home from Vietnam in a box. Everyone was angry with the government. No one was going to dwell on the story of a folk band hippy found dead in her tub.'

He looked away from her, his attention on the street where a mother had stopped to adjust the parasol on her baby's stroller.

'But what do *you* think happened, Jack?'

He shook his head, his expression slightly embarrassed.

'Over the years, I've asked myself that question a lot. But here's the thing. I was a kid given a break and I didn't follow through. I didn't ask enough questions, I didn't push hard enough even though my instinct was telling me that something wasn't right.'

'You don't think Verity died of a heart attack?'

'If that's what the autopsy said, I don't doubt it. But there was something else going on, I'm sure of it. And there's something else I never told anyone before.'

Lara leaned forward.

'I didn't stay in Verity's house long,' said Jack. 'The detective came back and threw me out –literally. Grabbed me by the scruff of the neck and almost hurled me down the back stairs onto the beach. So, instead, I went looking for witnesses. Knocked on doors. A guy called Mike Cohen was at home three doors down.'

Jack looked at her expectantly as if she were supposed to recognise the name. When she didn't react, Jack shook his head like a teacher who was disappointed in his student.

'Come on: Mike Cohen!' he said, sitting forward. 'Dark Noon? The Hindenburg Affair? Cohen was a screen-writing star of the Forties, blacklisted in the Fifties. A legend.'

He shrugged.

'Anyway, by the Seventies, Mike had retired to Malibu; he was in his eighties by now. I interviewed him twice about Verity, and he said exactly the same thing.'

'What? What did he say?'

Jack tapped a finger on the tabletop.

'He said he heard a gunshot.'

'A *gun*shot?' gasped Lara. 'What time was this?'

'Mike reckoned it was about midnight. He'd been up

watching a movie but was just going to bed and had switched off the TV. That's when he heard it.'

'From Verity's place? The shot came from the Malibu House?

'Mike swore it came from that direction – and back then, Verity's was the only house to the south.'

Lara frowned.

'But Verity wasn't shot.'

Jack grinned. 'Exactly.'

Chapter 10

Martha Riding's book club night had been a roaring success. Her friend Suzie Byers, a well-known Malibu caterer, had provided the food, and it had been outstanding: huge platters of cheese with olives the size of ping-pong balls, big rustic bowls of Greek, kale and Caesar salad, plus brownies, blondies and a Pavlova the size of a car wheel over-spilling with berries and cream. The evening's choice of book – Fifty Shades of Grey - had also been a triumph, prompting a riotous exchange of erotic scenarios, starting with the literary variety, then moving onto descriptions of the real-life kind, the women laughing and gasping at each other's tales. But the host herself was exhausted, and by 9pm, Martha wanted everyone out.

'Ladies, take whatever food you can fit in your Birkins,' said Martha, ushering them towards the spread on the kitchen counter. 'Bags are on the side. That watermelon salad won't last until tomorrow, so please, take everything.'

'What about the Blondies?' asked her friend Juliet, who lived a few doors down. 'I've got the grandkids all coming tomorrow, and they are always hungry.'

'Take the lot,' said Martha, bustling over to a kitchen

cupboard to find a tin and loading the leftovers into it. She opened the door and waved them off:

'Bye Melody…Cynthia, thank you for coming from Ventura…Tell Jeffrey I will never be able to look at him in the same light after that story about Amsterdam.'

Martha shut the door on them all and closed her eyes, her hand still pressed against the lock. 'Thank God,' she whispered. Martha's feet were aching, and she felt heady from the raucous conversation. 'Getting old…' she began but then jumped at a clatter from the kitchen. As she looked up, Lara Stone walked out carrying a stack of bowls.

'You frightened me,' breathed Martha, pressing a hand against her chest. 'I thought everyone had gone.'

'Oh. Sorry,' replied the young Englishwoman. 'I just thought you might need a hand tidying up.'

'Help gladly received,' said Martha, slipping off her shoes with a sigh. Of all her guests, she was happy her newest acquaintance had stayed. Lara had not been the loudest or the funniest at the gathering, but when she did say something, people turned to listen. It was too simple to say Lara Stone reminded Martha of her younger self, although there was a little of that. No, it was that Lara represented something Martha had once been: smart, driven and hungry for the truth. And when Lara was around, Martha could feel herself waking up again.

Martha stretched, wiggling her toes to ease the stiffness. 'I'm in my seventies, but I've still got to learn how to say 'no'. Like today, it was: 'Martha, do you want to come for breakfast? Yes, Barbara.' 'Martha, come and discuss your new book. Sure, Charles.' 'Is Book Club still on tonight, Marth? Of course. Come round for 6.30.'

Lara laughed.

'Well, I am glad you made the effort,' said Lara,

picking up plates and discarded napkins. 'It was the most fun I've had in ages.'

'Oh honey,' smiled Martha. 'You need to get out more.'

In the Seventies and Eighties Martha and Griffin's soirees had packed a powerful social punch – actors, producers, musicians, everyone came. Even now, if she squinted, she could still see a Rolling Stone on the terrace or Robert Evans lounging across her cream sofa. Martha and Griff had been considered erudite and smart back then. Perhaps, deep down, Martha felt she still was.

'And the food was amazing,' said Lara as she bent to stack the dishwasher. 'I can't believe you can cook as well as you write.'

'Well, I have to come clean there,' said Martha. 'I can just about manage pasta, but the salads, the cake - all made by my friend Suzie. She did it at cost in return for me giving a talk at her book club next month.'

'Well, your secret's safe with me,' said Lara.

'Coffee's all mine, though,' said Martha, holding up a jug. 'You want some?'

Martha took two mugs to the little seating area next to the terrace.

'Couldn't persuade Barbara to join us?' she asked Lara.

'I knocked on her door before I left, but there was no answer.'

'Probably hiding behind the drapes, with some TV drama on,' she said. 'Barb prefers watching The Love Boat to parties these days. She told me once that after 40 years of being a Hollywood wife, all those mind-numbing cocktail parties with Donnie, she promised herself 'no more small talk'. Sometimes, I don't blame her.'

'Talking of cocktails, weren't you seeing your agent today? How did that go?'

Martha looked away, taking a sip of coffee to hide her discomfort. It was a wonder that she had got through the book club, laughing and joking with her friends when all Martha wanted to do was curl up in a ball. She'd painted on a smile and joined in with the funny stories, but now and then, she'd get a flashback to her Polo Lounge lunch with Charles, and her mood would sink like a stone. She still couldn't believe that not one publisher had made an offer for her book. Not *one.* Three years of work down the drain. And worse than that, her agent had suggested she retire her typewriter. Like, forever.

'Martha, are you alright?'

'I'm fine,' she said, the words coming out sharper than intended. Martha pressed her lips together, trying to hold it all in. She didn't want to dump her disappointments onto a young writer who was in the prime of her career – why not let her keep dreaming? Besides, it was more than a little embarrassing too. Martha Riding, Pulitzer and Peabody prize winner and Columbia School of Journalism Fellow, had been dumped on the scrap heap. A fat tear rolled down her cheek.

'I should just have cancelled tonight,' said Martha quietly, pushing the tear away.

'But why?'

Just say it, Martha told herself. *Keeping it a secret isn't going to make it go away.*

So, drawing a ragged breath, Martha gave Lara a brief rundown of her depressing conversation with Charles in the Polo Lounge.

'*No one* wanted your book? God, then the industry is screwed,' said Lara fiercely. 'And Martha, it's not just books. Alex is always complaining that newspapers refuse to invest in talent. They throw money at trends and brands and their precious corporate ethos. But who's thinking about the *writing?* The opinions, the insight - the *words.* Those things will last long after you put down the book or the magazine.'

Martha appreciated Lara's passion, but it didn't change anything.

'You know, if I thought my book just wasn't good enough, I could have accepted it,' she sniffed. 'But it was some of my best work, Lara. I *know* it was. But then maybe they've got a point. If no one is reading any more, who cares what some old woman has to say?'

Lara practically growled.

'Seriously, Martha, listen to yourself,' she said impatiently. 'You have thousands, millions of fans. I'm one of them, and so is Alex; we all want to read your new work. Screw those publishers. Do it yourself. Go online and print your own books. Speak to Alex; he can serialise it.'

Martha gave a low, snotty chuckle.

'Maybe *you* should be my agent.'

Lara smiled. 'I don't think my rants about publishers would help.'

Martha turned to look out at the darkened beach. Somewhere out there, she could hear the swoosh of the waves. The sea didn't care about her problems, which somehow made her feel a little better. She reached across and forked up a mouthful of Suzie's carrot cake. That made her feel better, too.

'So, how's your day been?' she asked. 'Better than mine, I hope?'

Lara looked a little sheepish.

'I've been into the archives at the Globe, checking out the history of the Malibu House.'

'So the house has sucked you in,' said Martha. 'Yes. I can see it might do that.'

'You've got to admit it's intriguing,' said Lara, 'What went on that night after you left?'

Martha tried to picture herself talking it through with Griffin. The Verity Jones bug had also bitten him for a while. What did he say? What had he discovered when he had been investigating it? Martha couldn't remember; it was far too long ago to remember the details.

'Did you find anything in the archives?'

'Not much,' said Lara regretfully. 'But the archivist knew a retired journalist who worked on the original story, so I went to speak to him. Apparently, a neighbour named Mike Cohen heard gunshots.' She held up a finger. 'Now *that* has never been reported.'

Martha raised an eyebrow. 'Lara, you do know this is America? Three guns for every citizen – have you ever heard that? You're more likely to hear gunshots in the night here than hear an owl hooting.'

'But I thought gun laws were strict in California?'

'If you think owning as many guns as you like is strict. Anyway, this was the early 70s; they'd only just passed a law to stop people openly carrying loaded guns in public - and they only did that because The Black Panthers had marched into the State Capitol building waving machine guns.'

'Really?' said Lara.

'Look it up,' said Martha. 'Anyway, I knew Mike Cohen a little, and he must have been pushing eighty then.'

Lara gave a wry smile.

'And you're saying Mike must have been wrong because he was old?'

'Ah,' said Martha. 'You got me there. But even so…'. Her gaze trailed back towards the ocean, a big black hole of nothingness.

'I admit, it's odd,' she said finally. 'In fact, there's a lot about that night which was odd. But it was fifty years ago, and the police weren't even suspicious at the time. I don't know what you expect to dig up.'

Lara sat forward.

'One, the police barely investigated; they just took the doctor's assessment of a heart attack at face value. Two, the doctor was at the hospital, not at the scene, so his 'heart attack' diagnosis may have been correct, but there was no discussion over what *caused* the heart attack. And three, the post-mortem noted 'narcotics' and 'alcohol' as being present - but again, the police didn't think it worthy of further investigation. That's a start, isn't it?' Lara looked at Martha directly. 'And you admit it was odd: what else was off about that night?'

Martha sighed.

'I've always wondered why Verity threw everybody out when the party was just getting going. And the narcotics, that in itself was strange.'

'Why strange? It was the Seventies; I thought drugs were a big thing.'

'Sure, grass, maybe acid or peyote once in a while. And coke was starting to overtake the rock scene. But heroin?' Martha shook her head. 'Verity told me once she hated it and would never take it.'

It was one of the many things that Martha had admired about Verity. Despite her party-loving reputation, Verity didn't socialise for the drink, the drugs or the hedonism; she threw parties for the *people*. Martha had been the same. A tab of LSD at Berkeley had scared her so badly that she vowed never to touch it again, and even a puff of pot meant she couldn't think straight - and that interfered with her work. As for coke and heroin? She'd never gone near them, having witnessed too many Class A casualties, friends who thought they were in control of their drug taking but were lost in their grip. Verity always had a drink in her hand, but Martha had watched her; she was using the Dean Martin Method. If you had a hellraiser's reputation, everyone assumed you were drunk – while the glass stayed full.

'So what did Griffin think?' asked Lara. 'You said he was working on some drug angle?'

'Not for very long. And remember, the story got shut down.'

'But he must have told you something,' said Lara. 'Yesterday, you mentioned there was a bad batch of drugs going around, and Griff wondered if Verity had taken some?'

Martha could see the Englishwoman wasn't going to let this go. No wonder she was such a good journalist. And Martha could admit she was enjoying this, too. When she was a child, her mum and dad used to call her 'our born-storyteller' – an only child, Martha did remember sitting all her teddy bears in the corner of her room and telling them about her day. She had gone on to make a career out of it, and right now, Martha couldn't even tell you why it had taken her over three years to write another book because telling stories came as easily to her as breathing. She poured more coffee before she continued.

'Have you ever heard of China white?'

'It's a type of fentanyl, right?'

Martha sipped her drink. 'It might be what they call synthetic opioids now, but back in the 70s, China white was a very pure, very powerful heroin that came from the golden triangle in South East Asia. Griffin was looking at a guy named Jameson Bennett, some rich kid hanger-on who was in love with the celebrity life. He was also a dealer. His father was a diplomat and the rumour was Jameson was using Daddy's diplomatic bag to smuggle China white into LA via Marseilles. Two known clients of Jameson's died within two weeks of Verity's death. One a model, one a musician from West Hollywood, both in their twenties – and both suffered heart failure following heroin use.'

'And this guy Jameson Bennett had sold it to them?'

Martha nodded.

'Jameson was boasting about it: he said it proved just how pure his stuff was.'

'Did Bennett know Verity?'

'That's what Griffin was trying to find out. I mean, I never met Jameson or saw him at the Malibu House, but he knew some of the Laurel Canyon set, so Griff thought there was a chance Bennett might have dropped into Verity's last party.'

'Did anyone see him there?'

Martha shook her head. 'I know Griffin asked around, and it was a no. But even so, Griff felt there was still a possibility that some of Bennett's drugs made it to the Malibu parties. Drugs were passed around like candy back then.'

Martha felt a smile spread across her face, suddenly aware of how much she enjoyed talking about Griffin. Recently, Martha had found herself talking about him less and less as friends who remembered Griff died or simply moved on with their lives. It was good to reconnect with her husband, to remember who he was and why he was good at his job.

'So why did Griffin stop following the story?' asked Lara.

Martha shrugged. 'A week or so after it was commissioned, Harley - the editor - called him to axe it and gave him a kill fee.'

'How did Griffin feel about that?'

'Disappointed, maybe. But then he got another big-money Hollywood job and, well, you just move on, don't you?'

Lara was nodding thoughtfully.

'We should look into it,' she said. 'Make a list of the people who might remember something about that night.'

At first, Martha wasn't sure she'd heard her properly.

'We?' And look into what?'

'Into Verity's death. I've already been commissioned to

write about the 27 Club, but that's not the real story – the Malibu House is. Join me, Martha. Help me.'

'You want *me* to work on this?'

'Come on, admit it, there are so many questions about Verity's death. Don't you want to know what happened? Perhaps we could even finish off the story Griffin was writing.'

Martha knew Lara was manipulating her, but even so, she could admit she found the idea exciting. The younger woman looked at her with an expression of mischief and resolve. How she reminded Martha of Griffin—smart, tenacious, curious. But still, Martha was bruised from her meeting at the Polo Lounge, and the thought of concentrating on anything made her feel tired.

'Lara, I'm an essayist; I observe and then write it down. Investigative work was always Griffin's bag, not mine.'

But clearly, Lara was not to be put off.

'I thought Martha Riding could turn her hand to anything,' she said. 'And I know she wants to show the world what she's still got.'

'Ooh, you're a wily one,' said Martha, pointing a finger. 'You're just like Griffin, always knowing the right buttons to press. And…'

She started thinking. 'I guess we could talk to Eliot, Verity's husband, and Donna from the band, who was Vee's best friend. Maybe Willow Caan, too; she was friends with everyone.'

'So you're in?' said Lara.

Martha sighed.

'Well, I suppose I can make a few calls,' she said. 'Wouldn't do any harm to reconnect with some old friends.'

'Yes! She's in!' said Lara, offering her a hand.

And Martha reached out and shook it.

Chapter 11

9.30pm, and traffic was at a standstill. Alex drummed his fingers on the armrest and resisted the urge to look at his watch again. He didn't need to: he had been staring at it for the past hour, ever since he had finally left the office. Outside his window to the left was a stationary mini-van driven by a middle-aged woman with two children in the back. The driver was gazing straight ahead while the children, strapped into their seats, stared at their phones. Their blank expressions reminded Alex of a prison he'd once visited in Guatemala. Resignation and detachment: the lot of the imprisoned, even those with air-con.

Alex had, of course, heard all the horror stories about LA rush hour gridlock – in fact, 'Falling Down' was one of his favourite films, wherein Michael Douglas becomes so enraged about becoming trapped on the freeway, he abandons his car that goes on a murderous rampage. Alex could sympathise; it certainly felt like getting out and walking would be quicker. But Lara would not be happy – and Alex didn't blame her.

When she had booked her flight for her two-week trip,

he'd known that he would be busy, but he hadn't thought that getting Limelight over the finish line would be such hard work. Alex was still convinced that the idea of a glossy entertainment industry supplement was key to his plan of updating the Globe, but everything that could have gone wrong *had* gone wrong. It wasn't just the cover star dropping out; the magazine's design wasn't quite slick enough, and no advertiser had yet committed to the lucrative back page ad slot. Alex was so overstretched he needed to clone himself right now, and he only hoped his girlfriend would understand.

'Sorry about this, Mr Ford,' said Jake, his driver, over his shoulder. 'I never seen it this bad.'

Alex didn't usually use the Globe's driver service, but he was so tired right now that he was glad of it. He liked Jake, a salt-of-the-earth Italian Angelino and a huge Dodgers fan. Being around Jake was a refreshing change from the media liberals and Ivy Leaguers he spent his days with.

'It's not your fault, Jake,' said Alex, knowing it probably hadn't helped that Alex had asked him to stop in Chinatown to pick up a bag of pomelos. The giant grapefruit-like fruits were Lara's favourite. They'd discovered them almost a decade earlier when Alex had been posted to Hong Kong, and Lara had perfected a potent cocktail using the fruit – part vodka, part brandy, lots of freshly squeezed pomelo juice. But the detour to the Pan-Asian markets north of Union station had got them snarled in the middle of heavy traffic.

'Goddamn construction,' said Jake. 'If they are trying to screw with us deliberately, then it's working.'

Alex looked up, curious.

'What do you mean, deliberately trying to screw us?'

Jake's comment had been off-hand, but Alex sensed a deeper frustration in his words.

'Ah, just some chat I hear from the other drivers. Probably nothing.'

Or perhaps not, thought Alex. In his time as a foreign correspondent, Alex had found taxi drivers always had ground-level intelligence on whichever warzone he found himself in – even Los Angeles.

'What are the drivers saying?'

The chauffeur shook his head ruefully.

'Look, man, everyone knows that traffic in LA can get real backed up. But I hear City Hall is waving through projects that don't need doing – and it's like a domino effect. One snarl-up slows us up, but six, twelve of them? It's like drivin' through soup. And the planners know what's gonna happen, but they just don't care – 'coz it's making more business for the construction firm.'

'How do you know all this, Jake?'

'From my buddy Alfredo. He had someone in the back of his car telling him all about it. He said it sounded like they had insider knowledge.'

'Can I speak to Alfredo?'

In the rearview mirror, Alex watched the driver's expression sour.

'Me and my big mouth,' Jake muttered.

'Come on, Jake,' said Alex. 'No names needed; I'll keep Alfredo out of it. But if I know what's going on, I might be able to help do something about it. Otherwise, those fat cats at City Hall keep getting fatter, and we're stuck in quicksand for the rest of the year.'

He saw Jake rub his chin, then nod.

'Sure, I trust you, Mr Ford. Let me speak to Alfredo and see what he says.'

Before Alex could thank him, the car jerked into motion, swerving into the next lane and accelerating through a narrow gap between an oil truck and a Mustang with inches to spare, powering down the off-ramp and onto the inland canyon road. Alex knew this road would loop back and feed them onto PCH - but heading in the other direction, which would be far less congested: no one was heading into the city at 10pm.

'Now we cookin' Mr F,' said Jake, 'We'll have you back home in the blink of an eye.'

* * *

Alex pushed the key into the lock and walked into the beach house. He was surprised to find it in semi-darkness, just a shaft of moonlight slicing through to give the room a soft, silvery glow.

'Lara?' he called, slipping off his jacket and throwing it on the sofa.

Silence. Well, not quite: there was the hiss of the waves beyond the terrace and the hum of the giant freezer in the kitchen.

'Lar? Are you here?' he called again, walking into the kitchen to dump the bag of pomelos in the fridge.

Alex frowned and glanced at his watch. It was almost ten o'clock and he hadn't spoken to Lara since he'd cancelled lunch. He didn't expect Lara to wait around for him to come home – that wasn't Lara's style – but still, he was surprised she wasn't at the house this late.

He flicked on a lamp and slid the terrace doors open. The warm Pacific breeze smelt of seaweed and salt; at any other time, he would have welcomed being here, at the world's edge, with just the sound of the ocean for company. But this was strange. The car wasn't in the carport, so where was Lara?

Alex doubted she was still in the Globe archives. Had she gone to explore the Grove shopping mall or the Malibu Country Mart, perhaps? But Lara wasn't a shopper, and it was getting late. So, where on earth was she?

Alex pulled out his phone. Her number was just ringing when he heard a rustle at the door, and Lara almost tumbled through, holding a selection of paper bags and a large Tupperware box jammed under one arm.

'Grab these before I drop them!' she called as Alex ran over to help her.

'What is all this?'

'Food from Martha's party. I've got salmon skewers and chicken and salad. It's all delicious, and I thought you'd be starving.'

A party? In the middle of the week? Lara Stone was the kind of woman who could make a connection on a desert island, but that was fast work even for her.

'Martha's party? Who's Martha?'

'Martha Riding,' said Lara as she took food from the bags and spread it in various plates and bowls. 'I met her for breakfast this morning, and she invited me to her book club tonight.'

Lara spoke quickly, which she only did when nervous or excited.

'Martha Riding? The writer?'

Lara grinned and nodded.

'Alex, she's amazing, and we're going to work on a story together.'

Alex held up his hands.

'Wait, wait,' he said, utterly confused now. How had all this happened between breakfast and supper? 'Martha Riding – *the* Martha Riding - is your new best friend, and you've already been to her house?'

Lara opened a drawer, rattling through the cutlery.

'It's a beautiful place,' she said distractedly. 'Small but lovely, up on the Malibu Road. Do we have any little spoons?'

'Sounds like you didn't need to meet me for lunch after all,' he said, a little more sulky than he'd intended.

'Ooh, are you jealous?' she said, looping an arm around his neck.

He liked it when she flirted with him; Lara didn't do it often enough.

'Of course I'm not jealous,' he said, 'I'm glad you've had an amazing day. I just wish you would have told me where you were going. I was worried.'

'I sent you a message to say I was going to her book club tonight.'

Alex had spent an hour in Jake's cab, checking his phone every three minutes – he would have noticed a message, certainly one saying his girlfriend was going to meet the great Martha Riding.

Lara frowned, pulling out her phone. 'Ah, shoot. It didn't send - sorry. Anyway, I brought home half of Martha's feast. You hungry?'

He shook his head.

'We had pizza at the office. And I got you some pomelos.'

Her face lit up.

'Pomelos? Wow - where did you get those?'

'Chinatown. They're in the fridge.'

'Thank you,' she said, kissing him. 'Tomorrow, I'll make us a cocktail - if you're not home too late.'

She was teasing him, but Alex felt a creeping sense of irritation. He wanted to tell her how his detour to Chinatown had added another 30 minutes to his day and how guilty he'd felt leaving the tiny Limelight team still burning the midnight oil without him. And most of all, how he'd been rigid worrying about Lara's reaction - and yet she hadn't even been here! Alex crossed to the fridge and, pushing the pomelos aside, pulled out an open bottle of wine, splashing it into a glass.

'Want some?'

It was Lara's turn to shake her head. 'I'm bushed. If I

have a drink, I think I'll pass out.' She flopped onto the sofa, and Alex followed her over. *Be nice,* he said to himself. She's on holiday. And she had brought him skewers.

'So how were the archives?' he asked, sitting opposite her. 'Helpful?'

'They were. Stanley's great.'

'I don't really know him yet.'

'I guess the editor-in-chief doesn't need to go down to the basement much.'

She didn't say it unkindly, but again, Alex was needled by it. It was as if Lara was pointing out a divide between senior management and the worker bees.

'I was going to come up to see you, but I saw one of your reporters. Natasha, is it? She said you were busy.'

'Don't be daft; I'm never too busy for a coffee with you.'

'Natasha made it sound like you were.'

Natasha? Was that why Lara was winding him up?

'When was this?' asked Alex, but then shook his head – it didn't matter; he'd been in meetings all day. There was barely a gap when he wasn't in a meeting. That was the irony of being the editor-in-chief. You spent very little time editing the paper.

'So what's Martha helping you out with? That 27 Club story for Darius?'

Lara sat forward, her excitement bubbling over.

'No, listen - it's an amazing thing,' she said, 'Martha was friends with Verity Jones. And she was there – here - that night. The night Verity died.'

Alex looked away. He didn't want this to escalate into a big argument – and only twenty minutes ago, he'd been stuck out on the freeway, worried that Lara would be pissed off for being abandoned. Instead, she had made a new friend and found a purpose. He should be grateful for that, but it didn't quite sit right with him.

'And what? Are you going to include Verity in the feature?'

'Of course we are. Darius wants us to try and find a connecting thread between rock stars who died early, and there's an obvious one – drugs. You know there were opioids in Verity's system?'

Alex tried to resist shaking his head.

'Lar, it's just…this is Simon's house.'

'So?' she said defensively.

'I'm not sure we want to point the finger and brand this place as some sort of 'death house'.'

'Point the finger?' Lara repeated. 'You mean search for the truth?'

Alex squirmed.

'I'm just saying be careful. Simon has been generous in lending us this place. I hadn't heard of this Malibu House story before yesterday. It's old news, and for Simon's sake, I'm not sure we want to rake it up again.'

'Alex, You're a newspaper editor. If someone could prove JFK was murdered, wouldn't you splash it on the front page?'

'Lara, JFK *was* murdered. That's not news.'

'You know what I mean: there's a story here, and I want to write about it.'

Alex sighed. He couldn't fault her logic, nor could he ask Lara Stone to change how she was. He'd seen it so many times before; once Lara got her teeth into a story, it was like trying to prise a bear trap off your ankle.

'Just be careful, alright? I don't want to get fired for knocking seven figures off the boss's beach house. Being a newspaper editor is hard enough.'

'Okay, understood,' said Lara, crossing to his side and snaking an arm around his waist. Her closeness felt good, and he felt the day's stress start to leave his body.

'So when do I get to meet your new friend Martha?' he asked.

'Oh, so you're only interested in my literary contacts now? And here I was thinking you were interested in my brains.'

Her eyes twinkled - he was a sucker for it.

'Maybe it's not *just* your brains I'm interested in,' he said, raising his eyebrows.

'Tell me more about that,' whispered Lara, pulling him in for a kiss, the dramas of the day forgotten.

Chapter 12

Eliot Jones lived in Pacific Palisades, a leafy inland suburb just twenty minutes from Malibu, but Martha had barely seen him since Verity's memorial service nearly fifty years earlier. There had been the occasional snatched 'So-what-are-you-up-to?' conversation at an awards ceremony or a restaurant when they had bumped into one another. Eliot had also sent flowers when Griffin had passed away, for which Martha had been grateful. It was a stretch to call him a real friend, yet Martha still felt a connection to Eliot, a thread of shared history that still felt intact. Similarly, reconnecting with him hadn't been difficult. He still had the same number Martha had copied from an old phone, and Eliot seemed happy enough to meet up when Martha suggested it. That was often the way with friends her age; they were grateful for a face from the past and the opportunity to talk about the old days.

Martha stopped the car next to a yellow 'Beware! Mountain lion' road sign. She'd lived in LA for half a century, and yet the reminder that dangerous wild animals roamed the hills never failed to make her feel uncomfortable. It was much like Hollywood itself, she supposed –

behind the glitz and the glamour, there were always predators.

Martha walked up a short path almost hidden by shrubs and pressed the intercom, which was brightly labelled with an 'Armed Response!' notice.

'Mi casa es su casa,' murmured Martha.

The gate buzzed, and a disembodied voice said, 'I'm by the pool. Just follow the path.'

Follow the path, thought Martha with an ironic smile. Wasn't that what she was doing? This English girl, Lara Stone, had charged into her life and offered her the opportunity to take a new path. Lara's curiosity had reminded Martha of herself back when she had always wanted to know *why*. She had spent far too many years – since Griffin's death if she was honest – hiding from the world. Sure, she had written about it, but from a distance, like she was watching a movie. It was high time she got involved again.

Martha walked through lush gardens edged with Tree Poppy, Sagebrush and, if Martha remembered the name correctly, a big Manzanita with waxy grey leaves. As she turned the corner, the pool appeared, a bright blue rectangle overlooked by a statue of a man with a trident: *Poseidon, I presume?*

'Oh my Lord, Martha, it *is* you!' A squat man with a trimmed beard and a green Hawaiian shirt rushed towards her, his arms spread wide.

Martha hesitated before her brain caught up. It didn't seem long since Martha had last seen Eliot Jones, but it must have been over a decade, and he had changed considerably. If many of their contemporaries seemed much slimmer than they once were – Pilates, hot yoga, whatever the slimming drug of the moment was – then Eliot Jones had filled out considerably.

'You haven't changed a hair,' said Eliot, squeezing her and holding on.

'Still gorgeous and still…' He stepped back, grinning, '…Still Martha.'

'You look good too, Eliot,' she said. Remarkably, it was true. In his Virginian days, Eliot had been slim and stringy; his mop of dark hair and fondness for black polo-neck jumpers gave him a rather morose look, but now he looked like a jolly grandfather.

'Lucinda is a great cook and keeps me well-fed,' he said, patting his belly.

'Lucinda? I thought it was….'

'Terry? She left me ten years ago; Lucinda is the third Mrs Jones. You'll love her. Hey, Luce!' He said, calling into the house. 'Could you bring us some lemonade? The home-made stuff?'

Eliot led Martha to a table by the pool. It was a hot day and Martha was glad of the parasol that put them in the shade. Martha took a moment to look back at the house, which, from this angle, was particularly impressive. It had been designed in the Spanish Style, which meant white stucco walls, a red tile roof and, in this case, cute Juliet balconies on the second floor. Then again, Eliot Jones would hardly be stuck for cash. As Martha understood it, as co-songwriter, Eliot still held the publishing rights to The Virginian's back catalogue, along with Verity's solo stuff: they'd still been married when she had died. Plus, Eliot had parlayed his part in the Laurel Canyon myth into a low-key career as a songwriter, quietly pumping out B-sides and album fillers for some surprisingly big names.

A pretty dark-haired woman came out of the house bearing a jug and glasses and set the tray on the table, ice cubes tinkling. There were polite introductions between Martha and Lucinda and wife number three was diplomatic enough to exit quickly to leave the two old acquaintances to chat.

'She's lovely,' said Martha, taking a welcome sip of lemonade.

'She is, although she's been hinting at putting me on a diet this week. She's like the music press – they build you up then drag you down.' He reached over and tapped her hand. 'It's good to see you, Marth. Truly.'

Martha smiled. Not many people called her 'Marth' these days. Just the old gang.

'So, how've you been?' asked Eliot. 'Still writing? Still in Malibu?'

'Ouch – that word *still.*'

Eliot held up his hands.

'No offence meant. If it works, stick with it. I've never understood why we have to change.'

'What about you? Still the wild man of folk-rock?'

'That's one place I have changed. Thirty-three years sober,' said Eliot. 'Terry gave me an ultimatum the first year we married: her or the booze. The marriage didn't end well – she ran off with my lawyer - but for drying me out, I'll always be grateful.'

Martha smiled with pleasure. It wasn't until this moment that Martha realised how much she had shut off those early years and compartmentalised it all. She had lost too many friends, seen them wasted by alcohol, minds over-loaded by drugs or simply by the vicious realities of the industry. The literary world had the same snakes and ladders, but the slide down wasn't quite so bumpy when it came.

'So, you said you wanted to talk?' said Eliot, putting down his glass. 'I assume you're writing another book? What is the great Martha Riding turning her gimlet eye to this time?'

'The old days,' she said simply.

'The old days?' he repeated. She noticed a faint frown as he said it. Any other observer might not have noticed the micro-expression, but Martha had interviewed thousands of people over the years. 'Hasn't that been done?'

'Sure, but not well. Not as well as I can do it. Besides, this would be more about the Malibu scene. The house, in particular.' Martha didn't want to lie to Eliot; this wasn't untrue. After all, they didn't have a particular angle yet. 'I hoped you could fill in some of the blanks.'

'Blanks about what?'

'About Verity.'

For a moment, Eliot didn't speak and instead looked into his glass intensely. She didn't blame him for not wanting to talk about his late wife. She knew from mutual friends that Verity's death had hit Eliot hard, and that had been when the whiskey had taken over. He had moved to Montana for a while, although he returned to LA a few years later with Terry, a new wife he had met in a bar.

'Fifty years,' he said quietly. 'I guessed someone might write something for her anniversary. I'm glad it's you, Martha.'

'I'm helping a journalist,' she said, 'She's a British writer. Clever, trustworthy.'

'Journalists? *Trustworthy*?'

Martha bristled, then reminded herself that there had always been an invisible line between herself and her celebrity friends. Writers were different, a necessary evil: keep your friends close and all that. But Martha Riding had jumped the fence and become something of a celebrity herself. Over the years, she'd been profiled in Time magazine and the New York Times. The library at her old high school in New Jersey was now named after her, and a well-known fashion brand had recently asked her to model – although Martha had turned them down, suspecting that it was more of a publicity stunt than an act of genuine inclusivity. But for all her limited fame, Martha knew she was still on the 'other side' – sometimes useful, but never to be completely trusted.

'This had better not be some sleaze piece, Martha,' said Eliot.

Martha lifted her chin.

'Verity was my friend too.'

'She was my *wife*.'

Martha nodded.

'Exactly why you should want people to remember her as she was.'

'People do remember her, Martha - through her songs. Isn't that the best way?'

Martha waited. She knew an extrovert like Eliot would never be able to stand the silence.

'What do you want to know?' he sighed finally.

'Tell me about the parties at the Malibu House.'

'You were there.'

'Not like you were. As you point out, Verity was your wife.'

He shook his head sadly.

'Not really, not towards the end. We'd separated, remember?'

'Why was that?'

He let out a soft groan.

'It was that damn house,' he said, frowning to himself as if he was still bothered by the memory of it. 'We bought The Malibu House after the success of the first album. You sell a million copies and go to number one; you want to celebrate. For me, the Malibu House was a place to relax. Living in Laurel Canyon was fun; it was useful, but it was crazy, too, and sometimes I just wanted to escape it – hence decamping to the beach. Verity thought the same way, but then she started inviting people over. Before we knew it, The Malibu House was party central. She thought having a full house meant that people loved her.'

'People did love her, Eliot,' said Martha. 'Everyone did.'

'But there were so many hangers-on; Vee couldn't see they were just using her. So I wanted to sell the house. She didn't. And…well, it became a wedge between us. We split up, and the band went on hiatus.'

Martha had never heard that part of the story before. Many of her friends in the music or film industry had got divorced: most of them. It was almost one of those things you expected to happen. But she'd never heard of it happening over a house before.

'If you hated the Malibu party scene so much, why were you there the night Verity died?'

'Because she invited me,' he said with an anxious glance towards the house. Clearly, ex-wives were not a welcome topic in the Jones household.

'We'd separated the previous summer,' he said quietly. 'But honestly, I still loved Verity and think she felt the same way. There was a definite sense of us wanting to get back together. I certainly did, but we were both too proud to make the first move, so we kept in each other's lives at a distance until the time was right. Man, she was special, wasn't she?'

Suddenly, Martha could remember Verity so clearly. She pictured her in a long green kaftan, her red hair the colour of a newly minted cent. Martha had met many beautiful people in her time, but none like Verity Jones. She wasn't even considered particularly good-looking – her lips were a shade too thin, her nose too wide, and there were always cruel whispers about her weight. But it was because of these things, not despite them, that Verity stood out. It was her confidence and the warmth of her smile.

'What do you think happened, Eliot?' Martha asked. 'Why did Verity throw everyone out of the party that night?

'I don't know. But I wish I did because then maybe I could have saved her, you know?'

Martha sat forward, feeling her writer's instincts firing. It was like the 'whoomp' you'd hear when an oil furnace kicked into life.

'Eliot, come on. You must remember something. The autopsy found narcotics in her system. What was she on?'

Eliot looked away, sighing.

'Did anyone know what we were smoking or taking back then? We just wanted to have a good time.'

A line from a movie came into her head. The biker flick The Wild Angels, spoken by Peter Fonda and sampled into a song in the Nineties. Martha couldn't remember who it was by – some Brit band. Lara would know.

'Look, Vee would smoke a little pot,' said Eliot, 'Maybe a couple of pills to bring her down, nothing heavy. Whisky sours: that was her drug.'

Martha remembered; she could picture Verity sitting in her chair, surrounded by admirers while she held court, laughing and singing snippets of old spirituals, a tumbler always in her hand.

'So, was she feeling down? Depressed? Was she ill?'

Eliot shrugged. 'She seemed happy enough that night. Until she kicked everyone out.'

'But *why*?'

'I don't know. Her mood seemed to change quickly, and you didn't want to argue with Verity once she decided something.'

'Did you leave straight away?'

Eliot nodded. 'Someone suggested we go to The Troubadour – some band was playing. About ten of us piled into Jeff Wood's pick-up truck, and we drove to the Strip. We were there until about 2am, and then I went home.'

'Did you not think about calling Verity? To check she was okay?'

'God, Martha, don't you think I've wished I did that? But we were separated, and that made things complicated. I didn't know if she was upset about some other guy or something that wasn't my business. So I left it. That was a mistake.'

'But you think she was generally happy?'

A thin smile came to his face.

'Vee was excited about the future, I know that much. She'd released a solo single and had more stuff coming out. Someone in Vegas had even offered her a residency.'

'And how did you feel about that? I mean, The Virginians were only officially on hiatus.'

'I was pleased for her,' he replied without skipping a beat, although Martha thought he saw his eyes narrow just a fraction. 'Plenty of artists did their own work and then returned to their band. Look at George Harrison. Still, that could have been part of the problem.'

Martha looked at him with more interest.

'The idea of touring again made her worry about her weight,' said Eliot. 'Being on the road, on stage, it's pretty physical. On The Virginians Sing Together tour, she'd hurt her back and the docs suggested she get in better shape. Today, she'd have gone to a fancy Arizona spa, taken up pilates and hired a private chef. But back then, people saw pills as the answer to a few excess pounds.'

'You think pills brought on the heart attack?'

'It's a possibility.'

'What about the narcotics in her bloodstream? Opioids. There was some pretty lethal heroin going around.'

Eliot's expression changed. 'I heard that too,' he said tersely. 'But there is no proof that Verity took anything like that.'

He sat forward, lowering his voice. 'Come on, Martha,

what's all this about? Why are you poking around in all this now?'

'When would be a good time, Eliot?' replied Martha, her patience wearing thin.

'But what good will it do?' he asked. 'It's not going to bring Verity back, and the only people it's going to affect are those still around.'

'You, you mean?'

Eliot glanced around nervously.

'Yes,' he whispered. 'I'm *married*, Martha. And Lucinda doesn't like to be reminded there were…others.'

'Is that how you think of Verity,' said Martha. 'As just one of the many?'

Eliot's eyes flashed with anger.

'You want the truth?' he said. 'It was only ever Verity who truly got under my skin. I've *always* loved her, and I always will. But when you care for someone, you want to protect them, too. Even when they're gone.'

Martha saw Lucinda waving from the doorway.

'More lemonade?' she called.

Both Eliot and Martha shook their heads.

'I should go,' said Martha, rising. She watched Lucinda shoot her husband a quizzical expression and knew he was in for the third degree later.

'I'll walk you out,' said Eliot, guiding her down through the garden. At the gate, Eliot paused and took Martha's arm.

'Martha, please. Don't do this,' he said.

'Don't do what? I'm just asking questions.'

'But questions just lead to more questions.'

'Or they lead to answers,' said Martha, gently removing his hand.

'But it was all so long ago,' he said, 'Why not just let sleeping dogs lie?'

Martha looked at him. He looked stricken, like he was watching his house catch fire.

'What's going on, Eliot?'

'Look, I like this life I have. I love my wife. I like who I've become. Is that so bad?'

'No, not at all. But don't be afraid of who you used to be either, Eliot. Who all of us were. Looking back doesn't have to be negative; you might remember things you liked about yourself.'

'Sure,' said Eliot, opening the gate. 'And you might remember some things best left forgotten.'

Chapter 13

Lara sat outside the spa and flipped through her notebook. Martha had devised a list of people they needed to speak to, which wasn't long. As the great writer had pointed out to Lara, there had been plenty of casualties from those hedonistic times and too many of Verity's friends had joined the great supergroup in the sky. The few that Martha had been able to locate were scattered around the county – living in care homes in Florida or with family in towns that would take a three-hour plane ride to get to. Lara didn't feel Darius would authorise the expenses, especially when he was more interested in Kurt Cobain. However, Martha hooked them up with a former make-up artist named Willow Caan – they were due to meet her up in the hills the following day. As Martha was currently meeting with Eliot Jones, that left just one core member of Verity Jones' inner circle to contact. *Donna Phelps.* Even Lara had heard of her and she had very little interest in 'lifestyle celebrities.' A former member of The Virginians, Donna had pivoted from music to TV in the late Seventies, but it was in the Eighties that Donna's fame had accelerated, transforming herself into a wellness guru – a cross between legwarmer-era Jane Fonda and pre-jail Martha Stewart.

Lara locked the car, smoothed down her dress and checked her reflection in the gym's blacked-out window. The Xanadu Studio was the hottest gym and spa in LA right now, and it was important to get the tone right if she was going to get past the dogs on the door. Lara had gone for a little black dress with a matching blazer, and her hair scraped back in an unmistakable 'I mean business' bun. For once, Lara was glad she'd schlepped that big case to LA. She only hoped she hadn't misjudged it – what if everyone else wore gym bunny Lycra? But as she walked towards Xanadu's entrance, Lara relaxed just a little: LA gyms were like high-end hotels. Wide stone stairs and full-length glass doors guarded by a beefy man in an over-stretched suit. No one was wearing sweats to the Xanadu.

Let's do this, Lara thought, pulling her phone from her bag and pretending to be busy and important. She studiously ignored the security guy, striding confidently past into a stylish air-con blasted lobby. Lara breathed a sigh of relief and fought down a smile. She loved this, loved being in the thick of a story, doing whatever was necessary to get to the truth. Blagging and gatecrashing were skills investigative journalists needed in their toolbox —and anyway, if Donna Phelps hadn't stonewalled them in their requests for a meeting, then Lara wouldn't have had to take this approach.

Lara had caught wind of this glittering event to celebrate the launch of Donna Phelps' latest book 'Eat Yourself Well' barely an hour before. She had tried calling Alex to see if he could get her on the guest list, but apparently, he was incommunicado until the end of the day, which meant she would have to improvise.

And – *Dammit* – she was going to have to blag more than she would have liked because there was another barrier: long marble reception desk manned by two frosty-looking women. But there was no going back now.

'…Well, tell Marcus I paid for that house, and if he doesn't like it…' she said loudly into her phone, playing the part of an over-privileged Rodeo Drive habitue to the hilt, swanning straight past the guard dogs.

'Ma'am, your invite?'

Briefly Lara looked back at the girl, then gestured to the bag hooked over her arm. 'It's in there somewhere,' she said, still moving towards the door, but the girl stepped in front of her.

'I'm sorry, Ma'am, I'll have to see it first.'

Reluctantly, Lara pushed her phone into her pocket, her mind jumping to the various ploys she could use to gain entry. Lies? Charm? Kung fu?

'I can't see it,' she muttered, rifling around her bag. 'Can't I just give you my name?'

'Sure, I can look on the list,' said the woman.

The words came out of her mouth before Lara could think twice.

'Alex Ford.'

The woman trailed a manicured fingertip down her list.

'Alex Ford, I don't see that name.'

'Can you look again? My assistant said I should be on the guest list.'

The other PR woman was watching them, then came over.

'Alex Ford, did you say?' she said with a professional smile. 'From The Globe?'

Lara nodded, feeling a little hot despite the air-con.

'Do you have an identification?' asked the first woman with a mix of sympathy and steel.

Lara gulped hard. *Alex is going to kill me,* she thought,

pulling out the business card that Alex had proudly given her on her first visit to LA.

'Ah, Ms Ford, of course,' said the woman, breaking into a sickly smile. 'Please go through, it's just about to begin.'

She was pointed toward a waiter holding a tray of organic champagne and Lara took a moment to observe the glamourous scene before her. It was the most stylish gym Lara had ever seen, with blush-coloured décor and a vast chandelier made from shells cascading from the roof. At intervals, there were giant cardboard displays of the book featuring Donna Phelps on the cover, dressed all in white like an angel of well-being. A giant balloon announced, '50 million copies sold!' which Lara thought was a little premature, given the book wasn't on sale until the following week. Still, Lara couldn't help but be impressed at how Donna Phelps had transformed herself from a folk singer into some sort of modern shaman. She had a syndicated TV show, a podcast with a huge roster of celebrity guests, and a range of lifestyle products from yoga pants to woks, all artfully aligned to Donna's Californian wellness brand. It was a far cry from Donna's poverty-stricken early years – or at least, that was the backstory she claimed in interviews.

Accepting a glass of fizz, Lara allowed herself to be herded towards the front of the room, where there was a low stage with a pair of armchairs facing each other in front of another giant cut-out of the book. The rest of the audience was an assortment of Chanel-clad blondes and Bel Air housewives with frozen faces, but clearly, excitement was high.

Just then, a distinguished-looking man in his late seventies stepped up onto the stage to polite applause.

'Hi there,' he said into the microphone. 'For those who don't know, I am Stephen Savage. I don't usually do this kind of thing, but tonight, I wanted to help celebrate someone who started as a client, but is now one of my closest friends.'

Stephen Savage. He was an impressive host for the party. Lara was not an expert on the LA entertainment scene, but she knew Stephen Savage's name; he was a media legend. Having started his career with a wildly successful record label in the 1970s and 1980s, he had diversified into talent management, merchandising and even hotels – but five years ago, he had sold the lot, making Savage a billionaire. You didn't reach the top of a cut-throat business like the media without being a player, and if Stephen Savage had anything to do with Donna Phillip's career, then it was no surprise she was so successful.

'You will already know who I'm talking about,' continued Savage expansively. 'She's an author, broadcaster, producer and a passionate wellness advocate in every sphere of life. She is a pioneer and a disruptor; she is the point where health and entertainment meet – and she creates something entirely new. I'd like to ask you to welcome to the stage…the great Donna Phelps!'

As Donna stepped onto the stage, a huge round of applause rose, along with whooping and whistling from the back – Lara assumed the whistlers were Xanadu staff members because there was no way any of these Botox-ed trophy wives would be able to move their lips enough.

Donna was elegant but sexy, with long blonde hair and chunky bronze jewellery over a pale lemon dress. To Lara's surprise, Donna's face had wrinkles and lines; she looked like an ex-model who'd aged with dignity rather than surgery. And somehow, it made her appear more approachable and 'real.' Donna took a modest bow, then sat opposite Savage.

'So,' said Savage, 'Nice book.'

There was a ripple of laughter.

'I'm glad you like it,' said Donna. 'But I'll be honest, I didn't have you in mind when I was writing it, Stephen.'

More laughs.

'…No, I was reaching out to all those women who struggle with all those endless diets and faddy health kicks, and I wanted to say to them…'

Lara was listening, but she was mainly paying attention to Donna's voice, still as light and melodious as during her folk singing days. Lara could immediately hear it blending with Verity's on tunes like 'For Today' and 'When I Call'. Verity had been known as the powerhouse of The Virginians – her voice was a legendary instrument, and next to it, Donna's paled – but Donna still had something that made you sit up. Even today, she was still one of the most beautiful women in the room; her cheekbones were high, her cat-like eyes still bright. And having influential friends like Stephen Savage didn't hurt either.

Donna and Stephen discussed the benefits of kale and vitamins and the importance of fresh ingredients – Donna didn't seem to have much of a unique take on wellness, but then Lara supposed she didn't need to, having a zillion followers on social media and a range of stacking bowls in every Target. Success bred success. She turned to look at the ladies who lunch in the audience. They were sitting forward, hanging on Donna's every word. Her hippy past was never mentioned, but Lara supposed it added to her mystique; she'd been to the far side and had come back wiser. People listened to Donna Phelps; they wanted to hear what she said.

And so do I, thought Lara.

The short interview ended with more whooping and whistling. Lara clapped along, then waited as Donna's fans surged towards the stage, shaking hands, congratulating her, taking selfies. There was no doubt Donna Phelps was well-loved by the middle-aged one percenters - and given her social media numbers, every other demographic in America, too. Lara guessed it was a more rewarding last act than writing anonymous album fillers like Eliot Jones.

Lara tracked Donna's movements as the crowd dispersed, watching her working the room like a pro. She posed for more pictures with Stephen Savage and the rest of her entourage, then was led to a table piled high with books, which she started to sign for a long line of admirers. It was only when the queue had thinned and the PR was called away, that Donna Phelps was left on her own. Lara saw her opportunity.

'Donna? Ms Phelps?' Said Lara, approaching the table. 'I'm from the LA Globe. I wonder if I could have a few words?'

Donna hesitated, then glanced at her PR, busy by the juice bar.

'Just a couple of questions,' said Donna. 'I do have other guests.'

'Of course,' Lara smiled in what she hoped was a reassuring way. 'It'll only take a minute.'

She called up a voice recorder on her phone.

'Cute accent,' said Donna, filling the pause. 'I lived in London for a little while. Chelsea.'

'Really? That's where I live,' said Lara flashing the older woman another smile, trying to create a rapport. 'Most of the time, anyway. This week, I'm staying in Malibu.'

Lara thought she saw a flicker of alarm, but perhaps it was just the light.

'I'm renting a house you probably know: they call it 'The Malibu House'.

This time, Donna's expression didn't move.

'Verity Jones used to live there, I believe,' prompted Lara, 'You were best friends, weren't you?'

'Yes, we were. You're living in *that* house?'

'Well, I imagine it's changed a lot since those days. I believe it's been completely remodelled. Understandable after what happened.'

Donna closed her eyes and shook her head impatiently.

'So, you wanted to ask a question about the book?' she said, the previous warmth gone.

'What I wanted to ask was: why did Verity throw everyone out that night, Donna?'

'Sorry, I thought I was here to promote my book…' she said, her eyes searching for the PR.

'I'm writing a story with Martha Riding,' said Lara. 'I believe you know her from the Malibu days? It's the 50th anniversary of Verity's death, and we want to write a tribute to Verity's talent and the magic of The Virginians.'

Donna held up a hand. 'I think we want different things from this conversation. I am here to discuss my new book, not the past.'

Donna stood, but Lara moved to block her exit.

'Ms Phelps, please. We'd be grateful for any insight. Something upset Verity that night and if we knew what it was, perhaps we can finally understand her final hours. Of course, we can say you offered 'no comment' if you'd rather. But that might look a little *guilty*.'

'Guilty? Of what?'

'You tell me, Donna.'

Lara was pleased she had managed to get Donna off balance so quickly. She knew it was just a matter of time before someone shut Lara down.

'I will tell you what I told the police fifty years ago,' said Donna. 'I do not know why Verity threw everyone out of the party because I had already left myself.'

'But did anything strike you as strange? Please, Donna, you were best friends with Verity. You knew her better than anyone.'

The older woman lowered her voice.

'As I said. I'd already left,' she said, her voice almost a hiss. 'But, if you ask me to speculate, I'd say it was because of Benny Dean.'

Lara knew the name – Dean had been the fourth member of The Virginians.

'Benny was putting Verity under pressure to reform the band,' said Donna. 'But Verity didn't want that. No one did – Verity's solo career was beginning, and I was moving into TV.'

'But Benny did want to reform the band?' said Lara,

'Yes, because it was his meal ticket. It wouldn't have surprised me if Benny got aggressive. He would often get loaded at the parties and pick a fight with someone. Perhaps it was Verity's turn.'

'Or perhaps…' Lara began, but stopped as she felt a heavy hand on her shoulder. She turned to see the muscular security guard she had breezed past earlier.

'Ma'am?' he said to Donna, 'Is everything alright here?'

Lara could see the iPad-toting PR girl behind him, looking anxious.

'Our guest from the Globe was just leaving,' said Donna, giving Lara a thin smile. 'I think I've given you more than enough.'

Lara could see her cover was well and truly blown, so she shrugged off the guard's hand and straightened her back.

'Thank you, Miss Phelps,' she said. 'I'm sure we will talk again. I have plenty more questions.'

'This way, please,' said the security guard, nodding towards the door.

'I'm going, don't worry,' said Lara, not waiting to be manhandled. She walked toward the exit with as much dignity as she could muster.

I have plenty more questions, thought Lara. More questions than answers. Lara could understand Donna being defensive– Lara had ambushed her, after all – but she had seen something in Donna's expression: anger and fear. Why would Donna Phelps feel either of those emotions when Verity Jones was supposed to be her best friend? Sorrow and sadness, perhaps, but certainly not fear. At the door, Lara turned round and looked back into the party and as she did so, she saw Donna's face staring back at her.

'What do you know that you aren't telling me?' Lara whispered. One thing was sure: she couldn't ask Benny Dean. Because Benny Dean was dead.

Chapter 14

Summer Phelps watched as the security guards hustled the reporter through the door. Those guys were pros; muscles flexing under their suits, no doubt experts in kung fu and Krav Maga. It was like watching a sheepdog guide sheep. The threat was enough.

'What's going on there?' said Stephen Savage, nodding towards the woman being escorted out of the party.

Summer turned to face her boss. She hadn't wanted Stephen to see the fracas – she had worked for Stephen for over thirty years, and she knew he hated it when things didn't go absolutely to plan.

'Some hack reporter,' she said, flicking the business card reading 'Alex Ford' with her thumb. 'Gatecrasher.'

'A gatecrasher? To a book launch?' He said with amusement. 'Crashing the backstage of a Harry Styles gig, I'd understand - but this?'

'It sounds like she wanted an exclusive with Donna,' she replied, looking across the room to where her mother was berating her publicist.

'Oh dear,' said Stephen, exchanging a look with Summer. 'She doesn't look very happy.'

'She hasn't been happy all day,' said Summer, lowering her voice. 'Between you and me, she's pissed that Drew and Gwyneth took a rain check on the launch.'

Summer herself hadn't been surprised that the celebrities had stayed away. Donna's book publisher was handling the launch, and while their publicists were good at getting glowing reviews, snagging the presence of high-profile celebrities was an art on a much more rarified level. It hadn't stopped Donna from giving Summer both barrels about it. Summer had tried to explain that many of LA's top talent had their own wellness lines to promote and were unlikely to endorse a rival, but Donna hadn't wanted to hear it.

'I'll have a word with them both; make sure they come to the next one,' said Savage casually. Summer glanced at him. *Of course* Stephen would have the ears of the top A-listers. And, of course, they would be keen to do him a favour. Everyone owed Stephen Savage something.

'That aside, I think it went pretty well,' said Stephen, surveying the room; certainly, the guests looked in no hurry to leave.

'It's been a pretty hot party, obviously helped by being held here at Xanadu. Thanks again, Stephen, for making that happen.'

Savage had been one of the spa's early backers and hadn't hesitated when Summer asked him if they could host the book launch here. Across the room, Donna was once again posing for photos with the spa's clientele.

'And then all is calm,' Stephen whispered. Summer laughed at the in-joke. Savage had known Donna even longer than she had; he'd signed her to his record label after The Virginians had split for good, and even after Donna's solo singing career had faltered, Savage had stayed on as a de facto manager, advising her through the TV years and into the diet-boom of the 80s. So Stephen knew well what Donna was like; he'd seen all the tantrums behind the smiles.

'So, did you have a chance to look through that proposal?'

Savage groaned. Summer had been liaising with the current Savage Media senior management to create a 'legacy' package for its fiftieth anniversary. Stephen had sold a majority stake in the label five years earlier but still held the title of Chairman Emeritus. The schedule included a suitably retro vinyl box set of his artist's greatest hits, a ghost-written coffee table book showing Stephen shaking hands with Bowie and Lennon, and whispers of a possible Netflix documentary. The centrepiece, however, would be a televised extravaganza, 'An Evening with Stephen Savage,' when all the stars he'd launched would say nice things, then sing and dance. It would be cheesy but generate millions in revenue, so why was Stephen dragging his feet?

'I'm not sure about that TV thing,' he said. 'It all seems a bit… theatrical.'

Summer smiled. 'You remember that *Variety* once called you 'the consummate showman'?'

'Yes, but…'

'And remember that Super Bowl halftime performance where you persuaded Madonna to drape herself over Elton John's flying piano?'

Stephen chuckled.

'She didn't take much coaxing.'

'But Elton was not pleased, was he?'

'Furious would be a better way of putting it,' he laughed. 'Okay, yes, I take your point, but that was about selling units; this is about me. All those songs mean something to the fans, sure, but who cares about the producer?'

Summer herself could understand his reticence - she wouldn't want to be sitting on a throne while some music industry megastar crooned at him either - but for all his false modesty, Stephen Savage was a man who thrived on attention. Something was bothering him, but she would worm it out of him; she just had to pick her moment.

'Look, just think about it as a get-together with old friends, your version of a High School reunion. Having a singalong, just like the old days.'

Stephen wasn't in the mood for levity.

'Look we can discuss all this next week?' he said. 'I'm not in the office tomorrow. I'm out of town until Sunday.'

She frowned. Summer knew Stephen's schedule inside and out and wasn't aware of any trips. *You're his chief of staff, not his mother,* Summer reminded herself. She had spent too much time being around Donna, who required every detail of her life to be stage-managed.

'Monday, nine o'clock then?' said Summer.

Stephen nodded. 'Block off a couple of hours.'

Two hours? Despite being in his early Seventies, Stephen was still as busy as when he was at the heights of his powers as CEO of his record label. Summer couldn't remember being able to grab him for more than thirty minutes. Perhaps he was taking the TV show seriously after all.

'Time to head home,' he said, using two fingers to massage his temples, the sure sign of a headache.

'Are you okay?' she said, searching his face. He did look more tired than usual.

'I'm fine,' he said with a mischievous smile. 'I want to duck out before your mom finishes signing those books. I don't want her yapping at me about how Oprah should have been here.'

He meant that *someone* would have to listen to Donna's tirade – and he was nominating her. Delegation in action. Summer signalled Tansy, Donna's assistant, to call the car, then gathered up her mother, hustling her towards the door just as she had seen the security goons do. Donna was, as Stephen had predicted, whining about how the launch had been a wash-out, but Summer waited until the car had moved off toward Donna's Bel-Air home before talking.

'Is everything good?' asked Summer after they had both clambered in the back seat.

'No, everything is not 'good',' said Donna, her lips pursed. 'Where was everyone tonight? Where was *anyone?*'

Summer made all the right sympathetic noises, but even without the celebrity endorsements, Summer was confident Donna's cookbook would succeed. There had been no Gwyneth or Oprah, true, but there had been plenty of LA tastemakers in attendance. And more importantly, Donna Phelps was adored by the masses; the rural soccer moms who always pushed her books to number one in the New York Times bestseller lists.

'And what about that incident?' said Donna suddenly. 'That amateur PR team let some *ghoul* in to harass me.'

Summer frowned. 'You mean the journalist?'

'Of course I mean her. The British woman. The one who was asking all those questions about Verity Jones. *Verity.* Didn't she realise it was my party? Who *was* she?'

'Someone who talked her way in using the editor of the LA Globe's business card. The girls on the door didn't realise Alex Ford was a man and let her in.'

It would never have happened on Summer's watch; she made it her business to keep up to date on everything, so she had been aware of the man from the London Chronicle landing at the Globe.

'That must never happen again,' said her mother, eyes blazing. 'She was awful, Summer. We must contact the editor and tell him about this fraud. I'm sure he won't be happy either.'

Summer looked at her mother more closely: Donna

Phelps was the kind of woman who enjoyed drama - she could be reduced to fake tears by a spider in the shower stall – but for once, she seemed genuinely upset.

'Mom, what did this journalist ask you?'

'All sorts of questions. She was almost *accusing* me.' She said, firing an angry look at Summer.

'Accusing you of what?'

Donna crossed her arms, pouting. Summer had often thought Donna had the emotional range of a toddler. She was fine when she was being showered with praise or distracted by a brand new shiny thing, but ignore her or disagree with her, and Donna could go into a full-on tantrum. The trick was to behave like a parent.

'Mom, I'm your daughter, and you know how close I am to your business,' Summer said firmly. 'If it affects you, it affects me.'

It was true. Although Summer didn't have a formal position at Donna Phelps Inc., for the past twenty years, since she had graduated from Wharton with an MBA, Summer had kept a watchful eye over her mum's empire, advising, guiding and helping her mum make strategic business decisions.

'I don't see how it affects you, it was *me* she was trying to smear. Asking about the Malibu House that night – you know, at Verity's place?' Donna said in a rush, 'She wanted to know all the details… '

'What did you tell her?'

'I don't know; I can't be expected to remember everything this horrible woman said to me, can I? Why are you *grilling* me?'

Summer closed her eyes. This was classic Donna, going on the attack when she felt vulnerable. But why *did* she feel vulnerable? Of course, Summer had heard all the stories about Verity Jones and her tragic death - it was part of the mythology of the 70s. And, of course, Summer's father,

Todd Mayfield, and half of the musical royalty of the hippie movement had been present that night. No wonder people were interested.

'But why now?' Summer asked. 'It happened nearly 50 years ago. Why is this 'Alex Ford' suddenly interested?'

'She said she's on vacation,' Donna sniffed. 'She told me she was staying in Verity's house. Said she became curious.'

'Ah, I see.' Summer felt herself relax a little. So it was just mawkish curiosity, like those Greyline bus tours in Hollywood that took tourists around the sites of infamous celebrity deaths and murders. For one terrible moment, Summer had feared that some new evidence had come to light, something that had somehow implicated Donna in Verity's death. There had, of course, been plenty of the mad internet conspiracies down the years – a CIA hit, the Manson Family, a government cover-up involving LSD in the drinking water - but to Summer, Verity's death had always sounded like a terrible accident, nothing more. And while her mom could be a royal pain in the ass at times, Summer doubted she was capable of malice aforethought. Donna had trouble planning the day's wardrobe.

Summer turned towards the window as the car climbed the hills towards Donna's home. One of the ironies of her mother's life was that despite all her wellness exhortations to 'expand your horizons', she had never travelled more than a few miles from her starting point as a beatnik in Laurel Canyon. Talking about carbs and meditation on daytime TV had bought Donna a giant house overlooking the sprawl of LA, but it was just a fifteen-minute drive from where Donna had lived when she first arrived in LA, a little cottage just behind the Laurel Canyon Country Store.

Summer had been born in that house, but her memories were vague: running barefoot in the grass, surrounded by smiling adults in colourful clothes. The offspring of famous people often grew up with some sort of hang-up or addiction, but Summer had only felt nurtured and encouraged by creative people who constantly told her she could be anything she wanted to be.

Even after her parents split, Summer's father, Todd, had always been a steady presence, a happy, upbeat balance to Donna's many neuroses. *Had* been. Now, dementia was eating Todd away, and Summer wished she had spent more time with him. That thought stopped her, and she turned to Donna.

'Do you think that reporter will try to speak to Dad too?'

'How am I supposed to know…' Donna suddenly stopped, her eyes widening. 'Oh no. He could say *anything*, couldn't he? I mean, you know, with the dementia and all?'

She paused and then looked at her daughter more carefully. 'How is Todd?'

As far as Summer knew, Donna and Todd hadn't seen each other in years.

'You're concerned all of a sudden?'

'Summer, Todd is a part of my past,' said Donna, 'He's been a good father to you all these years and for that, I will always love him.'

It sounded like one of the soundbites she would trot out on Good Morning America. Or maybe she was softening in her old age now that Todd was not a threat to her.

'He's doing OK, I guess,' sighed Summer. 'Sometimes I don't think he recognises me, but other times he's pretty lucid.'

She looked at Donna. 'Listen, I'm going to Dad's place in Thousand Oaks on Saturday – there's a party. Nothing big, just a little get-together in the garden.'

'A party? What for?'

Summer tried to keep her expression neutral.

'It's Dad and Julianne's ruby wedding. Look, why don't you come? I know he'd love to have you there.'

'Would he?' She said it almost as if she wanted it to be the case.

'Todd never says anything bad about you, Mom. Isn't it about time you made friends again?'

Donna shrugged.

'Thousand Oaks is such a long way, and anyway – I'm not sure it's appropriate.'

'I get that, but …', Summer took a breath. 'This is a horrible thing to say, but I don't think Todd's got much more time. I think seeing a familiar face from the past would be good for him. He's a lot better with long-term memories.'

'Really?' said Donna. 'I mean, he remembers the old days? How much?'

Summer raised her eyebrows.

'Oh, I'm pretty sure he'll remember *you*, Donna.'

Chapter 15

Thursday night at Dodger Stadium, the sun sank behind this low-slung, open-sided ballpark surrounded by palms and about ten square miles of parking lot.

And lines of shiny cars, all trying to find a spot before the first pitch.

'Man, I love this,' said Will, practically bouncing in the passenger seat. 'Don't you love it?'

'I don't love these lines,' grumbled Natasha. They had been sitting in idling traffic, inching towards the gates for hours.

Will flashed her a grin.

'Come on 'Tash, you're from LA, how can you not love all this? Dodger Stadium *is* LA.'

'It's Natasha, not 'Tash' – and I'm from Brentwood. Brentwood is *not* LA.'

An overweight security guard in a neon yellow vest waved them over to the right, moving from one queue to another. *Great.* When Alex had told them they would find Alfredo, the taxi driver, at the stadium for the Dodger's play-off against the Houston Astros, Natasha's heart sank.

Baseball was almost a religion in Los Angeles, but Natasha was agnostic. She knew it existed, but she had no desire to get involved if she could avoid it.

'Space up ahead,' said Will as another operative with an orange stick directed them into a parking space next to a gigantic pick-up, all four doors open. The baseball fans spilling out wore sports jerseys and caps and grinned like idiots. It was as if they were about to see their favourite band play rather than a load of distant figures throwing a tiny ball around.

Within seconds, Will was shaking hands with their neighbours, high-fiving and exchanging snippets of sporting trivia.

'How's Chinzi doing?' 'That short-stop's on fire right now.' 'We're going all the way this season.' It was like they were speaking in some sort of secret code.

Natasha grabbed Will's arm and pulled him away.

'Do you know those people?' she asked as they began the trek towards the stadium.

'No, of course not,' Will frowned.

'So how can you high-five a total stranger?'

Will smirked.

'Remember how Alex said the best way to get information out of people was to get them to like you?'

'Hey! What's that supposed to mean?' said Natasha, 'People like me.'

'Sure they do…' Will cracked a grin. '…Na-*tash*-a.'

Natasha couldn't help but laugh. She threw a playful punch at his shoulder, which Will easily dodged. They followed the stream of spectators heading in through the security gates past a store selling endless merchandise: hats, clothes, signed balls and bags. There was nothing, it seemed, that couldn't take a Dodgers logo. Will started scanning an open-air bar.

'You think this cab driver will be here?' asked Natasha.

'Maybe. It's where the hardcore fans hang out: remember, Alex said this Alfredo guy lived for the Dodgers? Besides, the bullpen is right under the bar.'

'Bullpen?'

Will slapped a hand over his eyes. 'Have you ever *been* to a ballgame before?'

'Sure I have,' she said defensively.

The truth was, outside of high school, Natasha had only been to a baseball game once - and that had been the semi-pro Cape League out in Chatham. It had been on an abortive mini-break with a boyfriend just after college. He had thought to impress her with his connections to the Kennedys and his flash family summer place. The connections had been thin, and the summer place had been a rental. To hammer a final nail into a relationship already on the way out, the baseball game had been rained off, and Natasha had got sick on the chilli dog her date had insisted she sample. It wasn't her favourite memory.

'I just don't understand why grown men and women get so worked up about something so...'

'Stupid?' said Will.

She smiled at him. 'You said it - not me.'

'OK, come on,' said Will, taking her hand and leading her up a flight of stairs to a railing overlooking a little grassy enclosure.

'This is the bullpen,' he said. 'This is where the players warm up and practice a little batting before the game.'

The rail was crowded with families, guys with kids on their shoulders, Moms boosting their offspring up to see through the fence.

'Look at those kids' faces,' said Will. It took Natasha a moment to place where she had seen the expressions before.

'It's like Disneyland,' she said. It was the same look of

wonder and excitement she'd seen on children when the life-sized Mickey or Cinderella waved at them.

'Now look at the dads.' They were proud and happy, having the time of their lives.

'The game *is* kind of stupid,' said Will, 'but what sport isn't? It's all about hitting, kicking, or jumping over things real fast – it's all kind of dumb. But these people come every week with their families and have a good time together. Now, what's wrong with that?'

Natasha gave him a sideways look.

'You came with your dad, right?'

Will's mouth twisted. 'A couple of times, yeah. Sometimes, he'd get press passes, but mostly, Dad was out on stories or in some bar talking to cops. My Dad was an old school newspaperman, Natasha, always chasing the story, even on his off days. He wasn't big on fishing trips to the lake.'

She raised her eyebrows.

'So are you trying to give me some sort of warning about the lonely life of a reporter?'

He flashed her that cute smile again. 'I do not doubt that you will get to your news anchor job, your penthouse flat, and your investment broker husband - if that's what you want.'

She looked at him in surprise.

'You don't want that?'

Will shook his head slightly, then broke eye contact with her.

'Right now, all I want is to find this guy Alfredo. He always sits near home plate. That's…'

'I know where home plate is, Will,' she snapped and walked down the steps.

She wasn't sure why she was suddenly so annoyed with him. Natasha didn't want any of this - she didn't want any stupid family outings. She wanted what Will had just listed:

the anchor job and the uptown lifestyle. And she was going to get it. They were here to do a job, not wallow in hokey Americana.

Natasha walked up to a food vendor laden with peanuts and Cracker Jacks. 'Hey there,' she asked. 'Do you know Alfredo?'

The guy's expression didn't change.

'Alfredo? Lady, half the ballpark is called Alfredo.'

'He sits in this section. He's here every week.'

'What are you, looking for alimony?'

Natasha paused a beat.

'I left a suitcase in his cab: a million bucks in used bills. I'm hoping he'll give it back.'

The man burst out laughing.

'Sure, I know Alfredo. Everyone does.' He pointed to an empty seat with his chin. 'That's his seat, but right now? 'Fredo will be in Vito's.'

'Thanks.'

'Sure thing. And if you get those Benjamins from Alfredo, buy fifty bags of peanuts, okay?'

Natasha walked back up the steps to where Will was waiting.

'See?' he said, 'You're good at that.'

'At what?'

'Talking to people.'

Natasha shrugged. 'I just undid another button on my shirt.'

Will's eyes didn't even flick down.

'Don't sell yourself short, Natasha,' he said.

Embarrassed, she pushed past him. 'So what's Vito's? A bar?'

'Pizza place,' said Will. 'But before we go, I've got something for you.'

He produced a blue baseball hat and pushed it onto her head.

'What's this? A souvenir of our day out?'

'Think of it more as a disguise. Look around; everyone's wearing one.'

He walked off, and Natasha ran her thumb over the interlinked 'LA' logo. It was pretty cool—and it was sweet of Will. She followed him along the concourse, past the 'Dodger Dogs' concession and a surprisingly wide range of food outlets, including octopus rice balls and Korean barbeque ribs. Vito's wasn't hard to spot. It had a 3-foot-high neon sign above the door and a plastic model of a pizza slice the size of a surfboard.

'There he is,' said Natasha in a low voice as they pushed inside. The description from Alex's contact had been spot-on. Sitting at the corner of the bar with a frosty mug of beer in front of him, Alfredo, the cab driver, looked like he'd stepped straight out of The Sopranos. Shaved head, chunky rings and faded blue tattoos on his forearms; for a moment, Natasha felt relieved that she was with Will before dismissing the thought as a betrayal of her third-wave feminist principles. *This isn't the twentieth century*, she thought and slipped onto a stool near the cab driver.

'What can I getcha hon?' asked the bartender.

'Beer,' said Natasha. 'Two. And whatever our friend's having.'

Alfredo looked up, fixing Natasha with a questioning look.

'Any bleeding blue is a friend of ours,' she said. 'And let's face it, on gameday, we all need a drink, am I right?'

The cab driver pouted. 'Jack, straight,' he said before tipping an imaginary hat to Natasha.

'I haven't seen you here before,' he said, 'You folks from out of town?'

Natasha shook her head. 'LA born and bred, both of us. My Dad still lives in Westlake.'

She didn't feel bad about the lie. Her grandfather used

to run an accountancy firm with an office in Westlake. That was almost the same.

'You're locals?' said Alfredo, raising his glass, 'Saluti! We're getting thin on the ground.'

'No one's from here,' said Will. 'This whole place used to be Chavez Ravine, right?'

Alfredo pointed at him. 'You got that right. I love the stadium, but it's a crying shame what the City did to those folks.'

Natasha nodded solemnly; she had done her research too. When the Dodgers moved cross-country from Brooklyn in the late fifties, the City of Los Angeles sold the Chavez Ravine neighbourhood, earmarked for housing poor Mexican families, to the Dodgers, who bulldozed the settlements and paved them over. The scandal was still a black mark on LA's conscience.

'Same thing's happening now,' said Will, 'You ever take the freeway, you'll see how much the mayor cares about the people.'

'I heard that,' said Alfredo. 'I'm a cab driver; I spent the last six months out there breathin' in fumes.'

'So what d'you think's going on there?' asked Natasha. 'Same old same old, you think? The big guys screwing the little guys?'

Natasha watched Alfredo as he peered down into his beer. He seemed to be thinking it over.

'So I guess you're the reporters?' he said, looking up.

'No - hey buddy, we're just...' said Will, but Natasha cut him off.

'Yes, we are. Who told you?'

Alfredo nodded. 'Guy named Alex? He had the decency to call and ask me if I minded talking on the record.'

'Sorry about that,' said Natasha quietly. 'Honestly.'

'So what did you say?' asked Will. 'To Alex, I mean.'

Alfredo shrugged, then knocked his bourbon back, grimacing. 'I said sure. I'll talk.'

'You did?' Will's surprise was plain.

'Sure,' He looked at Natasha. 'I hoped someone would ask me about that broad in my cab. It's about time someone did something about that damn traffic.'

Natasha felt her shoulders relax and let out a silent breath.

'So who was she, this woman in your cab?'

Alfredo held up his glass to the bartender.

'Buy me a drink, and I'll tell ya.'

Chapter 16

Martha trailed her fingers in the rushing air, her head tipped back against the passenger seat of Lara's car. When Lara had picked her up in Malibu, she had been pleased to see the little red two-seater. It had been decades since she had travelled up into the Californian hills in a convertible. Years, in fact, since she had been on this particular road, which wound up past the Bohemian enclave of Ojai and decades since she'd been anywhere in a sports car. Nowadays, everyone was shuttled around in air-conditioned cubicles-on-wheels before stepping straight into an ice-box lobby: two or three steps in the open air at most. Martha missed the days when the sun had been seen as nourishing and inspiring instead of dangerous. What happened to '*let the sunshine in*'? When did everyone get so…removed?

'So, do you think you are going to move to LA?' said Martha, glancing over at Lara, who was frowning in concentration, dealing with the road's sudden bends.

Martha had enjoyed spending time with her new friend over the past three days, but she still knew very little about her beyond the fact that she lived in a houseboat on the

Thames and loved her work as an investigative journalist. Lara Stone was bright and passionate, but Martha could see she put up barriers; she was hanging onto some pain and sadness in her past, and Martha hoped she could draw it out over the next few days.

'There's no plans to move permanently. Not yet,' said Lara, still focused on the road ahead.

'Looks like you're enjoying yourself to me.' Said Martha with a smile. 'The house, the car, the story.'

'I am enjoying myself. I'm not seeing Alex as much as I'd like, but it's a couple hours more a day than if I was back in London.'

This time, she did glance across.

'Look, if Alex and I were married, it would be a no-brainer. But we've only been together a few months, and even though we were friends before that, I guess I want to make sure our relationship is strong enough to withstand the distance because, with the work we do, we're not always going to be in each other's pockets.'

Martha didn't reply. Lara was smart, but she still had the idealism of youth. Martha had thought the very same thing when Griffin had been lured out to LA by Hollywood work. They were engaged by then, and Martha had trusted Griffin. But it was other people you had to watch out for.

Martha could still recall going to LA one weekend and attending a party with Griffin on Malibu Colony Road. She had only turned her back for a moment to get a drink, but when she'd returned, a glamorous blonde had Griffin almost pinned up against the wall. Her fiancé had admitted to knowing the woman from the studio lot and had denied that anything had happened between them. But Martha had made plans to move to LA that same week, and whenever she told people that Malibu's beauty had made her relocate, she hadn't been telling the whole truth.

Lara took a hard left, bumping up from the twisting two-lane they had been following onto a dusty black-top cutting across the sun-baked hillside. The modern urban splendour of LA had been left long behind. It was practically a desert out here, and if you squinted, you could almost imagine you were back when the pioneers had arrived over the Sierras with their wagons and horses.

'Thanks for sorting this out, Martha.'

'It was just a phone call,' she shrugged.

'Two days ago, you promised me phone calls, but now here you are in the thick of it.'

'Yeah, I guess we're a modern Cagney and Lacey,' said Martha.

'Cagney and Lacey?'

'You're kidding me?' said Martha, turning in her seat. 'It was a TV show in the 80s. They were lady cops; one had a perm.'

'Martha, I wasn't even born back then.'

'Sheesh. You don't know what you're missing. Anyway, my point stands: we're like a crime-fighting detective duo.'

Lara gave a light chuckle.

'I could have done with you last night.'

Lara had told her about gatecrashing Donna Phillip's West Hollywood party. Martha would have accompanied her, but she'd had a physio appointment she didn't want to miss and had left Lara for what sounded like an embarrassing and unproductive encounter. That was part of the reason she was here now – guilt. Lara was driving the story, but Martha was a big part of it too now - she knew the players and couldn't leave everything to Lara.

'I'm sorry; I should have been the one to confront Donna.'

'Honestly? If Donna had seen you, she would have just turned around and run out of there.'

'Gee, thanks.'

‘I mean, Donna didn’t seem keen to talk about The Malibu House – and it was only because I could sneak under the wire that I got anything out of it.’

‘Which wasn’t much.’

‘I got a glass of organic champagne,’ smiled Lara.

‘Hmm. But if you move to LA, you’ll probably discover you’re blackballed from the Xanadu Club.’

‘I think they’ll get by without me,’ said Lara, pulling up at a rickety wooden fence. Almost hidden by an overgrown orchid tree, a hand-painted sign read ‘Folkvangyr’ in curling, playful letters.

‘Remind me who Willow is again?’ asked Lara.

‘She was Benny Dean’s girlfriend – you know, the fourth member of the Virginians? Lovely girl. A make-up artist, last I heard. She had the sweetest little shack on Kirkwood, one of the prime streets in Laurel Canyon.’

‘But she wasn’t at Verity’s final party?’

‘No, but given Donna told you Benny caused the argument that night, I still think we should talk to her.’

Willow had always been kind and open. In her years in the entertainment industry, Martha knew that makeup artists always had the best stories. Something intimate about the makeup artist’s chair made people share secrets. Maybe Willow had some of her own. And besides, despite his reluctance to talk about that past, Martha had enjoyed talking with Eliot. Too many friends had fallen away in recent years; this was a good excuse to reconnect.

Martha got out of the car and opened the gate. It gave a loud creak; either somebody wasn't maintaining the property well, or visitors were a rarity. Shielding her eyes against the sun, they followed a meandering path towards the house. It was a wood frame shack with clapboard sides painted a bright green. There was a mismatched red door and terracotta pots all along a peeling, sagging porch, wind-chimes tinkling softly. All the hippy cliches were present and correct. Martha stopped and paused for a moment, hands on her hips.

'What is it?' asked Lara.

'It's just…like stepping back in time,' said Martha. 'Have you ever seen the cover of the first Crosby, Stills and Nash album? This is what it was like. All the houses in the Canyon looked like this. This really could be Lookout Mountain Avenue, not Ojai.'

'Shall we…?'

WOOOF-WOOF! WOOF!

'Shit,' said Lara, immediately jumping back at the sound of furious roaring and claws scrabbling at the other side of the door.

'Is it a tiger?' asked Lara.

The noise was interrupted by an angry female voice.

'Wolfie, no, goddamn it. WOLFIE!'

There was a pause, then the door opened, and a woman stepped out, holding onto the collar of a huge grey German shepherd. Martha opened her mouth to speak, but before she could say anything, Lara stepped forward.

'Hey Wolfie,' she said, without fear, 'We're friends, aren't we?'

The beast growled at her, then sniffed the back of Lara's proffered hand. There was a suspended moment, and then the dog whined and licked her fingers.

'You're good with dogs,' said the woman, releasing Wolfie, who bounded around Lara happily.

'I grew up around animals. Dogs and horses mainly.'

'What are you, a cowboy?' whispered Martha from the side of her mouth.

'Rich girl,' replied Lara. 'We had stables.'

Seeing Willow was also like stepping back in time too. Her hair was silver now rather than blonde, but it was as long and unruly as it had always been. The Willow Martha had known had been tall and languid, not quite a model's physique but a girl-next-door version. The older version was still thin, and she wore the same clothes: a long Batik skirt and an embroidered waistcoat that showed off tanned arms. Willow stepped forward, and Martha embraced her; a proper squeeze, not the hands-free air kisses she got at her book clubs – and as she stepped back, Martha saw that Willow had tears in her eyes.

'It's been far too long,' she said, gravel in her voice.

'It has,' agreed Martha. She and Willow had never been particularly close friends; one of the defining characteristics of that Seventies scene was that it was fluid and ever-changing. People came and went, friendships rose and fell, and everybody was friends with – and sleeping with – everybody else. If you visited somebody's house, you might find a rock star strumming a guitar, and the next day, there could be some straight housewife in Pucci who had read about the scene in a magazine and wanted an adventure. All were welcome. Martha and Willow had shared that time, they had breathed the same air. And Verity had been the glue that had held them all together.

'Why don't you both come out back?' said Willow. 'It's a little more shady.'

Wolfie jumped at his new friend Lara as they walked through the house, a chaotic mishmash of thrift-store furniture, Eastern throws and an easel with artwork that appeared to be a multicoloured self-portrait of a naked Willow. As Willow had promised, the terrace at the back of the house was shaded by the huge leaves of a red oak.

'What do you want to drink? I have cactus tea in the icebox.'

Martha smiled to herself: she hadn't heard the term 'icebox' in years. In 21st-century Malibu, everyone had the latest thing – Sub-Zero fridges, electric lunch boxes or those foil boards that people used to skim across the sea. 'Icebox' felt reassuringly real.

‘Tea sounds good,’ Martha called as she and Lara settled into two rocking chairs. Beyond the porch, the sun-baked earth stretched out towards the distant mountains, broken only by an occasional outcrop of jagged rocks or a cluster of cacti reaching towards the bright blue sky. The tranquillity of the place was almost overwhelming; it felt like time couldn’t touch you.

‘You’re lucky; it’s not too hot today,’ said Willow, bringing out the drinks.

‘This isn’t hot?’ asked Lara. ‘Sorry, I’m English.’

Martha smiled. She, too, had noticed the car’s dashboard registering 93 degrees just before they had parked.

‘You wait a few weeks,’ said Willow, ‘It’ll hit 100 every day.’

‘Didn’t you use to live in Topanga?’ asked Martha. Topanga was a hippy-vibe town in the hills behind Malibu. ‘How come you moved?

Willow shrugged.

‘Topanga was amazing. Spiritual and magical, but it was still a little too close to LA. I moved here ten years ago when I stopped working in the business. I liked that Ojai was that bit further out, although we’re getting more and more people from West Hollywood moving in. It’s because of the vortex.’

‘Vortex?’ said Lara.

‘It’s like a sacred energy in the Ojai valley,’ said Willow. ‘It has the power to rejuvenate and recharge, you know?’

Martha wasn’t into crystals like Barbara, but Willow’s yard was certainly peaceful, just the chirp of cicadas and the almost audible hum of the hot rocks. They sat in companionable silence, just sipping their tea.

‘So you’re staying in the Malibu House and writing a story about Verity?’ said Willow, putting down her cup. Martha and Lara filled her in on the past couple of days: Eliot, Jack Anders, and Donna.

'So you met Donna, huh?' said Willow to Lara. 'How is she?'

'It was brief. She didn't exactly want to talk to me.'

Willow laughed. 'I heard she got pretty grand. Or should I say more grand.'

Martha and Lara exchanged a look.

'I thought you and Donna were good friends?'

Willow shook her head, smile fading.

'*Verity* was my friend,' she said with emphasis. 'And obviously, I went with Benny Dean for a while, but Donna? She always had a lot of negative energy about her. Didn't you ever feel it?'

Martha nodded. She wasn't sure about Willow's vortex, but Martha knew what she meant about Donna. It was often the way with the beautiful people. Winning the lottery in one area meant losing out where it mattered.

'So she didn't want to help, huh?' said Willow, looking at Lara.

'She kind of had me thrown out of her party.'

'Well, I'm not surprised she doesn't want to dwell too much on what happened that night. She was always saying she was Verity's best friend, but the only person Donna has ever cared about was herself.'

Willow started to stroke the top of Wolfie's head.

'Donna was having an affair with Eliot,' she said.

Martha almost dropped her cup. She thought Willow might shed some useful information on those Malibu days but this almost knocked her sideways.

'Donna and *Eliot*? When was this?'

'Like, a few weeks before Verity passed. Look, I know Verity and Eliot were separated,' said Willow. 'But still. It was typical of Donna to want to take something away from Verity.'

'Why do you say that?" asked Lara.

Willow was on a roll now, and Martha could see it. She

had waited years to tell this story and wanted to get it all out.

'I always got the sense that Donna was jealous of Verity. When they were in The Virginians together, Donna was the one the cameras were always on, but everyone knew that Verity was the talent and the band's voice. But it's not always about cheekbones, and Donna knew it: knew it and didn't like it.'

Martha was still in shock. She was shocked and annoyed that she hadn't gotten a hint of this when she had spoken to Eliot.

'But an affair with Eliot? That's pretty cold, even for Donna. How do you know?'

Willow picked up the teapot and topped up their cups.

'A few weeks before that last Malibu party, Verity organised a trip to the Joshua Tree for everyone, remember?'

Everyone? Martha and Griffin hadn't been invited. Then again, they weren't in the inner circle.

'There were about twenty of us, and we drove out to the desert in whatever cars and campers we could get hold of. Big convoy. We had a big bonfire on the outskirts of town on Friday night, just singing songs and howling at the moon.' Willow smiled at the memory. 'I can still picture that black sky; the Joshua Tree National Park is one of the best places in the world to see the Milky Way.'

She paused and took another sip of tea; Martha could tell the trip was about to turn dark.

'The next night, we all went to some bar together. The place was busy; everyone was in a great mood, Verity especially. I still remember her telling me how well she was getting on with Eliot. I asked her if she still loved him, and she blushed bright red. She admitted that it was why she'd planned the trip to the desert for everyone - because it's so romantic out there, those big skies and all the stars. Verity said she wished she'd had the guts to make it just Eliot and her. Get him out to the desert and tell him how she felt. But showing our vulnerabilities and sharing our feelings is never easy. There's safety in numbers.'

Willow looked towards the mountains, lost in her memories.

'We were staying at this motel on Main Street. Donna was with Todd Mayfield – her boyfriend, remember? - a couple of rooms along from me and Benny. That second night, I was real tired and went back to the hotel.'

She sighed before she continued.

'My room backed onto the pool, and it looked so pretty and so blue at night; I opened the patio door and went to sit outside for a little while. That's when I heard it.'

'Heard what?' asked Martha.

'Noises coming from Donna's room. I thought someone had broken in, so I went to look. The patio door was open; the net curtain was drawn back. That's when I saw Donna. She was on the bed, naked, astride a man. He was holding her hips, going real hard like he was hungry, you know? So I turned away, but then I remembered that I'd left Todd and Benny playing pool in the bar, so…I knew it wasn't Todd.'

She looked away, embarrassed.

'It was Eliot?' said Martha.

Willow nodded.

'The light was low, but it was enough to see them both. I was so upset for Verity. Angry for Todd as well. He was a sweet soul, a kind guy. Todd deserved more.'

'Did you tell Verity about what you saw?' asked Lara.

Willow gave a sad snort.

'No, and it's something I still think about. I mean, they were crazy times. Lots of drugs, lots of sex. Monogamy wasn't high on anyone's agenda, but people still have feelings. Maybe I should have said something.'

Lara and Martha exchanged a look.

'You didn't go to Verity's last party?' asked Lara.

'No, I went to see my mom in Oregon for her birthday. But…'

Willow pulled a pained face.

'What?' Martha prompted.

'I saw Verity the morning I left LA,' said Willow. 'The day before that last party at the Malibu House. I bumped into her at the Laurel Canyon General Store, buying some groceries. I swear I was about to tell her about Joshua, but then Vee told me she'd invited Eliot to the beach.' Willow shook her head, tears in her eyes. 'Verity looked so, so happy, I just couldn't tell her. And then…it was too late to tell her anything.'

Martha sat back in the wooden chair and blinked to clear her thoughts.

'Have you ever told anyone this before?' asked Martha.

Willow hung her head.

'No. That's why I was so glad when you called. You can live in this magical, spiritual place, yet you can never truly settle if you have something gnawing away at you. It feels good to share it. Set it free.'

It was Lara's turn to speak.

'Willow, do you think Verity found out about Eliot and Donna? Do you think that's why she was upset that night?'

'I don't know – I was a thousand miles away. But I've always wondered. That would explain it, sure.'

'Did Benny go to the party?' asked Lara.

'Yes, why?'

'That was Donna's explanation; she said Benny was the cause of the argument, that he'd yelled at Verity for splitting up the group.'

Willow frowned.

'Sure, Benny wanted the band to reform, and he was always asking Verity about it, but Benny was a sweetheart.'

She looked at Lara, bewildered. 'Seriously, Donna said that?'

Lara nodded, and Willow's eyes flashed with anger. Wolfie let out a low growl, picking up on Willow's mood. She reached out to soothe him.

'Benny had his demons, and sure, he drank too much, but it always made him sad, not violent,' Willow said. 'I don't remember Benny raising his voice unless it was to sing.'

She whispered Donna's name under her breath.

'I always knew she was selfish, but to paint Benny as the bad guy when she had done that to Verity?' she shook her head in wonder. 'So I'm guessing Eliot didn't tell you any of this either, huh?'

'No,' said Martha, feeling duped. She wasn't surprised Eliot had kept his affair in the desert quiet, but it was still quite an omission.

'What about Todd?'

'We're going to see him next.'

'I hear he's not been too well lately. Give him my love.'

'I will.'

'And be careful with him. He's a gentle soul.'

They stood up and, exchanging hugs, walked together through the sun and down to the creaky gate. Just before Martha turned towards the car, Willow stopped her.

'You know the other reason I left Topanga?' she said. 'Bad vibes. That's where Charlie Manson built his cult, did you know that?'

'Really?'

'Sure. It started as a commune, all peace and love, but…' Willow shook her head. 'Ambition and jealousy have a very bad energy. And if you let it, ambition will poison the well.'

Chapter 17

'Come look at the views, isn't it awesome?'

Jenna Brooks-Price clattered onto the apartment's narrow balcony in her five-inch heels with Pingu, her miniature Pekinese, tucked under one arm.

'It's amazing,' said Natasha, hanging back inside. She wasn't good with heights and didn't like how Pingu was wriggling – she could just see the yappy dog little leaping on her, claws like a buzz saw.

'Dental Hygienist Plunges To Death, Takes Reporter And Dog With Her': Not the headline she was looking for.

Natasha guessed Jenna was pushing fifty, although it was hard to tell precisely in LA. Her skin was unnaturally smooth, her blonde hair had an unearthly glow, and the way her breasts jutted forward, a surgeon's knife had to have been involved. But she did look good, slim and toned, like an athlete.

'Will, come and look at Jenna's view,' called Natasha.

'Sure thing!'

Will marched out and leant almost horizontally out over the barrier.

'Man, this is amazing!' he enthused, looking back at Natasha and winking. 'What is this, the fifteenth floor?'

'Sixteenth' said Jenna proudly. 'It's one of the highest in the zip code.'

'Got to be two hundred feet down, right?'

Silently, Natasha cursed him: she'd told him about her fear of heights in the elevator on the way up – Will was enjoying her discomfort.

'I wish my apartment were this high up, Jenna,' said Will. 'I'm *so* jealous.'

'Aw, hun, that's so sweet,' beamed Jenna. 'I just love showing it off.'

She click-clacked back into the open-plan living space.

'Have I shown you the TV? It's the biggest one they had.'

'It's lovely,' said Natasha and in fact, it was. The whole apartment was gorgeous. A multi-million-dollar high-rise condo with pristine fittings, everything slick, shiny and brand new. Natasha had friends who lived out here in West Hollywood, but their apartments were tiny and they needed wealthy parents to afford the rent. The reporter in Natasha wanted to ask Jenna, 'How can you afford all this on a dental hygienist's wages?' just to see her reaction. But Natasha already knew the answer: Jeffery Hanro, CEO of Hanro Construction, the firm with the contract for the Sun Valley Freeway Bridge and half a dozen other projects commissioned by City Hall, had bought the flat for her, along with the 4x4 down in the valet parking, the Cartier watch and, yes, even Pingu.

Finding Jenna's West Hollywood address hadn't been difficult with the newspaper's resources. Natasha had promised to keep Louie, the taxi driver, out of the story, so they had told Jenna that an unnamed 'whistleblower' had given the Globe investigations team her contact number. In truth, Jenna hadn't seemed to care who Natasha's fictional leak was. When Natasha had called, Jenna had insisted they come over at once. They all settled down on a pair of white suede sofas.

'Jenna, we're writing a story about the delays to the construction of the Sun Valley Freeway Bridge, and we understand you might have some unique insights,' began Will.

'Unique insights, is that what we're calling it now?' said Jenna, releasing Pingu from her arms.

Natasha looked at Will nervously. She had seen movies about things like this, and what would happen in the film would be some mobster would burst through Jenna's door with a machine gun. Natasha hadn't told anyone in the office where they were going, which, in hindsight, was a rookie mistake.

She watched Jenna's face. And to her surprise, she let out a laugh.

'Well, I'm happy to tell you anything. And I do mean anything.'

'You are?' said Natasha.

'Sweetheart, I've got an eyelash extension appointment in twenty minutes with Anastasia. If I miss it, I won't be able to see her again for another three months. Her schedule is crazy. So let's get this party started.'

Will nodded.

'Great. So we understand that you are in a relationship with Jeffrey Hanro?'

'Was, sweetheart. *Was*.'

She shook her head, highlighted blonde hair bouncing on her shoulders.

'You know Jeffery screwed me every way it's possible to screw a woman,' she said. 'He wined me, dined me, gave me gifts, and you know what's worse? He made me *promises*.' Jenna gave a theatrical sob, pressing a curled fist to her plump lips. 'He said we were going to be together, told me he was separated from his wife but couldn't divorce her right away because she was sick. And then – you know what I found out?'

Will shook his head.

'I found out that he'd been cheating on me. With *her*.'

'Her?' asked Natasha.

'With his *wife*. Is it too early for a drink?' she huffed, pushing herself back off the sofa, then disappearing into the fridge.

She returned with a giant pink Stanley cup. Natasha had no idea what drink was inside it.

'So you want a source, I'm your woman. I've never done this kind of thing, so you'll have to help me out here.'

'We just want to ask you a few questions, Jenna,' said Will, pulling a tiny dictaphone from his tweed jacket pocket.

'Sure thing, fire away,' she said, pacing around the room as if she were gearing up for a running race.

'Why don't you tell us how you met Jeffrey?' said Will, his voice smooth and reassuring. Back in the office, Natasha had always thought Will was a nepo brat who'd only got the job because his dad had been at the newspaper, but now she could see he was sharp. Dare she say it, he was pretty good at this stuff. She'd have to watch him.

'Oh, we met at the dental practice,' said Jenna, delicately wiping her eyes. 'Jeff came in for laser whitening – he's got a lovely smile - and you know whitening requires multiple sessions, so we got close.' She smiled. 'Real close.'

She ran a manicured nail along the lip of her cup.

'I'll give him this: Jeffrey knows how to treat a lady. He was spontaneous too, just turning up to take me to Catalina Island or Palm Springs – he's got his own place there,' she added with pride. She took a long sip from the cup.

'He didn't tell me he was married at first. He was

vague about those details. When I found out he had a wife, he told me they were separating. But I forced the issue when nothing happened, if you know what I mean.' She turned to Will and whispered. 'I started withholding sex.'

Natasha watched Will's cheeks turn pink.

'But still no word of any divorce. I ask him what the hold-up is, and he tells me his wife is sick. I feel bad until I find out she's not sick, she's in amazing shape; she goes to my girlfriend Shannon's hot yoga class. But you think that's bad enough? Then his wife tells Shannon that Jeffrey's taking her to Maui to renew their vows! Can you believe it?'

She started pacing again.

'So, do I have any loyalties to Jeffrey? *No.* He can go screw himself; in fact, we should let the cops do that because that bridge business is no good, and he just can't keep on getting away with everything.'

'What do you know about Jeffrey's business, Jenna?' asked Natasha. 'What do you know about the bridge?'

'I know that Jeffrey screws people. He screws the contractors, screws the suppliers, and now he's screwing the Mayor with those million-dollar kickbacks,' she said, her words coming out in a rush.

Natasha saw Will sit forward a little at that.

'Jeffrey told you he was paying the City to give him the contracts?'

'Told me? He *boasted* about it like he was the smartest guy on the block. Like he'd invented corruption all by himself.'

Will and Natasha exchanged a look. 'Are you sure you don't mind us recording this?' asked Natasha.

'Do what you like, sweetie. As long as you give Jeffrey 'I'm Separated' Hanro a kick in the nuts, I'm happy.'

'So, did Jeffrey tell you how it worked?'

Jenna snapped her gum.

'It's real simple. The mayor says, 'Hey, I'm up for re-election; I want to be seen to be building things'.

Natasha nodded, scribbling down shorthand notes in case the recording failed. Her heart was bumping; she didn't want to miss a word.

'So the City puts it out to tender – contractors pitch a price, all fair and square.'

Jenna shook her head, golden tresses shining.

'But that's all bullshit,' she said. 'Because Jeffrey's already hit 'em up with a suitcase full of cash.'

'So Hanro was always going to get the jobs?' asked Will.

Jenna held up a finger.

'Not just the jobs that need doing. Jobs that *don't* need doing. I've heard Jeff and his team laugh about it. *What can we get them to agree to next?* Jeff doesn't care if it's causing chaos around the city. He's just collecting jobs and money.'

Jenna gave a dramatic sigh.

'I guess I shoulda said something before – I guess?' she looked at Natasha, clearly hoping for understanding. 'I mean, I knew it wasn't right, what Jeffrey was doing. But what could I do? We were going to get married. But I got that wrong too, didn't I?' she added bitterly, stemming a tear with a bejewelled nail.

'Who is Jeff's contact at City Hall, Jenna? Do you know?' said Will gently.

It was the right question. Natasha knew they would need something more concrete than a disgruntled mistress spinning stories.

'She's called Elise DuBois. She works there. I met her at some fundraiser at the Broad. Jeffrey introduced us; she seemed real full of herself. I wouldn't be surprised if he wasn't screwing her too. And I tell you who else should you speak to? Helen Kampf. Works in DuBois's office. Jeffrey was real pissed with her before he went away to Maui.'

'What had Helen done?' asked Natasha.

'She'd worked out what was happening and threatened to go public. Jeff was furious. I heard him on the phone to Elise, saying she had to deal with it.'

'*Deal* with it?' said Natasha, the vision of a hitman with an Uzi leaping back into her mind.

'Don't worry. Jeffrey's not mob-affiliated.' She let out a cackle. 'He wouldn't last two minutes with those guys. No, Jeffery Hanro is just a greedy son of bitch who got lucky, but I wouldn't put it past him to apply some pressure on poor Helen. I guess she might speak to you, though.'

'Helen Kampf,' said Natasha, scribbling the name in her notebook.

'With an 'f',' said Jenna, then looked at Will.

'Now, how are we going to bring the bastard down?'

Chapter 18

Alex wasn't comfortable on Rodeo Drive. LA's premium shopping street was an alien landscape; Alex felt exposed like he was being watched. As if at any moment, someone would point and yell, 'Imposter!'. He walked past a woman in white skin-tight jeans and sunglasses bigger than her face. She was leaning on a squat man with Friar Tuck hair, carrying a yappy dog who didn't seem pleased by the experience. *These* were the people who belonged on Rodeo, the people who felt at home among these temples of conspicuous consumption. You needed platinum plastic and a Bentley prowling nearby to pick up all those cardboard carriers.

Or maybe Alex felt out of place because Rodeo was so emblematic of LA. It was, after all, where Julia Roberts had come to transform herself into Pretty Woman, to *become* part of LA. And perhaps that was why, if he was honest with himself, he'd been struggling. As much as he wanted to follow Julia's example, he knew this scene would never be him. Not really. And here he was, asking Lara to join him.

Alex tugged at his collar and squinted at the store

across the road, all gold and glass, practically glowing from within. Alex had been a foreign correspondent and had ventured into war zones, but right now, the urge to turn and run – or at least briskly stroll away - was strong. Then Alex heard his father's voice in his head. *Don't bottle it, son,* said Terry Ford. *It's only a bloody shop.*

So Alex crossed, dodging a slow-moving Maclaren in metallic orange – another native desperate to be seen – and pushed through the store's heavy doors. His feet whispered over the thick carpet, and Alex didn't know whether to remove his sunglasses; it seemed just as bright inside as out. He opted for the 'less flash' option and slipped them into his pocket as he approached the counter. Alex laid his hands gently on the thick glass. The treasures inside sparkled and shone. Rings like gulls' eggs and bracelets fit for a pharoah. Alex tried not to look at the prices, just at the jewellery. What would Lara like? What would be appropriate? This was a 'sorry' gift - a general catch-all to cover 'sorry I left you to move to LA', 'sorry I haven't been here for you during this break' and 'sorry I've been distant, I really don't know why'. But he also just wanted to get his girlfriend something lovely. Something that would make her smile. Something that might tell her how much he loved her.

'Can I help?'

A striking woman with shiny blonde hair had sidled up on the opposite side of the counter. Her name tag said 'Elise'.

'Just looking,' said Alex as a reflex.

'Looking for anything in particular?'

Alex carried on looking at the display cases. Elise was right; he did need help; otherwise, he'd drown in all these jewels. 'A necklace, I think.'

He thought of Lara's long neck. 'Gold. Not too big.' He knew he had to be careful here. Lara was not in any way flashy. Nor did she care about labels, but this jeweller had the reputation of making some of the most beautiful jewellery in the world.

'And what would you like it to say?'

Clever phrase, thought Alex. What *did* he want to say? Did he want to impress Lara? Tell her how much she mattered to him. To say 'please stay'?

He watched the woman assessing him, the cost of the suit and the shoes and watch, silently guessing his budget. It was better than embarrassing your customer, he supposed. She slid open a panel and brought out a velvet tray. 'Perhaps something like this?'

From a selection of four gorgeous gold pendants, Alex's eye was drawn to bright ruby encased in a delicate setting with a chain resembling a snake's skeleton. It was beautiful, but it wasn't Lara – plus Alex didn't know much about jewellery, but he did know big single stones cost *a lot*.

'It's not quite her,' he said. 'Perhaps something a little more simple and delicate…

From the corner of his eye, he saw another tray, catching the light like tiny fireflies. Winking at him. The assistant hadn't missed his reaction; she brought the tray onto the counter. A dozen rings twinkled and dazzled under the lights exactly as they were supposed to. The saleswoman didn't speak, didn't say the words 'engagement ring' - she could tell her customer was skittish enough as it was. But there was no denying what Alex had in front of him.

'May I ask the name of the person in question?' asked Elise.

'Who? Oh, um, Lara.'

Lara. He couldn't deny that he had just felt a surge of excitement, imagining her face as he pulled out the ring, getting down on one knee, asking that one question that would change their lives forever.

Of course, it wasn't the first time Alex had thought about proposing to Lara Stone. He thought about it a lot. Or at least thought about being married to her. It was the obvious next step. He flat-out loved her; his friends loved her, and his dad loved her. There was no one else in the world Alex Ford wanted to be with, not just since that first stratospheric kiss five months earlier, but since the very start – when they became close friends at journalism college. And wasn't it about time he told her that?

'If I may,' said Elise, picking a ring from the centre of the tray. As it moved, the facets flashed. Alex clutched the ring between finger and thumb, mesmerised. There was a reason the diamond was the jewel used for these special moments; it caught the light in a way nothing else did.

'So, what are we thinking?'

Alex was thinking this was going to cost him a fortune.

'Three carats,' said Elise. 'Asscher cut, almost flawless.'

Alex held it up to the light. As he moved it side to side, it was as if a hundred tiny butterflies had been released.

'Wow,' he breathed.

Elize just smiled.

'It's a 'D' for colour – ice-white, the best you can get.'

Well, Lara deserved the best, thought Alex.

Elise pulled out a small white card and slid it across. The price tag was discreet, but it was enough to make Alex's eyes pop. No matter. He was an editor-in-chief with a salary to match. He could afford it, and it was worth it. *She* was worth it.

'I'm guessing Lara is…unconventional?' Elise asked.

Alex looked up. 'Yes, very. She's not like anyone else, thank goodness. How do you know?'

'Oh, you can tell a lot from the ring you are drawn to. This ring's cut and setting are clean and elegant, but they're not ordinary, not at all.'

At the back of his mind, he knew there was another

option: his mother's ring, but Alex had once – foolishly – been engaged to another girl named Alicia, and he had given that ring to her. In his heart, Alex had always known Alicia was wrong for him, not least because she simply wasn't Lara. Alicia had returned the ring when their engagement fell apart, but it felt 'burned' – and the first ring on the tray, well, it just felt right. He picked it up and slipped it on his pinkie. Man, it looked amazing, even on his finger.

'Obviously, if you don't have Lara's ring size with you, just come back in, and we can re-size it.'

He was about to nod when his phone rang insistently in his pocket. 'Sorry, I thought I'd turned it off,' he said, looking down at the screen. *Gina.*

He frowned; he'd told his PA he had an important 'personal appointment' and that she should only call if it were an emergency.

'I'm Sorry, Elise. I need to take this,' he said, stepping towards the door.

'Of course,' said the saleswoman, meaningfully pointing to Alex's hand. 'If you could just…?'

'Oh. Oh, yes,' said Alex, twisting the ring free and placing it back in the tray. 'I won't be long.'

Putting the phone to his ear, Alex strode out into the shop. 'Gina, Alex. Is everything ok?'

'Not sure,' said Gina, tension in her voice. 'I've been fielding calls from Suzanne Genero for the past half hour.'

'The PR? Can't Dani deal with this?'

'She's demanding to speak to you directly.'

Over the past few months, Alex had been playing catch-up with the various media players in LA, but he knew Suzanne Genero; she was a powerhouse in the world of publicity, controlling many of the big-name celebrities and brands. She also had a reputation for being a ball-breaker if she felt her clients were threatened.

'What's her problem?' he asked, his thoughts turning to Limelight magazine. The launch issue was packed with celebrity interviews, and he could think of at least two on Suzanne's client roster.

Gina let out a reluctant sigh. 'She says someone from the Globe gatecrashed the book launch of one of her clients last night. Asked inappropriate questions and left the woman in tears.'

'One of our reporters? Who?'

'Suzanne only said they were female.'

He quickly ran through the possible candidates. The news team was too experienced to do anything like that, and why would they be at a book launch in the first place? This was more of a features kind of thing…Natasha? The young reporter was hungry, self-starting, and green. Natasha might have pushed too hard.

'Apparently, they used your business card to get into the party.'

Alex frowned. Of course, he was angry about someone using his business card fraudulently, but it also meant that this gatecrasher might not be one of his staff. After all, since he had arrived in LA, Alex had taken dozens of meetings and given hundreds of cards out.

'Who was the client?'

'Donna Phelps.'

'Donna.' He suppressed a groan. Alex was a music fan; he immediately made the connection. Donna Phelps had been in a band with Verity Jones. Which instantly led him to Lara. *Damn.*

Alex's fingers gripped the phone hard as anger flared. He had spent months schmoozing LA's media community, trying to convince them he was serious, switched on and reliable. He'd struggled to get the advertisers to believe in his vision for the new Globe – and he'd already had Simon Desai in his office this morning, openly questioning his approach. This was the last thing he needed right now. Alex rubbed a hand over his forehead.

'Okay, get me Suzanne's number,' he sighed. 'I think I've got some grovelling to do.'

'Right.'

'Oh, and Gina?'

'Yes, boss?'

'Can you call a saleswoman named Elise at the jewellers on Rodeo? Tell her I won't be back.'

Chapter 19

Lara shut the car door and turned, shielding her eyes from the sun as she took in the grounds of the Valley Pine Resort, 'the most exclusive retirement community in the Thousand Oaks area,' according to their website.

'Pretty, isn't it?' said Martha as they took a shell-pink path towards the main reception building. 'Pretty' was an understatement. The resort was spotless; the brickwork scrubbed, the hedges manicured, not a leaf or petal out of place. It was more like a film set than an old people's home. Thirty miles north of Malibu, it felt like Fifties suburbia; the saturated green lawns were hard-won via hidden sprinklers and the vigilance of an army of gardeners.

'Are you familiar with the novel 'The Stepford Wives?' whispered Martha as she and Lara passed residents in pastel leisurewear, each calling out a cheery greeting and beaming at them with cult-like intensity.

'Saw the movie,' said Lara, stopping to let a golf cart pass, driven by another senior with a rictus grin. According to Martha, this section of California was crowded with similar high-end settlements catering to elderly Californians who needed support but were still rich enough to care about appearances. Creepy or not, Valley Pine was certainly impressive, but it was a curious place for Todd Mayfield to have ended up. Willow's description of him had given Lara an image of some handsome youth in beads playing the bongos like a Seventies Matthew McConnaughey. But then, Lara's experience with the Book Club and Martha herself showed that people could change outwardly; but dig a little deeper, that beatnik was still in there.

'What do you remember about Todd?'

'He was gorgeous,' said Martha without hesitation. 'Like, super-gorgeous.'

Lara laughed. 'That's it?'

'Seriously, it was hard to get past that. Cheekbones, perfect teeth and a body…' Martha whistled. 'He used to wear a waistcoat or an open shirt, nothing underneath. I was happily married, but if you were a woman with a pulse, you'd…well, like I say, hard to get past it.'

Martha's eyes took on a faraway look.

'The funny thing is, Todd was a lovely guy, too. You know how some good-looking people get conceited and behave as if they deserve to go to the front of every line? Todd wasn't like that; he was just happy to be there. Maybe he was too laid back, too trusting, especially when it came to Donna. If you always go with the flow, you can find the current pulling you somewhere you never intended.'

Like me, thought Lara. Since leaving the Chronicle full-time several months earlier, she had been feeling lost and unsettled. Lara had thought that a more flexible arrangement with The Chronicle would be beneficial, allowing her to work for other outlets, but the truth was that few editors had an appetite for deep investigative stories. 'We'd love to, but it's too expensive,' she kept hearing repeatedly. Lara wasn't yet forty, but it made her feel like a weaver in the age of fast fashion. The industry was changing; perhaps Lara needed to change too.

'Are you sure you're comfortable with this, Martha?' she asked, giving Martha a sideways glance. Todd, Donna, and Willow were all pieces of her past—Martha's real past, not some semi-fictional characters populating a story—real flesh and blood, people she had a connection to. Was Lara being selfish? Was she using Martha? She wasn't sure anymore.

Martha raised an eyebrow. 'What do you mean by that? That I'm not up to the job?'

Lara held up both hands.

'Obviously not: you're Martha Riding. You were the first writer in Baghdad after the fall. But this story is your life – your past. It's different when you're on the inside. Believe me, I know.'

Martha nodded thoughtfully.

'Sometimes our real lives overlap with the story, and you know what? Often, that's where the best stuff is. *Every* story is personal, Lara; otherwise you're not doing it right.'

Martha stood still for a moment and just looked off into the distance.

'Seeing Eliot, Willow, and now Todd, I wonder why I didn't keep in touch with everyone. They were some of the best days of my life, and yet these days, my friends seem to be based on geography, not history.'

Lara remembered Martha's book club and the women she had invited. They had all seemed nice enough, but they hadn't seemed like Martha's sort of people, but, yes, most lived within a one-mile radius of Martha's house.

Martha pulled out a piece of paper and looked at the address. 'Todd's place should be one of these,' she said, looking up at the neat homes. 'So, what's our angle?'

'Angle?'

Martha lowered her voice. 'I mean, I'm ballsy, but I'm not sure I can go up to Todd, not having seen him for forty years and say, 'Hi, remember me? Oh, and by the way, I think your daughter is Eliot Jones' child.'

Lara understood her reluctance, but journalists sometimes had to ask hard questions, whoever it was. How you dealt with that grubby part of the job often dictated your success. Lara had met some reporters who seemed to have a 'sensitivity' chip missing from their circuits, but most just gritted their teeth and asked the question. It wasn't a profession for the squeamish. As if to prove the point, Martha peeled off and strode up to a woman pruning a bush.

'I wonder if you can help? We're looking for the Mayfield residence.'

The woman looked at them both, then pulled off her gloves.

'You've found it. I'm Julianne Mayfield, Todd's wife.' She put out a hand. 'And you must be Martha. Todd's told me a lot about you.'

Martha gave a tired smile.

'Only good things, I hope.'

Julianne paused and looked at them both. 'I really should have told you both on the phone.'

Lara and Martha exchanged a look.

'Told us what?'

'Todd is suffering from dementia,' she replied. 'He has good days and bad days, but…it can disturb visitors if he doesn't recognise them. Still, today is a good day, I think. And his long-term memory is usually pretty sharp. The doctors tell me it's good for him to exercise that part of his brain.'

Julianne led them along a path to the side of the house. In the garden at the rear, Lara saw a man hunched over a small patch of garden, tending to a collection of vibrant flowers. His hands were covered in soil, and his hair was a distinguished shade of silver. He looked up as Lara approached, giving her a warm smile.

Damn, Martha was right. Even in his seventies, Todd Mayfield was still striking, like a retired model.

'Todd,' said Julianne, 'This is Lara Stone. I told you she was coming to visit.'

He frowned. 'Really? I…'

His eyes drifted to the left, and his face lit up.

'Oh my,' he said. 'Martha?'

'Hello, Todd,' she said. 'It's been too long.'

Instead of answering, he rose and pulled Martha into a hug.

'It's so good to see you,' he said, a catch in his voice. 'Standing there, it was like…'

Martha nodded. 'Like a ghost, right?'

Todd let out a delighted laugh. 'You haven't changed. You were always sharp.'

'Well, nice to see where you ended up. It's lovely.'

'But not exactly the rock and roll lifestyle we all dreamed of, huh?' he said with a self-deprecating laugh, wiping his hands on his jeans. 'But it's peaceful here, and the garden keeps me busy. And…I…' Todd frowned, obviously groping for a word beyond his grasp. Lara's heart sank. She didn't know Todd, and even for her was hard to watch. It was like he was a shattered mirror, and tiny shards slowly fell from the frame each time he moved. Valley Pine *was* peaceful, but Lara couldn't shake the feeling that she was walking through a graveyard where dreams and ambitions long since laid to rest still lingered. Or perhaps she was just in a negative frame of mind.

'And who's this?' said Todd, turning to Lara. 'I'm sure I would have remembered you.'

His eyes twinkled with mischief, a remnant of the charming rogue he'd once been.

‘I’m Lara, I’m a writer from England.’

‘Writing what? Not my life story, I hope?’

‘I’m doing a piece about Verity Jones.’

‘Who for?’

‘I work for The Chronicle in London.’

‘Oh, Verity loved London,’ he said approvingly. ‘It’s a long time since I talked about those days.’

‘No, it’s not,’ said Julianne, rolling her eyes. ‘Everyone at Valley Pine wants to know what Joni Mitchell was like or whether Janis Joplin was that crazy. We get invited to barbeques so people can winkle the gossip out of him.’

Julianne gave them a warm smile.

‘I’ll leave you to talk,’ she said with a dramatic whisper. ‘Todd, why don’t you take them to the coffee shop? If you need me, I’ll be out front.’

Todd flashed Lara a smile as he led them through a side gate and up onto the road. ‘Don’t worry, I know the way – to the coffee shop, anyway.’

Todd chattered to Martha as they walked, happily filling her in on the missing decades. His acting career hadn’t lasted very long, and he had quickly moved into sales—‘I was an excellent photocopier salesman,’ he told them with some pride.

‘Well, this is a great place,’ said Lara as they weaved through the complex.

‘It’s not Laurel Canyon, that’s for sure, but we like it,’ shrugged Todd. ‘There’s a pool, an art studio, pickleball courts, and a movie theatre. Best of all, I’m one of the youngest people here. I wasn’t sure we were ready for it, senior living, but…’ He looked at Martha, pleading with his eyes. ‘They tell me I have dementia. So I guess no one wants me wandering off.’

‘Well, thank you for seeing us,’ said Lara, to fill the space.

‘Ah, it's no problem,’ Todd replied. ‘I don't get many

visitors these days. Fast living took its toll on most of my friends, one way or another. Only Bobby comes now.'

'Oh? Who's Bobby?'

'An old pal from the Malibu days.'

'You mean Bobby Franks?' said Martha. 'I haven't seen him in years. What's he up to?'

'Still working in the business. Remember, Bobby was younger than everyone else.'

They had reached the café now, so Lara left Todd and Martha reminiscing and went inside to order. When she came out with a tray, they were sitting at a table laughing. Just two old friends catching up.

'I was pleased to see they had tea here,' said Lara, handing out the drinks. 'Very sophisticated.'

Todd smiled. 'Summer suggested we move into this place,' he said, 'You know, Donna's daughter?'

'Isn't she your daughter too, Todd?' asked Martha.

'Yeah,' he said uncertainly, then a warm smile spread across his face. 'She's my little girl, my stars and moon. Summer's in fifth grade now, can you believe it?'

Lara exchanged a look with Martha.

'Does Summer live with Donna?' she asked.

Todd shook his head.

'I haven't seen Donna in years. I see her on Good Morning America more often than in real life.'

'No love lost between you then?'

He shook his head slowly. Again, Lara sensed he'd lost the thread. He looked at her quizzically. 'You wanted to talk about Verity?'

'Verity and the whole Laurel Canyon scene.'

'Well, Verity is a good place to start,' he said, brightening. 'Her house on Kirkwood was like fly paper for all the starry-eyed hippies like me, right Martha?'

Martha nodded with a soft smile.

'How did you and Verity meet?' asked Lara.

'I met her the week I arrived in LA. Twenty-one, fresh off the bus from Indiana. I had a guitar I couldn't play, twenty bucks and big dreams. Went straight to the Troubadour Club - and the first person I met there was Verity.'

Lara could guess why. She could imagine him fifty years before; Todd would have lit up the room.

'Verity was a good friend. Nothing more. I mean, I thought she was fantastic, but she was still with Eliot when we met. But she said I had talent. I'm not sure I ever did, but Verity saw something in me and introduced me to all the right people.'

'Did Verity introduce you to Donna?'

'Sure. I mean, you couldn't know Verity and not know Donna. They were tight. Like sisters.'

Lara thought back to their conversation with Willow but refrained from saying anything.

'So what do you remember about that night? The night Verity passed.'

Todd gave Lara a thin smile and tapped his temple. 'They say I have dementia, remember?'

'Anything would be helpful,' said Lara gently.

Todd stared down at his cup.

'Well, we'd been there most of the afternoon – everyone was having a good time - but I left early. I was in a play; something about Russians? I remember the costumes were funky anyway.'

Lara glanced at Martha and saw her disappointment. If Todd had left that early, he wouldn't have much insight into the drama that unfurled later.

'What time did you leave?'

'As late as I could,' he smiled. 'Verity's parties were always great; everyone was there that night. But curtain-up was at 7.30, and we had to be at the theatre an hour before. I had a motorbike, so it didn't take long to shoot down the PCH …I must have left around six?'

'When did you hear about Verity?'

Lara saw Todd wince, his face registering pain that looked new. Perhaps in the tangle of his brain, that was how it felt, like it had just happened.

'The next morning. Donna came to my apartment. God…' He looked up, eyes watery. 'I couldn't believe it. I mean, of all of us, why her? Donna was upset, too. We all were.'

'Did Donna stay at the party that night?'

Todd nodded and sipped his coffee.

'Did you know she had the baby? Little Summer. Like, the most joy I've ever felt. She's perfect.'

Lara could feel his mind wandering, and she knew she had to try to keep him on track.

'How long were you together with Donna?'

'Summer was almost four when it ended. Or three?'

'Why did you split up?' asked Martha.

He looked away, and for a moment, Lara wasn't sure if he'd just tuned out.

'I was never good enough,' he said quietly. 'Nothing is ever good enough for Donna. That's how she is: someone has a nice house? She wants a bigger one. Someone gets a new car; she wants a newer model.'

His shoulders gave a sad slump.

'My acting career never really took off. You know I did that movie with Bergman? Everyone said it was my big break, but it was the opposite. Suddenly, I was seen as avant-garde and European at a time when everyone wanted the clean-cut all Americans like Robert Redford. And when my career dive-bombed, Donna just stopped coming home.'

He looked up. 'Which, to be honest, was a relief.'

'So where was she? With someone else?' asked Martha carefully.

Todd flashed a look. 'No, she was working. Donna was

doing pretty well herself by then. Her solo singing career had gone nowhere, but she loved the parties I took her to, all that Hollyweird bullshit. That's how she got into TV – some producer picked her up to do 'Donna's Place': remember that?'

It had been well before Lara's time, but before their meeting at the book launch, she had researched Donna Phelps. 'Donna's Place' had been a fairly mainstream variety show with musical guests, the idea being she had invited them over to her 'swinging pad'. Donna would chat with the guests in a cosy kitchen area while she made them a cocktail or a sandwich, and then they'd sing a duet. The show hadn't been a hit, but Donna's kitchen segment had launched her career as a TV chef, leaning into all the hippy-Cali food fads like veganism, high-fibre and, of course, the Beverly Hills Diet.

'Donna got custody, of course. But I still see Summer,' he said, gesturing towards a manicured lawn across the coffee shop. 'We play catch or…' He frowned, then looked up at Martha. 'What was the question?'

Lara felt her smile fade. Pressing him on the details suddenly felt cruel. Todd seemed to find happiness in his memories, so who were they to spoil that?

Martha was obviously thinking the same. She placed a hand over Todd's, his fingers still stained with earth from his gardening. 'Isn't it time we got back?'

They walked the short distance back to the house, the fragrance of cut grass in the air. Lara could admit she had always seen these rich retirement communities in a negative light, as a way to separate the wealthy from their money when they were at their most vulnerable. But now she didn't think spending your last days surrounded by flowers and smiling faces would be so bad.

'You know who you should talk to,' said Todd after a moment. 'Bobby Franks. Remember he always had that

Super 8 camera with him? Told me once that the Malibu scene would make a great documentary. He might have some footage that could help you.'

'Great idea,' said Martha as Todd pulled his phone out of his pocket to give her Bobby's number.

'Say, we're having a party tomorrow,' said Todd, 'Do you want to come?'

'Todd, I'd love to,' said Martha, 'But I'll be in Carmel. One of my closest friends is 80 this weekend, and I've been invited to her birthday lunch.'

'Never mind, maybe next time,' he said, and Lara felt a sadness descend. She had seen dementia before, and it only went one way. 'Next time' for Todd might well be too late.

'Todd, can I use the bathroom?' asked Lara. She left Martha and Todd to say their goodbyes and followed his directions into the house. The inside was just as pristine as the outside, with all fresh paintwork and smudge-free windows – she imagined every house on the lot was the same, but Todd and Julianne had made this house their own. There were framed images of Todd in his prime, promo shots of him on set or stage, but the huge majority were sun-faded photos of pop stars: Eric Clapton, Joni Mitchell, and David Crosby, all sitting around playing guitars or lounging on the grass. Lara immediately knew they were from the Laurel Canyon days; she even recognised The Malibu House in the background of one in particular: Todd sitting on the steps down to the beach with his arm around a woman with a woven flower headband. Verity Jones. No wonder Todd and Julianne were so popular on the Valley Pine BBQ circuit.

As she leaned in to look closer, a door opened, and a woman in her early fifties walked out.

'Oh, hi,' said Lara quickly. 'I'm Lara. I was looking for the bathroom.'

The woman smiled. 'Sure, it's just down the hall. And I'm Ellen, I'm Julianne's daughter. Todd's my stepdad.'

Lara looked at her; she should have guessed. Ellen had the same dark hair as Julianne, the same nose, and the same high forehead. Ellen would be a little older than Summer, but not by much.

'Here for the big party tomorrow? Where have you come from?'

'New Jersey.'

'Long way for a party,' smiled Lara.

'Forty years of marriage. That's something to celebrate.'

Lara smiled. 'I couldn't agree more.'

In the bathroom, Lara washed her face in the small sink, grateful for the cool water. Slightly lost on her way back out, she stumbled upon Julianne in the kitchen, hulling strawberries.

'We're leaving now. It was lovely to meet you,' said Lara.

'Todd and Martha are still chatting, I see,' said Julianne, craning her neck to see through the window. 'I'm glad you came. It's good for him.'

'Congratulations, by the way. On your Ruby wedding,' said Lara.

Julianne's nose wrinkled. 'It makes me feel so old, but I can't wait until tomorrow. So many people are flying in, although I'm not sure how many we can fit in the house.'

'I've just met Ellen,' said Lara. 'She looks like you.'

Julianne gave a little shrug and pushed the bowl of fruit to one side.

'I was married to Ellen's dad before Todd. What do they call them now? A starter marriage? He was not a good man, but something good came out of it.'

'Is Summer coming?' asked Lara as casually as she could.

'I think so. She said she was bringing a cake. Some huge thing from a fancy bakery in Beverly Hills. I can't wait to see it. It will be good for the girls to see each other. Ellen is a nurse, so she doesn't get the chance to come to Cali that often, and obviously, Summer works so hard.'

'What about you and Todd? No other children…?'

It came out awkwardly, but she had a thin window of opportunity to learn about Todd's life.

'We tried, but it wasn't to be,' said Julianne gracefully. 'But we have the girls, and even though we are not all together that often, we are all still family.'

Lara stepped forward and gave the older woman an embrace.

'Good luck for tomorrow,' she said.

'I'll need it, catering for a hundred,' she said, pulling away and looking harassed. 'Ellen said she'd help make the brownies, but she's just gone out shopping!'

'I might be able to help there,' said Lara, having had a good idea. 'Give me your number and let me make a few calls….'

* * *

'The caterer from your book club. Do you have her number?' said Lara when they were back inside the car.

'Suzie? Why?'

'I wanted to send Julianne some of those tray bakes she made for you.'

'For their Ruby Wedding party? It's tomorrow, Lara. Suzie needs at least 48 hours notice for her catering services - if you're lucky. Usually, it's a month for big events like engagement parties and bar mitzvahs.'

'I think I can make it worth her while,' said Lara as Martha fiddled with her phone for the number.

'I forgot, you're rich,' smiled Martha, showing her Suzie's number.

'I forget myself sometimes,' said Lara.

'They are good people,' said Martha as Lara fired the car engine to pull away.

'Good and honest,' said Lara, voicing what her gut told her.

'Which is possibly more than can be said for Eliot Jones.'

Martha gave her a sideways look.

'Lara Stone, you know something,' she said, wagging a finger.

'I've got a theory, that's all. And if I'm right, I think you'll want to schedule another meeting with Mr Jones.'

Chapter 20

Alex stood on the balcony, staring out at the beach as the sun sank behind the horizon, casting orange and purple across the wet sand. After the panicked phone call from Gina at the office, Alex had rushed back from Rodeo Drive to the Malibu house to confront Lara – and had once again found the house empty. His anger had immediately flared; she wasn't answering her phone and hadn't replied to his texts – he had to guess she was avoiding him.

'So where are you now?' he murmured, checking his phone again. 'Out with Salman Rushdie and R.L.Stine?'

He snorted at his absurd outburst. After all, why shouldn't Lara be out enjoying LA? She would expect Alex to be at work until late, so why would she hang around the house? But clearly, Lara Stone's idea of enjoying her holiday was different to most people's, and if investigating the suspicious death of a singer floated your boat, then why not? That was just Lara; she could no more let a lead go than she could spread her wings and fly, but even so, that didn't give her the right to ride roughshod over his reputation. Alex had enough problems fitting into LA's closed media world without Lara coming along and causing outrage among powerful PRs like Suzanne Genero. He walked down the steps and onto the beach and took a deep breath. *Be calm, Alex. None of this matters.* It wasn't until Alex reached the edge of the water that Alex realised he hadn't been this far out before. The surf washed over his feet – it was surprisingly warm. Not like Whitehaven beach in Cumbria, the seaside destination of Alex's childhood. Your toes would go numb within a minute, even in the height of summer.

'Hey,' said a voice behind him.

He turned in surprise.

'You're home early.'

Lara was standing there. He had been brooding so much he hadn't even heard her approach.

'I got your texts,' she said quickly. 'I'm sorry. I've been driving or meeting people all day, so I didn't get a chance to reply….'

Alex squinted in the late afternoon sunlight. Usually, one look at Lara was enough to make him feel better, but he was still smarting from his terse call with Suzanne.

'You're sorry? What for exactly?' he said. His texts had been vague and hadn't mentioned the accusations from Suzanne Gennaro. He wanted to see if she would confess to gatecrashing Donna Phelps' party using his business card. After all, she hadn't mentioned it the previous evening when Alex had asked her how she'd spent her day. Now, Lara's lack of transparency felt duplicitous.

'Alex, what is it?'

'I got a phone call today from an angry PR. Donna Phelps' PR, in fact…' he said, squeezing his toes into the sand.

Lara looked down the long stretch of beach, then looked back at him.

'Yeah. I've got a confession to make.'

Yeah, I know, thought Alex angrily.

'I used your business card to get into a party,' Lara continued. 'I shouldn't have done it, but I was on the spot and thought it was our only chance to speak to Donna Phelps. I'm sorry.'

'But why? What was so important? Doesn't Martha Riding have her phone number?'

He said Martha's name with a hint of sarcasm, which wasn't big or clever, but he was upset.

'No, Martha doesn't have her number; they were friends decades ago. Anyway, Donna is a big star now – you know how hard it is to get to people like that. But I needed to speak to her. After all, Donna was here that night.'

Alex shook his head, trying to make sense of it all.

'Lara, I'm not being funny, but I don't see why you need to urgently speak to Donna Phelps for a 2,000-word feature about the 27 Club. Presumably, Verity Jones gets what, an extra paragraph because it's the 50th anniversary of her death? It's hardly big news.'

'Well, I'm sorry if my commissions don't meet your standards of investigative journalism.'

'Forget my standards, Lara. What about yours? Writing some cuts piece about a few dead musicians?'

He knew he had hit a nerve, but it was a cheap victory.

Lara looked down on the damp sand and then back at Alex.

'Look, I think there's something more to this story.'

'Lara, the 27 Club thing has been done a million times.'

'Not that; Verity's story. How she died. I think there's more to it than was first reported. I think there's a real possibility of foul play.'

The penny dropped with a think.

'Wait, you're not writing the 27 Club story, are you?

You're chasing Verity's death. Was this Martha's Riding's idea?'

Lara's face hardened, and she suddenly didn't look so apologetic.

'No, it wasn't Martha's idea,' said Lara tersely. 'But she is helping me, and we have already discovered some loose threads.'

Alex closed his eyes and held up a hand.

'Lara, you heard what I said the other day. We're living in Simon's house. He's my boss and I have to keep him on side. What is he going to think about Lara Stone poking around his house, pointing the finger and making accusations about dark things having happened here? Do you think he'll be happy, given he's kindly invited us to stay here?'

Lara snorted.

'Oh Alex, don't pretend he's doing us a favour. Simon is manipulating us. Yes, the house is amazing, but we both know the house is a bright, shiny thing to tempt me to move here, so you haven't got any distractions.'

Alex knew she was right – Simon had said as much - but still, it felt like a cold-hearted view of her holiday.

'And here's me thinking this was a lovely, romantic break,' he said sarcastically.

Lara moved a step close towards him.

'Look, you said be careful - and I am being careful,' she said.

'Careful? If you were careful, I wouldn't have had a PR yelling at me this afternoon. You're bored, you're a workaholic, and you need something to do. It's made you reckless, Lar. You can't gatecrash an A-lister's party using my business card and not even have the courtesy to tell me about it!'

'You think I'm bored?' she said. Alex knew he should back off and apologise, but he'd worked so hard to get here

– and now she was endangering everything by crashing around like a bull in a china shop.

'I don't think you know how to relax like normal people, no.'

'I'm not *normal* now?'

'I didn't mean that. Look, work is difficult. Simon can be difficult. Suzanne Gennaro can be very difficult and she can cause The Globe all sorts of problems. She can get us blacklisted from interviewing dozens of celebrities if she wanted to, and the first issue of Limelight hasn't even launched.'

'And you call *me* a workaholic,' Lara snapped. 'I'm left alone all day, so I find something to do – suddenly, I'm a selfish weirdo.'

'Not a weirdo, I never said that, but you *were* being selfish using my business card. I need to build trust with the film industry. And upsetting gatekeepers like Suzanne isn't going to help me.'

He saw Lara glaring at him as if to say his ambitions for the newspaper were pathetic. There was a hierarchy within news media: breaking news was right at the top, followed by investigative journalism of the type Lara specialised in, while the flashy flash of celebrity reporting was a long way down the pecking order. And yet Alex knew that the public – the people who bought newspapers or accessed the Globe's digital content - wanted stories about actors and influencers and reality TV stars. They *wanted* flash.

'Don't you want me to be a success? Is that what this is about?' said Alex quietly.

'I use your business card and now you think I'm trying to sabotage your career?'

'Maybe,' he said.

'What? Why?'

'Because then I'd have to come back to London,

wouldn't I?' said Alex. 'Then you'd get your own way.' He was being unreasonable, but still, he was hurt.

'Screw you, Alex,' said Lara with force. 'It may come as a surprise, but not everything is about you. I have a career, too. I have my own needs and ambitions and I'm doing my best to try and fit in with you.'

'*Are* you?'

'I'm here, aren't I? I'm sitting around waiting for you to come back like a good little girl, so that I can spend a few minutes with you before you pass out from exhaustion.'

'I have to work, Lara. This is my job; this is what I've always wanted.'

Lara nodded, her face a mask of contempt.

'And that's the truth, isn't it? This is what you've always wanted - to be a bloody editor - and screw what anyone else wants.'

'No, that's not it…'

'Isn't it? Truly? You've just been telling me how important it is for this powerful PR to be your friend so you can conquer Los Angeles and become king of the media castle. You used to know what was important, Alex. You used to have standards and priorities. You used to know that the story is king.'

'This isn't a *story,* Lara! You're talking to people about Verity Jones, a minor folk singer who died 50 years ago. No one cares.'

Lara's voice was low and measured. 'I care,' she said.

Alex shook his head.

'Even if this story was about Marilyn Monroe. If you followed the wildest conspiracy theories and proved that JFK murdered her – do you think that would be on the front page? No. It would be a feature on the inside.'

'So what *would* be a front page announcement for you?' she said tartly. 'Some new Marvel movie?'

'You're being unreasonable.'

'No, what I am doing is leaving,' she said simply. She turned and walked back towards the beach house.

'Lara!'

As her shape became smaller and smaller, Alex felt sadness grip his. This was supposed to be a happy, romantic break, and yet, right now, it felt as if she hated him.

'Lara, please,' he said quietly. 'Come back.'

But she didn't turn around, and soon she was gone.

Chapter 21

Lara kept going. Straight into the car – *bip-bip* – foot to the floor, heading away from the beach, back into town. As she drove, she banged her hand on the steering wheel, letting the rage out. *How dare he?* How dare he suggest she had no sense of what made a good story? How dare he suggest she would be happy if his career hit the skids? How dare he blow up the incident with the business card into what…an end of their relationship?

Lara let out a growl of frustration. Okay, yes, she did feel a bit guilty. Of course, she should have told Alex about gatecrashing Donna Phelps' party and what she was doing with the Verity story. She should have apologised properly for compromising his trust and reputation. But…

She felt a flutter of anxiety in her belly. Disquiet. There had been a huge number of changes in Lara's life over the past couple of years. The murder of her best friend Sandrine, leaving her full-time position at The Chronicle – and starting a relationship with Alex, only for him to leave London for LA. But the one thing Lara had been sure of when she had boarded that plane was that she and Alex would survive the separation. She loved Alex Ford unconditionally. Being in his company felt as natural as breathing. And yet, their confrontation at the beach house showed how fragile their bond was.

Green turned to amber, and Lara goosed the gas, zipping through the intersection with micro-seconds to spare. Screw it: Alex would be paying for the ticket anyway - it'd serve him right if he got one.

'You're in the way,' she whispered. Lara shook her head. He hadn't said that exactly, but it was what he meant. Alex Ford, The Great Editor, clearly cared more about his career than he cared about her.

So, some stupid PR was upset? So bloody what? The moment you started pandering to the PR machine, you were lost. It didn't matter whether it was a cookbook or a political party; you couldn't let the subject dictate the agenda; otherwise, democracy itself was at risk.

'Damn you, damn you, Alex Ford,' she said, accelerating again. It wasn't until she roared through another intersection that Lara realised she had no idea where she was going. Her instinct had been to get as far away from Alex as possible, but beyond that, she had no plan – but one thing she did know: Lara Stone did not back down. Alex might think the Verity Jones story was rubbish, but he was categorically wrong. And besides, what did Lara do when she was upset? She worked.

A gap opened ahead of her and Lara swerved into it, pulling away, the rising buildings a relief, LA folding around her like an embrace, anonymous and detached. She was just another car-bound commuter rolling through the city. Lara didn't want to think; she just wanted to move - and Los Angeles was the perfect place to get lost. They had drive-in banks, drive-thru coffee, 24-hour everything. You didn't need to leave your car or speak to a single soul.

But Lara did want to talk to someone – and now she knew where to head. She wanted to talk to Bobby Franks, Todd's buddy. The one with the big collection of video footage. No way was she going to back off this story. Alex might not think what she did was worthy of inclusion in his stupid new newspaper, but she'd show him. She would find out what happened that night in the Malibu House - then sell it to the LA Times, the Globe's biggest rival. Ha!

Up ahead was a giant doughnut sitting on top of a squat brick store. Randy's Donuts; Lara had driven past it many times—the donut shop was an iconic LA landmark you could sometimes see from the plane descending into LAX—but Lara had never been inside.

She pulled into the car park and looked up at the giant brown ring. It was hard to feel cross sitting under a 30-foot plastic donut. Lara pulled on the handbrake.

She knew what she needed: some carbohydrates. And she knew what she needed to do. Make that call to Bobby Franks.

* * *

Bobby's place was, ironically enough, only a few blocks from Alex's apartment. Not the borrowed beach house, but his actual apartment in the residential enclave of Echo Park in West LA, right on the edge of downtown.

Echo Park was edgy enough to feel Bohemian but gentrified enough to feel air-brushed; she rolled past a Vegan taco stall, an artisan drip-coffee cafe and a fixie bike store before turning into the tangle of residential streets. Alex had picked the neighbourhood for proximity to the Globe offices – just a ten-minute drive – and despite her irritation, Lara couldn't help smiling as she thought of her previous times here. They'd been flying visits, and the compressed timeline had given it an intensity and excitement, like a holiday romance, all bars and restaurants and time spent tangled together in the sheets.

A voice in her head wondered what this week would have been like had Simon Desei not loaned them the Malibu House. Would she and Alex be happier? But Lara was not the sort of person to dwell on the 'what-ifs'.

Despite its proximity, Bobby Franks' home was very different to Alex's smart duplex. The wood-framed bungalow had a pretty front garden and a short gravel path that led up to a small porch. Lara walked up to the front door and rang the bell. There was a pause – Lara had the distinct feeling she was being watched by the beady little spy hole in the door – then she heard the sound of locks unclicking and bolts being drawn. *Hey, welcome to LA.*

'Lara? Lara Stone?'

'That's me,' she called, trying to look as unthreatening as possible.

The door opened, still on the chain; Lara could only see one narrowed eye.

'Sorry,' said the voice. 'Just…you can't be too careful, can you?'

The door closed and then opened, revealing a short man wearing a purple bowling shirt. Lara had felt a flutter of concern over arriving at a stranger's house on a Friday evening, but Bobby's smile eased her worries.

'Come in, come in,' he said, 'I'm Bobby. Sorry for the mess.'

The house was brightly coloured—that was the first thing Lara noticed. One wall was canary yellow with a scarlet border, another pea green. But the colour scheme hardly mattered as most of the wall space was covered with framed film posters and seventies music memorabilia: there were cinema posters for Barbarella, the Manchurian

Candidate, and Woodstock: '3 Days of Peace and Music'. There was even a Bob Dylan 'Rolling Thunder' tour poster.

'I love the art. Is that an original?' she pointed to a large Dawn of the Dead poster.

Bobby nodded. 'Actually, I worked on that one.'

'On Dawn of the Dead? Really?'

'It was my first break,' said Bobby, 'Four weeks in that freezing shopping mall. George – that's the director – took me on because I was cheap, but I'm eternally grateful because, without it, I don't think I'd have had a career in the business.'

'So you work in film?'

'Oh yeah, for four decades, mostly in sound, some FX. Can't complain. It's a lot of fun.'

He waved her towards a sofa and sat on the edge of a chair, leaning forward, hands clasped.

'So you're a friend of Todd's?'

Lara pulled an apologetic expression. 'Not exactly. Earlier today, I visited him in Thousand Oaks, and he suggested I speak to you. '

Bobby gave a thin smile.

'He called and told me. He sounds in good form.'

'Look, I'm sorry for disturbing you like this…' said Lara.

'…But you wanted to see some footage from the Malibu days? It's okay: Todd told me that, too. Sure, I'll dig it out.'

Lara was taken aback, not expecting him to be so immediately accommodating.

It was a moment before she noticed his eyes were lingering on the front door behind her.

'Todd said you were working with Martha. Martha Riding?'

Ah. So that's why he is being so helpful, smiled Lara to

herself. Martha had called Bobby the 'little kid' from the fringes of their group, but she could imagine what a starstruck teenager might have thought of Martha Riding, who in her twenties was as beautiful as Lauren Hutton and Marisa Berenson put together.

'I have been working with Martha, yes,' said Lara. 'But dropping by was a spur-of-the-moment thing, and anyway, Martha is on her way to Carmel.'

'Shame, I would have liked to have seen her.'

He stood up.

'Beer?' he offered. 'It's Friday night.'

'Driving,' replied Lara, even though she would have loved something to take the edge off her nerves, her argument with Alex still raw.

'I've got some low-alcohol Guinness in the fridge. My American friends look at me like I'm nuts when I drink it, but you must know it, right?'

'I know Guinness,' smiled Lara. 'And the zero-percent stuff tastes just like the real thing.'

Bobby went to the kitchen and returned with two glasses, handing one to Lara. She took a grateful sip.

'So you hung out at The Malibu House?' said Lara after a moment. 'Excuse the question, weren't you a little...young?'

'Sure, I was still in high school when I first went. But it was *so* cool. I never wanted to leave. My folks were so pissed when I told them I didn't want to go to college and that I wanted to just get going in the business. But there was no convincing me. Meeting all those musicians and actors, directors and writers, I knew it was what I wanted to do,' he said, shaking his head like he could still barely believe he'd been allowed to tag along.

'So, how did you end up there?'

'My family's Mexican, and my mom had a taco stall near Trancas Market. Verity came there regularly. She loved my mom's tacos. She was so friendly and kind, and when I told her I was looking for some work, she said I could help out at the Malibu house. Answering fan mail, cleaning the pool, that sort of thing. I guess it went from there. After a few months, I'd saved up enough to buy a Super 8 camera, and given that I had already decided to be a director, I just hung around the house as often as I could, filming everyone.'

'Didn't people mind?'

Bobby waved a hand.

'No way. Either they were too stoned, or they just didn't care. It wasn't like today when a long lens shot could end up on the front page of the National Enquirer. We were all less careful back then. Besides, this was the counter-culture. The mainstream still didn't much care.'

'Todd thought you might have been at the party that night. The night Verity died.'

Bobby suddenly lost his bouncy enthusiasm.

'I was,' he said, looking away. 'I try not to think about it too much.'

'Did you stay til the end?'

'You mean when Verity threw us all out?'

'Yes. Do you have any sense of why she cut the party short?'

Bobby grimaced. 'I can say that Verity was in a really good mood that day, but at around ten o'clock, someone told me there were loads of cans floating in the pool, so I went to fish them out – always eager to help. That's when I heard Verity arguing with Donna.'

Lara sat up with interest. 'Arguing? What was it about?'

Bobby shook his head.

'Could have been anything; I edged away from it. It sounded heavy, and I didn't want to intrude.'

'Did you ever tell Todd this?'

'Once,' said Bobby, taking another sip of beer. 'I guess

he didn't mention it to you, huh? I don't blame him. Donna was a difficult woman. A nightmare. But Todd's a decent guy; he still wants to protect her. I guess he didn't want anyone whispering that Donna upset Verity that night.'

Bobby looked up and met Lara's gaze directly.

'Listen, this story about Verity? I want to know how I can help.'

'You do?' said Lara, unable to resist a chuckle. 'Sorry, it's just that almost everyone I've spoken to thinks it should all stay in the past. Even Martha took some persuading.'

'Well, I'll admit I Googled you when Todd called me. I read your stuff; you uncover the truth.'

Lara shrugged modestly.

'I try, but it's hard sometimes – often. Sometimes you can see the darkness immediately, but most of the time, it's wrapped in lots of layers.'

'I think there was darkness at the house that night,' said Bobby, his voice low.

'That's why I want to help you find the truth. Verity was like a second mom to me, and I still need to know what went wrong that night. It won't bring her back, but if you love someone, you have to go to battle for them,' he said passionately. 'You have to fight for them.'

'You're right about that, Bobby,' said Lara, thinking of Alex alone at the beach house. 'Listen, I should go. I've got someone else I need to speak to.'

She stood, and Bobby unlocked the door.

'Give me the weekend to dig out all the Malibu footage,' he said, 'Maybe come round for tacos on Monday night? Maybe bring Martha. No, definitely bring Martha.'

'Sure, I'll do that,' said Lara, already out the door. The moment she got to the car, she was on her phone. It went straight to message, and she could hardly blame Alex for that - but even so, she still wanted to connect with him.

'Alex, it's me. I'm sorry – I really am. I was in the wrong about all of it. And I wish....Anyway, I'm coming home.'

And she threw the car into a U-turn and headed for the beach.

Chapter 22

Summer buzzed down her car's window, wincing at the blast of heat from the late Saturday afternoon sun.

'Another one for Todd's party, am I right?' asked Gary, Valley Pine's sole security guard, stepping forward. 'Oh, hey Summer – didn't see you behind the tints. Big day for your dad, huh?'

'Let's hope so, Gary.' One of the pleasures of the Valley Pine community was getting to know people. Gary had been sitting in his booth working the barrier since Todd and Julianne had moved here five years earlier. There was something comforting about seeing people happy to be just where they were. The world Summer moved in was full of backstabbing and raging ambition, where nobody was ever really happy to see anyone unless there was something in it for them. Certainly, no one ever just came over for a cup of coffee and a chat.

'Big turnout?' Summer asked.

'What do *you* think?' grinned Gary. 'Todd's one of our favourite people. Maybe I'll see you later for a corn dog.'

'Look forward to it.'

Gary hit the button to raise the barrier, and Summer followed the familiar paved roadways to the parking lot. Pulling up, she reached into the back of her car to pick up her gifts: a photo book for Dad and a Xanadu gift basket for Julianne. She guessed at least Julianne would appreciate the hand cream after all that gardening.

Summer could hear the chatter and laughter long before she saw the house. There was music, too: The Flying Burrito Brothers' first album on some boomy speakers. Summer smiled to herself. She guessed only the offspring of a pair of hippies would recognise when 'The Gilded Palace of Sin' was playing.

The house's front door was open, but a sign in shaky handwriting saying 'This Way!' directed Summer to the back garden. As she approached the happy group standing on the shady lawn, she was glad Donna hadn't come. It would have been a nice gesture, but it would have unbalanced the day and made the whole thing about Donna. As it was, everyone was here to celebrate Todd and Julianne's marriage, which was just as it should be. Fairy lights had been strung between the trees; balloons had been tied to the back of chairs, and the air smelt of hot dogs and onions. And there was Todd, right at the centre of it, surrounded by family and a couple of dozen neighbours. Summer smiled to herself: Julianne had dressed Todd in a shirt with a collar instead of his usual ratty band T-shirts. He looked good.

'Summer!' cried Todd, rushing over, arms spread wide.

He pulled her into a hug, and Summer breathed a sigh into his shoulder, slightly guilty at her relief: being recognised was never a given with Todd.

'So great to see you, baby,' said Todd. 'Come and meet everyone. Do you know George?'

Summer smiled.

'Of course, I know George,' said Summer. George was Julianne's forty-something nephew who had six children himself, and from the happy squeals as they ran around, it sounded like most of them were here today.

'How's Maria getting on at UCLA?' she asked George.

'Top of her class, we're all so proud. She's only a sophomore but already considering applying to Yale Law when she's finished.'

Summer fell easily into conversation: she knew almost everyone at the party, and Julianne's side of the family had always treated Summer as one of them. Without a hint of snobbery, Summer loved the ordinariness of it; she had been brought up in a very rarified, if chaotic, environment. Summer remembered wearing someone's rhinestone boots as a child for an impromptu performance of Cinderella she had staged on Joni Mitchell's porch. In many ways, Summer's had been a dreamlike childhood, but there had been downsides too: Donna wasn't the kind of mom who'd bake cookies unless they had hash in them. Perhaps that was why Summer had grown up as a self-starter. Summer *had* to be self-reliant; it was a sink-or-swim situation.

'So your Mom didn't want to come, huh?' said Todd.

Summer looked at him in surprise.

'How did you know that?'

Todd chuckled. 'Because while you might pretend to be a ball-breaking girl boss…'

'Hey! I *am* a ball-breaking girl-boss!'

'…In fact, you are a beautiful soul, and you want the best for everyone, even your Mom,' said Todd, kissing the top of her head. 'And I bet you invited her because you thought it'd be good for *her*, too.'

Even with his crumbling mind, Todd could still shock Summer with how clearly he saw her. It was simultaneously wonderful and heartbreaking because she knew he'd cease to see her too soon. Even so, Summer wasn't sure Todd's assessment of her was entirely accurate - rose-tinted at best. You couldn't be Stephen Savage's chief of staff without breaking balls. But then, perhaps Todd's clearest memories of Summer were of that little girl in those over-sized boots.

The show on Joni's porch had happened just a few weeks before Donna and Todd had finally split up. Todd had stayed present in Summer's life, taking up the slack as Donna ran after a string of Hollywood executive boyfriends, convinced each one would boost her into the big time. Donna's success had come eventually, but it had been a long and very bumpy road; in fact, by the time Donna had reinvented herself as a 'Wellness Guru', Summer had been standing on her own two feet for some time.

'How's work?' asked Todd. 'Still running around after Uncle Stephen?'

'Dad, I know you worry about me, but I like what I do. And I'm good at it.'

'I know, Mermaid, but why work for a shark when you're the one running things? If you're working so hard, why not work for yourself?'

Summer felt herself tense at the casual insult for her boss, but bit her tongue. Her father was not the jealous type, but he never spoke warmly about Savage. Summer sometimes wondered if he resented their close relationship. Stephen wasn't just her employer; he was an unofficial godfather who had paid her college fees and given her a highly-paid job.

'Stephen's been good to me, Dad.'

'Hmm,' said Todd. 'But remember, it's good for him too.'

Summer had no desire to argue with Todd on his celebration day.

'Maybe, Dad,' she said. 'I'll think about what you said, okay?'

He squeezed her arm. 'You know you've always been my little girl, no matter what.'

Summer frowned.

'What do you mean?'

'I mean, you've always been the best thing in my life, even if….'

His eyes drifted, unfocused.

'Hey, have I introduced you to George?' he asked suddenly. 'I think you'll like him.'

Summer's heart thudded, and she pressed her lips together.

'Sure, that sounds great,' she said, smiling. 'But first, I need to get a drink. You want anything?'

'Thanks, babe. Get me a Bud, will you?'

Summer walked away from the crowd to the side of the house, making sure she was alone before she let out a sob. Todd hadn't drunk beer since the early Eighties, a poster boy for AA, sober for over forty years. It was only a small thing, but it felt like everything. Summer had fooled herself her Dad was okay, but he was never going to be okay, was he? She pressed the heel of her hand against her cheek to stem a falling tear.

'Here.'

Summer turned to see Julianne holding out a Kleenex.

'I always keep a few handy,' she said with a sad smile.

Summer dabbed at her eyes and gave an embarrassed laugh. She liked her father's wife very much. A former nurse who had met Todd when he had come to her clinic to fix the photocopier, she was warm and empathetic, where Donna was cold and selfish.

'I was just telling Todd what a badass I am. It's just…'

'I know,' said Julianne softly. 'He's just like the old Todd, then suddenly he's gone.'

'That's it exactly. It's so hard.'

Julianne put a hand on Summer's shoulder.

'But he hasn't gone yet,' she said. 'Even if he drifts off mid-sentence or forgets what year it is, Todd's still here.' She looked over at him, her eyes full of love.

Summer gave a crisp nod. She had thought she had made her peace with this. She had thought she was tough. But the thought of losing her father was almost too much to bear.

'You know I'm here to help where I can,' said Summer. 'You know I have money.'

'I think he'd like to see you a little more,' said Julianne. She said it with good nature, but she knew it was a gentle reprimand. Summer liked to think she saw Todd once a week, but the truth was it was nearer to once a month.

'Hey, is he upset with me?' asked Summer, but Julianne frowned.

'Of course not. Why would you say that?'

Summer looked over at Todd, who was now flipping burgers at the grill and chatting to Nelly, George's youngest.

'It was just something he said earlier. He said, "You've always been my little girl, no matter what." *No matter what?* What did he mean? Have I done something wrong?'

'You've done nothing wrong,' said Julianne, reaching out to stroke a strand of hair from Summer's face. 'You're the apple of his eye.'

Summer noticed her stepmother didn't blame the dementia for the obtuse remark. In fact, Julianne didn't meet her gaze at all.

'But he still said…'

'Damn! The grill,' cried Julianne. She turned and began running. Summer followed and could immediately see why. The grill was on fire. Todd had simply walked off and was now on the other side of the garden, embracing

Gary, the security guard who had presumably come for his corn dog.

'It's okay, it's okay,' said Julianne, throwing a fire blanket over the flames. 'Everything's under control.'

But Summer wasn't sure Julianne was right. She wasn't sure at all.

Chapter 23

Natasha had only been to Pasadena once before. She had met a boy named 'Karl' in the queue for In-N-Out Burger on Sunset Boulevard, and he had invited her to a party that night. The long drive hadn't been worth it. Karl had done beer bongs and turned into a leery jock; his house had been the only highlight. With white pillars on either side of the door and a wide lawn down to the sidewalk, it had been like an establishing shot in an eighties teen movie. It was perfect, assuming you could ignore the death metal rattling the windows and the reek of hydroweed.

'Are you okay?' asked Will, glancing across. They'd driven up in Will's not-quite-classic Volvo listening to a 90s mix tape – Eels, Teenage Fanclub, late-period Lemonheads – but Natasha had gone quiet as they approached downtown Pasadena. It wasn't just Karl; it was Natasha's memories of that whole period. Her college years hadn't exactly been happy. Ambitious from the outset, Natasha had spent too much time in the library and had failed to find her tribe in her freshman year. Over-compensating in her sophomore and junior years, Natasha had partied hard, then fallen into an ill-advised relationship with a very good-looking visiting professor who had left her gun-shy and cynical.

Her recent adventures into the LA dating scene hadn't bolstered her hopes for finding a hot, successful, decent guy. She knew that Los Angeles had a reputation for being brutal for single women. Too many men with Peter Pan complexes who didn't want to settle down and others who were only interested in relationships that could further their careers. Natasha had met them all.

'Sorry,' she said, looking across at Will. 'Just thinking about the story.'

It was a lie, but she wasn't about to share her sad tale with Will Anders. She didn't need sympathy; she needed a promotion.

'So what did you find out about this Helen Kampf?'

It had been Natasha's job to research the whistleblower's background, and Will's job was driving up north LA. It wasn't how Natasha wanted to spend her Saturday afternoon, but Will had convinced her that they needed to put in some overtime if they were going to keep up the momentum on the story.

'Didn't find much,' she said. 'Helen Kampf graduated from UC Irvine in the early noughties, she was a political science major, then she started out interning with congressman Bernie Hart.'

Will nodded. Hart had a reputation as a fair, dedicated politician.

'She moved to the LA county planning department a year later, and she's been there ever since.'

'Is she from Pasadena?'

'Close enough: Eagle Rock.'

He nodded. 'Explains the address.'

Natasha checked the map on her phone. 'Left at the stop-light, then two blocks down.' This part of town consisted of modest detached houses, the lawns far less clipped than she remembered in Karl's neighbourhood, but there were swing sets and bikes, hints of family life. Will had spotted it, too.

'Is Helen married? Kids?'

Their source, the wronged mistress Jenna Brooks-Price, had given them the whistleblower's name, but she had known very little else: she had got the information from her lover's rants about the 'Do-gooder turncoat' who was threatening to ruin his lucrative payday. Natasha had tracked down Helen Kampf's office extension, but it had gone straight to message and her email had bounced back with an ominous 'out of office' alert.

'Eyes left,' said Will, 'It's the grey house with the camper on the drive.'

He pulled up at the kerb and reached for the door-pull, but Natasha held up a hand.

'Let me,' she said.

Will frowned. 'You sure?'

'I'm guessing Helen's going to be jumpy. Two strangers turning up unannounced? She could bolt out the back door.'

'Then I can cover the alley at the back if you like?'

'Will, this isn't Beverly Hills Cop.'

'Am I Billy Rosewood in this situation?' he smiled. 'Because I want to be Axel Foley.'

Natasha grinned at him. She'd hardly spoken to Will Anders until this week. She had always thought he was a bit of a nerd, not surprising given he'd been to Yale and those ridiculous tweed jackets he wore to the office made him look about fifty. But she had to admit that he was good fun. Kind too, always fetching her coffee without even asking –her favourite kind too – decaf cappuccino with oat milk.

'Seriously, Will,' said Natasha. 'I think a single white female is the least threatening option here.'

'Single white female? You *have* seen that movie, right?'

Natasha rolled her eyes and popped the door, quickly crossing the empty street. Her logic was sound, but she also liked the idea of getting a solo interview. Alex Ford had challenged Natasha to show him what she could do, and she intended to fulfil that brief by hook or by crook.

'Let's see,' Natasha whispered, rapping loudly with a brass door-knocker. As she waited, Natasha rehearsed her opening line: 'Ms Kampf? Natasha King from the LA Globe.' No – that was too direct.

'Ms Kampf, could I have a word – off the record?' She shook her head at that one, too. No one believed reporters were ever off the record, certainly not whistleblowers.

'Helen? We're here to help.' Natasha almost laughed at that. Now that one *was* bullshit.

'Ms Kampf? Are you there?' she called. Natasha craned her neck to peer through the glass panel at the top of the door. Lights were off, no movement. Looking down, there were two rolled-up newspapers on the little porch. She knocked again and cupped an ear to the door. Nothing.

Walking back, she saw Will standing in the street talking to a young man on a bicycle who moved away as she approached.

'No answer at the house: who was that?'

'One of the neighbours. Says Helen told him she was 'taking some personal time' and has gone to visit her sister in Denver.'

Natasha sighed; her gut had already told her the bird had flown.

'When?'

'A few days ago.'

'Crap.'

Will gave her a sympathetic smile. 'Them's the breaks. Listen, I do have one other idea.'

Natasha tilted her head back to the sun, eyes closed. 'Go on.'

'Why don't we visit my dad?'

* * *

The Anders residence was about a ten-minute drive away, in a shady and well-heeled enclave of detached colonial houses that put Natasha in mind of the family home in 'Home Alone'; without the snow, of course. Will's father, meanwhile, was an older version of his offspring. Untidy hair, untucked shirt, but sharp blue eyes that missed nothing. Maybe being a good reporter was in the DNA.

Jack welcomed Natasha into the warm family kitchen at the back of the house, serving pastries and pouring her coffee. 'Newsroom priorities,' he said, winking as she took a sip.

'Ooh,' she said with genuine pleasure. 'Now that's good. I once did a story on a boutique coffee roaster in Los Feliz,' she said. 'The owner gave me a crash course in coffee tasting. This is a quality brew.'

Jack nodded. 'My first editor used to say, 'God is a journalist'. He meant that if you stick around in this job long enough, you end up knowing everything.'

He sat down and cupped his own mug.

'So the whistleblower has blown town?' he asked, getting straight to business. 'I can't say I'm surprised. Let me guess; she's out of town visiting a relative.'

'How did you know?'

He flashed a sour smile.

'It's classic. She won't be back.'

'You think she's been *killed*?' said Natasha, her eyes wide.

Jack gave a low chuckle.

'Oh, I don't think anyone would have Helen 'whacked'; it's City Hall, not the Sopranos. No, it's much more likely someone said, 'Here's a twenty grand pay rise and promotion to head of planning up in Oakland; now go and take a sabbatical until this all blows over.'

'Hush money? Do you think a whistleblower would take it?'

Jack shrugged.

'Whistleblowers have mortgages too.'

He sighed. 'Also possible someone put the fear of God in Helen Kampf, and she's just plain scared.'

It made sense, thought Natasha. It was depressing but logical.

'Even so. I'd like to speak to her,' said Natasha. 'When I called downtown, I hit a brick wall. Mr Anders, do you still have any contacts in that office?'

Jack looked at Will. 'She doesn't mess around, this one,' she smiled. 'You make a good team.'

He stood up and reached for his phone. 'Why don't you kids take your coffee into the garden? This might take a while.'

Outside, the sun was dipping in the sky. Will led Natasha to a wooden table beneath a bigleaf maple tree. Flowers were in beds next to the house, and a neatly trimmed hedge ran around the property. It was a beautiful place, exactly the sort of house Natasha had pictured herself living in when she grew up.

'I think he likes you,' said Will, raising his mug.

Natasha laughed.

'I think your dad is the kind of guy who likes everyone.'

'I'm not sure about that. My girlfriends used to get the third degree when I'd bring them home.'

Natasha didn't say anything. She hadn't imagined Will with a girlfriend, imagining him as the type devoted to his studies and work. But people could surprise you, even yourself.

'So this is what it's like?' she said, nodding towards the house. 'Growing up with a journalist for a dad?'

'I mean, Dad's good company and all, but he wasn't around much. Always out chasing some story, never home for dinner.'

'I know how that feels. My dad was a lawyer. So he missed your Little League games, too?'

Will gave a twisted smile. 'Sure. Not that I ever made the team.' He pointed at himself with a thumb. 'I run like a girl.'

'Yeah, but you know who Teenage Fanclub are, so it all evens out.'

Natasha looked away. Was she flirting with Will Anders?

'So, do you see yourself staying here?'

'In Pasadena?'

'No, working at the Globe.'

'For now. But I'd love to work for the New Yorker.'

'I can see you *editing* the New Yorker,' she said. Now she definitely was flirting. But to her surprise, Natasha could picture Will behind a big walnut desk in a corner office in Manhattan. He wouldn't even have to get rid of the tweeds.

'We have a cabin in the Adirondacks,' said Will. 'That's the dream for me: living up there six months of the year and writing for the New Yorker, the Paris Review, maybe working on a novel for the rest.'

Natasha couldn't think of anything worse.

'I just want to write words that last,' he said, sitting on the swing and letting it rock.

'Why are you working in news then?'

'Stories last too,' he shrugged. 'If they are important

stories, they do. I think that's why Alex picked us for this story.'

'Us?'

'You think the boss picked us at random for this assignment?'

Natasha hadn't given it much thought.

'Everyone else in that office is running the clock down,' said Will. 'They're all hoping they'll make it to retirement. You and me, Natasha, we're different. We're the future. And, you know, at a time when less and less people read newspapers, I think Alex wants us to learn how important this work is.'

Natasha looked at him, impressed with his conviction. Natasha's Brentwood friends worked for social media companies and Fintech and slightly looked down their noses at what Natasha did. But suddenly, Will had made her feel important.

'Any luck?'

Will called to his father, who stood at the house's back door, silhouetted by the indoor light.

'This isn't luck, son,' said Jack, walking across the lawn towards them. 'Fifty years of hard work building contacts. And a little charm, too.' He held out a yellow Post-it note. 'There. Helen Kampf's cell number. Now, which of you newshounds is going to call her?'

Chapter 24

Martha was very careful as she stacked the plates. They were delicate bone china, edged in gold with a delicate flower motif. Rebecca only brought them out for her 'special' lunches; she had once whispered to Martha that they were 19th century and worth more than her car - and considering Rebecca drove a beautiful vintage Mercedes SL, that was certainly saying something.

'Well, I think lunch was a success, don't you?' said Rebecca, gathering crystal glasses and carrying them through to the kitchen – the *entertaining* kitchen, that was: Rebecca's pied-a-terre had two. The rest of the guests left, leaving just the two of them, as Martha was staying at Rebecca's whilst she was in town.

'Lunch is always a triumph,' smiled Martha. It was true; her old friend was the consummate old-school hostess, and her lunch parties here at her Carmel-by-the-sea home were must-go events, from the exquisite food to the sparkling company.

'Although I was relieved no one insisted on singing 'Happy Birthday',' said Rebecca. 'So cringe, as the kids say.'

Martha had flown up to nearby Monterey for Rebecca's 80th the previous afternoon. There were lots of landmark gatherings within her circle these days - 75ths, 80ths, or funerals, mostly. Martha had been friends with Rebecca since the disco era, when Rebecca was the interiors editor and Martha was a star contributor for a magazine in New York. Rebecca had swiftly left journalism to set up a lucrative design consultancy in Manhattan, but her adored husband Rafe had died eighteen months earlier, so Rebecca had moved out west to be closer to her sister. Rebecca was now 'living her best life' with a much younger, much richer boyfriend named Tad. An outsider might have seen Rebecca as a social butterfly, someone who just lived to flit from party to party in this rarified upper strata of Californian society, but Martha knew there was much more to her friend. Sitting opposite them at lunch, in Rebecca's beautiful shady garden, she could also see that Rebecca was taken with Tad, and he with her. Even wealthy people were looking for love in later life – and Martha was pleased to see her old friend happy again.

'So what did you think of Bryson?' asked Rebecca.

Bryson had been Martha's blind date, a local single man Rebecca had positioned next to her at lunch. He was a veterinarian who specialised in circus animals; he'd been fascinating and hilarious. If only she'd been in the mood.

'Bryson was a good choice,' said Martha.

'But not the right choice,' said Rebecca, catching Martha's tone. 'I almost invited Harley, but he'd have dominated the conversation. And I wanted today to be about me, me, me.'

'Harley Stuyvesant?' Martha looked at her with more interest.

'He's just moved to Big Sur. Apparently, the house is amazing.'

Harley had been the editor of Skim, the underground

paper Griffin had worked on all those years ago – the one who had spiked his Verity story, in fact – but had gone onto much dizzier heights, launching Prestige, the premier arts and entertainment glossy in North America, a move that had made Harley a brand in his own right. Prestige had been absorbed into a media behemoth a few years ago, so it was no surprise he, too, had headed for the sunshine.

'You do know Harley's single now?' said Rebecca with a hint of a smile.

'Penelope died?'

'Nope. Left him.'

Martha barked out a laugh.

'Wow. At our age. Ouch.'

'Do you blame her? I ran into Penny in Amagansett last summer, and she said, 'Better late than never'. Honestly, after forty years, I think she was glad to be able to get a word in edgeways.'

Martha laughed. Rebecca had been right about the party invitation: Harley was great company, but always needed to be the centre of attention.

'Between you and me,' said Rebecca, lowering her voice, 'I think Harley was blindsided by the divorce. Devastated. And you know his restaurant went under, too?'

The restaurant had been Harley's great retirement plan: a chic, clubby French destination place in the heart of fashionable Manhattan where he could sit at the bar and welcome his many friends from show business. 'Harley's' had earned two Michelin stars and gushing reviews, so Martha wondered what had happened. Perhaps Penelope's divorce settlement had gobbled it up.

'Poor Harley,' said Martha. 'But enough about him. How are you?'

'You mean about hitting the big eight-oh?'

'No, I mean Tad,' said Martha as she filled two wine glasses with Chardonnay.

'Do you think it's too soon?' asked Rebecca, looking anxious.

Martha smiled sadly. She had thought her friend would ask if Tad was too young – Martha had put him at about 70 – but instead, she was still thinking about Rafe.

'Darling, at our age, it's never too soon. I like him.'

Rebecca looked mollified by her friend's words, leaning back against the kitchen island to take a sip of wine.

'I like him too,' she admitted. 'And I like it here in Carmel. I thought I'd always be a New York City girl, but I feel like I've lived here forever. Everyone is smart and interesting.'

'And successful. You have to be. It's not so different from the Upper East Side.'

'I think you should move here,' said Rebecca suddenly.

'Carmel?' said Martha, coughing on her wine. 'But I'm happy in Malibu.'

'*Are* you?' asked Rebecca with the bluntness of a true friend.

'I love Malibu.' Martha said it without even thinking,

'Marth, don't you want to keep moving forward? It's so easy to stay with what we know, but moving to Carmel doesn't just feel like a new life; it feels like a second life. You know I've taken up Kintsugi?'

'What's that?'

'Repairing broken pots by making them into new works of art. It's a Japanese technique – you can create something very beautiful.'

'Sounds like your move to Carmel,' said Martha, thinking about how devastated Rebecca was after Rafe's death, but how wonderful her new life in California now seemed – her new circle of friends, her beautiful home, just three blocks from the ocean, and a handsome new man. Rebecca had come back to life.

Martha picked some chocolate icing from the top of Rebecca's birthday cake.

'If you must know, I've been working on some new projects.'

'Ooh. Spill.'

'I'm dipping my toe back into journalism.'

Rebecca clapped her hands.

'Good for you. The industry has missed you. What are you doing?'

'Investigative work.'

'Really?' Rebecca looked surprised.

'As you say, you have to keep moving forward.'

Rebecca peered at her over the rim of her glass. 'What's the story, or aren't you allowed to tell?'

Griffin had always kept his work close to his chest, but Martha had never seen the point. If you didn't speak to people or share your information, you never knew what was happening or whether they could help you.

'It's something close to home,' said Martha.

Rebecca sat forward.

'This sounds juicy.'

And in that moment, Martha realised what had been holding her back. It *was* too close to home. Verity, the beach house, her rose-tinted recollections about those halcyon days – all of it. Martha was scared of what she might find out, scared that some dark revelations might colour a time she remembered as idyllic.

'It is juicy,' she said, smiling. She was thinking about how Lara Stone had brought her back to life and how Lara, Verity, and the story were her *Kintsugi*.

'In fact, it's so juicy, I think you can help me. All you need to do is lend me your car.'

Chapter 25

Martha drove Rebecca's beautiful red Mercedes SL south, hugging the deep curves of the coast, the sea sparkling to her right. She was glad that the birthday lunch had ended early, and she was glad for the loan of the Merc. Rebecca was a good friend: understanding, perceptive and even more connected than Martha, supplying her with Harley Stuyvesant's number within a minute.

Martha hadn't seen Harley for a long time – and only then at the occasional awards season party, when he had been too busy schmoozing to pay her much attention. Following Harley's directions, she turned off the highway onto an unmarked driveway. There were gates, but they were already open; Martha drove through, and in her rear-view, she saw them slide shut. Somehow, that was more unsettling than having a gatehouse filled with armed guards. The drive wound up through pine forest until Martha's ears popped and the car turned into a clearing – and the house was finally revealed.

'Oh man,' she sighed. 'Maybe I should have stuck with magazines.'

It was a faux French chateau with a blue slate roof and

symmetrical wings on either side of a central tower—it was unnecessarily big. Harley was single, yet here he was, rattling around in a vast mansion with arched windows looking out onto formal gardens.

'Status is a bitch,' said Martha. For decades, Harley Stuyvesant had been the king of New York, invited to every opening and gala. People had jockeyed for his favour, asked his opinion, and showered him with gifts. This palace in the clouds was exactly the sort of house a master of the universe would own. But what was the point in having it, if no one was here to see it?

'No one except me.'

Martha pulled a lipstick from her bag, popped open the sun-visor mirror and applied a slick of colour across her lips. Martha knew modern-day feminists – fourth wave, or whatever number we were on now – would probably find fault in her touching up her Chanel Rouge before meeting a man. But Martha had been a feminist in the eighties when women dressed sexy, kicked ass and left men in their wake. And she wasn't about to change now. She smacked her lips with a satisfying pop and headed for the door just as Harley Stuyvesant stepped out, waving.

'Martha, so wonderful to see you! It's been too long.'

He was wearing a silk smoking jacket and opera shoes. Martha guessed it was supposed to look casual—a European prince post-chukka—but there had always been a sense of the theatrical about Harley like he was playing the role of a media mogul and trying to project it to the back row.

'Come through, come through,' he said, beckoning her into the double-height entrance hall. 'Shall we go into the study? It's a bit more cosy.'

'Cosy' wasn't quite how Martha would have described it. In square footage, Harley's den was bigger than Martha's house, and the décor appeared to have been based on Ralph Lauren's Madison Avenue flagship store. Inlaid wood panels, leather upholstery and sheepskin throws: there was even a stuffed bear. *Of course* there was a stuffed bear. And a drinks bar with an array of decanters. It was like he was playing the part of Hugh Hefner circa 1964.

'Amazing place, Harley.'

No other journalist she knew lived in such a splendid property. Then again, Harley's salary in the 1980s had been legendary, and he had undoubtedly made wise investments.

'Cocktail?' he asked.

'I'm driving.'

'Back to Malibu?'

So he knew where she lived. Interesting.

'No, I'm staying at Becky Martin's in Carmel. It's her car.'

'Shame, it suits you.'

It had been a while, but Martha knew when she was being flirted with. Harley was no Todd Mayfield, but Martha couldn't deny he was magnetic. It came from a lifetime of being listened to, she supposed, the expectation that people wanted to be close to you. Harley went to the bar, clinking bottle against glass, pouring Martha a soft drink and himself something with a twist.

He sank back into a suede sofa, resting his arm along the back cushions.

'To what do I owe the pleasure?'

Martha took an armchair opposite.

'Verity Jones,' she said.

Harley nodded as if it was the answer he had been expecting.

'You knew?'

'LA is 500 square miles, but it might as well be a village,' he smiled. 'Donna Phelps is cornered by a British journalist asking all sorts of questions about the Malibu house. The journalist says she is working with you. Donna complains to her PR, who rages about it to her wife, who happens to be a director at the Getty, where I am attending an opening. And then Martha Riding turns up out of the blue.' He took a drink. 'I was wondering when I'd hear from you.'

Harley was boasting, letting her know how connected he was, but Martha knew she should have expected it. Harley did know everyone; that was how he had become such a titan of the media world. She'd never known him to write a single word, but Harley had grasped early that journalism was about getting the best stories. You could always hire someone to write it – someone like Martha Riding, for example – but the important thing was securing access or getting the tip-off for that headline-grabbing scoop. And yes, he might be sitting in his castle miles from anywhere, but Harley still had his finger on the pulse. Martha could see she needed to sharpen up.

'So what's your interest in all this?' Harley asked. 'Is it such a slow news week?'

Martha looked at him with more focus and saw the hint of amusement at the side of his mouth. He was enjoying this. Of course, Harley Stuyvesant was a player and always had been. His semi-comic playboy schtick was designed to put people at ease and drop their guard. But he knew something. Martha could feel it.

'I wanted to talk to you about Griffin's story,' said Martha. 'The one he pitched to Skim magazine a few months after Verity's death. It was about how hard drugs were overtaking the music scene and how a connected dealer might have been involved in Verity's death.'

Harley pouted. 'It sounds vaguely familiar, but that was long ago. Forgive me if I can barely remember…'

'You spiked it,' she interrupted. Harley grunted.

'Martha you've been in this game as long as I have. You know that stories get spiked all the time.'

'*Bullshit,* Harley, you do remember it.'

His bushy eyebrows shot up, and then the corners of his mouth followed. 'Oh, Martha,' he chuckled. 'I *have* missed you.'

He felt around in his pockets, then pulled out a leather cigar case. 'Do you mind?' He asked.

'It's your study,' said Martha. She liked the smell of a cigar; it reminded her of her grandfather, who had smoked Cuesta-Rey no. 7s. Harley went through the ritual of clipping, warming and lighting, finally emerging from a grey cloud with a smile.

'So?' he said, brushing a speck of ash from his jacket.

'So Griffin was writing a story about some trust-fund drug dealer – I forget his name – '

'Jameson,' said Harley. 'Jameson Bennett. But he was known as 'Bird' for reasons lost to time.'

'So you *do* remember.'

Harley nodded, settling back.

'I don't forget much; it's a curse,' he said. 'Anyway, Griff wanted to write an expose about this guy, the idea being he was smuggling heroin in his father's diplomatic pouch, then selling it to musicians, including Verity Jones. All horseshit, of course.'

'Was it?'

He shrugged.

'The smuggling thing? Hogwash. Griff looked into it and discovered that this Jameson kid had barely spoken to his father in about three years. Daddy didn't approve of the beads and the sandals.'

Martha frowned. 'So that's why you spiked it - because it wasn't true?'

'Griffin wanted to keep on digging, but the story was thin. Take out the ambassador; all you're left with is a private school kid with a drug habit. Hardly headline news.'

'But wasn't it connected to Verity?'

'Maybe it was,' said Harley, blowing on the end of his cigar.

Martha tipped her head back and let out a howl. Harley looked up in alarm.

'God, can't you just stop being so damn…' she curled her hands in frustration.

'So what?' he asked.

'So *Harley*,' said Martha. 'Like you're this media emperor with the

power of life or death over every story in the world. Maybe that used to impress people at Prestige, Harley, but let me tell you, here and now, you're driving me up the Godamn wall.'

Harley blinked at her, obviously shocked by her reaction. Perhaps he wasn't used to people calling him on his bullshit. Perhaps he wasn't used to people questioning anything he said. There was a long pause, and then he sighed.

'Look, I spiked it because Savage called me,' he said.

'Savage?' Martha repeated. 'Stephen Savage?'

Harley nodded. 'Remember, this was nearly a year after Verity died, and by then, Savage was managing Gene Henderson.'

Martha nodded. Everyone had been surprised when the young Stephen Savage had signed Gene Henderson to his fledgling record label – but not as surprised as they had been when 'Time For Change' had been a massive, international hit. It was a great tune, but it was a tune Henderson could have taken to any major record company. Instead, he'd chosen Stephen Savage, and the song had kick-started Savage's label and set him on a path to global domination in pop music.

'Why did Savage want you to kill the story? Verity wasn't one of his acts.'

'No, but Gene was part of Verity's gang. She used to pick up all sorts of waifs and strays at the Trobadour or the Whisky a Go Go, take them under her wing, introduce them to people who might help them. Gene was one of those people.'

Martha nodded, remembering Todd telling her how he had met Verity and how supportive she had been.

'Savage had heard that Griff was writing a piece about drugs – and how this kid Bird had started supplying hard drugs to the parties at the Malibu House. Verity's official cause of death was a heart attack, but Griffin thought it might be linked to her opiate use that night. Savage did not want that getting air-time.'

'Why was he so sensitive to it? Drug use isn't exactly unusual in the music business.'

'No, but Savage was doing a distribution deal with one of the majors, and Henderson was his trump card. He didn't want his star client associated with heroin– and he certainly didn't want Gene associated with a scandalous death.'

'So Savage bribed you.'

Harley shook his head.

'We cut a deal. If I pulled Griffin's story about the Malibu House, Savage said he'd give me Gene for my front cover.'

'So he *did* bribe you.'

Harley sighed.

'Martha, you know how this works. It's the old 'bait and switch'. Happens all the time. Muffle one story, and get a better exclusive in return.'

'Call it what you like, Harley; Savage twisted your arm.'

Harley snorted.

'Don't be so naïve. At that point, Gene Henderson was poised to blow up into a huge star - everyone wanted an interview. It was an offer I couldn't refuse.'

'And screw the hard-working writer, yes?'

Harley gave her a cynical smile.

'Griff's preppy dealer story was a dead duck, remember? And I think Griffin did pretty well from me – you too, Martha.'

Martha couldn't deny that. Over the years, her words had appeared in many of Harley's publications; Prestige Magazine, in particular, had high cultural status. People were impressed if you were a 'Prestige' writer. But it was still depressing to hear that the free press was only free as long as no one in power willed it otherwise.

'Besides, not running that story was better for Verity,' said Harley.

'As if you care about that,' huffed Martha.

'I'm not a cold-hearted monster Martha. I loved Verity's music, too. And honestly, would it have done her any favours if the world saw her as a drug casualty? Not when it was accepted that she'd had a cardiac arrest.'

'So you did Verity a favour, is that what you're saying?'

'Didn't I?' said Harley, his eyes flat, the sparkle gone. 'Tell me, Martha, how do people remember Verity Jones?'

'As a wonderful singer who died far too young.'

'Exactly,' said Harley. 'Poetic, tragic and wholesome. And what happened after she died? Big surge in sales for her solo stuff and The Virginians' back catalogue too.'

'Verity was dead, Harley,' said Martha. 'I'm not sure she exactly benefited from the marketing boost.'

Harley raised his hands to indicate his mansion. 'But life goes on, no?'

Martha flexed her jaw and fixed him with a glare.

'Don't you miss it, Harley?' she said.

'Miss what?'

'The truth,' said Martha. 'That's how we both started, isn't it? Before the parties and the gala invitations and the restaurants – that's what we both got off on. You used to love digging out new stories, exposing bullshit, calling out the bullies. Where did all that go?'

Harley puffed on his cigar.

'Things change, Martha,' he said. 'Haven't you heard? We're in the post-truth era now.'

Smug prick, thought Martha. *Stupid of me to think he might be anything else.*

She stood and carefully placed her glass on a coaster. She didn't want to leave a mark on the beautiful walnut table.

'Well, thank you, Harley,' she said. 'This has been surprisingly illuminating.'

Harley looked up in surprise.

'You're leaving?'

'Time to be going. It's a long drive back to Carmel in the dark.'

'But…I thought you were staying. I thought…'

'Places to go, people to see,' said Martha briskly, walking towards the door.

'Martha, this is silly,' said Harley, jumping up, ash cascading down his jacket. 'Stay, we can talk about the old times.'

Martha stopped at the door.

'I prefer to remember the *good* times, Harley.'

And she left him alone in his vast castle.

Chapter 26

The Savage Foundation building was a post-modern LA landmark, a silver Camelot of curved glass and steel nestled just behind Hollywood Boulevard. Back in the 1980s, it had won countless architecture awards, but Summer had always thought it was ugly, like a shiny bug squashed by an angry God. She walked in through the main entrance, then turned a sharp right, bypassing the grand, art-filled foyer by taking the express elevator straight to the fifth floor: the nerve centre of the Foundation. It was the natural next step for Stephen Savage. Her boss had sold the recording and publishing arm of the Savage empire five years earlier, making him an instant billionaire. But instead of taking a foot off the gas, he had immediately set up the Savage Foundation, a charitable organisation dedicated to the 'actualisation and promotion of the arts' in Savage's name. It was philanthropy writ large: The Savage Gallery in the arts district and the Stephen Savage Theatre built to house the newly-minted Cine Awards were already up and running – and it was Summer's job as Savage's chief of staff to 'actualise' more promotions in the same vein: big, splashy and no-expense-spared.

‘Good morning, Miss Phelps,’ called her PA Wesley, meeting her in the hallway. ‘You have a nine o’clock with Mr Savage and an eleven with…’

Summer held up a hand, not breaking her stride. ‘Cancel everything to lunch, Wes. We’re planning Mr Savage’s 50th. No calls unless Dylan dies.’

With a curt nod, Wesley peeled off, and Summer continued down the corridor and through the double doors into Savage’s inner sanctum.

‘Ah, Summer, take a seat,’ said Stephen, waving towards a pair of teardrop sofas facing each other over a Donald Judd coffee table strewn with music magazines.

His voice was brusque, suggesting he did not want to discuss his weekend and just wanted to get down to business.

‘So,’ said Summer, flipping open her folder. ‘Let’s talk legacy. I think it’s time we decided on the ghostwriter for the coffee table book; how did you feel about going with the guy from London?’

‘Summer.’

She looked up. Stephen was standing next to the sofa, his face grave.

‘We need to talk.’

‘Okay,’ she said uncertainly. Was she being fired? *Could* she be fired? Summer knew enough about Stephen’s business practices to have him in litigation for decades.

‘I’m dying,’ he said.

‘You’re…you’re what?’

Stephen handed her an envelope stamped with the Cedars-Sinai logo.

‘I have colon cancer,’ he said. His dark eyes were dry, his voice steady. It was as if he was delivering her the Second Quarter financial report.

‘Everything’s in the envelope. It’s stage four, already

spread. I'm not sure how' - he took a breath - 'Not sure how long I have.'

Summer swallowed.

'Christ,' she said. 'Stephen, I'm so sorry.'

He held up a hand. 'No platitudes, please. I've decided to face this squarely and would appreciate you doing the same.'

'Of course, of course. But, how long have you known?'

Summer's mind raced. He had been unwell; she had been aware of that. He'd lost weight and seemed tired more often. He'd taken more 'personal days' and, now she thought about it, she had seen him taking pills quite regularly. But Summer had put it down to being in his seventies; most men his age had retired to Cape Cod, whereas Savage seemed to be taking on more and more work. Now, of course, it made sense.

'I've known for a couple of months,' he said, sitting down with care. 'I think I suspected something was wrong for much longer. I was in denial,' he said with a grim smile.

Savage was very good at denial; some might say he had effectively built his empire on that basis. Dream big, then make it happen. Donna would call it 'positive manifestation'.

'What do the doctors say?'

'Too late to operate – it's spread too far. Lymph nodes, liver. Lungs.'

'What about treatment? Chemo or drugs or something?'

Stephen shook his head. 'I was in Zurich this weekend taking various appointments. The consultant suggested a new line of treatment, which might give me an extra six months.'

'Well then, you have to try.'

'And be sick the whole time?' he said. 'I don't think so.'

'But we can get you the very best specialists.'

'Don't you think I've already tried? No, Summer. I appreciate the sentiment, but I'd rather do this on my terms. I'd like to be as well as I can for as long as I can, and bow out with as much dignity as possible.'

Summer gaped at him, mystified. If she had been given the same diagnosis, she was sure that she would fight tooth and nail, do anything that she could just to squeeze one more day from life. But of course, she hadn't had his diagnosis, and how could she possibly know how she would react? And she supposed that Stephen had reacted in a way that matched his personality. Straightforward, well-considered and utterly ruthless.

'Well,' she said with a weak laugh. 'I guess that puts a different complexion on this legacy discussion.'

'No, Summer, not at all,' said Stephen emphatically. 'It doesn't change what we've achieved or what we want to do, although we just might have to do it all a little quicker.'

'Okay,' said Summer, opening her notepad. Her head was reeling, but she knew she might fall apart if she stopped to think about it. So she did what she was good at: she went into fire-fighting mode.

'We should accelerate your estate planning. Is the will with Grant Klein? Do the lawyers know?'

'My lawyers know nothing yet. No one knows except me, Dr. Statham and a few specialists at Cedars-Sinai. And now you. Anyway, you leave the estate to me. I'm still of sound mind – as sound as it ever was.'

'Fine, but shouldn't we send out a press release, perhaps brief Sara Naim at the Post? She's always been sympathetic.'

But Stephen was already shaking his head.

'No press, no publicity. I don't want the last twelve months of my life to be a freak show, people looking at me thinking, 'Is he about to keel over?' Tilting their heads in fake sympathy, asking how I am. No – that's the last thing I want.'

'So how do we handle it?'

Stephen looked at her for a long moment.

'That's up to you now.'

Summer frowned.

'What do you mean?'

'I mean, you're in charge. I want you to take over as CEO of the Savage Foundation.'

Summer gaped at him.

'CEO?'

'Why not? You've been my right hand for over a decade, and no one understands what I'm trying to do with the Foundation better than you.'

Summer was stunned. It was true that she had been deeply immersed in Stephen's work in the record company and more recently with his philanthropy, but…

'It's just that I always assumed you would be directing this work.'

Stephen pointed at her. 'Which is exactly why you are the perfect candidate to run it after I've gone. I don't want some careerist executive who will prioritise fund management and shore up his position. I need someone to get this money where it needs to go.'

'But where do you want it to go? What do you want the Foundation to be after…well, after you've gone?'

He spread his arms.

'Just continue doing what we've been doing these past five years. Keep it simple, Summer. Use the Savage Foundation to make a lasting impression on the world.' He raised his finger. 'And *that* we can accelerate. Let's spend it all.'

'Spend it *all*?'

Summer hadn't been involved with the sale of Savage Media – her job had been running the day-to-day, not the intricacies of mergers and acquisitions, so she wasn't entirely sure how much money 'all' was. She knew that with the construction of the Savage Gallery, the theatre and a film school attached to the Cine Awards, the Foundation had already allocated nearly $500m. How deep did the pot go? Multiple millions, possibly approaching a billion, given that most of the sale's proceeds had been invested in high-yield bonds, stocks and commodities. Savage had always been good at making money, even when he was giving it away.

'That's a lot of money, Stephen.'

'Which is good, right? It means all those schemes and ideas we've talked about for years can happen,' he smiled for the first time. 'Come on, let's have some fun.'

'Fun?' She rubbed a hand over her eyes. The idea of 'fun' did not compute right now. 'Sorry Stephen, I'm finding all this a bit…'

'I know,' he said gently. 'It's a shock, but think of it as an opportunity. No boundaries, no limitations, not any more.'

Logically, Summer could understand that Stephen was dealing with it the best way he could, but inside, Summer was screaming. Stephen Savage had always been in her life, right from when she was a little girl, as 'Uncle Stephen' who would come over for Thanksgiving. Then, when Summer had come to work at Savage Media, he had been her boss and mentor, the rock beneath all her schemes. But most of all, he had been a surrogate father, and over the years, she had spent far more time with him than her own father.

'So, how was your weekend?' he said more briskly.

Summer needed a few moments to collect her thoughts. She was stunned by Stephen's health announcement, stunned by the fact she was soon to be a CEO.

'Good, great. It was my dad's Ruby wedding anniversary. They had a party.'

'How is Todd?'

'He's up and down. Sometimes he seems fine, sometimes he's...it's tough.'

'Can I do anything?'

'I don't know, Stephen.'

She wondered if you had unlimited pots of money as Stephen did; there were ways you delay your demise. Then again, those billions weren't helping Stephen.

'At least send him a fruit basket. A good one. For his anniversary. See if you can get hold of any Crown Melons. They've just come in season.'

They sat there in silence for a few moments.

'What was he like?' asked Summer.

'Who?'

'My dad. I mean, you knew Todd back when you were all just hanging out at the beach.'

'He was a good man,' said Stephen simply. 'Talented too, I never really understood why Todd wasn't a huge movie star.'

Summer appreciated his empathy; it wasn't usually Savage's style. Maybe the illness would make him a better person.

'Why do you never see people from back then?' she asked. 'I mean, back in the seventies, you were all so close, weren't you?'

Stephen shrugged. 'You move on, you change. Different experiences, different lives. People have kids or whatever.'

She watched him consider the question.

'I guess I've always looked forward, searching for new things: new music, new trends. I think too many of those guys live in the past. Hanging onto their glory days, you know?'

'But friends are friends whatever you do,' said Summer. 'You were concentrating on building the company, but you could still meet up.'

He looked at her, his face serious.

'If you want to be as successful as me, Summer, you must make sacrifices,' he said. 'And you know what? After a while, some sacrifices don't feel that way anymore.'

Summer wondered what he was thinking of when he said that. It struck her that she should ask because very soon, she wouldn't be able to ask him anything. But not now. She looked at her watch and flipped her notebook closed.

'Dammit, I have another meeting. Let's book a dinner. Somewhere nice. Just me and you.'

He stood, moving back towards his desk. 'Schedule it in for next week,' he said

as if nothing had happened. Business as usual. But it wasn't business as usual, was it? Summer walked briskly through the double doors, down the corridor and into the executive bathroom. It wasn't until she had checked all the stalls were empty that Summer locked the door, sat down and cried her heart out.

Chapter 27

Martha left the maze of LAX and looped past the marina, turning right at Santa Monica, threading up into the hills. She reached for the coffee she had picked up at the airport, hoping the caffeine would work its magic. As a younger woman, she had just shrugged off air travel, but the short hop from Carmel combined with a late night at Harley's place had left her wiped out.

'I'm getting too old for this,' she murmured, turning off the highway and pulling up at the tall gates of the golf course. The Portofina Country Club wasn't Martha's usual environment. She was no stranger to expensive restaurants and fundraisers where men wore black tie and women wore pearls, but she had never truly felt at home there. Perhaps it was her roots in the Sixties counterculture, or perhaps it was the air of exclusivity that hung over these places like a gas leak. It was as if these shiny golf clubs revelled in their WASP conservativism, flipping the bird at the real world outside their high walls.

Negotiating past a monosyllabic security guard – her name, thankfully, was on the list – Martha parked next to the roll-call of elite European cars, their flawless paint giving off heat, then strolled towards the clubhouse. Here was the country club clientele writ large: white teeth, tanned skin, cashmere sweaters draped over the shoulders. We've been to prep school, they seemed to say, Ivy League and Wall Street: we fit in, do you?

Of course, none of this was a surprise. Rumour had it that it cost a quarter of a million just to join this club, plus annual subs and course fees. Luckily, Martha wasn't here to play golf—and she hoped Eliot would pay for lunch.

She loitered in the lobby, sending him a text.

Standing next to a giant golf ball. Where are you?

A golf cart pulled into a bay just outside as she looked up. Eliot climbed out and shuffled towards her.

'Sorry, sorry,' he said, ducking for an air kiss. 'Thought I'd have time for a round before you arrived, but got caught behind…' he shook his head. 'Sorry, you don't want to hear about that, do you?'

Martha looked at her old friend. She had, of course, seen Eliot's house, but she'd had no idea Eliot Jones had become part of this world. He wore an expensive branded golf shirt with a popped collar and matching slacks. Single white glove on one hand. Not a hint of natural fibre anywhere.

'So shall we go to the clubhouse?' he asked, eager to please. 'Is it too early for lunch? I know I could do with a drink.'

At the clubhouse entrance they were shown to a private booth surrounded by blousy hydrangeas, which gave an uninterrupted view of the golf course. This was the equivalent of a box at the Opera; the primo seats were meant to impress. Martha couldn't help grinning as Eliot accepted the waiter's glass of white wine and went into the whole swilling and tasting performance.

'What's so funny?' he said after approval had been given and the waiter had backed away.

'All this,' she said, gesturing towards his fancy golf attire.

'What did you expect? That I'd still be wearing that Indian tunic and sandals? Times change, Marth. Fashions too.'

'Not here, it seems.'

Chinos, blazers and tea dresses: Martha doubted there would have been a jot of difference if you'd visited the clubhouse when Jack Nicklaus was king.

'Am I being accused of joining the establishment?' asked Eliot with a raised eyebrow.

'I just didn't ever see you playing golf.'

'Hey, Alice Cooper is the poster boy for golf. And if you recall, he was there in the canyon, living next door to Zappa.'

'Alice plays it off as irony,' said Martha. 'And it works mainly because his day job involves wearing a boa constrictor around his neck.'

Eliot frowned. 'You're not exactly a rebel yourself anymore, Martha.'

'Touché,' she said, taking a sip of her wine. She supposed she wanted things to stay the same, and they kept changing, whether you liked it or not. Perhaps she should quit turning over rocks.

'Listen, thanks for seeing me again, Eliot,' she said. 'I know it's only been a few days since we last met.'

'Yeah, sure. It's always great to see you, Martha, but what's urgent? I don't see you for years and then it's twice in less than a week.'

He added a laugh, but it didn't quite land.

'It's this story I'm working on,' said Martha. Eliot's expression grew more serious.

'Verity,' he said.

'Yes, we dug up some new information, and I thought you should hear it. In person.'

'New information from whom?'

'First, I went to see Willow,' she said.

She dropped the 'first' in deliberately, wondering if Eliot would catch the implication. Evidently not: he just swilled his wine thoughtfully, then took a long drink.

'How is Willow?'

'The same. Pretty much exactly, actually - it was like time travel. Like she'd transported the Canyon up into the hills behind Ojai.'

Eliot shrugged.

'Well, personally, I have no desire to go back there. I'm happy here, Martha.

Willow might want to stay in the Seventies, but that was a bad time for me. I was drinking, strung out and don't forget the rest: I lost my brother in Vietnam.'

Martha nodded, conceding the point. The truth was that after Verity's death, the Malibu crowd had scattered to the four winds. Martha chose to remember the good times, but there had been darkness there, too – for all of them.

Eliot gave her a sideways look.

'So what's this information Willow gave you?'

Martha took a breath. This wasn't going to be easy. She was a practised interviewer—she had been face-to-face with senators and despots—but felt out of her comfort zone here. These were her friends.

'Willow told us about that trip to Joshua Tree,' she said and waited for Eliot's reaction. A slight flare of the nostril, nothing more. If he had been expecting it, he hid it well. Martha continued.

'Willow said she went back to the motel and saw you and Donna together.'

She watched the colour slowly drain from Eliot's face. He snatched up his wine and took a gulp.

'Jesus, Martha.'

He was practically squirming in his seat. 'Willow can't have…' He turned to face Martha, eyes wide. 'What did she say?'

So Martha told him. How Willow had seen them through the window, how they'd been so engrossed, they hadn't seen her. And how she had quietly withdrawn and had told no one. Until now.

'She knew all this time?' Eliot offered no denial, but then Willow had always been the most straightforward of the Malibu crowd. She was the last one you'd expect to tell a lie.

'Why didn't you tell me, Eliot? The other day, I gave you the opportunity, and you said nothing.'

He barked out a laugh.

'Why? Are you kidding me? Like I'd go around boasting about screwing Donna.' He shook his head. 'If I could jump in Marty McFly's Godamn DeLorian, that's what I'd go back and change. The one thing in my life I truly wish I could erase.'

Martha felt sympathy, but keeping quiet about it hadn't done anyone any good. And there was something else to consider, too.

'Are you Summer's father?'

Eliot bristled.

'Goddamn Martha! What is this? Are you writing a Vanity Fair expose about me? Can't you leave this shit alone?'

'But it's true, isn't it? I've checked out Summer's date of birth. The dates work exactly. And we've been to see Todd Mayfield too. He's been married for forty years but couldn't have children with his wife, although she has a daughter from another marriage.'

She looked at Eliot and saw that his hand was shaking. He looked old, but she pressed ahead anyway.

'Eliot, I think Donna fell pregnant that night in Joshua. And I think she told you. You are Summer Phelps' father, aren't you?'

'That's what Donna claimed,' said Eliot, his voice almost a whisper. 'But I can't have been the only one she was screwing back then.'

'So you *have* spoken to Donna about it,' said Martha. 'When did she tell you?'

Eliot had shrunk back into the booth like a cornered animal. He raised his glass and swallowed, tears in his eyes now.

'That night…' his voice caught. 'That last night at the Malibu House. She told me then.'

Martha could feel her heart pumping harder.

'*That* was what the argument was about?'

Eliot pulled a pained expression, then let out a long breath.

'I was down on the beach. It was about ten o'clock. It was dark, mellow. And then Donna came over. I didn't want to speak to her or see her at all after the Joshua Tree thing, but she kept calling me, and up until that night at the Malibu House, I'd managed to avoid her.'

Martha knew Donna well enough to know she wouldn't tolerate being ignored. Eliot couldn't have chosen a better way to make her mad.

'I was polite to her,' he said, 'But I told her I didn't want a relationship. I made that clear. But Donna kept pushing – let's meet for dinner, go to Catalina for the weekend. I said no, no, no.'

He turned to look at her. 'I said no because I was still in love with Verity.'

Martha almost laughed. If Eliot had loved Verity, he had a funny way of showing it. Eliot looked at her as if he had read her mind.

'Nothing should ever have happened between me and Donna. Never. But I know why she came on to me.'

'Why?'

'Because she was jealous of Verity, of course. Donna thought she was better than Verity because she was thin, blonde, and beautiful. She wanted to prove she could take anything from Verity whenever she wanted. And that night in Joshua, she did. I was drunk, high. I made a mistake, and I paid a terrible price.'

A tear slipped down his cheek, and Eliot dashed it away.

'How did the news go down?' asked Martha. 'When she told you that night?'

Eliot's mouth twisted.

'I called bullshit, obviously.'

'You didn't believe her?'

'Why would I? She was with Todd back then. But she said they'd stopped ballin'. She said Todd was more interested in acid than her.' He was probably avoiding her, too. Donna was sexy as hell until you discovered what a bitch she was. That kinda took the wind out of your sails if you follow me.'

He took another drink and waved at the waiter for another carafe.

'So, guess what happened next?' he asked bitterly. 'You know, considering what a piece of work Donna was? How jealous and vindicative she is?'

Martha knew right away.

'She told Verity.'

Eliot nodded.

'Donna told me she was leaving the party, but she didn't go immediately. No, first, she went to find Verity and told her about the baby. And that's when the bomb went off.' Eliot traced a mushroom cloud in the air. 'Like nuclear war.'

Martha tried to remember the night, to picture the scene unfolding. She knew the house and the people so well that it suddenly felt real and vivid in her mind. It didn't take much imagination; given the amount of booze and stimulants circulating at the Malibu House, arguments flared up regularly at Verity's place. So, Donna telling Verity about Eliot would have been like tossing gasoline on a bonfire.

'So that's when Verity threw everyone out?'

'Sure. I tried to explain it to her, but Verity didn't want to listen. I couldn't blame her. I'd fucked up, about as big as it was possible to fuck up.'

'You left too?'

'Man, I was out of there, along with everyone else. Some of us drove up to the Troubadour - some band was on - then we got trashed at an after-party at my place up in the Canyon. I didn't even hear about Verity until the next morning.'

He trailed off, and they sat silently for a moment, watching the golfers rolling past in their carts.

'Why are you doing this, Martha?' asked Eliot finally. 'Seriously. I mean, how does this help anyone?'

It was a good question, one Martha had been mulling since her encounter with Harley. She had been pulled into this investigation by Lara Stone's enthusiasm and curiosity – and Martha didn't regret that part at all. However, unearthing old stories was never a neutral process because there were always consequences. People would be revealed as liars and cheats, and relationships would be changed forever. And more than that; everyone had their own version of the past, especially when there had been a tragedy. Everyone found a way to get through it, to feel comfortable in their skin. Something as explosive as this could undermine the very ground they all walked on.

'Maybe you're right,' said Martha quietly. 'Maybe it won't help anyone. But don't you think Verity deserves the truth?'

'Verity is *dead*, Martha,' said Eliot with feeling. 'How does the truth help her now? Jesus, I know what happened that night, and the thought of it has almost killed me, too.'

Martha frowned.

'What do you mean? You 'know what happened'?'

'What do you think? The news about the baby destroyed her,' he whispered. 'Verity wanted kids so bad. We'd tried, but it hadn't happened; that was one of the things that pushed us apart when we were first together. But then Donna tells her about me, about the pregnancy and boom! In one moment, her entire world shatters. She finds out her husband has cheated on her, and right at the moment she thinks we're getting back together, too. That has to be a dagger to the heart, right? But then comes dagger number two – I've cheated on her with her so-called best friend. You want to know about the truth, Martha? The truth killed Verity.'

Martha felt the breath stop in her throat as the full implication hit her. She turned to look at Eliot, eyes wide.

'You think…you think Verity killed herself?'

Eliot nodded slowly.

'She was more sensitive than people knew. I broke her heart, Martha. *We* broke her heart. Hard drugs were floating around that night; there always were. I think Vee got hold of some. I think she wanted to just slip away.'

'Oh, Eliot,' said Martha, putting her hand over his.

Around them, the diners laughed, and the glassware tinkled. She looked at her old friend, his skin grey, weighed down by this burden he'd carried for half a century. She was glad they were in a discreet booth where he could relive his agony unseen. That, at least.

'Does Summer know?' she asked. 'That you're her father, I mean?'

Eliot shook his head.

'I don't think so.'

'You have to tell her, Eliot,' she said. 'Summer deserves to know.'

Eliot snatched his hand away.

'I thought we'd just established that honesty isn't always the best policy? Summer *has* a Dad, Martha - a good one. Do you think it will improve her life to hear her biological father is a cheater? Some guy who has practically ignored her for fifty Godamn years? And what about Todd Mayfield? He has a daughter he's loved and raised his entire life. You think *he* wants to know it's a lie?'

She saw Eliot had a point. All her professional life as a writer, 'the truth' had been an absolute. As a writer, you exposed the truth; you yanked it from the darkness into the light. But when the people were your friends, when you saw how it could change people's lives, it was different. Perhaps it shouldn't be, but it was. And most of all, Eliot was right that Summer hadn't asked for any of this.

'I was adopted,' said Martha. 'I don't tell many people. You won't find it on my Wikipedia entry or author biography. But when I was 21, my parents told me. They said to truly know who you are, you must know where you came from. And it was hard, but I believe that. So I tracked down my birth mother, and we met. She was called Mary, and she was 16 when she gave birth to me. She couldn't cope, so they found me a family that could give me everything, which they did. My mum and dad were wonderful. But I liked finding out that Mary could paint and that she was a talented artist. I liked finding out that despite her lack of education, Mary loved books, and I think that my creativity, my love of words, came from her. Meeting Mary didn't change my relationship with my mum and dad; it deepened it. And it deepened my understanding of myself.'

'So you think I should tell her?' said Eliot quietly.

'I don't know, Eliot. But you should certainly think about it. She might already know. Donna might have told her too.'

She touched his hand again. 'But I think she might like to hear it from you.'

Chapter 28

The Mayor didn't fit the brief at all. Throughout his childhood, Alex had watched American TV cop shows about maverick detectives who would, at least once an episode, enrage the city's mayor. The actors playing the mayor were almost always middle-aged, overweight, and spitting angry. Mayor Jonathon Durante was none of those things. He was in his late forties, gym-trim and groomed, and, as Alex was shown into his office, he walked around his desk and greeted him warmly, shaking with both hands.

'Alex, so good to finally meet you,' he said, 'Can I get you anything? Ice water? Tea?'

'No, thank you, mayor,' said Alex, slightly thrown. It was the first time he'd been offered tea since he'd been in LA.

'Please, call me Jon,' said the mayor, gesturing towards a pair of leather armchairs in keeping with the office's art deco style.

'You told my press secretary that you had a specific issue you wanted to discuss?' asked Durante. 'Obviously, I'm always keen to help the Globe in any way I can.'

Particularly right now, thought Alex. Mayor Durante was

coming to the end of his first term and already gearing up for re-election. Having a major newspaper in your corner would be a huge advantage. But that also gave Alex an opportunity. He hadn't liked taking the bridge story back from Natasha and Will, but this move needed to come from the top. Durante needed to know the Globe meant business. Even if, in reality, the story was thin: one pissed-off mistress and a whistleblower who had refused to talk. But the mayor didn't know those details, and right now, the threat of an expose into City Hall corruption was potent. Assuming Alex could sell it.

'My issue is traffic,' began Alex. 'We're getting a huge amount of complaints – about the Sun Valley bridge construction and the new Shadow Hills bypass.'

Jonathon sat back in his chair, tapping his chin in a gesture of thoughtfulness. Alex suspected this was the result of media training; that, or Durante had practised it in front of a mirror.

'Traffic, yes,' he said with a knowing smile. 'I won't say it's the biggest issue facing Los Angeles, but it's the one that has caused me the most headaches since coming into office.'

He sat forward. 'You know what it comes down to? Money.'

Yeah, I figured, thought Alex, suppressing a cynical smile.

'Here's the problem: unlike New York and Chicago, I don't control the city's whole budget. I have to share power with Los Angeles County and the municipal districts –87 of them, each controlling their own schools, water and public services, each with their own slice of the budget, each with their own officials – *eighty-seven*, Alex.' He gave Alex one of his winning smiles. 'Imagine trying to untangle all that.'

Alex made a show of pulling out a notebook and flipping to a new page.

'So you're telling me your hands are tied? That the mayor can't help the commuters in his own city?'

Durante's smile dimmed a little.

'Not at all. I'm just saying it's complicated. But rest assured, I am fully committed to addressing the problem.'

Alex paused a beat.

'Addressing the problem,' he repeated. 'As my readers see it, Mr Mayor, 'Addressing the problem' seems to involve endless roadworks which only make things worse.'

Durante was in full media charm mode now.

'I get it, Alex – I do. I feel your readers' frustrations.' He gestured towards the office. 'People imagine I live in this building, but I have to endure that commute every day, too.'

Alex wrote down the word 'endure' and underlined it.

'Progress is never easy,' said Durante, his eyes on the notebook. 'But Los Angeles has never been afraid to reinvent itself.'

It was a soundbite Alex guessed he had used many times before and was already tired of the game playing. The uncomfortable irony was that was exactly what he was here for: chess moves on a loaded board. In fact, it was worse than that because today, Alex found himself playing the role of Darius. Alex had never rated the Chronicle's editor-in-chief, seeing Darius as a self-promoting bullshitter who spent his time hobnobbing with politicians and celebrities. But the connections he had formed at those endless back-slapping parties had enabled Darius to make moves just like this: to use the power of the media to bend events to his will. To make a difference.

'Shall I lay my cards on the table, Mr Mayor?' said Alex. 'The Globe is keen to support you in your bid for re-election.'

Durante's grin was back. 'Well, that's very welcome news; I have always read the Globe ever since...'

'But,' said Alex, holding up a finger. 'The Globe wants to support a candidate who has the power to fix our readers' problems. The Globe is not looking for someone whose 'hands are tied'. Our readers want action.'

The mayor peered at him.

'And what would that action look like – from your readers' point of view?'

'One, they would want an end to these criminal road schemes.'

'Criminal?'

'I use the word deliberately, Mr Mayor. Rest assured I have information which will back up that statement.'

Alex paused to let that sink in.

'And two, our readers want to know who is responsible for making them sit in traffic - and they want to see those people held to account.'

Alex watched the mayor's bonhomie dissipate.

'You're talking about a scapegoat?'

'No, Jon,' said Alex, losing his patience. 'I'm talking about naming names, exposing whoever is responsible for this clusterfuck. If it's not the Mayor's office, then there has to be someone else in City Hall who is bringing LA to a standstill. For the money.' He added with emphasis.

'And you say you have information about who that might be?'

'In journalism, we have a maxim I always find useful,' said Alex, 'We ask ourselves, 'Who would benefit?' In this case, it would seem to be the contractors who are raking in millions building these bridges which benefit no one but themselves. But someone at City Hall has to give out those contracts, right?'

Durante looked at him for a moment.

'And I'm guessing the Globe will benefit from exposing this 'crime'?'

'Of course,' said Alex. 'As a crusading newspaper, we

champion the issues close to Angelino's hearts and, yes, if we can be seen to ease their daily pain…'

'…And stick it to The Man?'

Alex smiled. 'Never a bad thing either.'

He tapped his pen against his notepad.

'And a mayor tough on corruption is also a mayor the Globe would be happy to support.'

Durante looked at him, then seemed to make a decision. He stood up and offered Alex his hand.

'It seems we have a common goal. I will be in touch very soon.'

Chapter 29

Lara and Martha sat in the car outside Bobby's house, listening to the ticking of the cooling engine.

'Are you sure I'm invited?' asked Martha, looking across at the little red door.

'Martha, Bobby set this whole thing up for you,' said Lara. 'I don't think you have anything to worry about.'

'I'm not worried,' said Martha with a little too much force. 'It's just…I haven't seen Bobby in maybe a dozen years.'

Lara hadn't known Martha long, but this was the first time she had seen her even close to flustered.

'When was the last time you saw Bobby?' she asked gently.

'Some film party in the hills, one of those horrible concrete boxes hanging out over space,' said Martha. 'Bobby was working on an arty movie, maybe a Spike Jonze, Charlie Kaufmann – something like that?'

Lara saw an unbidden smile creep across her friend's face.

'So you enjoyed his company?' said Lara with amusement.

'Not that way,' Martha said with a warning tone. 'But he was funny – and you don't know how rare that is in this town. And you could trust him too. I remember Verity saying that's why she let him run around with his little camera. 'He's one of the good ones', she said.

'Well, he won't have changed.'

Martha hesitated before she got out of the car.

'What's wrong?' asked Lara.

'Let's not go too heavy on the Verity thing,' said Martha. 'Let's just try and have a nice night.'

Lara tried not to react. Martha had told her about her meeting with Eliot Jones and his belief that Verity had killed herself that tragic night at the Malibu house. Lara thought the overdose theory was possible - even if it had been accidental - but a good journalist had to consider all the angles. Even so, these were Martha's friends.

'Okay. Maybe Eliot is right,' said Lara. 'But let's see what Bobby has to say, too?'

They walked up the short pathway to Bobby's front door, and Lara pressed the doorbell. As she waited for the clunks and clicks of Bobby's security system, Lara found the nerves were contagious. She wanted Martha to enjoy her reunion with an old friend but was also excited at the prospect of seeing Bobby's home movies.

'Ladies, thanks for coming.'

Bobby was wearing a shirt, and his hair was combed flat. Lara guessed he'd spent a long time getting ready; he hadn't looked this smart when she had visited on Friday. To be fair, she hadn't given him much notice.

'Martha,' said Bobby. 'It's…it's wonderful to see you.'

Lara could see he meant it.

'You too, Bobby,' said Martha, clasping his hands. 'Or is it Robert now?'

'Always Bobby to you. Please, come on in.'

Lara could see he'd done his best to spruce up the

place, too; there were fresh flowers, scented candles and more pillows on the couch.

'Oh, I love these posters,' said Martha, crossing to a one-sheet featuring a distinctive painting of a young Gwyneth Paltrow in Great Expectations. 'Isn't this Clemente? Didn't he do all the art for the film?'

'Yes, my friend worked on the sound design.'

She looked at him in surprise, impressed.

'Listen, make yourselves at home,' said Bobby, backing towards the kitchen. 'I've got a few things to deal with. Sorry, I should have prepared cocktails or something...'

When he was gone, Lara raised her eyebrows at Martha, who just pointed a finger at her and mouthed, 'Don't.'

Lara raised both hands. 'Never said a word.'

'What's cooking?' Martha called towards the kitchen as she continued to examine the pictures on the walls.

'Oh. My Mom's burritos,' Bobby shouted. 'It's all under control. Put some music on.'

Martha was already flicking through his stack of vinyl.

'Gosh, this is a trip down memory lane. Don't you have anything after 1975?'

Bobby's flushed face popped around the door.

'It was the best time,' he said.

He caught Lara's eye and surreptitiously beckoned to her. Lara left Martha with the record player and slipped into the kitchen – to be met by a scene of complete disarray.

'Jesus, Bobby,' she gasped. 'Did you drop a grenade?'

The floor was wet, a mountain of chopped vegetables was spilling over the counter's edge, and something charred was smoking in the skillet on the stove. Bobby had a tortilla stuck to the bottom of one shoe.

'Bobby, what's going on?' she laughed. 'I thought this was your speciality?'

'My *Mom's* speciality, not mine,' he grimaced. 'I thought 'how hard can it be?' But the answer seems to be 'pretty darned hard.' It's like the kitchen has declared war on me.'

Just then, hot fat spat at Bobby, and he jumped back, shaking a hand and dashing across to run it under a tap.

'Let me help', said Lara, stepping forward confidently. 'I live on a boat with the world's smallest kitchen – I should be able to salvage something.' She peered into the pan, then looked up. 'Okay, we should go again with the onions and peppers.'

'We're all out,' said Bobby miserably. 'This was my second attempt.'

Lara suppressed a laugh. She could see how important it was to Bobby, but he looked like a drowning man.

'Listen, you go and hang out with Martha.'

'No, I can handle it…'

'Seriously,' said Lara firmly. 'Go set up the film. That's the important thing.'

Lara turned to the fridge and plucked off a flyer pinned there.

'I'll order pizza, okay?'

Bobby began to object but then seemed to see the carnage around him for the first time. He began to nod. 'Yeah, maybe that's not a bad idea.'

'Go on and talk to Martha,' said Lara kindly. 'I'll deal with this. That way, you can catch up without setting off any fire alarms.'

Bobby nodded, removed his apron, and disappeared into the other room. Lara dialled the pizza place, over-ordering to cover any dietary kinks, then peeked around the door into the living room; Martha and Bobby were already deep in conversation over a pile of records.

'The burritos are off,' called Lara.

'Good, I get a bloat from beans,' said Martha, not

looking up from examining the back of a Creedence Clearwater album.

'Anyone want a drink?' asked Bobby.

Lara shook her head. 'Driving.'

'I'm not,' said Martha. 'I'll have the strongest thing you've got.'

Bobby brought her a bottle. 'These days, it's a Bud Light, I'm afraid.'

'Perfect,' said Martha, flashing him a smile.

Lara gave them space, lurking by the kitchen door as Bobby fussed around connecting a screen to a pair of speakers.

'Right, I think that's got it,' he said nervously. 'Ladies, if you'd like to assemble on the sofa?'

Lara and Martha eagerly snuggled down on the slightly squishy couch, grinning anxiously. Bobby lifted a box onto the table. 'Okay, so these are the originals. I arranged the Super8 reels by date and subject but concentrated on any I could find from around *that* date.'

Martha peeked into the box. 'Wow, Bobby, there are hundreds of them. How much did you shoot, exactly?'

Bobby pulled a face. 'A lot. Like, a *real* lot. I guess I had some idea of turning it into a documentary, but…well, after Verity, it didn't seem right.'

Lara admired his loyalty. She felt someone would have paid handsomely for Bobby's intimate footage of a golden musical era.

'Anyway, let's start with this one…'

Suddenly, a happy, smiling face appeared on the screen, Verity Jones beaming into the camera. In the background, Lara could see a very familiar view.

'Hey, that's our balcony!' she said, recognising the Malibu House behind Verity. It looked a little different – it had been remodelled since the Seventies, but over Verity's shoulder, the beach, the sea – even the seabirds lined up by the water's edge, it was all the same.

'Hi Bobby,' Verity called, waving into the camera in that slightly sped-up way Super 8 had. 'You having fun?'

Wow, thought Lara. *What a smile.* Verity was dressed in that famous green kaftan and threw her arms wide, spinning in a full circle in front of Bobby's camera, laughing. 'Isn't it a beee-uu-tiful day?' she said, then held up a beer bottle and pretended to sing into it. 'Summertime and the living is easy…' That smoky voice came through loud and clear. Real. Alive.

'This is amazing,' whispered Martha. 'It's like looking through a window into the past. Look, there I am,' she gasped, pointing at the TV. 'And Griffin too.'

What a great-looking couple they were, thought Lara. Griffin was every bit as handsome and dynamic as Martha had described.

'You look like Taylor and Burton,' said Bobby as Martha blushed.

Lara was transfixed. Now, she had made the connection to the Malibu House of the present day; suddenly, the images came to life. In Bobby's footage, she could see a young woman in a bikini top lounging in the wicker chair; she would be sitting in the modern-day kitchen. In 1970s Malibu, Verity's piano sat against the outside wall where, right now, a flat-screen TV stood. And the same idea applied to the people in the movies. Where before they had appeared to her as actors in an over-saturated costume drama, now they felt real. Flesh and bone, as vital and vulnerable as the three here, clustered around Bobby's TV.

'There! At the back - is that Dennis Hopper?' she said as a man in a denim shirt wandered past. That was the other remarkable thing: even the celebrities seemed normal, just ordinary hippy kids who had swung by Verity's place to hang out. Which, of course, was exactly what they had been. If some of their faces later became legendary, that was incidental. Even with her limited knowledge of the late 60s music scene, Lara had recognised David Crosby, Carly Simon and Mickey Dolenz from the Monkees.

'Oh my God, do you remember that Godawful clock Verity had?' said Martha, pointing at the screen. 'It always used to run about fifteen minutes too slow. She used it as an excuse for being late for everything.'

'Wasn't it a present from Dennis Wilson?' said Bobby. 'I think he brought it back from tour.'

'Dennis Wilson from the Beach Boys?' asked Lara, and Martha nodded. These global superstars were just part of the gang to Bobby and Martha. 'Remember when Eric brought Dylan over?' said Martha. 'They spent the whole day just watching Joni play the guitar, open-mouthed'.

Lara kept one eye on the footage but mostly watched Bobby and Martha. Martha had said that she didn't know Bobby all that well, but despite the decades they'd been apart, Bobby and Martha were so comfortable in each other's company, joking and teasing. There was a spark that was for sure.

'Hey, there's Verity at the piano,' said Lara, leaning forward as the footage kept spinning.

Bobby paused the film and looked at Lara and Martha. 'Sorry to stop it, but this footage is from *that* day,' he said. 'Mid-afternoon.'

'Are you sure?'

He nodded. 'I was an anal kid. I wrote the times, dates, and the camera settings on each reel.'

He set it running again. In the shot, you could only see Verity from behind, her shoulders moving as she played the piano, but knowing that in a few short hours, she would be lying cold and still in the bath gave these sunny scenes a sudden dark aspect.

'Who's she singing with?' asked Lara. 'Wait, is that Gene Henderson?'

Even in this sea of big names, Gene stood out. It was partly his distinctive look: With his wild mane of hair and flashing eyes, he looked to Lara like a tiger prowling around at the edge of his cage. But there was another layer to Henderson, an imagined dark cloud hovering above him too, because Henderson had been another casualty of this scene, spinning down into addiction and, ultimately, death only a few short years later.

'Gene was another of Verity's discoveries,' said Martha. 'Verity found him in some bar. I'm not even sure he was a singer then, just another Laurel Canyon stoner who used to come and hang out, but she spotted his charisma straight away.'

Bobby leant forward to increase the volume but they could barely hear anything from this distance.

'It's not great sound,' he shrugged, 'You had to be up close for it to be clear.'

'What a shame. It would be great to hear her and Gene sing. Especially as...well, you know.'

Especially as it might have been the last time Verity sang anything, thought Lara. But as the film continued, Lara found it hard to stay too gloomy. Martha had been right: it was a unique look into a time that was almost lost. In their bell bottoms and headbands, goofing about on motorbikes, bicycles, or surfboards, having a barbeque on the beach, or holding piggy-back races—they were just a load of young kids having fun.

Bobby moved the footage forward. It was now dark at the Malibu house. Many of the big names had disappeared, but the party was bigger.

'Who are all these people?' asked Lara.

Bobby shrugged.

'I'm not sure who many of them are – we never were.

Once word got out that Verity was having a party, all sorts of people would drift in and out. But you might know him,' said Bobby, pointing. 'Stephen Savage. The music mogul?'

Lara looked closer. With his long hair and skinny limbs, he was hardly recognisable from the commanding figure she had seen at Donna's launch party.

'Savage was the other kid who liked hanging around Verity's place. I think she liked me more than him, though,' Bobby smiled. 'Savage was a little too pushy.'

'Pushy?' asked Lara. 'Was he trying to get into the music industry?'

'Of course. Savage was a hustler even then,' said Bobby. 'His uncle was an artist and had a ratty trailer near Verity's place. He used to let Stephen stay there at the weekend, which meant he could hang around at the parties. He was a year or two older than me, and I thought we could be friends, but he wasn't interested. He was laser-focused on networking with the people who had already made it, not the wannabes.'

Bobby pointed at the screen again.

'You might know these two as well. Donna and Eliot. They were in the band with Verity.'

Lara stood up and crossed to the TV for a good look. Eliot was sitting near the shore, drinking a beer, and Donna watched him near the bonfire. Lara felt a shiver and turned to Martha.

'Do you think this is where Donna and Eliot had their conversation?'

Bobby looked back and forth between them.

'What conversation?'

Martha bit her lip.

'Look, we should tell you something…'

'Martha,' warned Lara, but there was no stopping her friend. 'I spoke to Eliot Jones earlier today, Bobby. It seems that Eliot and Donna Phelps had become *entangled* romantically. Donna told Verity, and Verity was understandably distraught at the betrayal.'

'You mean she told Verity that night?'

Martha nodded.

'There were drugs in Verity's system. Eliot thinks she might have overdosed intentionally.'

Bobby frowned.

'Surely the autopsy would have shown that?'

'Maybe it did. All we know is the cause of death was heart failure. Perhaps it was intentional, or perhaps it was the unintended consequences of Verity trying to dull her pain.'

'I told you I saw Verity and Donna arguing,' said Bobby, turning to Lara. 'I didn't have my camera with me just then because I was going to clean the pool, but Verity was upset – definitely.' His face was pale now. 'It all makes sense if….'

BANG! BANG!

Martha flinched, and Bobby creakily tried to rise from his chair. '*What the hell?*'

But Lara was there first, pulling back the drapes. The civilian in her breathed a sigh of relief: not an assassin with a rifle. 'It's just the pizza delivery guy.'

The journalist in her, she had to admit, was disappointed. Bobby went to unlock the door. A young man with his crash helmet cocked back on the top of his head was standing there wearing a 'Pizza Planet' sweatshirt.

'Man, you scared us,' said Bobby, 'What was that bang?'

'Sorry, Dude,' the delivery guy drawled, handing over a stack of boxes. 'It's my scooter, keeps backfiring. The boss says he'll get me new wheels, but it's whatdotheycallit? Surplus labour value. Capitalism, man. It's a bitch.'

Bobby carried the pizza back to the living room,

shaking his head. 'I think a kid on a scooter has just given me a lecture on economics,' he said, handing out plates.

But Lara wasn't listening.

'What is it?' asked Martha.

Lara turned back to her friend.

'The noise,' she said.

'What noise?'

Lara gestured towards the street.

'The motorbike. Those 'bang bang' sounds when it backfired.'

'What about it?'

Lara tried to quickly gather her thoughts, piecing together snippets of detail she had heard over the week, trying to connect them all.

'Jack Anders told me that he spoke to Verity's neighbour – some screenwriter, remember? He said he thought he heard gunshots at around midnight.'

'Sure, but the police dismissed it,' said Martha. 'Verity died from a heart attack, not a gunshot.'

'But what if it *was* a motorbike?' said Lara. 'Like the delivery guy's bike? What if someone came back to The Malibu House after the party?'

Martha waved a slice of pizza.

'Well, Todd Mayfield had a bike. He told us, didn't he? That's how he got to the theatre for his play.'

Lara nodded. 'But it was Chekov's Three Sisters. I checked after we spoke; it's a long play. Wouldn't have finished until after eleven. He would have had to change out of costume and get up to Malibu by midnight. It's possible, but not likely.'

'Gene had a motorbike too, didn't he?' said Bobby, addressing Martha.

Bobby put down his garlic bread and, wiping his fingers, cued up another tape.

And there he was: Gene Henderson, just wearing

shorts, zooming up the beach on an old Triumph, a girl on the back, both laughing. The bike looked beaten up and rusty; it certainly looked like a kind which might backfire. Lara looked at Bobby.

'Who is she? That girl on the bike? Wasn't she in the room with Verity and Gene when Verity was playing the piano?'

Bobby rewound the footage to look at the girl. She was striking with long black hair, like a pre-glam Cher.

'Cora Bryant, Gene's girlfriend,' said Bobby, his voice flat. Lara guessed he didn't approve, but the name sounded familiar.

'She's a photographer now,' said Martha. 'Quite a celebrated one. Owns one of LA's high-end studios.'

'Well, we need to speak to her,' said Lara, feeling the familiar exhilaration when she uncovered a new lead. 'What if Gene had returned to Verity's after the party had ended? She might know.'

'Although if she did, Cora wouldn't necessarily tell us,' said Bobby. 'After all, she ended up as Gene's wife.'

Martha was shaking her head. 'And Lara, remember what Eliot said. Verity's arguments with Eliot and Donna - that's what led her to do what she did.'

Lara could see Martha was struggling with it, and she could sympathise. Verity had been Martha's friend, too, and if she had indeed taken her own life, intentionally or otherwise, Martha would be weighed down by guilt. Lara put her hand on Martha's arm.

'Maybe Eliot's right,' she said gently. 'But the gunshot – or motorbike - at midnight is still a loose end.'

Martha looked at Bobby for backup, but he just shrugged.

'It's worth a conversation,' he said, then looked at Lara. 'Although rather you than me. Cora Bryant was always pretty scary.'

Chapter 30

Natasha lay on her bed, looking at the pictures pasted onto the side of her closet. Nick Jonas, Liam Hemsworth from 'The Hunger Games' and Ross Lynch from 'Teen Beach Movie'. She supposed she should have taken the cuttings down when her dad moved the closet down here, but since there was no way she would ever bring a date back here - *Not even Will – especially not Will* – it didn't matter. And if she was really honest, Liam H was part of the reason she wanted to work on Limelight. Their eyes would meet at a promo junket, Liam would fall madly in insta-love, and they would make beautiful babies together.

Natasha shook her head. She was twenty-six and still entertaining fantasies about guys she liked when she was in eighth grade. It would be laughable if it weren't so depressing.

'And if you think that's depressing…' she muttered, getting up to fetch her laptop from her desk. The desk, incidentally, she had used in high school and to study for her SATs: *God.*

While Natasha told people she lived in an apartment in

Brentwood, the truth was that it was the converted garage to the side of her parent's home. Yes, she had left home to go to college, but post-college had been brutal. Natasha had tried sharing tiny apartments with friends after graduation, but the rent in the city was extortionate, and the pay in journalism was scandalous.

When she had finally asked her parents for help, instead of ponying up the cash, they had offered to remodel the garage, at the time her father's 'man cave', complete with a bar and poker table. A triple bypass three years ago had forced Tony King to give up both Miller and high-stress card games, so Natasha had moved in – along with furniture from her childhood bedroom. Fast approaching her thirties, Natasha had managed to move roughly five yards to the east.

She fired up her laptop and clicked open a document called 'Bridge.' Natasha could admit now that she hadn't relished being assigned to this story initially, but over the past few days, it had started shaping up into something intriguing. Driving back from Pasadena with Will, she had almost felt like she was starring in The Pelican Brief, with herself in the Julia Roberts role, obviously - the glamorous ingenue solving an international conspiracy. But then there had been the scene with Alex Ford in his office. She and Will had dashed in, eagerly telling the editor about Helen Kampf, the whistleblower at City Hall. How they also had a witness willing to go on the record to point the finger at the contractor. Natasha hadn't expected a pay rise, but she had expected some praise, even a gruff 'Well done, kids.' But no.

Alex had stroked his chin, nodded, then said, 'I'll take it from here.'

Like if he was doing them a Godamn favour!

Natasha sighed heavily and, not for the first time, thought about looking for a new job. But then she glanced up at the Liam Hemsworth poster and imagined how cool it would be to work for Limelight. She could see herself now, interviewing him over a cosy dinner at Spago, the Dictaphone between them only adding to the intimacy of the situation.

'I'll take it from here?' Natasha whispered. What did that even *mean*? That Alex was going to write the story himself? That he was dropping it? What?

Natasha groaned, rubbing her eyes until she saw stars. Why was this all so hard? There had to be another way to get noticed. Will's dad had described City Hall as 'Capitol Hill in miniature,' but he could equally have been talking about an organisation like the LA Globe. People spent more time protecting their position and keeping hold of their jobs than doing the actual work. Dani on features ignored Natasha because she didn't want any competition, and Alex Ford took this slam-dunk of a story 'off their hands' once they'd turned it from nothing to a potential front page splash.

Natasha looked up at Liam Hemsworth again: he didn't survive the Hunger Games by giving up. You found a way to turn the odds in your favour.

'It's not about politics, it's about power,' Natasha murmured to herself, opening the computer. If Alex was going to take her story, then she needed something else, something attention-grabbing. She tapped in a search request: 'Verity Jones, cause of death'. She was sure there was something in that story. If there wasn't, then why was Lara Stone so interested? During their visit to Pasadena, Jack Anders had mentioned Lara had been in touch asking questions: the Great Lara Stone wouldn't have bothered making the journey unless she had an angle. 'But what?'

Natasha hit return, and her screen was flooded with Verity-related hits, mostly from various social media platforms. Causes of death: Drugs, suicide and Russian mob executions were all offered up as fact, and Natasha quickly found herself yearning for the dusty certainty of the Globe archive.

She pushed the laptop away and fell back on the bed. Perhaps she wasn't cut out for journalism after all. Some stories never made it over the line; you had to accept that. But…they had done such good work. There was a scoop there; she could feel it.

'Ah, who am I kidding?' she said out loud. She lived in a garage and wrote about 'aromatherapy for seniors'. Even Will Anders seemed ahead of the game. Natasha had barely started.

'Knock knock.'

She looked up as her dad put his head around the door.

'Hey,' he said. 'Your Mom – that is *we* – were wondering if you wanted to join us for dinner? It's meatloaf.'

Natasha gave an ironic smile. It was as if the universe was making sure she got the message: don't go thinking you're an adult - you really do still live at home.

'Thanks, Dad,' she said, 'But I'm not hungry right now.'

'Not feeling well?' he asked, stepping inside. She could tell he was aching to feel her forehead for evidence of a fever but managed to restrain himself, and for that, at least, she was grateful.

'No, I'm fine. Just a little tired from work.'

'Breaking some big story?'

Natasha snorted. 'No, just had one spiked, actually.'

'Ah.' He sat on the edge of her bed. 'Happens in every job, I'm afraid.'

Tony King was an employment lawyer. While it sounded deadly dull to Natasha, it suited his personality; he liked representing the little guy who'd been screwed over by their big bosses. And right now, Natasha could relate.

'Is this it?' he asked, looking at her laptop. 'Verity Jones? Now she could sing. No auto-tune in those days, just raw talent.'

She looked at him with interest.

'Do you remember this then? Do you remember when she died?'

Tony chuckled. 'I'm old, honey – but I'm not that old. I think I was in elementary school…' He trailed off, frowning like he did when mulling over a crossword clue.

'What is it?' she asked.

'Wasn't Verity Jones on Savage Records?'

Natasha shook her head.

'Don't think so. Although Donna Phelps was on the label – and she was in a band with Verity.'

'The Virginians!' said Tony. 'Your Mom used to love 'Sing Together'.'

'She did?' Her mother was so straight-laced that Natasha had never been able to imagine her younger than middle-aged.

'Yeah, she loved all that seventies hippy stuff. She even had the knee-high suede boots. I keep asking her if she'll bring them out of storage, but she never obliges.'

'*Any*way,' said Natasha quickly, eager to head him off before he went into one of his tales about their dating years: Tony had a bad habit of over-sharing. 'Why did you ask about Savage?'

'Oh, because we represented Jacob Anstey a few years ago.'

The name didn't ring a bell.

'Anstey was Stephen Savage's right-hand man in the early days,' said Tony, 'But they had a nasty fall-out when Savage sold the media company. We get this a lot: founder directors getting manoeuvred out to avoid giving them their slice.'

Natasha sat forward. It was one of the many things she loved about LA. It was fuelled by gossip and scandal.

'So what did this Anstey guy tell you?'

Her dad shrugged. 'That Savage was an operator, a total shark. No big surprise, I guess, but Jacob spoke darkly about how Savage had come from nowhere and that there was some huge secret, but he wouldn't say what.'

'Did he say what Savage did? I mean, how was he a shark?'

'God, there was so much. Like how Savage would gather dirt on potential clients, honey traps, and hidden cameras. Anstey claimed Savage blackmailed Sonny Cisco to sign for the label. Can you believe that? Unless he gave the company 'Love Zone', he'd tell the press that Sonny had a long-term boyfriend.

'Love Zone'? That was the theme of that Eddie Murphy movie, right?'

Tony nodded. 'Sold seven million copies – I checked.'

'Interesting…' said Natasha. Maybe this was why Lara Stone was so interested. Maybe the story wasn't about Verity Jones, after all.

'Anyway,' said her dad, standing up, 'Are you coming for meatloaf?'

He held out a hand. 'Please? You know your Mom will make my life hell if you don't.'

Natasha giggled and took his arm. 'Well, if you put it that way. But I can't stay for dessert.' She looked longingly towards her laptop. 'I've got lots of work to catch up on.'

Chapter 31

It was already approaching dark when Summer pulled into her little driveway, although that wasn't unusual for her. Working for the Savage Foundation demanded commitment in both focus and time, but it was well rewarded, as the home in front of her attested. A certain class of Angelino would kill to live here in the swish 'Bird Streets' enclave, so-called because of the names of the roads: Swallow Drive, Thrush Way, Warbler Place. The Bird Streets were close enough to the Strip for the nightlife but deep enough into the hills to give privacy and, of course, that all-important whiff of exclusivity. It was, currently, one of the most desirable square miles in Los Angeles – and only the most well-heeled could afford it.

Summer dropped her keyfob on the Italian sideboard - sourced from the achingly desirable Olive Ateliers - and walked through her double-height open-plan living space. The house was comparatively modest for the area: two beds, two baths, 3,000 sq feet of contemporary glass and white marble. But then, there was only Summer here. Now that she thought about it, she wasn't entirely sure whether the second bedroom had ever been slept in. Most homes clinging to the hillsides up here had status-driven bolt-ons like cinema rooms, bowling alleys and steam rooms – but they also had space for growing families.

Family. The word hit her like a jab. Was her own family history why Summer had never been able to hold down a relationship? A selfish mother who deliberately – and gleefully - undermined her father and now in Stephen Savage, a substitute parent whose time with her was running out like sand through a cracked hourglass. It wasn't exactly a solid base on which to build her own home life. Hence the sterile gated bolthole with the walk-in wardrobe, she supposed. What else did a successful single girl need?

She opened her Sub Zero fridge with a satisfying hiss and took out a plastic box of salad, freshly prepared by her housekeeper, Mrs G, who spent more time in Summer's house than she did. Pouring a glass of white wine and grabbing a fork, she walked out onto the terrace.

'Ahh,' she sighed out loud. *That* was why houses in the Bird Streets cost so much: the view. The wide, flat plain of the City of Angels shimmered with lights, the hazy mountains spread under a vivid purple sky, and, just glimpsed if you squinted right, the ocean.

Maybe it wasn't too late, she thought, spearing a slice of cucumber. Summer was touching fifty, but maybe she could still meet the right guy; maybe they could love a pair of cockapoos as much as her friends loved the children they out-sourced to nannies and elite boarding schools. The truth was that Summer still lived with a vague hope of falling in love, but she simply didn't have the time to devote to meaningful connections. *And when you're CEO,* said a voice in her head. *You're going to have even less time.*

Summer was in no illusions about the demands of being a CEO – she had spent enough time a few steps from power to know what it could do to you, and yet she was excited over the prospect, even if the opportunity was only being given to her because of very sad circumstances. She flattered herself that Stephen was right: no one else understood the potential of the Savage Foundation. She – they – could do great things. She wanted to make sure that Stephen had a legacy to be proud of.

There was a low chime, like a gong being struck: it was the sound to tell her that someone had arrived at her gate. She picked up the unfinished salad and took the wine back to the kitchen to pour away. Better to have a clear head for this.

She walked swiftly to the front door, swinging it open as he walked from his car.

'Eliot,' she said. 'Hope you found it okay?'

'Sure, no problem. We all used to live around here, remember? Laurel Canyon's just over that ridge.' He looked around in wonder. 'All changed, though.'

Summer stood back to let him inside. Eliot was shorter and wider than she remembered. Then again, she had only ever seen him on album covers or at the odd industry event when they'd had hurried introductions. Nobody stayed the same, especially after fifty years. She steered him out to the terrace, where he sat waiting, knee jiggling, as she brought out a tray of coffee.

'Thanks for seeing me,' said Eliot when she was sitting across from him. 'I wasn't sure you would agree to it.'

'Neither was I.'

'So…why did you?'

'Curiosity, I guess,' said Summer. 'It didn't strike me until you called; how weird it is that we've never had a proper conversation.'

'Well, not so weird. Your Mom…'

'Oh,' she smiled. 'Yes.'

The young Summer Phelps had unsurprisingly been curious about Donna's career as a singer: after all, how many kids had a mom who had been on TV, let alone was on first-name terms with a Beatle? But every time Summer had brought The Virginians or Laurel Canyon up, Donna had changed the subject. Once, as a teenager, Summer had pushed harder, asking flat-out why she had never been introduced to Eliot, by then the last remaining member of the group. Donna had become tearful, saying as Verity and Benny Dean were both dead, seeing Eliot was too painful – so Summer had dropped the issue.

'I guess your Mom was protecting you,' said Eliot quietly, pouring oat milk into his coffee with a shaking hand. 'But now you're working in the music business too? It's good to see you do so well, even if it's only from afar.'

Summer looked at him.

'Eliot…'

He held up both hands.

'Yes, I know, I know. Cut to the chase, right?' He barked out a nervous laugh. 'This is weird for me as it is for you.'

Summer wasn't entirely sure about that. After all, a whole section of her life was missing, like a black hole. Todd had done his best to fill the blanks, but he could only really talk about the time before Summer was born. 'We must have met when I was a kid, right?'

Eliot shook his head ruefully. 'About the time you were born, your mom and I kinda fell out. So when you were living in the canyon, we didn't socialise. The hippie dream was over by then anyway, and everybody had gone off into their own little careers. I moved to Westwood Village for a little while after my wife died, then out of LA entirely for a few years.'

By 'wife', Summer assumed he meant Verity. She could imagine Verity's death would have hit him hard.

'So why are you getting in touch now? Is this something to do with that journalist?'

'Martha Riding?' asked Eliot, looking uncomfortable. 'Has she spoken to you too?'

Summer kept her face neutral. She didn't know the true identity of the gatecrasher at Donna's launch, but she certainly had not been Martha Riding, the iconic essayist of the 1970s. She knew Martha had been part of the Malibu set, but nothing else. How was *she* involved? And why now? Summer felt a flutter of unease rising. *Something* was going on here, and she wanted to know what it was. Summer was starting to think she should have arranged to meet him in a bar on Sunset, not here alone.

'Eliot, you called me. I assume there was a point to this beyond reminiscing?'

'Yes, yes. Of course.' He took a deep breath, his eyes fixed on his coffee cup. 'Your mother – Donna – told me that I was…' His eyes finally met hers. 'She said I was your father.'

His words were like a punch to the gut. For a moment, Summer couldn't speak. Her *father*?

'Donna and I had a fling,' Eliot continued. 'Just a one-time thing, but the dates line up with you coming along.'

Summer's heart was beating, her stomach churning, but she kept her expression calm.

'And it's taken you fifty years to tell me this.'

Eliot at least had the decency to look ashamed.

'I didn't *know*, Summer. Not for sure. Your mother…'

…Was unreliable; Summer completed the sentence in her head – and that was putting a polite spin on it. Donna Phelps was not above lying her ass off to get what she wanted; Summer had fifty years' experience of Donna's manipulation and emotional outbursts, so she could understand Eliot's scepticism. But even so, if Eliot had believed Summer was his daughter, half a century was a long time to wait before sending a birthday card.

'So let's take it at face value,' said Summer. 'Let's say

you were unconvinced you were my father – well, it seems you are convinced now, at least enough to have this conversation with me. So what's changed? Why are you here, in my home, suddenly confessing fifty years after the fact?'

Eliot grimaced.

'Martha Riding is writing a story about Verity Jones.'

'But why? Wasn't she tight with all of you guys? Is she trying to revive her career by dredging up the past or something?

Eliot looked pale and sick – and instinctively, Summer knew there was more to this story.

'What happened, Eliot? What has Martha found out?'

He looked away and shook his head.

'Was this something to do with Verity?'

That was what Donna had said in the car after the journalist had gatecrashed her book launch. She hadn't mentioned Eliot; she had said the reporter had been asking about Verity. But why? Summer knew even less about Verity Jones than she did about Eliot. She had been the songwriter for the Virginians, and she had been Donna's best friend - Summer had gleaned all this from pop music lore: it was just another one of those subjects her mother had refused to discuss.

'You were married to Verity, right?'

Eliot nodded. 'Separated, but we were getting back together.'

Summer's eyebrows shot up. 'Oh, I see. And a baby…' Summer's hand strayed to her throat. 'Oh shit. Did Verity know?'

Eliot nodded. He seemed even smaller than he had when he had walked in the door like a tortoise retreating into his shell.

'So Verity loved you, but you cheated on her with her best friend – does that about sum it up?'

'Yes,' he said, his voice gravelly. 'And, well, Donna told her that night. Told her she was pregnant.'

Summer's hand had curled into a claw.

'The night she died? Jesus,' she whispered.

Eliot's eyes were haunted, full of pain.

'We didn't mean to hurt her.'

Perhaps that was true; perhaps Eliot had just been weak - she didn't know him at all. But Summer did not doubt that hurting Verity was exactly what Donna had intended. She knew her mother far too well.

'If Donna hadn't told Verity that I was the father, the party would have carried on,' said Eliot, his tone pleading. 'Then Verity wouldn't have been alone that night.'

'Oh, I see,' said Summer tersely. 'And then none of this would be your fault?'

'No, that's not what I meant.'

But Summer had heard enough. She stood.

'I think it's time for you to go,' she said.

Eliot blinked at her. 'After everything I've just told you?'

'I think I've heard enough,' she replied, her voice tight.

'Summer, we should find out for sure. DNA tests these days are simple…'

Summer closed her eyes and snorted softly.

'We won't be needing a paternity test.'

'No? But why?'

'Because I *have* a father, Eliot. His name is Todd Mayfield. He is a wonderful man, and I am lucky to have had him in my life for the past fifty years. No blood test will change a single second of that. And now I would like you to leave.'

Eliot looked like he had been slapped. He blinked twice, then his shoulders slumped. 'Yes, of course,' he said, getting unsteadily to his feet. 'And I know it sounds hollow, but I *am* sorry.'

Summer followed Eliot through the house and waited

as he got into his car. Just as he started the engine, she had a thought. She crossed the drive and tapped on the window; it purred down, Eliot's face expectant.

'One more thing,' she said. 'If you ever breathe a word of this to Todd, you truly will be sorry. Are we clear?'

Wide-eyed, Eliot nodded.

'Good.'

Then she turned and walked back into the house, closing the door behind her.

Chapter 32

'You cut a *deal*?'

Alex walked to the balcony overlooking the ocean, inky black in the low night-time light. He hadn't exactly expected Lara to congratulate him on the outcome of his visit to City Hall, but he certainly didn't want anyone overhearing her outrage. The beach, happily, was deserted.

'No, I didn't cut a deal,' he said, turning to face her. 'I negotiated a solution.'

'Alex, what the hell?' said Lara incredulously, 'That's not how it works.'

'That's exactly how it works, Lara.'

'Bullshit,' she said. 'We're journalists. Our job is to expose the truth, not to dictate how that information is used.'

Lara had been spoiling for a fight but from the moment she had walked in from yet another soiree with Martha Riding. To think, Alex had been excited when Lara had said she'd made friends with Martha Riding, but now Alex could pinpoint the day when things had started to get fractious with Lara: when she had met Martha.

'Lara, you're being naïve,' said Alex. 'Taking on City Hall is like trying to fight the whole government. You can't expect to bring down the house of cards in one go. Sometimes you just have to be satisfied with a small victory.'

'This isn't a victory, Alex!' said Lara with feeling. 'If anything, it's a defeat. You could have punished that bloody mayor, exposed him as the worst kind of manipulative politician, but instead you promise to give him a leg-up to another term.'

'We have no evidence that Jonathon Durante had any idea about the corruption,' Alex said, his anger rising again. 'All we know is that Jeffrey Hanro was boasting about giving kickbacks to someone in City Hall and that he was funding his girlfriend's lavish lifestyle on the proceeds. That could just be that pissed-off mistress trying to drop Jeffrey in it.'

'Of course it could, but the whistleblower confirmed it. She can bring them down, Alex.'

He shook his head in disagreement.

'Lar, I told you the whistleblower refused to confirm *anything*. Yes – we managed to speak to her, but she wouldn't go on the record.'

'Then you have to *persuade* her to go on the record or find another way to prove what she has to say.'

Usually, Alex loved Lara's passion for truth-seeking journalism, but he was just tired right now.

'Lar, the Globe news team is under-resourced, and they don't have this much investigation experience. We could spend weeks or months on this story and still not have anything which can get past the lawyers. At least this way, we get the mayor to root out the corruption in City Hall – the person responsible for this mess, the one taking the bribes. We might even get these pointless roadworks cancelled. Isn't that a victory?'

Lara just grunted. Dissatisfied, angry. These days, she

seemed determined to dump on everything he did. Alex turned back to the sea, hoping the roar of the waves would soothe him.

'God, I'm tired,' he whispered, leaning on the rail. Staying in Malibu had added three hours to his daily commute, and everything seemed to be catching up with him. He understood Lara's frustrations, but it *was* how business was conducted. Alex couldn't count the times in his career when a story had been spiked because someone had whispered in the editor's ear in exchange for a future favour. That didn't mean he had to like it, but now Alex was editor-in-chief; he was the one who had the power to choose what stories were told and which were not – and he was determined to make the best of that. Had he really won this time? Alex wasn't sure. He felt a presence at his side.

'I'm sorry,' said Lara.

He nudged into her playfully.

'I'm sorry too.'

'Let's not let work get in the way of all this,' she said, gesturing towards the beach. 'Please?'

Alex let out a small chuckle. Coming from Lara, that *was* an apology. Lara would never let anything divert her from a story. That was why she was so good.

'I think we should plan a holiday,' she said. 'A proper one. You know, like Saturday, but longer.'

After their argument on Friday night, Alex had taken Lara to Santa Barbara for the day. He'd had VIP passes for a polo match, but they'd ditched the hospitality tent early and sat on the beach with a make-shift picnic from a really good deli. It hadn't been a holiday, but it had made them both relax, laugh and remember who they were.

'How about Rome, or Stockholm or Marrakesh?' she said with excitement in her voice.

'We should try somewhere new, someplace neither of us has been before,' he replied.

'That'll narrow it down,' smiled Lara. 'I think we're left with one of those all-inclusive holidays where you just move between the sunlounger and the buffet.'

'How about the Orient Express?' said Alex, imagining Lara in a long, silk dress with that Rodeo Drive ring dazzling on her finger. He pushed the thought away; right now, he just wanted to get through the next week without splitting up.

'I just want to spend more time with you,' Lara whispered, resting her head on his shoulder. They stood there for a long while without speaking.

'So how's Martha?' he asked.

'I think I've fixed her up,' said Lara, glancing at him.

'What? With a man?'

'A guy named Bobby, an old friend of hers,' she grinned. 'I say old friend. He was 19 when they knew each other, she was like 27 and married. But I think she's started to see him with new eyes.'

'Like you with me,' he said.

'Oh, I always liked you,' she replied, looking out at the sand. 'Right from the start.'

Alex looked at her in surprise. Lara Stone was not the type for gooey, romantic talk. He wanted to ask her more about this, from what *exact* moment Lara had fancied him, but she turned to face him, the shift in the mood palpable.

'I want to be honest with you,' she said.

Ah, crap, thought Alex. *And it was all going so well.*

'Martha and I were together tonight to discuss the Verity Jones story. We're making progress.'

'Well, that's good,' said Alex, not wanting to inflame the situation again. Everything he'd said during their argument on Friday, he still believed. Lara was poking at a hornet's nest looking into Verity Jones's death, and he wasn't sure it was worth her while. It could certainly land Alex in trouble – with the PRs of LA and with his boss at the bare minimum. Even so, he knew this was Lara Stone. If she had the scent of something, she just had to run it down.

'It turns out that Verity was heartbroken the night she died,' said Lara. 'She'd just discovered that her best friend, Donna from The Virginians, was pregnant with Verity's husband's child.'

'Eliot Jones?' Said Alex with more interest. Now, that *was* a story. Alex wasn't sure where it would fit in the paper; Hollywood Scandal from fifty years ago wasn't exactly front-page news, but it was certainly intriguing.

'So remind me: you're thinking Verity might have overdosed?' he asked.

'It's possible. We are still looking at all angles. I have to say that Martha is amazing. I can tell that she doubts herself - you know her publisher has turned down her latest book? But I'm learning from her every day.'

'They turned down Martha Riding?' said Alex. 'God, the media industry really is screwed. She should write for the Globe.'

Alex said it without thinking, but Martha Riding was exactly the kind of journalist he had been thinking of when he had persuaded Simon Desai to stump up for respected heavyweight writers. And right now, it sounded as if the Globe budget might even be able to stretch to her word-rate.

'You should meet Martha,' said Lara. 'You'd like her.'

Alex pulled her closer.

'Let's sort it out then.'

'It's a deal. And in return, I need a favour from you.'

'Go on,' he said.

'I need you to find me an address and cell phone number.'

Alex nodded cautiously: newspapers had resources for this sort of thing – within reason. 'Who?'

'Gene Henderson's sister.'

'Gene Henderson, the rock star?'

'Apparently, the sister lives here in LA. Must be in her mid-to-late seventies.'

'Okay, I think I can sort that,' Alex said, hooked despite himself, keen to discover what Henderson's involvement was.

'Thank you,' said Lara, kissing him on the neck. Alex felt it right down to his toes. He turned to her, kissing back. Maybe there was something in this story after all. And maybe it was worth risking the wrath of LA PRs and Simon Desai. For the moment, at least.

Chapter 33

Point Studios was a surprise. Martha had been to plenty of photographic studios over the years – with celebrity profiles, magazines liked to kill two birds with one stone and do their cover shoot at the same time as the interview. In Martha's day, studios were usually converted city centre lofts with wooden floors, high windows, a couple of tripods, and a plate of sandwiches if you were lucky. Point looked more like a high-end car showroom. Hidden behind automated gates in an industrial area on the outskirts of West Hollywood, it was a low white box with shiny glass doors. Martha felt under-dressed just approaching the front.

'Ms Riding?' the security guard flashed her a perfect white smile. 'I'm Jason, welcome to the studios.'

None of this would have been remarkable in any other corporate environment, but this security guard was gorgeous. With perfect cheekbones, flawless hair, and a smooth complexion, he should be emoting from the cover of a million-selling album rather than guarding the door.

'I'm here to see Cora Bryant,' she said. 'The photographer?'

'Of course, if you just like to head up the steps to reception,' he said. 'Emily will take care of you from there.'

'Oh, uh. Thanks.'

Martha walked up the wide white stone stairs and into the perfectly chilled box of the reception area. It was as calm and airy as a high-end spa, the minimal reception desk a solid black slab uncluttered by anything as passe as a computer screen or appointment book.

'Ms Riding!' said the receptionist, standing to greet her. 'I'm Emily, it's good to meet you,' she added in a way that, incredibly, sounded sincere.

Of course, Emily was also model-grade beautiful. Martha was beginning to feel a little like that one time she had tried peyote: it was as if the world had tilted slightly on its axis. With an open gesture, Emily invited Martha to walk with her along the corridor, her five-inch heels clicking as they went.

'I'm afraid Cora is rather busy this morning,' she said. 'A shoot starts at ten. She's already prepping, and the models have just arrived, so she can only spare a few minutes. But she can't wait to see you.'

Martha glanced across, surprised.

'She said that?'

'Absolutely. I understand you are old friends?'

'Yes, I suppose…yes.'

Martha and Cora had never been friends. In the Malibu House days, Cora made it clear that she believed journalists were part of the establishment, lap-dogs of 'The Man' keeping the hippies down. Martha meanwhile saw Cora as a hanger-on who got lucky, sinking her claws into starry Gene Henderson and riding him all the way, ending up as his defacto manager, a classic rock Svengali and ultimately his wife. Martha's assessment hadn't changed much when, after Gene's death, Cora had leveraged Gene's contacts to reinvent herself as a rock photographer, swiftly side-stepping into the world of art and fashion. So Martha had been slightly shocked when Cora had agreed to speak to her about Verity. Or perhaps it was just business: Martha could admit that her name still had some clout and yes, she was connected. Cora was the sort who would never upset someone if they could one day do something for her.

'Must have been exciting times back then,' said Emily as if she were reading Martha's mind.

'Yeah, it was pretty cool. But it looks like things have changed quite a bit since then.'

'Oh, I think it's pretty much the same. Cora likes to keep it 'old-school' – Emily framed the phrase with finger quotes. 'Just point the camera and shoot, that's what she says. It seems to work pretty well.'

That was an understatement. Photography had been 'working' for Cora for the past few decades. Her speciality was now portraiture, making her name for coaxing unexpected or spontaneous poses from her subjects. Her subjects were a who's who of popular culture past and present: Kanye, Debbie Harry, Sidney Poitier. Even Martha had to concede Cora's shot of Kurt and Courtney entwined in bed was hauntingly beautiful.

Martha turned as she heard a shout from the open double doors at the end of the passage. 'More light on the left! No, MORE!'

Martha felt a tingling along her scalp: that voice transported her back. Cora shouting at Gene, shutting him down. Emily gave Martha a rueful smile as they stepped into the studio. 'Cora knows what she wants.'

Emily's assessment of 'old school' was either wildly modest or things really had changed since Martha was last in a photographic studio. It was cavernous, like an aircraft hangar and lit up like a movie set, cables snaking back and forth across the pristine concrete floor. Marooned in the centre was what looked like an oasis: palm trees, ferns, and a dune's-worth of sand had been artfully laid out in an Arabian Nights fantasy.

'It's a shoot for Impala, the beauty brand,' said Emily. 'Technically, I should get you to sign an NDA, but as you're an old friend of Cora's...' She gave Martha another winning smile. Just then, Cora walked into view, carrying a camera with a huge lens, twisting to fire off a buzz of shots from different angles while barking instructions at her entourage. Seeing Martha, Cora handed her camera to an assistant and clapped her hands. 'Five minutes, everyone, then we need to begin.'

'Martha,' she beamed, pulling Martha into a brief hug, then held her at arm's length, inspecting her.

'God, you haven't even aged a day. Seriously.'

There was a pause, and then Martha snorted.

'Still full of shit then,' she said.

In the corner of her eye, Martha saw Emily freeze, and then Cora burst out laughing.

'Yeah, sorry,' Cora chuckled. 'It gets to be a habit in this world.'

Martha took a moment to assess her. Cora had changed, of course, but she still had the same long dark hair, albeit now streaked with grey. Cora had always been tall and thin, but she seemed even more angular, bones jutting from tanned skin, the effect emphasised by her clothes: a crisp white shirt with the sleeves half-rolled and wide-legged pants over scuffed motorcycle boots. For a thirty-year-old, she would have looked achingly chic, but Cora must have been around seventy-five, and the look fitted perfectly with Cora's minimal but high-tech studio. Martha felt a stab of envy: Cora Bryant was still making it happen for Cora; she was at the peak of her powers.

Meanwhile, Martha Riding barely inspired a shrug from the publishing world.

'Come on, I can give you ten minutes,' Cora barked, striding past Martha through another doorway and onto an open terrace shaded by giant sculptural umbrellas.

Cora threw herself down on a white sofa and, as if by magic, another gorgeous operative appeared with a tray of what looked like iced health drinks, then melted away.

'So. I have to say I was surprised when you called,' said Cora, 'Pleased, but surprised. Why has it taken so damn long?'

'I guess we had to wait for the 50th anniversary of Verity's death.'

This was the cover story Martha and Lara had concocted: they were working on a retrospective that would run in the London Chronicle, a celebration of Verity's music, her style, and the people she had nurtured into countercultural icons. The idea had been flattering enough to get Martha past Cora's PR guard dogs. Ice cubes tinkled as Cora took a sip of her drink.

'Do you see anyone else from those days?'

'Not really,' said Martha. 'Griffin and I went off down the literary avenue, Todd Mayfield went into acting, you went – well, here. It's easy to lose touch.'

'Ain't that the truth?' said Cora, all business now. 'So what can I tell you about Verity you don't already know?'

Martha took a beat, then smiled. 'Honestly? I don't want to know about Verity; I want to know about you.'

Flatter, flatter, flatter: that had always been Griffin's approach to interviewing. Martha's style had been more abrasive, more point-blank, asking the difficult questions, but Cora was far too savvy for that. Martha needed to slide up on her blind side.

'Why don't we start by telling me how you got here.'

'Luck, I guess.'

'Luck?'

'When Gene died, I moved to Paris and hung out with artists and poets, but I didn't speak the language, so I'd take photos of them instead,' she shrugged. 'Then I came back to LA, set up this place in an old bus garage, and God, forty years on, we're handling some of the biggest editorial and commercial clients in the business.'

This was Cora's official story, worn smooth in the telling, but Martha still couldn't separate her from the Cora of the Canyon years. That girl had been quiet, bird-like, sitting in the background, her smoky kohl-lined eyes always watching Gene, frightened to let him out of her sight. Martha remembered hearing the sharp admonishments from behind closed doors – 'Gene, no!' – but in public, she barely spoke. There had been little hint of the confident, cocky Cora lounging in front of her. Although the eyes were still watching, Martha felt that strongly.

'I think my lucky break was when I met Andy just before he died.'

'Andy Warhol?'

'Who else? Those pictures were used a lot after he passed, and showed people what I could do.'

Martha nodded. Cora was obviously talented, but it can't have hurt that, as Gene Henderson's next-of-kin, she had inherited his estate. The ongoing royalties to some of the most played songs of the decade would have given her industry contacts and the money to buy this studio. But was that just cynicism? Martha had to admit she'd felt a touch of envy as she'd watched Cora working. Her minions hung on her every word, and Cora herself had the air of an artist, someone with magic at her fingertips. Over the past decade, Martha had begun to suspect her own career had fallen off due to ageism, the belief that older people lacked relevance or an artistic cutting edge. And yet here was Cora, thriving in her 70s; the fact that she was older gave her more gravitas, not less. It didn't feel like Cora Bryant was at the end of her career; it looked like she was just beginning.

'Man, 50 years on, and I still can't believe Verity's gone,' said Cora.

'You were there that day, right? What do you remember?'

Martha kept it light and casual, just getting context.

'We got there early,' said Cora. 'Hung out on the beach. I remember burning my nose in the sun, so I had to go inside.'

Martha thought of the footage she had seen at Bobby's place: Gene and Verity singing around the piano, Cora lurking at the back, sticking to Gene like glue. But then why wouldn't she? Gene Henderson was handsome, charismatic and going places. She could hardly blame Cora for wanting to hold on. Maybe success was that simple: aligning yourself with the right people.

'Why are you asking anyway? Weren't you there too?' asked Cora.

'No, Griff and I had been for dinner, we turned up just as everyone was leaving. Do you know why Verity cut the party short?'

'I heard she'd had a row with Benny,' said Cora in a gossipy tone. 'You know, Benny Dean, from the band? I didn't see them argue, but someone told me they were at each other's throats again.'

Martha nodded. It matched the story Donna told Lara, although Eliot's version of events still made much more sense.

'Then what? The Troubadour? I heard everyone went on there after Verity's.'

'No, Gene and I went back to my place after the party. I think someone told me about Benny at Verity's memorial service. People tried to be discreet, but it was all anyone wanted to know. Why did Vee end the party?'

'And what did you think of the rumours of an overdose?'

Cora sipped her drink.

'I don't know, but whatever happened that night was such a waste,' she said quietly. 'Verity drank but didn't really do drugs. But if she did, I think it had to be an accident. And believe me, I know how easily that can happen. One minute, I had Gene; the next minute, I'd lost him, and I never even got to say goodbye.'

For a moment, Martha could see Cora's pain. She knew how Gene Henderson had struggled with fame, dying of complications related to alcohol and drug abuse in a New York hotel suite just a few years after Verity.

Martha reached across and touched Cora's hand.

'We could all have done things differently. No one is to blame.'

Cora nodded sadly. 'I just wish…Oh crap!' She looked at her watch and jumped up.

'It's been great seeing you, Martha, genuinely, but I've got to finish this Impala shoot on time because I've got a Korean boy band coming in this afternoon to shoot their album cover.' She clutched Martha's arm. 'And it's great we're celebrating everything good that came out of that beach house. That's how Vee should be remembered.'

She steered Martha back towards the studio where, inevitably, Emily was waiting, smile in place.

'Listen, why don't you come along to the opening of my show?' said Cora. 'It's at the Savage, the new gallery downtown? Kind of a retrospective. It'd be great to see you again – and dumb if we left it another fifty years.'

'Absolutely,' said Martha, 'I'll be there.'

But Cora was already off, moving on to the next thing, leaving Martha in her wake.

Chapter 34

Summer sat with her hands on the steering wheel, willing them to stop shaking. The morning sun slanted through the trees in front of her mother's house, dappling the hood of Summer's Merc.

'Dammit,' she whispered. Summer wished she'd thought to have coffee before she had driven over. She wished she had managed to sleep after the visit from Eliot Jones the previous night. She wished fate had gifted her a different mother.

'If wishes were horses…' Summer squeezed her eyes tight. *What was the rest of that phrase*? She banged the flat of her hand on the dash in frustration.

She had been angry with her mother before; of course she had. Donna Phelps was the kind of woman who often inspired rage, especially if you had to live with her. Donna was a narcissist, prone to emotional manipulation and sudden outbursts if things didn't go her way. It was like riding a rollercoaster without seatbelts: Summer's fingertips were raw from clinging on. But this thing with Eliot? This was something else.

'How could you?' Summer whispered out loud. 'How *could* you keep this from me?'

And, of course, she knew the answer to that one. Donna had lied – to her daughter, to Todd and to the world – simply because it suited Donna. Just like everything else in her life. And because Donna was her mother, Summer had always indulged her because it made life easier. But this was too big to ignore.

'No more,' she said, popping the door and heading into the house. Summer had her own key. Donna had given it freely because it allowed Summer to water the plants, to adjust the temperature, and to deal with pool maintenance. Because it allowed Summer to act like Donna's PA.

'Mom?'

The big entrance hall echoed with Summer's footsteps. It was a roomy Colonial with a red slate roof and cool terracotta floor tiles, bought with the proceeds from her last licensing deal, Donna Phelps Gourmet: chopping boards and spiralisers for the suburban earth mother.

'MOM!'

Donna walked down the curved stairway, tying a silk robe around her. Her blonde hair was in disarray.

'Don't shout, Summer,' she groaned. 'Mommy has a headache.'

Donna pressed three fingers against her forehead with a theatrically pained expression. 'And what time is it anyway?'

'Early,' said Summer. 'Come down here, we need to talk.'

She saw Donna pause momentarily, just a hitch in the rhythm as she descended the steps, then she tightened her robe.

'First, I need my juice,' she said. 'And where are those pills? The big green ones not the blue ones, they make me all fuzzy.'

‘Just come and sit down,’ said Summer, heading her off as she crossed the living room.

‘What? I’m not going to…’

‘I said *sit down*!’

Summer never shouted. She never needed to. But right now, she felt like she was standing on the edge, all ten toes over the abyss. Donna blinked in surprise, took three rapid backwards steps, then fell into a caramel suede sofa, arms splayed, like she’d dropped from the top deck of the Titanic. No opportunity for drama was ever missed.

‘Well!’ Donna huffed, ‘I don’t know what makes you think you can talk to me like that.’

‘Let me fill you in, shall I?’ said Summer. ‘Guess who came to visit me last night? Eliot Jones. He told me all about that night at the Joshua Tree.’

Donna’s face froze in an open-book expression of shock and fear. And immediately, Summer knew it was true – all of it. If Summer had doubts about the truth of Eliot’s revelations, they disappeared at that moment like a soap bubble popping.

‘God, it’s true, isn’t it?’ said Summer. ‘He *is* my father.’

Summer saw Donna’s mind working, wondering if she could wriggle out of it and Summer let out a bitter laugh.

‘Don’t bother dreaming up some excuse, Donna,’ she said. ‘I’ve had enough of your lies.’

‘Lies? How dare you!’

‘Why not? You told Eliot he was the father, but when he didn’t bite, you let Todd believe he was my father.’

‘Todd *is* your father, Summer!’

‘Yes, he is, and thank God for that,’ said Summer with passion. ‘And whatever typical screwed-up Donna Phelps scenario this is, it will change nothing: Todd will always be my father. But I think, after fifty years, I deserve to know who my biological father is, don’t you?’

Donna looked sullen and defiant, a child caught

stealing a lollipop. Suddenly feeling drained, Summer sat down on the sofa opposite her.

'Why didn't you just tell me, Mom? I've given you so many chances over the years, asking about my past.'

Donna crossed her arms like a toddler building up to a tantrum. She glanced at Summer and immediately saw that particular approach wouldn't work, so she changed tack.

'Yes, something happened between Eliot and me in the desert; he had always loved me. And yes, I got pregnant around that time. But I kept it to myself because I was just a scared young woman,' Donna cried, her voice suddenly wobbling.

'You didn't keep it yourself, Mom,' said Summer, crossing her arms. 'You told Eliot.'

'Yes, I suppose,' she said vaguely as if it were a minor detail, 'And yes, when he decided not to further our relationship, I let people believe Todd was the father – but I *had* to, Summer. In those days, Society said you had to have a partner.'

Summer snorted.

'Don't try to make this a feminist issue. It was 1970s California, not 1920s Alabama – and you were a pop singer. No one would have even raised an eyebrow if you were a single mother.'

'I went with Eliot because my relationship with Todd was failing,' she said. 'I needed to support you.'

'More like Todd's career wasn't taking off in the way that you thought.'

'It wasn't like that.'

'Oh no? Then what was it like?' asked Summer.

Donna's bottom lip started to wobble.

'Imagine how I felt. The band had split up, I felt low, I had no direction, no future, and Todd was never at home, always hawking himself around the studios trying to get noticed. But Eliot was always around; from the beginning, he always made me feel better. You know he discovered me?' she said, looking up. Summer didn't – she hardly knew anything. Donna had always been vague about how she had become part of the Laurel Canyon sound, preferring to cultivate the myth that celebrity had just *found* her.

'I moved to LA when I was just 17,' she said. 'I thought I would become a model or a beauty queen, but they said I was too short for fashion. I was thrown out of two apartments for not paying the rent, but there was no way I could afford it. Sometimes, I just slept with men, so I had somewhere to stay.'

'Mom…'

'For a week, I roughed it in Venice Beach, and I got assaulted twice.'

Donna paused, a tear swelling in her eye – genuine this time, Summer thought.

'And then I met Eliot in a bar on Sunset. He told me he was in a group, and I told him I could sing. The next thing I knew, he had introduced me to Verity and Benny Dean, and we were a hot new foursome. Eliot and I…we always had a connection, and that weekend in the Joshua Tree, it just got the better of us.'

'He wasn't in love with you though, was he? It was a one-night stand, and he regretted it. Isn't that what really happened?'

Donna looked down, playing with the hem of her robe.

'He was under Verity's spell.'

Summer vividly remembered all of her mother's previous lovers. They were either extremely wealthy and powerful or very handsome, almost beautiful men. Eliot Jones didn't fit into either category.

'Isn't the truth that you were just jealous of Verity?' said Summer. 'You weren't attracted to Eliot. You just wanted to get back at Verity for leaving the band and starting to have success?'

Donna shot a look of spite at Summer.

'Is that what you think of your mother?'

Summer gave her a level look.

'Yes, Donna. It is.'

'Then well done,' she said, clapping her hands sarcastically. 'You're right. So you want the truth after all this time? Alright then – sure. I was sick of all the attention Verity got, the plaudits and the recognition of her 'genius'.' Donna made finger quotes around the word, and her face twisted into a sneer. '*I* was the one who got The Virginians noticed,' she insisted. '*I* was the magic ingredient in that band. Before I came along, they were nothing, but when I stood on that stage, suddenly, everyone wanted to know our name. But then Verity wrote a few stupid songs, and I was just some pretty face. Do you know how it feels to be dismissed like that?'

Are you kidding? Thought Summer. Her mother had spent her entire life dismissing and undermining her – she knew exactly how it felt. But Summer was intimately familiar with her mother's strategies, and she knew if she called her out on them, Donna might well shut down and give her the silent treatment—and Summer needed answers right now.

'Please, Mom,' she said, trying to take the heat out of the conversation. 'Tell me: is Eliot my father?'

Donna shrugged. 'Probably,' she said.

'Just probably?'

'Alright, yes. It had to be Eliot because Todd called me up years later. He said he was trying to conceive with his new wife.'

'Julianne.'

'Is that her name?' said Donna innocently. 'Anyway, the doctor said Todd was the problem because Julianne already had a daughter from another marriage. So, I told Todd about Eliot. Actually, I think that's the last time we spoke.'

Summer swallowed. Todd knew? He'd known all this time, and he'd never said anything? Then Summer felt her heart swell because this was different. Donna and Eliot had kept quiet to protect themselves, but Todd had kept quiet to protect *her*. She turned back to Donna, a cold fury taking hold of her.

'Tell me about Verity,' she said.

She saw another flare of anxiety in her mother's eyes.

'Verity? I told you about her. I don't see what else she's got to do with any of this.'

'You told Verity that Eliot had got you knocked up on the night she *died*, Mom! That sounds pretty damn significant to me.'

'I hope you're not suggesting I had anything to do with her death!' Donna instantly became emotional. 'Because Verity was my best friend,' she said, her bottom lip wavering. 'I loved her.'

To her surprise, Summer felt nothing as her mother sobbed.

'Best friend?' she said. 'Gleefully telling Verity that you'd screwed her husband doesn't sound very sisterly.'

Donna's tears immediately stopped, replaced by a twisted smile.

'And what do you think I should have done? Kept quiet about it? Let Eliot get away with it? All I wanted was for that cheater to stand up and take responsibility for what he'd done. And I wanted to let Verity know what sort of man she was still married to. I was *saving* her from heartache, don't you see? Showing her what a rat he was before she got hooked back up with him.'

Summer had enough experience with Donna's mind games to know that, at this moment, Donna believed this completely: an innocent princess seduced by the beast in the woods. Seeing Summer's stony face, Donna barked out a laugh.

'Oh, you wouldn't understand. Little Summer, always had it so easy. Everything handed to you on a plate.'

'Easy?' gasped Summer. 'You think I've had it easy? I've spent my entire life looking after you, Donna. Dealing with your overblown catastrophes, cleaning up your petty little dramas, lying for you again and again - when I should just have been growing up.'

'You see? Still so selfish. Everything has to be about you.'

Finally, it hit Summer like a blow. Summer had always told herself that Donna was damaged, thin-skinned and artistic; she had done her best to help her, shield her, to fix her endless screw-ups – and she had guided her, managed her, negotiated her contracts, rubbed her Godamn shoulders - and never once had Donna thanked her. Never once had she acknowledged Summer's part in her success. And now she knew why. Her mother could only ever think about herself.

'You know, it's amazing,' said Summer.

'What is?'

'It's amazing that I've turned out sane. After a lifetime following you with a shit-shovel, I should be a total basket case, in rehab or on my second marriage.'

'Like Todd?' sneered Donna.

'I wish,' said Summer. 'Todd has a loving family around him who care for him because he's a wonderful man, no other reason. That's a role model, right there.'

Summer stood up.

'You're going?' said Donna. 'But I'm having a *crisis*. You can't just leave.'

Summer smiled at her.

'Yes, I can. All this time, I could have just walked away – and I never did. Wow.'

'Summer!' Donna wailed. '*Summer, come back*!'

Summer stopped, felt in her pocket, and then dropped her mother's keys on the coffee table with a clatter.

'From now on, you can water your own plants,' she said.

Chapter 35

The Venice canals were strange but beautiful. It was as if an alien hand had scooped up an entire section of another city and dropped it into Los Angeles. Connected to the 'mainland' by a series of elegantly curved foot-bridges, the only vehicle you could use to access the canals was a canoe or maybe a pedalo, and consequently, it felt wonderfully disengaged from 21st century life. Lara paused at the mid-point of the bridge in the far eastern corner, taking in the palms reflected in the green water and cute little houses clustered along the edges. Some were tiny, little more than summer houses, but given their location, Lara guessed they all had hefty price tags. She didn't know how Della Henderson could afford such a desirable home; then again, she knew plenty of older people back home in Chelsea who had bought a flat on Flood St or Cheyne Row for less than £10,000 in the Swinging Sixties.

'Number 24. Here we go,' said Lara, stopping outside a quaint cottage painted a bright yellow and surrounded by bamboo plants, their spear-shaped leaves waving in the breeze. She unlatched the white gate in front of Della

Henderson's house, walking up the short path to the front door, already open.

'Hello?'

A woman rose from a sofa and Lara was immediately struck by the family resemblance. Dark hair fell in curls, high cheekbones and sharp blue eyes. She came forward, hand extended.

'Lara? I'm Della, did you find it alright? It's a maze, isn't it? Can I get you a drink? I'm drinking iced tea, but I have Pepsi somewhere, I think… '

The questions all came at Lara in a rush. Lara had expected hostility and resistance from Della, declarations that it 'was all a long time ago', that she didn't have anything to add to all the other blood-sucking journalists she had encountered over the decades. Instead, Della Henderson was as welcoming and warm as the interior of the little house. The living room was cosy, with soft couches and photos adorning every wall.

'Let's sit by the water, shall we?' said Della, bringing a jug of tea and leading Lara to a section of raised decking with chairs upholstered in leaf green.

'It's funny,' she said, settling down and sipping her drink. 'Yours was the second call I had this week about Gene.'

'It was? Who else called you?'

Della frowned.

'Oh, some online retailer wanting to use Gene's music to sell cars or pop tarts, whatever. I'm like' – Della made a chopping motion with her hand – 'No way, Jose.'

She smiled at Lara.

'Not that I own a single note of Gene's music; I just hope it will put them off. Because people love those songs, you know? People fell *in* love to those songs. Gene's songs mean something. Advertising Lucky Charms would demean the whole thing, don't you think?'

Good for you, thought Lara.

'So what can I do for you?' asked Della, taking a drink. 'You're a journalist?'

'I'm sorry,' said Lara, and Della laughed out loud.

'It's the first time I've heard that.'

'It's the first time I've apologised,' Lara smiled.

She immediately felt an affinity with the woman – also not a given with interview subjects – as Della quickly filled her in on the Henderson family history. Della was two years older than Gene and had never had anything to do with the music industry. Instead, she had gone straight into academia, just like her parents, after completing her doctorate at USC.

'I was as straight as Gene was rebellious,' she said. 'My parents just couldn't understand when Gene announced he wanted to be a rock star, although my friends immediately understood - Gene was so handsome. He announced it at dinner one night: 'Mom, Dad? I'm going to be a star!' Mom was like: 'That's nice dear - more mashed potatoes?'

'But didn't he go to college?'

'Oh yes. He got a place to study at UCLA, but I think that was just a cover story to get him out west with his guitar. Predictably enough, he dropped out after his first year and moved to Laurel Canyon. My Mom and Dad used to worry so much about that; they'd heard stories about these hippy communes. Mom used to send him socks and toothpaste as if it would somehow save him.'

She paused and looked straight at Lara with a kindly smile.

'So you're doing an anniversary piece on Verity?' she said.

Lara simply nodded, hating all the subterfuge necessary to interview anyone for her Malibu House story.

'I heard Gene and Verity were close.'

'Oh yes, Verity was like part big sister, part mentor. She

spotted Gene singing at some bar – apparently, he'd got drunk and jumped on stage, but Verity took him to one side afterwards and told him that he had talent and should stick at it. From what Gene used to tell me, she encouraged his songwriting, came to his gigs, persuaded him to stay solo when he lost faith and started looking for a band. You've got to remember Verity was a star then, so her support meant a huge deal to Gene and all those other kids in the canyon. He was devastated when she died.'

That made Lara think of her night at Bobby's.

'This is a weird question, but did Gene have a motorbike?'

Della blinked in surprise. 'Sure. You want to see it?'

Lara gaped at her.

'It's here?'

'Sure. Just next door – come on.'

Putting down her glass, Della beckoned Lara into the house. Passing through the living room and into a little kitchen, Della opened a side door into a tiny garage. It smelled of oil and grass cuttings, tools neatly lined along the walls.

'It's under here,' she said, pulling off a dusty tarpaulin to reveal an old Triumph. *The* Triumph: Lara immediately recognised it from Bobby's video.

'Does it still go?'

Lara entertained a fantasy of kicking it into life and immediately hearing it backfire in confirmation of her 'gunshot' theory – something like JFK's magic bullet or OJ's gloves.

'I haven't started it in years. Gene left it at my place once when he was on a break from Cora. They'd have a screaming row, and he'd crash at mine. Then he'd go crawling back and leave stuff behind. The bike was one of those things that just stayed.'

'Cora: that's Cora Bryant, his wife?'

Della snorted.

'If you can call her that.'

'You wouldn't?'

'Put it this way, when I think of Cora, I see one of those carrion birds hunched over a lion.'

Martha seemed to have a similar view of Cora Bryant. The way Martha and Bobby had explained it over pizza, Cora had been one of the many pretty hippy chicks hanging around the periphery of the Canyon-Malibu scene; Cora had been lucky enough to latch onto Gene Henderson. And, rumour had it, to introduce him to drugs. Della ran a hand over the bike's dusty black tank. 'I guess it should be in a museum or something, but…it's hard to let it go. It feels like part of him, you know?'

Lara did. She'd had enough of her own personal pain over the years, and there were certain things she treasured, too. Her mum's silver hairbrush, her dad's copy of The Wasteland, annotated in the margins, even her cat's milk saucer. She'd never part with any of them.

'Luckily, I have this place to store it,' said Della, looking up at the garage's shelves.

'It's a great house,' said Lara, deciding that it reminded her of her Chelsea houseboat.

'Did you know Gene bought it for me?'

'Wow. That's generous.'

'Gene was like that. When he started making serious money, he paid off my parents' mortgage and bought me this place. I like to think of it as half his. He always loved the water.'

Della covered the bike again and led Lara back into the kitchen, filling a kettle. Lara gave her space, turning to the framed photographs on the walls. They were mostly conventional family shots – young Gene and Della cross-legged under the Christmas tree, Gene and their parents posing on a beach – but there were also shots featuring a slightly older, hippy Gene, bearded and careworn, but his eyes still shone.

'Where's this photo from?' she called. Della popped her head around the door.

'God, I don't know, maybe when he was at The Chelsea? I visited him there once. Near the end.'

'Did you get his effects afterwards?'

'No, all that stuff from the hotel mysteriously disappeared. All his guitars and his clothes. I guess Cora sold them for smack.'

That stopped Lara: she'd heard the rumours about Cora's involvement in drugs, but no one had come out and said it before.

'Was Cora an addict?'

'Always was. Certainly as long as Gene knew her.'

Della's words were harsh, full of anger.

'Do you blame Cora for Gene's addiction?'

Della took a breath and let it out.

'No,' she said finally. 'Gene was a grown-up; he made his own choices. To be honest, I don't think he ever recovered from Verity's death. That was when he started drinking heavily. Not just on a Saturday night, but all the time. His drug use escalated then, too. Gene was so powerful and magnetic on stage, but he was so sensitive underneath.'

As his sister made tea, Lara walked around the room, stopping at a gold frame. Inside was a single sheet of paper covered with slanting handwriting and chords written above. Lara felt her heart jump.

'O.M.G.' She breathed, 'Is this what I think it is?'

Della looked up and shrugged.

'The original music and lyrics to 'Time For Change'? Yep – at least I think so.'

Lara gazed at it wide-eyed, her scalp tingling. The notepaper inside the frame was a little creased, and the writing was careless, as if it had been dashed off quickly with multiple crossings-out. Also, curiously, it was written in purple ink; perhaps Gene had just grabbed the nearest pen when the muse struck. But it was unmistakably the song that had launched Gene's career and remained his best-known tune. A song which defined a decade.

'I found that in a suitcase Gene left at my place once when he came to stay after another row with Cora,' said Della. 'I just pushed it under the guest bed and didn't even open it until...well, until he was gone.'

'Gosh, Della. If this is the actual paper that Gene wrote the song on, it will be worth a fortune,' said Lara. She remembered reading that Bob Dylan's lyrics for 'Like A Rolling Stone' had sold for millions. 'I'm not sure you should have it on your kitchen wall like this, anyway.'

Della smiled and shrugged.

'But what good is it stuck in some climate-controlled vault? This way, I get to have a little bit of Gene in my life every single day.'

Della looked at it, tilting her head. 'It's pretty cool though, isn't it? Funnily enough, I always thought he wrote it about Verity.'

'Really?'

Lara looked more closely at the lyrics. She'd never thought of it that way, but it made sense. The key line in the chorus: *The clock on the wall is moving too fast.*

Lara thought of Bobby's Super 8 film, Gene and Cora sitting under Verity's clock, that oddball gift from Dennis Wilson. It was a perfect metaphor for a life run out too soon.

'Can I take a picture of it?' said Lara, holding up her phone.

'I'd rather it didn't go in any newspaper.'

'No, no - I wanted to show it to my friend Martha

Riding. She was friends with Gene back in the Malibu House days.'

'Martha Riding the writer?'

Lara nodded.

'My goodness, I love her work. Of course, snap away.'

Lara took a photo of it and sent it by text to Martha.

'You know, it's been good to talk,' said Della after a moment. 'I don't have many people I can talk to – not about Gene, anyway. His whole life was that music crowd, and I don't know any of them.'

'I take it you don't see Cora?'

Della's lip curled.

'No. It all got a bit unpleasant after he died. Cora contested the will. Gene had left something to me and mom and dad, but Cora challenged it and the judge ruled in her favour because she was his wife, even though it was some ceremony in Bali that didn't sound particularly legal.'

She sighed.

'Still, at least I have Bert.'

'Bert?'

'Bert Walters, Gene's roommate at UCLA. I guess you'd say he was Gene's best friend. Remained close with Gene until the end. Bert's a good guy, a scriptwriter. We see each other now and then, talk about…' Della squeezed her eyes shut. 'Sorry,' she said. 'Forty-some years on, you'd think it'd get easier, wouldn't you?'

'I should go,' said Lara, touching her arm. 'If I have any more questions, can I call you?'

'Anytime,' she smiled. 'The only thing I ask in return is to be kind to Gene when you're writing your story. My brother was brilliant, but he was lost. And when we're lost, we're easily led.'

Chapter 36

'He's just an old friend, Becca,' said Martha. She took the phone away from her ear as her friend laughed down the line. It was just past sunset on Martha's balcony and the beach ahead was deserted, just a gathering of plovers at the waterline, the birds' elegant shapes silhouetted by the orange light of a near-drowned sun.

'Sure, Martha,' Rebecca deadpanned. 'Just an old friend you've seen twice in two days. And what is it tonight? An intimate dinner, just the two of you?'

'Well, if you put it like that,' said Martha, a smile in her voice. She had to admit that she was excited about the prospect of Bobby coming over. She had enjoyed the taco night at his place, even if it had been a culinary disaster. 'But it's not a date.'

'That so? Well, let me ask you this: did you spend more time than usual choosing your lingerie?'

'Rebecca!' gasped Martha.

'I'll take that as a 'yes'.

Martha had spent more than an hour getting ready, which was about an hour longer than she usually spent. Bath, hair, make-up and, yes, underwear, then a beautiful blue Yves Saint Laurent dress from what Martha liked to call 'the carousel' – the walk-in wardrobe from which nothing was ever banished: eventually, it all came around again.

'I have no plans for anyone to see my undergarments,' said Martha primly. 'My undergarments are in full retirement. I am still a married woman.'

'Hmm, yes,' said Rebecca with disapproval. 'Well, that's always been your problem, hasn't it?'

Not always, Martha wanted to say. She hadn't meant her mourning to stretch into years; she just hadn't been able to adjust to life without Griff. And then suddenly, one day, Martha looked around and found that's exactly what had happened - she had become used to living alone. The idea of bringing anyone else into her life just didn't compute. Girlfriends like Rebecca had gently suggested dipping a toe into the dating pool, but Martha had ducked the subject and made excuses. There just wasn't room in her life for anything like that.

'So anyway, I was talking to Sylvie,' said Rebecca, clearly tired of her teasing.

Martha's ears pricked up: Sylvie was one of their more gossipy friends – and one of the most connected. She always had scurrilous tales about celebrities who had some secret kink or mutual acquaintances who were having ill-advised affairs with senators.

'What's Sylvie heard now?'

'No scandal this time – well, not really. Sylvie bumped into Harley in Carmel today and he was asking after you. Seems you made an impression on Sunday.'

'Really?' Martha was genuinely surprised: she had rather expected Harley to cut her dead after her hurried exit from his grand mansion. 'I thought he would be furious.'

'Treat 'em mean and keep 'em keen,' said Rebecca.

'Anyway, Harley wanted to know if you were going to the Limelight launch?'

'Why? Is *he* going?'

'Sounds like it. Maybe you could go together?'

'Together? Like a date?'

'You could do worse,' said Rebecca. 'Come on, you've seen the house. I looked on one of those satellite apps and it barely fit on the screen.'

Martha sighed.

'I think I'd be exhausted just walking from the kitchen to the bedroom.'

'Ah-ha!' said Rebecca. 'So you *are* thinking about the bedroom!'

Ding dong.

Martha turned as her doorbell chimed.

'Oh, that is sad,' she said to Rebecca. 'I must go – someone at the door.'

'So *are* you going to Limelight?' said Rebecca quickly. 'Harley wants to know. Says he will be in LA for a couple of days.'

'Let's see how tonight goes, hmm? One man at a time.'

'Oh honey, at our age, we *do* need to speed up.'

Smiling, Martha clicked off and hurried down to the entrance, pausing to inspect her reflection in the full-length mirror. She supposed she didn't look too bad. Misery had kept her lean, and nature had done the rest.

'It'll have to do,' she whispered and opened the door. Bobby was wearing a sports coat and holding a huge bunch of sunflowers.

His smile said everything: he was just pleased to be there. Martha smiled back.

'These are for you.'

'Well, thank you, kind sir,' said Martha, taking the bouquet and ushering Bobby inside.

'I'll admit I froze in the florist,' he said, 'Then I saw

those, and I just thought 'Now, they are *so* Martha.' He stopped, obviously thinking he had said too much. Martha touched his arm. 'They're lovely. My favourites.'

Peonies were her favourites, but there was plenty of time for Bobby to find that out. She buried her face in the flowers to hide a blush; was she really thinking about Bobby in such a long-term capacity already?

Go with the flow, Martha Riding, she thought to herself. Maybe Rebecca was right; maybe it was time she got back on the horse. *That* thought brought on another flush, and she practically ran into the kitchen to put the flowers in water.

'Oh, and of course - this is yours too.'

Bobby held up her orange scarf, which she had left at his place the night before. Bobby had volunteered to return it, and Martha saw it as a perfect excuse to cook supper.

'I didn't leave it deliberately, you know.'

'The thought never crossed my mind,' he said with an innocent expression.

Martha poured them both generous glasses of wine and Bobby sat at the breakfast bar to watch as Martha busied herself fixing a simple pasta dish.

'So how have you been spending your day?' she asked.

'I was in Burbank working on a movie,' said Bobby. 'Technically, I'm retired, but one of my pals asked me to come over and help with an edit. It was fun to get involved again.'

'What was it? Some gigantic blockbuster?'

'I'm sworn to secrecy, I'm afraid,' said Bobby, 'But no, not a blockbuster. More of an art house kind of thing: Oscar bait.'

'Sounds right up my street.'

Martha realised why she enjoyed talking to Bobby: he had no side. In her social world, even at the book club, everyone was showing off, trying to impress everyone else, to make sure everyone knew how wealthy or connected they were. Bobby just said what he thought. It was refreshing in the extreme.

'And you?' he asked. 'More detective work?'

'Well funnily enough, I was in the studio too: different kind though, photographic.'

She recounted her encounter with Cora at the space-age Point Studios.

'So you managed to get an audience with her. How was she?'

'Cora does seem to have grown into her skin. She's certainly not in Gene's shadow anymore.'

Martha told Bobby about the revelation she'd had watching Cora, how she was feted for being the grand dame of the visual arts. 'Meanwhile, my career feels as though it's on hiatus. Like I'm retired.'

'I didn't think writers ever retired.'

'Not willingly, but sometimes they *get* retired - put out to pasture. It's like suddenly, for no real reason, the volume of your voice gets turned down, you know?'

Bobby nodded.

'Yeah, I think that's a common theme amongst our generation. Back in the sixties and seventies, we could do no wrong. The world loved our energy and our new ideas, and for once, everyone seemed happy to sweep the old guard aside. But we're the old guard now, aren't we? We're the fuddy-duddies with our lame songs about peace and love. We're over the hill, Martha.'

She smiled. 'Speak for yourself, Bobby Franks. If Cora Bryant can still be cool at 75, I'm sure going to have a go too.'

'That's more like it!'

Bobby raised his hand for a high-five, and as Martha clapped against it, he let out a whoop. 'Flower power, baby!'

They broke out laughing. As she cooked, they began chatting about films and books, memories and dreams. Martha found it so easy to talk to him.

'The thing is, we know more stuff,' said Bobby as he forked up the last of Martha's ravioli. 'That's why my buddy Jonno called me up today. When he speaks to these hot young bucks just out of film school and mentions Bernard Hermann's work on Psycho…'

'Those shrieking strings in the shower scene?'

'Exactly,' said Bobby, pointing at her with his fork. 'Jonno says he's lucky if they've even heard of *Hitchcock* these days. The 80s is like their year zero: Blade Runner is like us watching Harold Lloyd.

Martha leant across to top up his wine.

'Well, here's to experience,' she said, chinking glasses. Bobby took a drink.

'So tell me, what did Cora have to say?' he asked. 'I'm guessing you asked her about Verity?'

'I did, but you'd guessed right: she wasn't forthcoming. She rattled out that same story Donna had about Benny getting drunk and yelling at Verity for splitting up The Virginians.'

'But?' Said Bobby, his eyes bright. 'I'm sensing here that Martha Riding's world-beating journalistic instincts were detecting something else?'

Martha shook her head; she wasn't sure. She had never liked Cora and feared that was colouring her judgement. Besides which, Martha wasn't all that sure she wanted there to *be* a story any more. She had been shaken by her visit to Eliot at the golf course, and his question still rang in her ears: what good did the truth do if it just made people miserable?

'So if you're doing all this high-class Nancy Drew stuff, what's Lara doing?' asked Bobby.

'She went to see Della Henderson, Gene's sister. And actually, she did find something pretty cool.'

She clicked on messages on her phone and showed Bobby the screen.

'Look what was on the wall of Della's kitchen. A piece of rock and roll history.'

'Damn, my reading glasses are in my jacket,' said Bobby, still squinting.

'It's the original composition of Time For Change.' Martha used her thumbs to increase the size of the image.

'Oh man…' he breathed. 'That is *awesome.*'

Martha laughed out loud.

He looked up. 'What d'I say?' he asked, embarrassed.

'Don't worry,' Martha grinned, 'It was a laugh of pleasure. Do you know how rare it is to see someone have such a reaction of excitement to anything these days? People are so cynical and reserved. It was lovely to see.'

Bobby blushed a little, then tapped on the screen.

'But why *wouldn't* you react that way? This is like the Dead Sea Scrolls or something. 'Time For Change' is the song of our generation. Even these kids that don't know 'Psycho' have heard 'Time For Change'.

Bobby gave her a sideways look.

'You should write about this,' he said. 'This is like Howard Carter opening Tutankhamun's tomb.'

Martha laughed. 'Not quite, but I suppose it *is* a treasure.'

'Seriously, it's an artefact that people of our generation would love to see. And who better to write about the significance it has?'

Martha felt a stab of sadness.

'I'm not sure anybody is interested in my words anymore, Bobby. You know, I thought my words would last forever. But then I thought the years would last too, but they just fly by now.'

'Hey,' said Bobby with a hint of reproach, 'Concentrate: we were talking about you and your genius, remember?'

Martha shook her head. 'I just don't feel *potent* any more. There was a time when I truly thought I could do anything – that we could do anything – when Griff and I would hold these salons full of artists, directors, and designers and it felt like the world was following in our wake.'

She looked at him, hands on hips.

'Do you know I was once even on the cover of Esquire magazine?'

Bobby's eyes opened wide, and he began choking on his wine.

'I'm sorry,' he spluttered. 'You were on the cover of... how? When?'

Martha laughed.

'Oh, don't get too excited; it was one of those group things they used to do, remember? 'Great American Writers' or something equally bombastic. There were six or seven of us: John Irvine, Don, and Griffin. I was the only woman. They stood me in the middle wearing a fabulous ballgown.'

'How did I miss this? What year was it? I must have been on location. Let's see if we can find it online,' he said, reaching for his phone.

'Why don't I show you the real thing?' said Martha impulsively. 'We have a library in the basement. I'll bet it's there somewhere, maybe even the contact sheet from the shoot: Griff kept everything. Come on, let's have a look.'

She could hear the glee in her voice; Bobby's enthusiasm had infected her. She led him downstairs to the lower level. Griffin had been a hoarder, filing every paper, photograph and piece of research he had used down the years in rows of cabinets. Shelves were neatly stacked with magazines and newspapers they had contributed to, and cupboards were filled with letters and notebooks.

Bobby whistled.

'Well, you're organised, I'll give you that. It puts my cardboard cartons of film reels to shame.' But Martha could see he was excited as he walked over to a shelf piled with envelopes full of developed photographs.

'Do you think there are any of me in there?' He asked, eyes shining.

'Maybe,' she shrugged.

'I doubt it,' said Bobby. 'No one wanted to take pictures of the scrawny kid from the Taco stand.'

'Everyone thought you were cool.'

'Did they?' he said, doubtfully.

'Okay, maybe not cool. But everyone liked you. I did. You were kind.'

'Just what every 19-year-old guy wants to hear.'

'But now we're older and wiser, we know it's the best compliment you can give.'

They didn't find the Esquire cover, but they found plenty of other magazines and newspaper articles Martha had completely forgotten about: essays about the fall of Saigon, about Apollo 17, a day out in Disneyworld, the rise of Disco and the panic over Video Nasties. To Martha, they'd each been a month or a week's work; then, they had slipped from her mind to be replaced by the next assignment. Not only had she forgotten writing them, but she had forgotten how she had thrived on the variety of it all. Her face ached from smiling. She and Bobby sat on cushions on the floor, spreading notes and papers around them, occasionally picking up a magazine and marvelling at the cover or the dated adverts. There were also endless amateur snapshots of people leering at the camera at party after party, some wearing beads and fringes, some wearing black tie and pearls.

Martha liked how Bobby was not shy about praising Griffin's work, too.

Some men would have tried to write her husband out of the narrative, but Bobby seemed to understand how important that part of life was to Martha.

'Man, this an amazing piece on Nixon's resignation,' he said. 'Griff's nailed Tricky Dick here.'

He looked up. Martha had fallen silent.

'What is it?' asked Bobby.

'It's just...you're right,' said Martha. 'We did do some amazing stuff here. We wrote about our world, dissected it and analysed it. When did we stop doing that? When did we stop thinking it was important, Bobby?'

'Your work has always been important. And the fight-back starts here, with your story about Verity.'

He paused.

'Hey, you mentioned that Griffin was writing a story about the Laurel Canyon scene but it got nixed. Did he keep any notebooks that could offer any leads?'

Martha shook her head.

'I'd already thought of that. Griffin was organised, but he liked to keep some things up here,' she said, tapping her temple. 'Most of these notebooks are mine.'

'Shame.'

He turned to look, then stopped.

'Oh wow,' he said, reaching over to pick up a piece of notepaper. 'Check this out. One for your current article, perhaps?'

Martha took the paper from him. It was a letter - or rather, a 'thank you' note. And her heart jumped: it was from Verity Jones.

Dear Griff,

Thanks for the loan of the books. I loved the Whitman poems and

Bonjour Tristesse. I guess I can identify with Cecile – maybe I never stopped being that awful teenager; maybe none of us did! Hope you like the record. I'll see you at Charlie's party next week?
Vx

'Typical Verity,' said Bobby. 'She was so sweet. Old fashioned manners, too.'

But Martha wasn't really listening; her heart was beating hard now, and suddenly, the air felt charged.

'Don't you think they look the same?' she said.

'What does?' said Bobby distractedly, having already moved on to a 1976 issue of Sports Illustrated.

Martha reached for her phone and quickly brought up the photograph of the 'Time For Change' lyrics Lara had sent over. The quality wasn't great, but the similarities were obvious.

'Pass me that thank-you note,' she said. 'My God,' she said quietly, holding them side-by-side. 'I mean, I'm no expert, but look.'

She turned the screen and held up the thank-you note so Bobby could see.

'It's the same handwriting on both. The same purple ink and everything.'

She watched Bobby's dawning understanding.

'You're right. God – you are!'

Martha tapped the screen. 'Which means – what? That Verity wrote those lyrics on Della's wall?'

Bobby clambered off the floor, holding the thank-you note to the light.

'Did Verity and Gene ever write songs together?' he asked.

'Not that I ever heard of.'

'But remember that footage from Verity's party,' said

Bobby. 'The stuff we were looking at last night. Verity was sitting at the piano. Gene was there beside her. I'd have to look back at the footage, but maybe they were writing it together then?'

'Or maybe it's simpler than that,' said Martha, feeling the hair rise on her arms. 'Verity was at the piano. Della's song sheet is in her handwriting. Do you think…' She looked at Bobby. 'Maybe Verity Jones wrote the biggest song of the decade?'

'And if she did?' said Bobby.

Martha's mind was already racing ahead.

'Then that gives somebody a very big motive to keep her quiet.'

Chapter 37

The cake was made in the shape of a number '1' and decorated with stars and stripes. Alex would have preferred a Union Jack, but even so, he smiled when Natasha brought it in.

'My Mom made it,' she said with a hint of embarrassment. 'She kinda insisted.'

'Tell her it's much appreciated,' said Alex. 'And thanks to everyone else for the chips and dips. And for the beer.'

He raised his can of Budweiser to muted cheers from the staff. This get-together in the boardroom – paper plates, plastic forks and, yes, those little party hats with elastic that made your chin itch – was an impromptu launch party for the Limelight supplement, which had finally been sent down to the printers. There was a sense of forced jollity to the celebration, but right now, Alex would take any kind of merriment. He had spent all day thinking about his last argument with Lara over his meeting with the Mayor and the look on her face when she said 'You cut a deal?' Every time he saw Lara these days, they seemed to be at each other's throats.

'I would also like to thank the entire team,' he continued, 'For all your hard work and dedication over this project, and particularly to Peter, our ever-present deputy,' Alex turned to give the grey-haired veteran a grateful smile. 'Don't you ever go home, Pete?' He quipped, to amused laughter, 'Peter has, of course, managed the insane feat of working on the Limelight supplement, while also keeping the main paper going at its customary high standard. Also, we should add hearty thanks to Dani for having pulled off the exclusive interview with Ryan Reynolds in which he failed to adequately explain the offside rule in British soccer. I know none of you understand it either, but reading it gave your editor-in-chief a great deal of pleasure.'

He raised a hand towards Dani.

'A round of applause and perhaps some American 'whoops' for them both.'

Alex waited until the clapping had died down to deliver the real point of his speech.

'Now, I know not everyone was completely convinced when I pitched the idea of an entertainment supplement,' he said. 'But I think you might all change your mind when Tom Cruise parachutes into the official launch party at the weekend.'

There was more laughter, but that could have been because the staff had been drinking since five that afternoon when he had 'pulled the trigger' and sent the digital files to the printer.

'But seriously, our world is changing. Newspapers don't have the luxury of being first with the news any more, but we do have two huge advantages. The first is that the readers - crazy bastards that they are - still trust us to give them the real truth.'

'Fools!' shouted Peter, who had been mixing his own cocktails.

'And the second is that we happen to be right in the heart of the biggest, most influential entertainment town on earth.'

He held a finger to his lips in a gesture of thoughtfulness.

'Oh, and we also have secret weapon number three: the best goldarned newspaper team IN THE WORLD! Give yourselves another round!'

There was cheering, toasting, and Cheetos thrown in the air as Alex threaded his way out and down the corridor, pulling off his party hat. It was important to acknowledge hard work and encourage the team to let off some steam, but Alex had no desire to spend any more time in the boardroom. Besides, no one wanted the boss around cramping their style. Crossing the lobby, he wandered into the street, taking a moment to breathe real air. Alex sighed; he knew he was just putting off the inevitable. He had to get back to Malibu and make up with Lara - if she was still there. He had invited her down this evening, to take her to dinner but he hadn't heard from her. Alex had known Lara Stone since her early twenties, and he was well aware she could make big gestures – like flying straight back to London – just to make a point.

'Ah, Alex,' he whispered to himself. 'Why are you such an idiot?'

'Oh, I wouldn't say that.'

He looked around to see Natasha standing there, framed in the backlit doorway.

'Shit, sorry. I was speaking to myself,' he said.

She giggled. 'Yeah, I guessed. Anything I can help with?'

'No,' He smiled, 'But thanks for asking.'

'Are you looking for a cab?'

'Yeah, it's probably wise – I've only had a couple of

those fizzy things you call beer, but I don't want to top off a crappy day with an arrest.'

Natasha nodded her understanding, and Alex appreciated her not probing why his day had been so bad.

'So, are you heading out west?' she asked. 'If you *wanted* to detour via Brentwood, it'd save me forging an expense claim.'

Alex laughed. 'Sadly your timing is off – I need to get home ASAP tonight.'

'Ah.' Natasha pulled a pack of Marlboros from her bag. 'Shame.'

She shook out a cigarette and offered it to him. Alex hadn't smoked in years, but wouldn't this be the perfect excuse for a relapse?

'Ah, go on then,' he said, 'This might be my last chance before they ban everything fun.'

'That's the spirit,' said Natasha, raising a suggestive eyebrow. She clicked a lighter and they both blew smoke towards that not-quite dark sky.

'So tell me if it's none of my business,' said Natasha, 'But did anything happen with the bridge story?'

Alex looked down at the dancing tip of his cigarette. He figured it couldn't do any harm to tell her – and after all, she had been actively involved.

'I went to see the Mayor,' he said with a half-smile.

'*The* Mayor? Durante?'

Alex nodded, then laid out the whole tale. When he had finished, Natasha grinned. 'You actually said 'clusterfuck' to the mayor?'

'I'm afraid so.'

'Man, that's…awesome,' she laughed. 'Not just the cursing – although that's pretty cool – the whole negotiation thing.' She squinted up at him through cigarette smoke. 'Very slick.'

'You think?'

'Are you kidding me? Look, I'll admit I was pissed that you took the story off our hands...'

'I *did* notice, Natasha,' he said.

'Yeah, sure. But I can also see we didn't have enough to print. A cab driver who spoke to a gold-digger, who led us to a whistleblower who wouldn't talk. It's not Wikileaks, is it? But then you stroll into Jon Durante's office and turn that into a scoop? That's pure seat-of-your-pants journalism in action.'

'I should point out that I haven't heard back from the Mayor,' said Alex modestly, but he was still pleased, noting the stark gulf between Natasha's reaction and Lara's.

'Seriously though,' said Alex, 'I couldn't have done any of that without the groundwork you and Will had done. And don't worry, Natasha: your time will come. Getting noticed in this business isn't just about having your byline printed.'

She dropped her cigarette and ground it out with the toe of a shiny black pump.

'And have you noticed *me*, Alex?' she said.

Alex stopped mid-breath. He might be out of practice, but he wasn't so ring-rusty that he couldn't tell when a woman was coming on to him. And she was attractive, no question about that, but Natasha was, what, ten, twelve years younger than him? – and he was her boss, not to mention he was committed and...*ah, shit.*

'Yes, I have noticed,' he said. 'And I'm flattered, but there's a big problem – well, lots of them, actually - but the big one is that I'm in love with someone else. Big time, head-over-heels love. So I'm sorry, Natasha, but it's a no.'

In a split second, Natasha's expression ran between crestfallen, embarrassed and angry before settling on sad. 'Well, you can't blame a girl for trying,' she said, laying a hand on his arm and leaning in closer.

‘Lara’s a lucky girl,’ she whispered, then stepped back. ‘And you know what? I think I’ll get my own taxi after all.’

Alex was in the process of muttering awkward thanks when he stopped dead.

‘Oh shit,’ he said.

Lara was standing on the other side of the road.

Chapter 38

Lara kept walking; she didn't even know where she was going. She just needed to get away, but she heard heavy footsteps behind her.

'Lara, please,' Alex called, 'Stop.'

Lara whirled to face him.

'So this is why you invited me down here?' she snapped. 'So I could watch you seducing some girl?'

She saw the hurt in his eyes but couldn't help herself. She was lonely, lost and unsure of her future, but Alex had always been the one thing she could rely on – and now she couldn't even trust him.

'Lara, it wasn't…' he began.

'Wasn't what? It wasn't what it looked like?' She asked in a mocking tone. 'Is that the best you can come up with? You're such a bloody cliche.'

She turned to walk on, but he caught her arm.

'Don't you touch me!' she hissed, yanking herself free, 'Don't you *dare*! Not when I saw her kiss you.'

Anger crossed Alex's face, and he stepped across Lara's path, blocking her escape.

'She didn't bloody kiss me!' he shouted. 'And if it's any

of your business, I just told Natasha that I was head-over-heels in love with you, and she told me you were a lucky woman.'

Lara blinked at him. 'You said that to her?'

'YES!' he cried, throwing both hands in the air. 'Because God help me, I do love you. And you know what else? I'd give up this damned job in a heartbeat if you asked me to because I don't want anyone else - ever. I never have, and I don't think I ever will.'

Lara opened her mouth, then closed it again. Her heart was pounding in her chest. 'Really?' she said quietly.

'Yes, really.' Alex let out a held breath. 'Do you think I would have invited you over tonight if I was planning on kissing another woman?'

'No,' said Lara. 'I suppose not.'

'So stop being so stupid and…DAMN!'

A ringing in his pocket made Alex break off to angrily pull out his phone, jabbing at the red 'reject' button.

'Look,' he said, his eyes meeting hers. 'I love you with all my heart; you're the only thing that matters. Not the job, not the story, nothing else. Whatever you want to do from here on in, I'll do it. Quit the job, go back to London, whatever it takes for us to be together. Just tell me and I'll do it.'

Lara couldn't help smiling.

'Well, you could start by taking me to dinner like you promised.'

Alex threw his head back and laughed. 'Yes, I think I can do that…'

They both looked down as Alex's phone started ringing again. He glared down at the screen.

'It's the bloody mayor.'

He moved to turn the phone off, but Lara quickly put her hand over his.

'Take it,' she said.

'What?'

'Take the call – do your job. Go on.'

He looked at her, his eyes wild with confusion.

'God, woman, you're maddening.'

'I know,' she said, leaning forward to kiss him. 'Now go, talk to the mayor, finish your story. I'll get the car and meet you at the front of the office. Then we'll talk.'

Growling in frustration, he shook his head, then strode off, putting the phone to his ear. 'Mr Mayor, so nice to hear from you…'

Lara snorted to herself. *Well, he loves me.* That was something, wasn't it? It was more than something. It was pretty good. She stood at the kerb, watching Alex talk into his phone, pacing up and down, pushing his free hand through his hair.

'Ditto,' she whispered to herself, a sad smile creeping across her face because all those things he'd said, they applied to her, too. She loved Alex Ford; she always had. And she would give up her job too – such as it was – to be with him.

Funny, she thought, looking up beyond the Globe building to the night sky. Funny how we let things get between us and what we need when it's so often right there in front of us. She turned and walked back past the Globe's entrance – just as Natasha stepped out, almost clattering into her.

'Oh God,' said the girl, tottering a few paces back, looking ready to run if necessary. 'Lara, I'm so, so, sorry,' she said in a rush. 'It was all my fault - really. Alex didn't lay a finger on me; in fact, he told me…'

'That he loves me,' said Lara. 'Yes, I know.'

Confusion crossed the young woman's face. 'So why…?'

Lara glared at Natasha. She wasn't about to let the girl off the hook that easily.

'*Why?* Because I just saw you coming on to my boyfriend, Natasha. Isn't that what really happened?'

Natasha looked suitably ashamed.

'Yes,' she said softly. 'I just…' She closed her eyes and shook her head. 'I don't have an excuse.'

'No. You don't,' said Lara. 'It's not a good look trying to seduce the boss.'

She took a deep breath, trying to calm down. It wasn't as if Lara didn't understand; she had been young and ambitious once, too. But Lara always ensured that every opportunity she was given was 100% down to her work.

'What do you think would have happened if Alex had gone for it, Natasha?' she asked. 'What if he had dumped me and given you a big promotion – or whatever it was you wanted from this? Would you have felt good about that?'

'No, I guess not,' sighed Natasha. 'But it's so hard these days, Lara. So few jobs, so few newspapers, and I'm drowning at the Globe. I'm almost 27; am I supposed to sit here for another ten years waiting for a non-existent section editor's position? What the hell do I do?'

Lara stepped closer. She thought she could trust herself not to strangle the girl now.

'You're a bright girl, Natasha. Alex told me you did good work on that traffic story.'

She looked up eagerly.

'Really?' said Natasha. 'He said that?'

It wasn't true: Alex hadn't said anything of the kind, but Lara remembered what it was like to be at the start of your career. Praise from the top was a huge deal for a new writer.

'Alex rates you – and Will,' she added quickly. 'So why not try and impress him with your work? Show him what you can do. That's what any editor wants from their staff. People they can trust.'

She saw the idea sink in. Natasha looked stricken and slumped against a wall.

'Goddamn it,' said Natasha, covering her face. 'He'll never trust me now, will he? I've messed it up, haven't I?'

Lara gave her a half-smile.

'I'll be honest, it hasn't helped, no. But like I said, Alex is only really interested in people who can help him. So do the work. Do the research. Find your own stories. He'll soon get over it.'

Natasha looked up at her, eyes glassy.

'Thanks, Lara,' she said. 'That's good advice. And more than I deserve, considering.'

'Agreed,' said Lara. She paused, looking at Natasha.

'So why don't you go for Will? Assuming he's single. He's cute.'

Natasha snorted out a laugh. 'He is, but the irony is…I was worried about mixing business and pleasure.'

Lara had to laugh at that.

'Actually,' said Natasha. 'I was at Will's family place yesterday, and his dad, Jack? He told me you'd spoken to him about Verity Jones.'

Lara frowned, and Natasha caught it. 'No, no, I'm not about to step on your toes – I wouldn't dare. It's just I mentioned Verity to my dad, too, and…'

Natasha told Lara about her father's experience with the Savage organisation, the dirty tricks and accusations of blackmail, and how Savage had cut his old partner out of the sale.

'I was just thinking - if Stephen Savage was as ruthless as that when he sold the company, then maybe?'

Lara nodded, following her train of thought. Then maybe he'd been equally ruthless in his dealings with Verity.

'See?' said Lara. 'Now you're thinking like a journalist. Help people, and they'll want to help you.'

‘Sorry,’ said Natasha again.

Lara shrugged.

‘Da nada.’

They both looked up as Alex walked back.

‘So you didn’t kill her then?’ he said, looking at Lara warily.

‘Not yet,’ she said with a half smile. ‘But the evening is young. Now go and flag us a cab. We need to get Natasha home. ’

Chapter 39

'I can't believe you have an original David Hockney,' said Lara, staring at the picture on Barbara's wall. Coloured lines of blue and green wove across the paper, denoting the movement of water on the surface of a swimming pool, a pair of legs from an unseen body lazily kicking in fractured shapes below.

'It's only a drawing,' said Barbara from her kitchen, where she, Martha and Bobby had all gathered to discuss the discovery of Verity's handwritten note. 'David did it for Donny when he lived in LA; when was it? '69? 70? He was such a baby then.'

'Who, Donny?' teased Martha, leaning over the breakfast bar to snatch one of Barbara's freshly baked cookies.

'No, Hockney – although Donny was quite a youngster himself back then. We all were, weren't we?'

'I don't want to make you feel old, Barbara, but I was still in middle school,' said Bobby with a smile. Still, Lara could picture it: Donny, Barbara, Martha, and Griff, fresh-faced and hungry for success, all bathed in perpetual sunshine, all forever young.

Lara smiled as she watched Barbara pouring them all

coffee. She was glad she had included her neighbour in their pow-wow. As an investigative reporter, Lara often worked alone, but her father, one of the most talented journalists of his generation, had always impressed upon his daughter the importance of taking advice from people who had an objective viewpoint. It was sound advice: you could be too emotional when you were too close to something, unable to see the wood for the trees. Often, Lara talked through her investigative work with Alex because he would always add a fresh perspective and make observations she hadn't even thought of, and now she was keen to hear Barbara's thoughts. Besides, Barbara cooked an amazing breakfast.

'Lara sweetie, come and help me carry the eggs to the table,' Barbara called. The cook, somewhat disconcertingly, was wearing an apron featuring the semi-naked body of a Chippendale – 'a souvenir from the 90s', she had trilled with a wistful look – but her breakfast goodies were much more mouthwatering. Fluffy scrambled eggs with chorizo, silver dollar pancakes with Canadian bacon and 'country fried potatoes' featuring peppers, onions and big chunks of Kielbasa sausage.

'It's like Thanksgiving,' smiled Martha, pulling up a chair. Lara noticed her casually touch Bobby's hand. Lara knew he'd been over to Martha's for dinner but didn't know if he'd ever been home since.

'So,' said Lara, as they all filled their plates, 'Shall I officially convene the meeting?'

'Oh yes, please,' said Barbara. For someone who disliked social gatherings, she seemed to be enjoying the faux conference more than anyone. 'Why don't you all fill me in?'

Lara smiled. When she had worked full-time at The Chronicle, Lara and her assistant Stella were billeted in the basement, which lacked the buzzy collaborative atmosphere of the main newsroom but was a great place to strategise. Lara would create an 'evidence wall' for each story she was working on - a patchwork of Post-it notes and photos - which helped her clarify her thinking and link pieces of information that would otherwise appear unconnected. There was no whiteboard today, but Lara was surrounded by people whose judgment and intelligence she trusted.

'Verity died of heart failure with opioids in her system,' Lara began. 'Overdose, suicide, or misadventure, we don't know exactly, but let's start with the *why*.'

She looked around the table.

'On the night of Verity's death, Donna Phelps told her she'd had an affair with Verity's husband Eliot and was pregnant with his child. Verity was distraught, ended the party and everyone left the beach house.'

'Or did they?' said Bobby.

'Well, exactly,' replied Lara. 'Perhaps Verity wasn't alone when she died. Her neighbour heard a gunshot at around midnight.'

Bobby looked at Barbara.

'We've been thinking that might have been the sound of a back-firing motorbike - someone coming back to Verity's place.'

'So who would want to go back and why?' said Barbara, cutting a little corner off her pancake.

'The obvious people are Donna Phelps and Eliot Jones,' said Martha. 'But Eliot was seen at The Troubador at one in the morning and I believe him when he said he went there to get loaded and forget about his argument with Donna. Remember, Eliot was a pop star; people would have remembered it if he'd left.'

'What about this back-firing motorbike?' said Barbara. 'Do you know who had one?'

Lara nodded - her neighbour was asking all the right questions.

'We know that Todd Mayfield and Gene Henderson had motorbikes. But we think Todd's unlikely because he was in a play that night. And why would he go back?'

Barbara tapped her lips thoughtfully.

'Todd was in a relationship with Donna, right? Well, if he knew about her affair with Eliot too, maybe he wanted to talk it through with Verity?'

A wicked smile spread across Barbara's face.

'Or maybe it was a booty call,' she said. 'You remember what those days were like, Martha; I once heard that Warren Beatty would see two, three women a night.'

'Couldn't that apply to Gene too?' asked Lara, but Martha shook her head.

'My recollection is that Gene was completely under Cora's thumb. I don't think she ever gave him the opportunity to stray.'

'Gene Henderson?' said Barbara. 'Why do you mention him?'

Lara quickly filled Barbara in on the purple handwritten lyrics while Bobby pulled a backpack from under his chair.

'Gene and Verity were working on material together, I'm sure of it,' he said, pushing his plate aside and spreading some print-outs across Barbara's kitchen table. 'These are stills from the footage I shot on the night of the party. Look; you can see Verity and Gene together in the music room.'

'But what's that got to do with Verity's death?' asked Barbara.

'Well, Lara began this conversation asking why Verity died,' said Martha. 'Was she sad or depressed or reckless with her drug taking? But what she is also asking is did anyone have a reason to want Verity dead.'

'You think someone *killed* Verity?' said Barbara, her eyes opening a little wider.

'We are just exploring all the options,' replied Lara, but she smiled to herself a little. This was what she had missed over the past few months; the camaraderie of a tight-knit team working together on a puzzle. How remarkable that she should find something so similar here, on the far side of a different continent, among a group of feisty pensioners.

'What if Henderson and Verity were in dispute over the song?' asked Bobby. 'Verity isn't mentioned on any album sleeve, I checked. There's not even an acknowledgement.'

Barbara clapped her hands together.

'Yes! This is just like that episode of Magnum PI.'

Martha frowned. 'The Tom Selleck TV show?'

'Well, *obviously*,' said Barbara. She pulled off her apron and walked down to the lounge area. One wall was entirely taken up with shelves: there were some books and a few little sculptures – including, Lara noticed, a Golden Globe award – but most were filled with neatly labelled VHS cassettes and DVDs, like a little flashback to the past.

'It's here somewhere,' said Barbara, putting on a pair of reading glasses and peering at the spines. 'Magnum, Magnum, Magnum…no!'

She stood up suddenly and looked back towards the breakfast table. 'It's not Tom Selleck, it's Dennis Schultz.'

'Who's that?' asked Lara.

'Becker Private Eye!' said Barbara, looking shocked. 'You've never seen the show?'

'I'm not sure it made it across the pond.'

'He was a shambling detective like Columbo,' said Martha, deadpan, 'But Dennis Schultz was no Peter Falk.'

'Well, I enjoyed it,' pouted Barbara.

'Actually, I know a couple of people who worked on it,' said Bobby. 'You can't beat a gentle afternoon mystery.'

Martha gave a good-humoured roll of the eyes.

'Don't say you're another connoisseur of the corny TV drama.'

'Hang on, slow down, everyone,' said Lara, patting the air. 'Can we just rewind? What has Becker Private Eye got to do with anything?'

Barbara gave a dramatic sigh.

'Becker Private Eye always followed the same structure. They'd spend the first ten minutes showing you the bad guy doing the murder, then Becker would turn up, and he'd spend the rest of the show working out how the killer had done it.'

'A how-dunnit,' said Martha.

'Exactly,' smiled Barbara.

'Anyway, there was this one episode about a stolen song,' said Barbara. 'I can't remember the exact details, but it was about an up-coming rock star who killed his friend at a showbiz party because she'd written this amazing song and he wanted it for himself.'

With a cry of triumph, Barbara plucked a DVD off the shelf and brought it back, held aloft like a prize.

'Here it is. Season Three. It's called 'Killing Me Softly – brackets – With Her Song.'

'Let's look,' said Bobby, pulling out his reading glasses and peering at the credits on the back of the box.

'This was directed by Brad Hurst,' he said. 'You know he went on to win an Emmy? And they had Ricardo Mendez doing sound. We worked together for a while.' He read out the list of credits. 'James Link…Ray Reynolds… Bert Walters.'

That made Lara look up.

'Wait, what was that last one?'

'Bert Walters: screenwriter. He wrote most of the series.'

Lara was good with names, but placing it took her a moment. Then it struck her. Della!

'Gene Henderson had a friend called Bert Walters!' she said excitedly. 'Bert was his roommate in college. Della said he was a screenwriter.'

Bobby looked back at the DVD case.

'Well, it looks like he wrote Barbara's episode.'

Martha looked at Lara, and Lara knew she was feeling the same excitement. They had

'I think we need to track this Bert Walters down and see what he has to say, don't you?' she said. 'Because it sounds to me as if he's trying to tell us something.'

Chapter 40

Lara was back at the beach again: Long Beach this time. On the map, it looked just a short hop down the coast from Malibu, but in fact, it was a brutal hour's drive across LA. The atmosphere here was a world apart, too. Malibu was pristine, clipped and swept by an army of gardeners and discreet maintenance people. Lara remembered that old joke about how the late Queen thought everywhere smelled of fresh paint – Malibu was like that. Long Beach, meanwhile, was high-rise, concrete and towering palms: Snoop Dogg's home town. It smelled of ganja and gasoline, and the paint came from a spray can. Even so, the beach was still Cali-cool, unfeasibly wide and dotted with pastel lifeguard shacks. Lara walked along the boardwalk, looking for 'Flavios', the taco stand near the pier. Lara had easily got hold of Bert Walters's number from Della Henderson and he had been quick to respond, choosing Flavios as their rendezvous point. Lara had been happy to follow his suggestion; she'd been jonesing for Mexican food since Bobby's burritos had gone up in smoke.

She spotted Bert Walters straight away, leaning by the

order window. In his mid-seventies, he was tall, with a grey beard, plaid shirt, and red Angels baseball cap—like an undercover cop or an off-duty screenwriter.

'You must be Lara,' he said, holding an awkward hand.

'I hope you don't mind, I already ordered. Best fajitas in the city.' He nodded towards one of the brightly-painted picnic tables next to the stand.

'Are they good?' asked Lara.

'You'll soon find out,' he grinned. 'I ordered you one too.'

'Number 23,' shouted the server at the hatch, and Bert went to collect his order.

'Thanks for coming…' Lara began as Bert tore open the sack.

'Eat first, then we'll talk.'

Bert had been right about the food. It was heavenly. Salsa, guac, and just the right amount of chilli. When she had finished, Lara sat back, groaning with pleasure.

'Good, huh?'

Lara pointed to the detritus of their meal. 'That's the best food I've had in LA. Seriously.'

Bert raised a Jarritos Lime in salute.

'So you keep in touch with Della Henderson,' she said.

'Della's great,' said Bert. 'I don't flatter myself she enjoys my sparkling personality; she stays in touch because I was Gene's buddy. And without me, her only connection to her brother is Cora.'

'I got the sense Della wasn't keen on Cora.'

'That's an understatement,' he said with a snort.

'So you were Gene's roommate at college, right?'

'In our Freshman year, yes. Then we got an apartment together near campus, although by the end of sophomore year, Gene had met Cora and was spending most of the time with her in Laurel Canyon.'

The sour tone of his voice told Lara that Bert didn't much like Cora either.

'Della told me she thought Gene's life might have turned out differently if he hadn't met her,' said Lara gently. Bert crushed the paper wrapping of his fajita into a ball and tossed it into a nearby bin.

'You know, I often wonder why schools don't teach you how to choose the right friends because if you get mixed up with the wrong sort, all those qualifications, all that learning? It's meaningless.'

Lara kept quiet and let Bert keep talking.

'If he hadn't met Cora, Gene could have been a famous novelist or poet,' said Bert, his voice wistful. 'Maybe even a politician. Before the drugs, Gene was so engaged about causes and issues. I'll never forget seeing him at an anti-war rally in our first few weeks at college – man, he could hold an audience even then. The problem was that Gene was passionate about *everything*. And that included Cora and the drugs, too.'

'I'm sorry,' said Lara, seeing the pain on Bert's face as he remembered his friend.

'I tried so many times to get him into rehab,' he said, shaking his head. 'I tried to get him away from her, but Cora was like a guard dog, at least until the last few weeks of his life.'

'You saw him then?'

'Yeah. I went to see him in New York – he was in a bad way, but I finally got him to say yes to going into a treatment centre but then…' He shrugged. 'Then there was the overdose.'

Over the past few days, Lara had read up as much as she could about Gene Henderson. She knew all about his death – in a hotel in Gramercy Park just days before he was due to begin recording a new album.

'You were a good friend to him.'

'I tried,' he said simply. 'I tried to be a lot of things.'

'Well, Della said you were a good influence.'

Bert laughed. '*A good influence* makes me sound so dull. And anyway, how could I dissuade Gene from becoming a rock star? He had the voice, the stage presence - and you couldn't walk down the street without girls coming on to him. He was a natural star. He just couldn't cope with it – too much attention, too much stimulus.'

'Do you think that's why he became a heavy drug user?'

Bert grimaced. 'Maybe.'

It was obvious Bert found this hard to talk about, so Lara took a step back.

'So you're a screenwriter?' she asked.

He glanced back at her.

'Sure, when I can get the work. It's a young business.'

'You used to write for Becker PI, right?'

'I did,' he said, absently rubbing at a spot of dirt on his trousers. 'It paid the bills.'

'Didn't you write an episode called 'Killing Me Softly', about a rock star stealing a song from a songwriter? I watched it this morning.'

'Ah. You know about that, huh?' he said quietly. 'It was a good episode.'

'It was,' replied Lara. 'But it was funny because I'm looking into the life and death of Verity Jones and, well, that Becker PI episode reminded me of her story.'

Bert didn't reply. Just took off his cap and combed through his grey hair with his fingers.

'Bert, I'm pretty sure that Verity wrote 'Time For Change'.'

He glanced at the diners at nearby tables, then nodded towards the pier.

'Come on, let's take a stroll.'

Lara followed Bert onto the concrete walkway, jutting

out into the sea like an accusatory finger. This wasn't like Santa Monica Pier, filled with buskers, hot dogs, sideshows, and a Ferris wheel. The Belmont Pier was just a jetty standing out over the water with a few locals fishing from the end.

'I wondered when someone would come and speak to me about this,' said Bert as they walked. 'I hoped it would be soon after Verity died, but Gene was never linked to the story. And then after that Becker PI episode transmitted, I thought someone might start asking questions.' He gave a sad, low laugh.

'I guess Becker PI wasn't all that popular.'

Lara had spent many years interviewing people. Some people were guarded, some guilty, but others were desperate to unload their burden. She had a feeling Bert Walters fit squarely into that camp.

'So I was in my final year at UCLA, living in a studio just off campus when Gene turned up one Sunday morning,' said Bert. 'I was about to graduate; Gene had dropped out 18 months earlier, chasing the dream, living with Cora. So I hadn't seen him much.' He glanced across. 'And I had no idea it was the morning after Verity Jones died.'

Lara looked at him.

'How was he?'

'Upset. Agitated, pacing around – he couldn't sit still.'

'Did he say why?'

'He said he'd had an argument with Cora and that he just wanted to get away from the city, to get away from everything. I had this little car and he was like, 'Let's just GO, man!' – like we were characters in a Kerouac novel.'

'So that's what you did?'

Bert flashed a sad smile.

'Burned straight down to Tijuana and got stoned; total hippy cliché.'

Lara and Bert stopped at the rail, staring down at the waves rolling in one after the other.

'Did your boys' trip away cheer Gene up?'

'At first, sure. He seemed relieved to be out of the country, said he never wanted to go back, talked about moving to Paris or London. It wasn't until later that I realised why.'

He paused.

'By the time we got to Mexico, the radio was reporting Verity had died, so of course, I asked Gene about it. I knew they were friends. At first, he was vague, but later on, when we went down to the beach and got drunk on tequila, he…well, he broke down and told me everything.'

Lara waited, but Bert seemed to have shut down, just picking at some flakes of rust on the rail.

'Bert, what did Gene tell you?' she prompted. He turned to look at her.

'He told me that he'd killed Verity.'

Lara could hardly breathe. This was huge. Her instinct that Gene Henderson was involved in Verity's death had been correct.

'What did he say?' she said, trying to keep her cool.

Bert shook his head, looking out to sea, the view blighted by a line of off-shore oil rigs.

'It all started when they went to Verity's to hang out for the day. By the sound of it, most people were on the beach, but Cora didn't like the heat, so they retreated to Verity's music room and she joined them, sat down at the piano and started playing this song.'

'Time For Change,' said Lara – a statement, not a question.

'Yep. Gene said he knew it was a stone-cold classic the moment he heard it. They all knew it was special, even Cora. Maybe Cora most of all.'

Bert walked on, Lara jogging to keep up.

'Did they compose the song together, or was it something Verity had done already?' Lara's gut told her the answer, but she had to confirm it.

'It was all Verity, 100% her song,' said Bert. 'But even so, Gene still asked her – no, begged her – to let him record the song. Gene had that wild rock star voice and the stage presence, but his career wasn't taking off because he didn't have the songs.'

'Did he even have a record deal at this point?'

'Nothing. No deal, no manager. Just a dream.'

'And what did Verity say?'

'Verity said sorry, but no. I mean, would you give away 'Candle in the Wind' or 'Yesterday'? Besides, Verity was launching her own solo career, and she must have known 'Time For Change' could take her back to the top of the charts.'

Bert glanced at Lara.

'But Cora wouldn't take no for an answer.'

Lara felt a growing sense of disquiet. This was ancient history, of course - no spoilers on the outcome - yet she felt like she was hearing this from Gene, confessing to her the day after the tragedy.

'Cora was persistent, but she didn't have long to persuade Verity because the party finished. They all had to leave.'

Lara touched Bert's arm.

'But Gene and Cora went at about midnight on Gene's motorbike, am I right?' she said, remembering the pizza delivery guy.

'Sure, that's what Gene said,' said Bert, his voice flat. 'They knew Verity would go to see her record company on Monday and 'Time For Change' would be lost.'

They stopped at the end of the pier and perched on a stone bench, just watching the fishing, the rods flashing in the sun.

'When they got back to the Malibu House, Verity was drunk,' Bert continued. 'Drowning her sorrows about whatever made her nix the party. So, of course, that worked in Cora's favour. She was good at manipulating people, and people who are sad and drunk are easy to manipulate.'

'So *did* Verity give them Time For Change?'

Bert gave a hard little laugh.

'Lara, Verity didn't give them the song - they *took* it. Verity was still saying no, so Cora thought she needed to be loosened up a little more.'

'Loosened up? How?' But Lara had already guessed.

''Just a line' – that's what Gene said. Verity thought it was coke.' Bert looked at her. 'But it wasn't.'

'They gave her heroin?'

Bert nodded.

'There was some hardcore stuff going around, and Cora had some. You've seen 'Pulp Fiction', right?' he said, looking up at Lara. 'That scene where Uma Thurman ODs? That's how Gene described it: eyes rolled back, foaming at the mouth, jerking on the floor. Then she went still.'

'Shit.'

'Cora and Gene both freaked; didn't know what to do. Cora had the idea to put Verity into a bath of ice-cold water – it's an old junkie trick – but Gene wouldn't touch her. Gene told me he just retreated into a corner. Cora screamed at him, called him pathetic, and then she went for help.'

'Did she call 911?'

Lara knew the answer was no, but she had to ask.

'She went to find Stephen Savage,' said Bert. 'Stephen stayed at his uncle's trailer just a few minutes walk from Verity's house - less if you ran.'

Lara could picture it vividly. Moonlight slashing across

the white sand, a desperate Cora running to save her own skin as well as Verity's. As for Savage, he must have been barely twenty at the time. But such a ruthless and ambitious man would undoubtedly have been a safe pair of hands in a crisis even then.

'But I don't understand,' said Lara. 'Why did Gene tell you he killed Verity? Cora was the one who gave her the overdose.'

Bert shook his head sadly.

'After Cora was gone, Gene felt terrible for not helping, so he picked Verity up and managed to get her into the bath.'

With a lurch, Lara understood.

'He thought the shock of the cold water brought on Verity's heart attack?'

'Yeah. I mean, maybe it did, or maybe Verity was already dead – we'll never know, but my guess is that the heart attack thing was a narrative Cora played on, whispering in Gene's ear. Either way, when Cora and Savage arrived, Verity was dead.'

Lara was a news reporter, she had seen plenty of crime scenes, even murder sites, so she could imagine how it looked. She also remembered Jack Anders' description of the Malibu House the morning after, how he had felt the cold bathwater. He hadn't, however, mentioned a flooded floor. Did Savage mop it up? Clean the site of prints? In the event, the police had chalked it up to a routine heart attack, but Savage wouldn't have known that. It must have taken nerve. Lara thought of Natasha's father and his account of Savage's dirty tricks. Cora had chosen her helper well.

'So Savage engineered a way for Gene and Cora to get away, and to take Verity's song with them.'

'Not just that,' said Bert. 'Savage went on to manage

Gene and used Time For Change to launch his new record label – and his entire career.'

Lara nodded. Stephen Savage was even smarter than she thought. Cora Bryant had asked for help, but Savage had been quick-thinking enough to use it to his advantage. Over the past week, Lara had researched all the main players of the 70s Malibu scene, and one thing had stuck out – how Savage had gone from star-struck hanger-on to record industry mogul in a few short years. Lara always thought of it as 'the grey' area – the part of an origin story that didn't quite add up. People who liked to put their overnight success stories down to luck and hard work were often secretly supplemented with deep-pocket investment, or those 'chance meetings' were actually the result of months of heavy-duty networking or nepotism.

Bert looked at Lara. 'I know Savage looks like a villain here, but in a strange way, I was grateful to him.'

Lara frowned.

'Grateful? He stole that song from Verity as surely as Cora - he built his whole empire on it, he made millions.'

Bert nodded. 'Sure. But he kept my buddy out of jail. That night in Tijuana? Gene decided he was going to confess; he was from a decent straight-shooting background and felt so bad about Verity. But if he'd told the cops what happened, they would have locked him up and thrown away the key.'

Lara grimaced: she knew it was the truth. Some long-hair hippy confessing about dosing Verity with smack? They'd book him with murder one in a heartbeat. They sat in silence, watching the birds circle, hoping to scavenge from the fishermen.

'As it was, by the time we got back to LA, the dust had settled,' said Bert. 'No cops, no suggestion of foul play, just a terrible tragedy. And of course, Cora was waiting on my front step and Gene's resolve to report their crime just… disappeared.'

'And you never said anything to the police?'

'I think you know the answer to that,' he replied.

'But you wrote a version of the story in Becker Private Eye.'

Bert gave a hollow laugh.

'I mean, come on – it's a great storyline, and I wanted to impress the director. But for me, it was also atonement. It was my way of shining a light on what had happened. I really thought people would notice the similarities of the characters to Verity and Gene – they'd see it and go: 'Ah-ha! So *that's* what happened with Verity Jones! Let's reopen that case.' But obviously, that never happened.'

Lara didn't want to point out that Bert could have gone to the police himself, but she had seen enough of life to know that people were complicated.

'Don't judge me,' said Bert, as if reading her mind. 'I only wanted to protect my friend. And Gene got his punishment anyway, didn't he? Rock folklore might say that Cora got him into drugs, but I don't think he ever really got past that night. Every time I saw Gene after that, there seemed to be less of him, somehow.'

Bert looked at Lara, dark smudges under his eyes.

'Maybe I could have done more. Maybe I should have. But I guess that's something I'll have to live with.'

Chapter 41

Stephen Savage was not shy; that much was clear. The Savage Gallery was one of the largest commercial galleries in Los Angeles, a purpose-built modernist sculpture dropped right in the middle of the arts district downtown, right between the prestigious galleries of The Broad and Hauser & Wirth. Tonight, the Savage looked like a palace, lit up with roving spotlights. It was hard to miss at the best of times, but they'd pulled out all the stops for tonight's 'Cora Bryant: Icon' exhibition. There was a red carpet up the stairs and waving flags of solid red bearing a single word in bold black text: 'Icon'. But it was all dwarfed by the sign reading 'Savage', a ten-foot-high neon statement. Self-image was not something Stephen Savage struggled with.

Lara and Martha had to walk the last block to the gallery: there wasn't much choice given the gridlock of limos and town cars queuing to deliver the great and good to tonight's see-and-be-seen gala opening.

Lara had dressed up for the occasion, and Martha had supervised the transformation at her house, giving Lara full access to the walk-in wardrobe she called The Carousel.

Lara had chosen a classic black Halston maxi dress with fluted sleeves and a plunging neckline. It had just cried out for some bling, and Martha had dug out a chunky neckpiece with a citrine centrestone. 'You look a million dollars,' said Martha as they approached the receiving line, the paparazzi flashbulbs popping.

'So do you,' Lara replied. Martha was glowing in a deep orange evening kaftan, and she had to lift the hem of the dress to avoid heel tangle as they negotiated the steps.

'I wish Griffin were here,' said Martha. 'He used to love things like this.'

Lara nodded; she felt the same way about Alex. He looked sexy as hell spiffed up in a suit and tie, but more importantly, Alex often relaxed at a formal party, perhaps because he could always find the humour and ridiculousness of such fancy events. Alex had got hold of two tickets for tonight's launch party, but sadly, it was not date night. Not only did Alex have to work late that evening – the Limelight launch was imminent - but Martha and Lara needed to try and talk to Savage and Cora Bryant. That wasn't going to be anyone's idea of fun.

To add to the pressure, Lara had already called Darius at the Chronicle in London to break the news that she wouldn't be filing the '27 Club' story, placating him with the promise of 'something much bigger'. They really needed to pull this off.

At the top of the stairs, they handed their tickets to a security guard and were waved inside. A waiter in a red waistcoat handed them each a scarlet cocktail, fitting with the evening's colour scheme.

'Thank you,' she said, clinking her glass against Lara's.

'You're welcome,' said Lara. 'But what for?'

'Oh, just everything. The dressing up. Making me part of your story, introducing me to Alex.'

Lara smiled. She knew Martha and Alex had met for

breakfast, and he had offered her a column. There was nothing altruistic about it for Alex – he was getting one of the great writers of the last century – but even so, it was a boost for Martha after her recent literary rejection.

'Thank you for bringing me back to life…' she whispered.

'Martha…'

'No, seriously,' said the older woman, looking emotional. 'For too long I've hidden away in my little beach house.'

'That's not true, Martha,' said Lara. 'You're hardly a hermit.'

'The occasional book club or lunch with my editor, sure. I was just sticking with the familiar, wishing it was the Seventies, the Eighties again. But meeting you at Barbara's forced me out and brought me back.' She waved her glass towards the gallery. 'To all this. Life. I'd forgotten it was all here.'

Lara reached out and squeezed Martha's hand.

'Come on, let's pretend we're looking at the pictures.'

The exhibition consisted of 100 vast portraits of people who, in Cora's opinion, fit the title of 'Icon'. Movie stars - of course – artists, writers and even politicians, juxtaposed with 'ordinary' people – a nurse, a priest, an undertaker - all shot in dramatic grainy black and white. Each image had been blown up and hung from the roof, all cleverly orchestrated for maximum impact. Martha and Lara walked the circuit, focusing less on the art and more on the guests. Lara recognised two Hollywood stars, a news anchor and at least three East Coast heirs.

'I wonder if the undertaker has been invited,' said Martha, taking a sip of her cocktail. Lara could tell she was nervous, and she sympathised. Martha Riding was an experienced journalist; she had been to El Salvador,

Beirut, and even Tiananmen Square, but that had all been a long time ago, and tonight's plan would be difficult.

'Uh-oh,' said Lara from the side of her mouth. 'Target, twelve o'clock.'

'Twelve O'clock? What's that mean?'

'By the giant balloon animal.'

Cora Bryant was standing next to a bright pink Jeff Koons sculpture, surrounded by well-wishers. She had dressed up too; a Simone Rocha balloon dress in, of course, bright red. It was edgy, chic and on brand. If she hadn't had another mission in mind, Lara would have gone up and congratulated her.

'She's moving,' said Lara. Cora had left her group and was walking towards the back of the gallery. 'But I doubt she's leaving. The party has only just started and I think she's the sort to want to soak up all the attention.'

'We don't want to take any chances,' said Martha. 'We'd both better be quick in any event. Cora will certainly throw us out once I speak to her, so if you want to catch Savage, now is your opportunity.'

Lara squeezed Martha's arm in reassurance. She was experienced enough to know this was a long shot. Savage was heavily protected and Cora Bryant was savvy.

But they had to try. Lara watched her friend set off towards the back door through which Cora Bryant had just disappeared. Martha had been kind to say how grateful she was for Lara's friendship, but the feeling was mutual. Ever since her relationship with Alex had turned romantic and he had moved to LA, Lara had missed close companionship. Looking back over the past few months in London, Lara had spent her time working on her houseboat on the Thames, researching new story ideas, writing the odd piece for Darius and the Chronicle team, but she could see how she had been so lonely.

'Alex Ford, I presume,' said a voice behind her. 'Or should we start using your real name?'

Lara spun around to see Summer Phelps standing there. She wore a shimmering white gown, her hair piled up to show off a long neck. She might be almost fifty, but Summer looked at least a decade younger; a combination of her mother's bone structure and Eliot Jones' dark eyes made her one of the most attractive people in the room.

Lara didn't answer. Summer had obviously recognised her from Donna's launch – perhaps she had even ordered Lara's eviction from that party. Summer Phelps had the cool, knowing gaze of someone with both street smarts and intelligence, and Lara knew there was no point telling her anything other than the truth.

'Don't worry, I'm not going to call security,' said Summer.

'Good. I hear that Mace can play hell with your mascara.'

Lara thought she saw the hint of a smile on Summer's face. She extended a hand.

'Summer.'

'Lara Stone.'

'So you're the person who has left me repeated messages over the past week?'

'I've been trying to get in touch with Stephen Savage. I figured you were the way in.'

Summer cocked her head slightly, assessing her.

'What do you want from Stephen? The same thing you wanted from my mother?'

Lara shrugged.

'I'm a journalist.'

'I know. I Googled you. Look, why don't we go somewhere we can talk,' said Summer. 'The sculpture garden will be quiet.'

Lara hid her surprise - she hadn't expected Summer

Phelps to be quite so ready to talk to her – but followed her through the back of the gallery and down a shallow flight of steps into the garden and immediately felt herself relax. Lara had spent her teen years in a grand English stately home, a bright ray of light in a time of dark clouds. The garden had been her Aunt Olivia's domain who, for all her many faults, also had an eye for statuary – fauns and goddesses emerging from foxgloves and allium – and in Lara's memory, those days had been full of sunshine and flitting butterflies. The sculpture garden at The Savage was equally lovely, a surprisingly lush courtyard with artful gaps cut in the shrubs to display the beautiful curves of Rodin, Hepworth and Moore.

Summer stopped at a pair of curved benches and sat delicately. Lara crossed to perch opposite, trying hard to read Summer's face.

'So, do you want to tell me what story you are working on? Something a little more than a retrospective of Verity Jones' life and times, I'm guessing.'

'I'm staying at the house where Verity died. I thought I'd look into it,' replied Lara.

Summer gave a low laugh.

'Really? I was in Dallas on business last month but I didn't feel the urge to start investigating JFK.'

'Maybe that's because you're a music industry executive, not an investigative reporter.'

Summer was holding a flute of champagne and took a quiet sip.

'What do you want, Ms Stone?'

'I want someone held accountable for the death of Verity Jones.'

'Lara, Verity Jones died of heart failure. It was tragic, but there has never been any suggestion of foul play.'

Lara took a breath.

'Verity Jones was deliberately administered pure,

potent heroin by Cora Bryant for material gain. Stephen Savage helped cover it up. In return, Gene Henderson joined his record label, and from there, Savage built his empire.'

The garden was entirely silent, like the pause after a gunshot. Lara tried to decipher Summer's expression, but it was a perfect poker face—cool and devoid of emotion.

'I thought you were a journalist, not a fiction writer,' said Summer finally.

'It's all true, Summer. But then I think you already knew that.'

'You can't prove any of it.'

Possibly not, thought Lara. But it was also interesting that Summer Phelps hadn't denied a single point.

'I have witnesses.'

There was a pause.

'Do you?'

Summer had said it as a challenge, yet Lara detected a hint of something else—curiosity. Martha had urged Eliot Jones to tell Summer that he was her father just a few days earlier. Had he done it? Was Summer questioning the events of that Malibu weekend herself? Certainly, Summer did not seem surprised by any of this. Perhaps it was time to appeal to her better side.

'Summer, I've asked around,' said Lara. 'You have a reputation as one of the few fair and dedicated people in this business. There are plenty of sharks and monsters in LA, but you're not one of them. Everyone I spoke to said the same thing – you have integrity. Stephen Savage is your boss and mentor, and I thought you should know what sort of man you're working for.'

'That's right, he is my boss,' said Summer, her voice gathering more steel. 'And it's my job to protect him. I don't know who your *witnesses* are, but let me tell you this. Do not trust them. Stephen Savage is a very wealthy and powerful man – which makes him a target. If you succeed in this town, one half of it can't leave you alone, while the other half wants to drag you down. And this accusation sounds like the kind of hit job I deal with every week of my working life.'

'You want an accusation – I'll give you one,' said Lara. 'Verity Jones was murdered.'

'Murdered?' Summer laughed, but Lara carried on.

'Verity Jones wrote 'Time For Change' the day of the party - the day she died. We know she wrote it because we have her handwritten lyrics. She played the song for Gene Henderson and Cora Bryant – again, we have evidence, a film of the moment it happened. Cora and Gene wanted the song for themselves, so they went back to The Malibu House after midnight and tried to soften Verity up with drugs. But they gave her too much. Cora went to get Stephen to help, but it was too late. She died. So – yes, it was tragic. But it was also deliberate.'

Summer glared at her.

'If you print a word of that, if you utter one word on a podcast – or if I even hear you passing this off as a joke - then Stephen Savage will sue you, and he will ruin you.'

Lara looked the woman directly in the eye.

'Do you really want to protect a man like that?'

Summer's perfect lip curled.

'Why come here, Lara?' she said. 'Even if it was true, do you honestly believe Stephen would admit to any of this?'

It was a good question. Why *was* Lara here? When she first contacted Summer, she wanted an audience with Stephen Savage simply because he was one of the few surviving members of Verity's core group of friends who had been at the Malibu House that night. Now she suspected – no, she *knew* – that Savage was involved in the events surrounding Verity's death.

But Summer was right: Savage would never confirm anything. So, what did she hope to achieve by telling Summer? She simply had to hope the woman had as much integrity as people said.

'I came here to appeal to you. Ask Stephen and see what he says. Perhaps he might tell you something.'

That amused smile was back.

'And if he did,' said Summer, 'Do you expect me to come running back to you with an affidavit?'

Lara knew she had to take a chance. She didn't know whether Eliot Jones had spoken to Summer about her true parentage, but either way, the facts remained: Eliot was still married to Verity at the time of her death, which made Verity Jones Summer's step-mom. Perhaps deep down, Summer felt a little of that connection.

'Verity Jones was a good woman,' said Lara, 'Just like you are, Summer. She always tried to help people; she gave dozens of people a break, including people close to you. Now I think it's time we paid some of that debt back by telling the world how and why she died.'

Summer bowed her head.

'Do you think it matters now, after all this time?'

'I think the truth always matters.'

She watched Summer think it over.

'So what do you propose?'

Lara stood up.

'I think we need to speak to someone else.'

Chapter 42

The door at the back of the gallery led to a corridor with grey walls and a poured concrete floor. Martha knew enough architects to guess it would have been designed at great expense, but still, it reminded her of a prison, which was where Cora Bryant belonged.

Where have you gone? thought Martha, peering past plate glass into a sterile meeting room. In her directional vermillion dress, Cora had been hard to miss at the party, but backstage, it was as quiet as a mausoleum, and the photographer was nowhere to be seen.

A door at the end of the passage was slightly ajar. Martha slipped off her shoes so she could pad across the concrete quietly. Martha had felt the cold acutely for years, and the iciness underfoot sent a shiver up to the back of her neck. She could hear Cora's voice, ending a phone call – 'Don't give me excuses, just make it happen' - and her tone indicated she was in a bad temper. *Great start.* But Martha only had herself to blame; it had been her suggestion to directly confront both Cora and Savage. Martha had received some advice from a Washington Post friend in the early days of her career. If your story gets *stuck*, he had told her, challenge all the main players. Poke the hornet's nest. The advice contradicted editors she trusted– cautious men who liked to run everything past lawyers and not give people a right to reply until the final moment - it had served her well throughout her career. Ask the question; don't be afraid.

She peered through the crack between door and frame and could see expensive art on the walls – a Lichtenstein and a Pollack –beneath them, Cora leant against a metal desk, rolling a joint. *Old habits die hard,* she thought, stepping into the room.

Cora looked up and blew out a stream of grey smoke.

'Oh. It's you,' she said, then held out the glowing joint.

'Just taking the edge off. Want some?'

Martha shook her head. She had tried grass at Graham and Joni's place on Lookout Mountain in '68. It had made her jittery and uncomfortable, exactly the opposite of what she needed right now.

'So you got yourself a ticket to the party,' said Cora. 'I said I'd get you one, didn't I? I've been busy. I apologise.'

Martha felt exposed, standing in front of this confident woman in her bare feet.

'Congratulations on the exhibition,' she said awkwardly. 'It's wonderful.'

Cora gave a satisfied little laugh.

'People are calling it a lifetime retrospective, but I'm not even nearly ready for that.'

'Still, over forty years of work,' said Martha. 'You have shot everyone.'

Martha let a heavy pause hang between them.

'No photographs of Gene, though.'

Cora gave a one-shoulder shrug.

'I thought it would be too obvious.'

'Obvious? Or do you just want to forget about him? Forget about how you got here.'

'Excuse me?' said Cora, her dark eyes narrowing.

'Without Gene, you might never have discovered photography, right? You studied fashion for a year before you dropped out to hang out with Gene. And when he got famous, you sold some photos of him to Rolling Stone. '

'Yes, it was a break,' said Cora, her smile slightly more brittle. 'But I was always creative and ambitious. I would have made it without him.'

'Ambition. It's the quality that nobody ever talks about in LA. People talk about starlets arriving at Union Station with nothing but their drop-dead gorgeous looks. But nobody talks about the drive and the ruthlessness you need to make it here.'

'What do you want, Martha?' said Cora, stubbing out the joint.

'I wanted to talk about Gene's big break. Writing Time For Change, releasing it on Savage's label…'

'You can read about that in any rock biography.'

'True. But I wanted to discuss it with someone who was there. And I thought this might help jog your memory.'

Martha opened her clutch bag and took out a piece of paper. Cora unfolded it, then lifted her gaze to frown at Martha.

'Song lyrics for Time For Change?' she said. 'Where did you get this? From a student's bedroom wall?'

'It's a copy from the original. Which is in a vault.'

It wasn't strictly true, although Martha had sent Bobby round to Della Henderson's place that afternoon to persuade her to put the framed lyrics into safe storage. Della had asked all sorts of questions and demanded Lara Stone wouldn't drag her brother's reputation through the mud. Martha only hoped the reassurances they'd given were true.

'The original?' said Cora. 'I doubt that very much.'

'Della Henderson seems to think it is.'

'Della?'

Martha nodded.

'Gene tried to leave you many, many times, didn't he? Once, he moved in with his sister for a couple of weeks and left a suitcase behind. That lyric sheet was in it.'

'I'm surprised Della hasn't sold it.'

'Really? But Della loved Gene – really loved him. This song sheet has a lot of sentimental value.'

Martha paused, keeping her eyes on Cora's face.

'Although I'd guess she wouldn't be quite so attached to it if she knew her brother hadn't written it.'

She watched Cora absorb the information and saw her mind working, looking for those angles. Then she reached for the butt of the joint and tucked it into a matchbox she had been holding. Still careful about disposing of the evidence, Martha noted.

'I thought I was the one who had been smoking something,' said Cora. 'If you're trying to imply that Gene didn't…'

'A graphologist – a handwriting expert – compared it with a sample of Gene's writing,' said Martha, interrupting. 'It's not a match. Those words – and the music - were written by Verity Jones.'

Cora's eyes narrowed. 'Bullshit,' she sneered.

Now that's the Cora I remember, thought Martha; cool, vicious. Utterly convinced she would win.

'This was written at the Malibu House, wasn't it?' said Martha, tapping the lyric sheet. 'The afternoon of that last party.'

Cora snorted.

'That's not true.'

'Yes, it is. We have a home movie of Gene and Verity sitting at the piano dated to that day. And you know who's in the background? You are, Cora.'

Martha watched Cora's eyes flick towards the lyric sheet. The smoking gun.

It wasn't an admission, but Martha could see it was eating her up: How much did they know? What evidence did they have? She was off balance, and now it was time to start pushing.

'Your relationship with Gene was volatile, wasn't it? Passionate, yes, but unpredictable. Some might even call it co-dependent. So you persuaded him to steal Verity's song.'

Cora's expression soured. 'Not true,' she snapped. 'Never was, never will be.'

'And, of course, you're entirely unbiased?'

Martha had checked: as his wife and next of kin, Cora Bryant received all of Gene's royalties – and the income from a perpetual hit like 'Time For Change' would certainly be enough to set up Point Studios and keep her in film for the rest of her life. A motive enough, even without Cora's raging ambition.

'Okay, let me tell you what actually happened,' said Cora, rattling the matches absently. 'Yes, Gene and Verity hung out together that afternoon, jamming at the piano. That happened all the time; musicians throwing ideas around, it was a collective atmosphere. Even you won't deny that? Then Gene got a tune in his head and played it to Verity. She could see it was good; she could hear the magic, so she wrote it down for him.'

She pointed to the lyric sheet still lying on the table.

'That music, those words? They came from Gene's head. It may be Verity's handwriting, but that's because it was a transcription, Martha. As a journalist, you should know all about that.'

Martha tried to keep her cool. This was a plausible recollection of events to an outsider, and since the two main players were dead, Cora was the only witness.

Martha could see Cora had regained her swagger, but still, she pressed on.

'What 'really' happened is that Verity wrote the song, and you recognised it was a hit. You begged her to let Gene record the song, but she said no. So you decided to steal it.'

Cora threw her head back and laughed.

'You are a scream, Martha. You really are.' Then, her cold eyes met Martha's. 'But don't imagine I'm going to let you go around spreading this fiction.'

Over the years, she had moved among plenty of bullies and dictators: Mugabe, Pinochet, even Nixon. They all had one thing in common: they liked to intimidate. Martha knew Cora Bryant had money and fame; in the main gallery, hundreds of people were fawning over her work, and she would never jeopardise her status by allowing anyone to shine a light on her origins story. But how far would she go to protect her position? Just then, Martha remembered another piece of advice from an old editor back in the sixties. *Audacity*.

'Don't underestimate audacity, Riding,' he'd say. 'Sometimes audacity is the only thing which will get you in the room.' Her editor had been talking about getting past police lines or over-zealous press people, how you found your way into an exclusive face-to-face with a politician or celebrity, but now Martha knew it might apply here too.

'I'm just repeating what Gene said.'

Martha saw alarm flash in Cora's eyes.

'What *Gene* said? What did he say? When? You barely *knew* Gene.'

It was the smallest of giveaways. When Cora was anxious, her voice rose a tone. A 'tell', as they said in poker.

'No, I didn't know Gene,' said Martha with more confidence. 'Not really, not enough for him to confide his deepest, darkest secrets. You needed to be a true friend for that. A friend like Bert Walters.'

'Bert Walters?' she scoffed. 'That jealous loser?'

Martha didn't move her gaze from Cora.

'Perhaps. But even you wouldn't deny Gene loved Bert like a brother. He didn't see him much, not once Gene was famous, not once you told him you hated him seeing his 'jealous loser' friends. But Gene saw Bert when it counted.'

Martha opened her clutch again and took out an envelope, slightly yellowed at the edges. *Audacity*.

'Gene left you the morning after Verity's death, didn't he? He felt awful about what happened at the Malibu house and blamed you.'

Bert hadn't exactly said that to Lara, but Martha was improvising, imagining Gene's sorrow and regret.

'Gene and Bert drove down to Mexico. And Gene told Bert everything.'

'Says who? Bert? Have you paid him to sell his story? I hear that work is hard to come by for washed-up writers like Bert, and desperate people are unreliable people, Martha. Years in journalism must have taught you that, surely?'

A note of panic had entered Cora's voice now. Martha held up the old envelope.

'Bert had a lawyer in his family.'

It was pure speculation, but Bert went to UCLA, and most middle-class people knew at least one lawyer.

'So Bert knew the importance of protecting yourself. He got Gene to write everything down. A just-in-case-I-don't-come-back kind of letter. A confession, really. We all knew you could be terrifying, Cora, but I think Gene really was scared of you.'

'This is bullshit,' she spat. 'Bullshit!'

The word echoed in her head again. *Audacity*.

'Really? Because I have the letter here.'

Cora stared at the envelope Martha was holding, her face pale now. It was, of course, a bluff. There was nothing in the envelope. Martha had left the clutch bag hanging in The Carousel for decades, and its contents were like a flashback to the Nineties—a compact mirror, a tarnished old quarter, a receipt from a long-dead coffee shop, and this brown envelope, which had once contained tickets for an event just like this one.

'Your lawyer will argue that the three of you were just hanging out and that narcotics were part of the mix. But Verity didn't touch heroin, did she? So you told her it was coke. 'Just a line', that's what you said, wasn't it?'

It was the phrase Bert had used, and Martha saw Cora's eyes flare.

OMG, she thought. *She really did it.*

'Jameson Bennett was your dealer, wasn't he? He knew how potent the drugs he was selling were. You knew, too. A junkie like you could handle it, Verity couldn't.'

'It wasn't like that,' Cora. *And there it was.* The unguarded moment that Martha had been waiting for. Cora might be protesting, but she was confessing, too.

'We know everything, Cora. You tricked Verity into taking heroin, and when she'd had a fatal overdose, you ran to find Stephen Savage to help clear it up.'

'Enough!' shouted Cora. She made a swipe at for envelope, but Martha snatched it back.

Martha shook her head. 'It won't do you any good. We have notarised copies.'

To her surprise, Cora stood perfectly still and started clapping.

'Oh, well done, Nancy Drew,' said Cora, her voice dripping with sarcasm. 'So you've worked it all out: well done. But so what? No DA would pursue a case against someone with nothing but a crazy letter written by a hippy who was high as a kite.'

Martha conceded she had a point. But then she reminded herself there wasn't even a written confession in the first place.

'It's all true though, isn't it?' said Martha quietly. 'Come on, tell me. As you say, it won't change anything. But I was there that day, Cora. I need to know.'

Cora leaned back against the table, opening her matchbox and firing up the rest of her joint. She looked arrogant and in control—a narcissist feeling her power.

'Okay, so Verity wrote the song,' she said, shaking out a match. 'But it doesn't matter. Gene recorded it and it was Gene's voice and his charisma which made it a hit. Gene made a lot of people a lot of money.'

'That's right. Gene, you, Savage. But not Verity. Verity paid for it with her life.'

'I was helping her!' Cora snapped. 'When we got there on Gene's bike, Verity was a mess, drunk as hell. Do you know why? Because Eliot was screwing Donna – that's why she broke up the party that night. And so yes, I gave Verity some of Jameson's dope, but I was just helping her dull the pain. I didn't know she had a weak heart.'

'Would you have cared ?'

Cora smiled and blew smoke in Martha's direction.

'I guess not. But, y'know - it all worked out, didn't it? Gene got the song. Stephen Savage became rich, and the cops bought the heart attack story.'

She gestured dismissively towards Martha's envelope.

'And fifty years on, do you really think you can prove otherwise?'

'Maybe not, but we are certainly going to try,' said a voice behind them.

Summer Phelps was standing there, her face a mask of cold fury. Martha could see Lara lurking behind, holding the door shut.

'How…how long have you been standing there?' said Cora.

'Long enough,' said Summer.

Cora's pale face twisted into a nasty smile.

'Tread carefully, honey. You know your mother is up to her neck in all this.'

But Martha was pleased to see that Summer didn't flinch.

'It's your neck you should be worried about, Cora,' she said.

Cora's eyes blazed.

'I will be fine, I always am,' she said, raising her chin. 'And if you'll excuse me, I think I am needed in the gallery.'

Her dress rustled as she strode for the door.

'And fuck you, Martha,' Cora hissed as she pushed past. 'You always were a nosy bitch.'

Martha smiled.

'Oh, you ain't seen nothing yet.'

Chapter 43

Summer slammed the door of her Porsche and strode towards Stephen Savage's home. The night was still warm and fragrant, the cicadas in full chorus, but Summer was in no mood to appreciate any of it. She hadn't climbed to the heights of the cutthroat media world without knowing this basic rule: never go into a meeting angry. But after her encounter with Lara and Cora Bryant at the gallery, Summer knew there was no way she could leave this until morning.

Despite being the host of Cora's party, Stephen had left early and retired to his estate in the Bel Air corner of the Platinum Triangle. Wanting to catch him before he turned in for bed, Summer had taken corners at speed and skimmed through stoplights. *Screw the tickets*, she thought as she jabbed at the brass bell. She'd charge them to The Foundation. Savage could afford it, as this angular modernist house would attest – it was a virtual twin to the Foundation building and had cost almost as much to build.

She rapped impatiently with the black iron knocker, and the oak door swung open on silent hinges. Hong,

Stephen's Vietnamese butler, stood to one side, his expression unreadable.

'Miss Phelps,' he said with a bow. 'Is Mr Savage expecting you?'

'Oh, I think he'll want to see me,' she said, stepping inside.

'Mr Savage is in the stables. If you'd like to follow….'

'I know where it is, thanks Hong,' she said briskly, brushing past. Savage had lived in the house for almost twenty years, and Summer knew every room and passageway. Her heels clicked on the polished Honoki floor, imported from Shikoku in Japan at huge expense. Savage's whole mansion had a muted elegance that whispered, 'I also collect Rothko and Fontana' – which, of course, Stephen did. Every detail had been meticulously curated, from the art to the carefully arranged colour-matched books on the shelves, all the work of interior designers. Summer was willing to bet Savage had never once opened a single one. She pushed out onto the rear terrace at the end of a corridor and turned left down to the low stable block. Savage kept ponies but rarely rode; he just liked grooming them. It was his way of relaxing, and given his illness, she wasn't surprised that he had left the party early and come here.

She found her boss in the first stall, brushing a snow-white gelding named Dylan; all the horses were named for musicians who'd refused Savage's advances. The joke was that he got to make them jump anyway.

'Summer,' he said as she walked in. Savage was wearing jodhpurs and riding boots, his grey hair worn long, like it was still the 1970s. 'You do know what time it is?'

'We need to talk.'

He glanced across at her.

'Sounds ominous.'

'It is, Stephen.'

Considering his illness, Stephen Savage still had a commanding presence about him. His sharp, piercing eyes locked onto hers.

'So I take it you've been speaking to Martha Riding.'

Summer frowned.

'How did you know?'

'Cora called me. She's…unsettled by the whole thing.'

'*She's* unsettled? Cora's had fifty years to get comfortable with it.'

He didn't reply; he simply put down the brush and patted the horse's neck affectionately. *Who are you?* She wondered. *What kind of man are you?*

Summer couldn't stop thinking about how Lara Stone had described her. 'You have integrity'. She realised the reporter was trying to flatter her, but Summer had always tried hard to do the right thing, even when swimming with the sharks. And she had to do the right thing now.

'I can't believe you are involved in this, Stephen,' she said quietly. 'Why have you kept this from me all this time?'

'I've never told anyone, Summer, because I've always wanted to forget that night.'

'So it's true,' she said simply. 'All of it.'

'All of what, exactly?' asked Savage. Taking a deep breath, Summer gave Stephen a precis of everything she knew – or at least everything Lara Stone had told her: Verity writing Time For Change, Gene and Cora wanting the song, returning to Verity's house after the party, the overdose, the clear-up.

'Yes, that's about the sum of it,' said Stephen, not looking at her, stroking the gleaming pale horsehair, quite ghostly in the low light.

'So that's how you managed to sign Gene as a client. I always wondered why he went with you, the inexperienced teenager.'

'I was twenty, and I was good,' he said, his tone harder now.

'It was still payback though, wasn't it?'

The horse snorted and shuffled sideways, unsettled by Summer's raised voice.

'Let's find somewhere to sit,' said Stephen, his voice almost a whisper.

She followed him out of the stable block and into an outdoor seating area overlooking the estate. The terrace was subtly lit with hidden bulbs, which gave the area an eerie glow, but the eye was drawn to the distant lights of the city. Savage eased himself onto a sofa, and Summer sat opposite him. Stephen took a breath; Summer noticed he wasn't filling his lungs. She felt a stab of guilt, but this conversation needed to happen.

'You have to understand, I was some geeky kid from the suburbs,' he began quietly, 'My Dad was an accountant; our lives were Wonder Bread and Little League. But my escape was rock music. I adored it and had a good ear, too. I could spot a hit from the first few bars on the radio. I was desperate to get into music, for it to become part of my life, but there was no way in for a kid like me until my mom's brother, Uncle Shep, came back into the picture.'

A fond smile played across his face.

'Shep was an artist. He'd been living in Brazil for years but returned to California and got a trailer in Malibu.'

'My mom and I visited him one day, and he told me about Verity, how she lived just a few yards down the beach, how all the music industry legends would come to party there. Then Shep got a new boyfriend, some lawyer who lived in Palm Springs, so he gave me a key to the trailer, told me to get out to Verity's and network my ass off.'

Savage had always been a hard-nosed businessman; even in his social life, he was efficient and cutthroat, but when he talked about getting the keys to Shep's trailer, he lit up.

'So I got busy, making contacts, learning everything I could. I was younger than most of that crowd, but it was obvious I loved the music. I'd badger them with questions, asking them how it all worked; they liked having a kid around who was so into it. Your mom in particular.'

Summer gave an ironic laugh.

'Well, she always liked attention.'

'Sure, but the others never really took Donna seriously as a musician - only I could see her potential as a performer. Anyway, Verity, let me hang around, and for that, I'll always be grateful.'

He took a long breath, then started coughing, yanking a handkerchief from his pocket to muffle it. Summer tried not to let sentiment sway her.

'That night, Stephen,' she prompted. 'What happened?'

Savage looked out over the treetops towards the bowl of Los Angeles.

'I was on the beach having a drink around the fire when I saw Donna running away from the house. She was obviously upset, so I followed her. She was crying hard, bitching about Eliot and Verity, but not really making any sense. So I took her down to Shep's trailer, gave her a couple of drinks – she passed out.'

Summer nodded; that, at least, was a familiar scenario for her.

'And then?'

'I went back to the party, but by then it was over, Verity was kicking everyone out. So I went back to the trailer, too. Read a book, listened to some music, made sure Donna was okay. But at around 12:30, there was a banging on the door.'

'Cora.'

Stephen nodded.

'She was white as a sheet, make-up running down her face. She kept saying 'Oh fuck, oh fuck' on a loop, then babbling about Verity, Gene and some song. Saying she needed my help.'

'Did you know Verity had overdosed?'

He shook his head, his eyes starting to get misty with tears.

'But when I got back to Verity's place, I immediately saw something was wrong. Overdose, heart attack, I don't know. Gene had put her in a cold bath, trying to revive her, but I felt for Verity's pulse. There was nothing.'

'So she was dead when you got there?'

Stephen nodded, his face grave.

'There was nothing I could do,' he said, a note of pleading in his voice. 'We were just kids, Summer. We were scared, we panicked. And they looked to me because I was the only one who could think straight. So I got Cora and Gene out and removed anything that linked them to the scene.'

'Including the song?'

He looked at her. And in that moment, Summer knew that Lara Stone had been right about everything. It might not have been Stephen's idea, but he had gone along with it and used the situation to his advantage. He'd conspired with Cora to keep quiet all these years. Summer felt choked by a feeling of sinking disappointment. Music was a ruthless business; Summer knew that - she had the scars to prove it, but she had always thought Stephen was different. He was ballsy, daring. He took risks. But Summer had always felt he'd pulled it all off through sheer brilliance. It was crushing to hear that Stephen was just like everyone else: greedy, impatient and happy to step on fingers if it got him what he wanted.

'And what about my mom?' she asked, remembering

Cora's words at the gallery. *She's up to her neck in this.* 'How does she fit into all this?'

Stephen avoided her gaze and Summer gaped at him.

'She *is* involved, isn't she?' Until that moment, she hadn't quite believed it, even though she knew Donna would do anything if it helped Donna.

Stephen took another gulping breath.

'Remember Donna was still holed up in Shep's trailer? When Cora hammered on the door, she must have woken her up. And by the time I got back, Donna was awake, wide-eyed and told me she had heard everything.'

In the distance, Summer heard the snorting of horses.

'She blackmailed you, didn't she?'

'Nothing was said, but we understood one another. She wouldn't say anything about Verity in return for me keeping quiet about her affair with Eliot.'

In return for keeping quiet about me, thought Summer, a sick feeling in her stomach. 'You've known that Eliot Jones is my father all this time?'

His face was grey now.

'I suspected.'

'Bullshit, Stephen,' said Summer, anger rising. 'Even now, you can't admit it. Even now, you're in denial about what you've done.'

'What? What did I do?' he pleaded.

'Stephen, you covered up a murder!'

'Not a murder, an accident,' replied Stephen, but there was no force to his words. 'Even the police put Verity's death down to natural causes. We were all devastated that she had passed; of course we were, but what could we do? We didn't want to be dragged into a police investigation; our lives would have been ruined just as they were getting started.' His voice trailed off. 'And it was an accident. It was.'

Summer shook her head in disbelief. Together, they

had brought about Verity's death, and together, they had profited from it. Even her mother.

'So what did Donna want from you? More than your silence, I am guessing.'

He stared out at the dark city.

'After 'Time For Change' had gone to number one, Gene Henderson was the hottest new singer in the world - and I was hot too. That was when Donna came to see me and said she wanted me to manage her. Said I owed it to her.'

Summer had always known how self-centred her mother was, so it was zero surprise to discover Donna had used Verity's death to her advantage.

'I always wondered,' she said quietly. 'Why you spent so much time and attention on a washed-up folk singer.'

Savage shook his head.

'Don't underestimate her, Summer. Maybe she wasn't going to make it as a singer, but I knew from the start that Donna would always do what it takes to succeed. And as history has shown us, Donna is nothing if not adaptable.'

Summer closed her eyes, willing herself not to buckle. All of the people in her life, all the people she trusted: her mother and her mentor, they were all out for what they could get. She supposed it was why they were the ones left standing.

'Have you ever felt guilty?' she asked.

'I feel it every day of my life.'

Summer wasn't sure she believed him.

'You need to do something, Stephen,' she said. 'It's not too late. 'Time For Change' has generated millions of dollars in royalties for Cora Bryant over the years, and she doesn't deserve one cent of it.'

'But what do I do, Summer?' he said, lifting his hands. 'I can't tell the truth about what happened that night. My career, my business, everything I've worked for. It would all come crashing down.'

'Fix it, Stephen. I know you can.'

'Fix it?' he said incredulously. 'How?'

'You're a clever guy, and we've spent months discussing your 'legacy.' Well here's your opportunity – your *real* legacy. You can make this right.'

She stood up.

'Because if you don't, I will.'

Chapter 44

'Dammit, closed,' said Lara as she walked past the Downtown donut shop. She had been meaning to visit ever since she'd read about 'Glazed and Confused' on the flight over, but there was no arguing with the business-like padlocks on the shutters.

'Ah well, I'm not dressed for donuts,' she murmured, looking down at Martha's Halston gown. Instead, she ducked into a corner bodega and picked up take-out coffee, where Lara's glittering neckpiece didn't even raise an eyebrow.

The arts district – and the Savage gallery – was only a couple of blocks from the Globe office, and Lara wanted to surprise Alex. Coffee was always welcome when you were working late.

'Evening, Miss Stone,' said Earl on reception. 'Been a while.'

When she'd left Heathrow on this two-week vacation, Lara had imagined herself popping by all the Globe offices all the time, bringing Alex sandwiches and meeting for after-work cocktails in funky hipster bars. But it hadn't quite worked out that way and she was surprised the receptionist remembered her at all.

'Hey, Earl. Here's my pass,' she said, fumbling in her bag for the visitor's card, but Earl waved it away.

'Just see if you can persuade Mr Ford to leave,' he said with a toothy grin. 'He's been putting in fifteen, sixteen-hour days all month. I'm expecting to see a bed delivered to his office any time now.'

'I'll try. No promises.'

The lift was empty as she rode it up to the tenth floor of the Globe editorial offices, and the doors opened onto a quiet, industrious newsroom, a skeleton staff hard at work at their computers; the lights of the office reflected on the black windows overlooking the city. The door to the editor's office was open, and Lara raised a hand to knock on the doorframe but stopped herself at the last moment. Alex was sitting at his desk, chair half-swivelled away from her, a copy of 'Limelight' in his hands. Lara held her breath, watching him, not wanting to spoil this moment. This was why Alex Ford had come all this way - five thousand miles and a huge cultural leap - to see if he could breathe life into an ailing newspaper. Had he pulled it off? Was it even possible, given he was swimming against the technological tide? In the end, Lara knew it didn't matter. The point was he'd come, and he'd tried. It hadn't quite struck Lara before this moment just how brave it had been for Alex to come here, leaving a prestigious job at one of the UK's top newspapers, leaving his home, his father, his friends – leaving her. That took guts.

'I'm proud of you,' she said.

Alex looked up, and that insta-smile came to his face. No hesitation, no ifs or buts. How could she ever have wanted anything, anyone else?

'Proofs just came in,' he said, lifting the magazine.

'And what do you think?'

'Pretty good,' he said, but his face betrayed his anxiety. Lara could sympathise. However much you put into a publication, however perfect you thought it was, the only opinion that mattered was the man in the street, the people who paid to read it. 'Hit and hope' was how Alex always described it, some old football metaphor meaning 'just get it out there and trust it'll work'.

Lara put down the coffee, took a copy from an open box, and flipped through the magazine. It was glossy, bright and full of energy, but at the same time, there were longer in-depth articles: the signs were certainly good.

'It's going to be a huge hit,' she said, walking around the desk and slipping her arms around his neck.

'Yeah. Fingers crossed, touch wood,' he said. 'And we've been getting a lot of enquiries for the launch party tomorrow night, so that's a good sign, isn't it?'

That's the man I love. Lara wasn't sure what the future held for her, but she didn't want to be anywhere else. She handed him his coffee and perched on the corner of his desk.

'Listen, I wanted to apologise,' she said.

'What for?'

She laughed.

'God, everything. I've been such a brat since I arrived. For spending so much time on the Verity Jones story, for not supporting you, for being grouchy and never even making pomelo cocktails when you went to all that effort to find them.

'No, no…'

She held up a hand. 'Seriously, Alex. I've given you such a hard time about everything. And I wanted to tell you: it's not you, it's me.'

'Oh God,' said Alex. 'Isn't that what girls say just before they're about to dump you?'

She bent to kiss him. 'Not this girl,' she said softly. 'Not ever.'

She hadn't planned a big speech, but now she was here, she wanted to explain her behaviour.

'When I found out about Verity Jones, I wanted to know what really happened to her. I knew there was a story there, and I wanted to get justice for her. But honestly? I chased down that story for myself. I wanted to prove I still had worth as a journalist, to remind myself that I was still good.'

Alex chuckled.

'Lara, you are the most talented journalist I have ever met. You could be an editor tomorrow if you wanted it, but we both know you're better off out there in the field. Using your instincts, making a difference. It's what you love. It's one of the many, many things I've always loved about you.'

His words meant a lot to her but Lara still wanted him to understand everything she was feeling.

'For a long time, I was on my own; well, near enough.' Her twenties and thirties had been marred by a string of one-night stands and short-lived relationships; Lara didn't need a shrink to tell her that she had been scared to get close to anyone because of the death of her parents when she was twelve.

'And because I've been alone, I've always thrown myself into my work. School work, university, the Chronicle. You were right when you called me a workaholic.'

'Come on, Lar…'

She clutched his hand.

'No, seriously, even now we're together, I still can't relax and enjoy life. I feel as if I don't work, then maybe my world will fall apart, and I will be exposed.'

Alex gave a soft smile.

'I get it, Lar, I do. I'm hooked on work too. I grew up

in that tiny town in the Lake District and I longed for excitement and adventure. That desire eventually brought me here, to this corner office in the most glamorous city in the world. But do you know when I was at my happiest?'

She shook her head.

'When I was with you, at dad's house in the Lakes over Christmas, even though that turkey dinner was a dry as a bone.'

Lara laughed and lifted his copy of Limelight. 'You might win Editor of the Year for this, but Gordon Ramsey has nothing to fear.'

'So I guess we're stuck with each other, huh?'

'I hope so.'

She reached back and handed him his coffee, taking a sip of her own drink.

'How was Cora Bryant's launch?' asked Alex. 'You look amazing by the way.'

Lara told him about her meeting with Summer Phelps and witnessing Martha and Cora's confrontation. Alex's mouth opened wider and wider as she spoke.

'Cora really confessed?'

'Alex, she knew how strong those drugs were. Surely it's murder?'

Alex shook his head sadly. 'I'd have to check with the lawyers, but I'd guess involuntary manslaughter at most. Verity took the drugs willingly, remember? And there's a statute of limitation on manslaughter: three years. It came up in another case a few weeks ago, where a producer had someone OD in his bathroom back in the noughties. They had to let him go.'

Lara had suspected as much; a statute of limitations – the time span in which a crime could be brought to trial – meant that many suspected criminals had avoided justice simply because after all this time, who would believe the witnesses, even if they could be found?

'What about murder? I thought you could be tried for a capital crime after any length of time.'

'Sure, but without witnesses and physical evidence? Honestly, I think it will be nearly impossible to pin anything on Cora, let alone Stephen.'

Lara knew he was right. What she had in the way of evidence was so thin, but she couldn't let everything she had found out be a waste and her mind groped around for ideas.

'What about getting it in front of ambitious deputy district Attorney or a minor politician. Someone might want to champion the case if they thought the publicity might help their campaign to jump up to Congress.'

Alex looked doubtful.

'Cora Bryant and Stephen Savage are exactly the sort of high-rollers ambitious politicians want to keep onside.'

Lara looked at him hopefully.

'Do you know *anyone?*'

Alex gave a sigh. 'Look, the mayor has a background in law. He might be persuaded he owes me a favour after the bridge business.'

Lara gave her boyfriend a soft smile. 'Maybe you are going to be good at this media mogul thing after all.'

Alex gave a sideways look.

'I thought you loathed all that boardroom game-playing?'

'Right now, I'm thinking 'whatever it takes to bring the bad guys down'. And besides…'

She slipped into his lap.

'All this power-playing? It looks kinda sexy on you.'

Alex pulled her closer.

'Really?' he smiled. 'Tell me more.'

Chapter 45

The rooftop bar of the Galaxy hotel was one of the highest in Los Angeles, giving a spectacular view of the city. The sky was dark blue, just past sunset, and the yellow-orange lights shimmered like a Christmas garland waving in the breeze. Alex stood at the edge of the terrace, smiling. *This* was what he'd come to LA for. A vibrant city full of energy in front of him, while behind him, spread over the top two floors of the hotel, was the biggest party in town. His party, the one he'd been planning since before he'd even moved to LA: the launch for 'Limelight', the Globe's brand new entertainment supplement.

Alex turned to look at the bar, the party-goers already spilling out onto the roof, around the small pool, a slab of glowing turquoise in the dark. Actors, agents, musicians, socialites, everyone who wanted to be seen was here. The Globe's PR agency had done an amazing job.

'It's pretty impressive,' said Lara, slipping a hand around his waist. 'See? I said you didn't need to worry.'

He grinned, kissing her neck.

'Hey,' she laughed. 'Don't let Donna Phelps see us

together. She'll work out my connection to the real Alex Ford.'

'Is she here?' he said, looking around anxiously.

'I'd imagine she's keeping a low profile, but Stephen Savage just arrived. I saw the convoy of Bentleys pull up; it was like the POTUS motorcade.'

'Stephen Savage? *Really?* We invited him, but I didn't think he would show.'

Alex felt a stir of anxiety. Savage's people knew of the link between Lara Stone and the Globe – she had used his business card to get into Donna Phelps' book launch, after all. Had he come to deliver a warning to Alex: stay away from the Verity Jones story?

'Do you think he's here to shut us down?'

'I doubt he'd have bothered to wear a Tom Ford suit to do that,' said Lara. 'No, he's here for the party.'

Perhaps she was right. The Limelight party was simply the place to be tonight. Alex could admit he'd been almost rigid with apprehension all day. Would anyone come? Would any of them be the kind of people he wanted to pay attention to Limelight – the industry players who, in turn, could give him the exclusives he so desperately needed? In the end, they all came: chatter and laughter was thrumming from the bar where cocktails – lime-themed, naturally – were oiling all the wheels.

'So can you relax now?'

'Are you telling me I'm uptight?'

'Only most of the time.'

He gave her an affectionate squeeze. 'But no,' he said. 'I can't relax because in…' - he looked at his watch – 'Ten minutes, I've got to make a speech.'

'What about?'

'Oh, you know. Entertainment is the lifeblood of this city, the Globe is here to help. Enjoy the canapes.'

'And by 'here to help', you mean 'run the Hollywood Reporter out of town'?

'Well yes,' Alex chuckled, 'But I won't put it like that.'

In actual fact, Alex had been surprised by the genuine enthusiasm he'd felt as he'd circulated among his guests. Agents were offering him their clients, studio heads were offering exclusives on up-coming projects: they wanted in. And why? Because in a world blighted by venal social media and fake news, the one huge advantage newsprint had over digital was its authority. Newspapers were old-fashioned, sure, but readers knew they could trust them. The Globe might print a negative review of a movie or TV show, but you knew the critic meant what he said, he wasn't just trolling you – and his views would be consistent and sane. The same went for the news and the sport and everything else. Except perhaps the horoscopes. Now all Alex had to do was keep people reading the Globe – and to keep paying for it. But that was a problem for another day.

'So does this mean you can take a holiday?'

'The fifteen hour days might become twelve hour days,' he smiled.

'Well, in that case, I might stay another couple of weeks,' said Lara.

Alex felt his heart leap, his mind immediately thinking of how he could make it up to her, all the places they could go – maybe Catalina Island or Newport Beach for the weekend, perhaps up to Francis Ford Coppola's Vineyard in Geyserville or one of the other delicious wineries in Sonoma and Napa.

'Lar, that's amazing. Oh.' He felt his enthusiasm fizzle out. 'But I'm not sure we'll be able to stay in the Malibu House.'

'Not necessarily a bad thing,' said Lara with a touch of

wistfulness. 'I think maybe we're done there. And speaking of which, here comes Simon. I'll leave you to it.'

Simon, for once, had a smile on his face—the smile of someone basking in adoration and the glow of high status.

'Alex, I have to say, this is spectacular party.'

'Have you tried the macadamia mini eclairs yet? They are something else.'

'And have you heard that Rolex want to take the back page ad for the next twelve months? And they are paying rate-card: the ad team are thrilled. Even Hermes is coming on board.'

He threw an arm around Alex's shoulder. 'Alex, it's a slamdunk - so you have my full backing to run this any way you like.'

Uh-oh, thought Alex. In political circles, 'my full backing' was usually a euphemism for 'I'm about to sack you.'

Still, if ever there was a moment to ask for what he wanted it was now.

'I need more budget for top-class columnists we talked about. I'd love to get another couple of staff onto the Limelight team – Natasha and Will are due a promotion - and I'd need a few days off next week. Just to regroup,' he said thinking of hibernating in a vast bed somewhere with Lara.

'All fine,' said Simon with a wave of the hand. 'However, there is one thing.'

Alex steeled himself.

'Go on.'

'Okay, so you're about to give your big speech, right? Well, I was hoping you might be able to add a little extra announcement to the end...'

Chapter 46

'Martha, you are looking incredible as ever.'

Harley Stuyvesant appeared at her side, offering a flute of champagne.

'It's a long way to come for a party, Harley,' she said, taking the drink.

'Oh, this isn't just a party, Martha. This is an opportunity,' he said, nodding towards all the heaviest hitters. 'Agents, managers, studio heads,' he said, practically rubbing his hands together. This was Harley's playground and he'd dressed for the occasion, tonight opting for 'Cary Grant in North By Northwest' in a pebble-grey three-piece suit and gold cufflinks. You had to hand it to Harley; he knew how to make an impact.

'So a little bird tells me you've been offered a column for the Globe.'

'It wouldn't be for me to say,' said Martha. 'But an announcement is imminent.'

Harley nodded.

'It's about time. You were always the best of the best, Martha. And you've inspired me to get back in the saddle: perhaps you could introduce me to Alex Ford?'

'Perhaps,' said Martha, although she doubted Harley Stuyvesant needed her help to get into print. He could just launch his own newspaper – and after the excitement surrounding the Globe tonight, it wouldn't have surprised her if he did.

'The other rumour I hear is that you've landed a huge scoop. Anything to do with Verity Jones, by any chance?'

Martha saw the twinkle in his eyes. He was fishing for information, but of course, given the questions she had been asking at his house, it was an obvious guess.

'Once again, you'll just have to wait and see.'

Martha wasn't entirely sure their Verity Jones story would ever see the light of day. There were too many holes and too many powerful people with the means to snuff it out, but truthfully, Martha wouldn't mind. Two weeks ago, she had walked out of the Polo Lounge feeling her career was over: she'd been sidelined and dismissed. But this investigation had given her a new lease of life; it had pushed her out into the world and reminded her who she was. She was Martha Riding, the writer. And no, perhaps this particular story would peter out, but as they used to say at the end of that 1950s TV cop show, 'There are eight million stories in the naked city.' All she had to do was find them.

'So I'm at the Waldorf for a few days,' said Harley. 'I have a box for Don Giovani at the opera on Saturday; I was wondering if you would do me the honour of accompanying me?'

She looked at him in surprise. Rebecca had warned her that Harley had been making enquiries, but she still hadn't expected him to ask her out quite so soon. But then, what had Rebecca said about getting a move on in later life?

'Saturday? Oh, Harley, I think I'm tied up. My book club runs until early in the evening…'

'Not a problem; I checked the tides. I can pick you up

from the beach in the Sikorsky; the Tower Heliport is only a few blocks from the Opera.'

Martha could see he was serious, and for a moment, she allowed herself to entertain the idea. She had certainly loved dressing up for Cora's opening; it was another side of herself she had shut off since Griffin had passed – she imagined herself in a swishing gown, walking under those glorious chandeliers on Harley's arm, every eye turning to admire them. Oh, it *would* be fun.

But across the room, she could see Bobby. His suit was off the peg, the knot of his tie slightly too fat, but when she caught his eye, he smiled. A warm, uncomplicated smile that said nothing more than 'I'm happy to see you.'

And when Bobby looked at her, Martha knew she was *seen*. Bobby liked her for who she was, not some fantasy or trophy.

'Sorry, Harley,' she said, touching his wrist. 'It's a wonderful offer, but I will have to say no.'

'You're…no?'

'No,' she repeated. 'But thank you.'

She walked across the floor and as Martha approached Bobby raised an eyebrow and nodded towards Harley.

'Is that man bothering you?' he said with amusement.

'No, he just offered to take me out in his helicopter on Saturday night.'

'Oh,' said Bobby, disappointment in his voice.

'But I told him I couldn't go.'

'Oh?' a hint of hope this time. 'What are you doing instead?'

'Staying in, eating pizza and watching a movie.'

'Any particular one?'

'Great Expectations. The Gwyneth Paltrow one.'

Bobby raised his glass.

'I'll see what I can do.'

Chapter 47

Alex Ford wasn't exactly Chris Rock, but he got a few laughs. Standing on a low stage, he thanked Simon, the staff and the guests for coming. Then he played the bumbling Englishman abroad for all it was worth – mix-ups with valet parking, tipping and the term 'fanny pack' all went down well, so he quickly slipped in the serious point about his commitment to making the LA Globe a modern fast-moving newspaper for a modern fast-moving city. That brought a ripple of heartfelt applause, so Alex figured he'd quit while he was ahead.

'But before I leave you, I'd like to announce our first signing – our first pick draft, I believe you call it over here.'

There was a twitter of interest.

'This writer is undeniably one of the greatest journalists the United States has ever produced. She has won a Pulitzer, a Peabody award and an Orwell Prize – and possibly more importantly, she's my boss's neighbour.'

Alex rode the laughter as he extended an arm across the room, 'Ladies and gentlemen, the Globe's new columnist, Martha Riding.'

There were excited 'Oohs', followed by whoops and

generous applause. Martha nodded modestly as the spotlight shone down on her. Alex could see she was pleased.

'...And now,' he said. 'I would like to introduce someone else I think you might know, who would like to say a few words. Please welcome to the LA Globe stage... Mr Stephen Savage.'

The applause was enthusiastic, although many expressions were bemused, and he couldn't blame them; why on earth would Stephen Savage be speaking at a newspaper party? Simon had given him very little hint what Stephen wanted to announce – other than the 'details had been worked out' and that Alex would be delighted. Alex's first thought was that Savage was about to buy the LA Globe – that would be an easy way to shut down any inconvenient stories about Verity Jones - but Simon had assured him it was not anywhere near that seismic. Even so, Alex's heart was thumping hard as Savage bounded on stage like a talk show host. Alex was stressed enough – the last thing he needed was any surprises.

'Thank you Alex, and may I quickly say how happy I am to be sharing a stage with you and your new team. We at the Savage Foundation are super-excited about where you're taking the Globe.'

He paused to smile at the audience. Where Alex had played on his all-in-this-together charm, Savage was slick, a man used to giving keynote speeches, a man used to being listened to. He was impressive, but Alex noted the dark smudges under his eyes. Maybe the guilt was finally getting to him.

'As many of you will know, it is the fiftieth anniversary of Savage this year.' Stephen showed a mouthful of even white teeth. 'Okay, so maybe I'm a *little* older,' he said, holding up finger and thumb to polite laughter. 'But when you reach my age, it is a time for thanks and reflection and tonight, I just wanted to point out to some of the most successful people in this crazy industry that my business would never have got off the ground if it were not for the encouragement and mentorship of my dear friend, the late great Verity Jones.'

Alex glanced at Lara. Standing at the front of the crowd, she looked as uncomfortable as he did.

But everyone else had started to wildly applause, and Savage waited until it died down. 'So why am I telling you this at an LA Globe party?' he asked.

Just tell us, thought Alex, wishing he had forced Simon Desai to tell him more than Stephen's announcement would be 'good for the paper'.

'Behind the scenes, I have been working with the Globe to exclusively launch The Verity Jones Scholarship for the arts.'

Alex looked over to Simon, who was beaming like a Cheshire Cat, and gave Alex a discrete thumbs-up sign.

'The scholarship will be dedicated to finding and nurturing new talent in music, literature and art. We don't want money to be a barrier for creativity, so I will be starting the scholarship program by personally giving an endowment of two hundred million dollars.'

There was a collective gasp, followed by cheering. Alex looked at him with a kind of horrified respect.

Oh, well played, he thought. Stephen Savage had a reputation for being a sharp operator, but this was a masterstroke. From this moment on, Verity's name would be associated with positivity and creativity, not drugs, death and deceit. More importantly, no one would be motivated to ask questions about Verity's final hours, for fear of robbing young people of their million-dollar windfall. Whatever the truth of Lara's investigation, with this one announcement, Stephen Savage had effectively washed his hands clean. He looked over to where Lara was standing, but she had gone.

Chapter 48

Lara was furious. If looks could kill, Stephen Savage would be toast. Martha tried to calm her, but Lara was too wound up, pacing back and forth across the Galaxy's roof-top bar, past the fairy-light lit Tiki bar and the swimming pool muttering curses.

Martha could understand, of course. She had watched Stephen Savage's speech open-mouthed, feeling their entire investigation slip away with each word. If she hadn't loathed Savage's self-seeking motivations, Martha might have given him a sort of grudging respect. He had stood up in front of LA's media community and created his own alternative narrative to the Verity Jones story – then dared them to contradict him. It was a high-risk, high-reward strategy, but Martha guessed it would work. The whole crowd was atwitter with excitement at this enormous act of generosity. At a stroke, Verity Jones had become a byword for kindness; no one was going to want to hear any alternative, especially not one involving drugs and grand larceny.

'He just outplayed us,' said Lara, two hot pink circles appearing on her cheeks.

'You have to hand it to him,' said Martha trying to be

the one to keep her cool. 'It's sneaky, but it's also kind of brilliant.'

'Brilliant?' gasped Lara. 'All Savage did was bury the truth beneath a giant pile of money. There must still be a way to tell the real story. All this can't have been for nothing.'

From the moment Martha had met Lara she had been impressed by the woman's single-minded pursuit of the truth, but Martha knew she had to give her honest opinion.

'Any negative spin on the Verity Jones story would look mean-spirited at the very least and might possibly strangle that scholarship at birth. And anyway, now the Globe has this exclusive link to the programme, I doubt even Alex is going to print a word against Savage. Right now, Stephen is bulletproof.'

Lara's mouth was in a firm line – she was not the sort to give up without a fight.

'So we publish it in the UK. The Chronicle has no connection to the scholarship or to Savage.'

Martha sighed: she had already run the alternatives in her own head.

'That's even worse,' she said. 'England has such strict libel laws; you can't print anything you can't prove and, frankly, we can't prove anything.'

Lara moved closer to Martha, glancing around the terrace to make sure no one overheard.

'Cora Bryant is a killer and a thief,' she hissed. 'And Savage is almost as guilty.'

'Perhaps,' said Martha. 'But honestly? I'm not even sure Stephen knows what happened at the Malibu House that night - and the only two witnesses are dead. No DA would take this on.'

Lara let out a quiet groan and Martha grabbed her hand in solidarity. When you'd worked in the media for nearly sixty years, you knew you were going to meet professional disappointment. Stories sometimes didn't stick, no matter how much you wanted them to. Lara Stone was undoubtedly a brilliant investigator – perhaps she had never encountered defeat before. Perhaps this was the assignment when she had to learn that sometimes the bad guys got away with it.

'Remember how you told me Alex said something the other day? About how you couldn't take down the whole system; the best you could hope for was to disrupt it a little?'

'Small victories,' said Lara. She closed her eyes. 'But Stephen Savage has won the whole game here. In fact he's come out as the *hero* in all this.'

A deep voice came from behind them.

'It's good of you to say so, Ms Stone.'

They both turned. Savage was standing there, a sardonic smile on his face.

'If I were you, Stephen, I wouldn't be smiling,' said Martha. 'We know what you did, we know what Cora did. Do you really think money is going to wash all that away?'

Stephen's smile faded.

'My money won't bring Verity back, no. But it can help thousands of other people become the new Verity.'

Lara snorted.

'And Mussolini made the trains run on time. One good deed doesn't make up for a lifetime of guilt.'

'And you must be Lara Stone,' he said with a solemn nod. 'Summer Phelps has told me all about you.'

Martha and Lara glanced at each other. Had Summer persuaded Stephen to do all this? Had the scholarship been her idea?

'Believe it or not, Verity meant a lot to me,' Stephen continued. 'I'm simply trying to do something to make amends.'

'A noble sentiment,' said Martha. 'Only slightly undermined by the fact you 'made amends' because you were about to be exposed.'

'What else would you have me do?' he asked.

'Tell the truth about what really happened. Take the consequences.'

'I can't. To 'tell the truth', as you put it, would hurt people not involved in this. My entire artist roster, my employees. Every one of them worked so hard for their success. Do you want them tarnished with a scandal, because this could take the whole company down.'

'Don't pretend you care for the artists,' scoffed Lara. 'You've made plenty of money from them all.'

'I've only ever tried to protect my artists,' he said cooly. 'Starting with Gene Henderson.'

Protecting Gene Henderson. Martha knew it was as near to a confession as they would get.

'Alright, then I have a proposal for you,' said Martha after a moment. 'One more of those good deeds you've become famous for.'

'I'm listening.'

'Time For Change was the song of a generation, right? But the writer didn't get any credit. Wouldn't you like to see that terrible oversight corrected?'

Savage frowned.

'You're suggesting we have Verity Jones listed as the song's author?'

'Co-author. I imagine Gene's sister and friends would support the idea. And now Verity is getting all this positive publicity? Well, I doubt anyone would object.'

'I think Cora would,' said Lara.

Martha looked meaningfully at Savage. 'Yes, I imagine she would, but perhaps one of her close friends might persuade Cora that it's the fair thing to do?'

'Unlikely, but perhaps,' said Stephen. 'If I have your

word that any story you write about all this will be about the song rather than the circumstances of Verity's death?'

'You won't stop us writing a story?' she asked, unable to hide her surprise.

'I won't sue – that's the best you're going to get.' His smile faded. 'I doubt I'll be there for a court case anyway.'

As he said the words, Martha noticed that he looked quite unwell. His eyes were rimmed with pink, he had lost his hallmark plumpness from his cheeks.

'Stephen…' she said, but he just gave a sharp shake of his head.

'It's good to see you, Martha. It's a shame we all lost touch. I guess Verity was the glue that held us together.'

'And drove us apart,' said Martha sadly.

Savage crossed the lobby and got into his waiting Bentley. As he drove away, Lara stared at the empty space.

'How can one man be both villain *and* sympathetic male lead in the same story?'

'Aren't we all like that?' said Martha. 'When it comes down to it?'

Lara shrugged. 'I still wish someone was going to prison.'

Martha squeezed Lara's hand. 'That's why you're such a good reporter.'

'Yeah right: great reporter,' said Lara sarcastically. 'I don't even have a story.'

'What? But Stephen practically gave us permission to write it.'

'He gave it to *you*, Martha. And it's a story you need to write: after all, you were there the day the song was born. And if Alex won't print it, I'll put you in touch with Darius. He'll bite your hand off.'

'Thank you,' said Martha.

Lara smiled.

'No problem. And actually, there is one thing you can

do in return. Ask around and find me a house at the beach. But preferably not one with a ghost.'

Martha gasped.

'You're staying?'

'I told Alex I'll stay another couple of weeks, but we can't expect Simon to let us stay on. And I like Malibu. I like London too, but I could rent somewhere for when I come over.'

Martha beamed.

'So I can sign you up for book club on a permanent basis?'

'Oh, I wouldn't go that far.'

Chapter 49

Lara walked up the staircase to the top floor, weaving her way across a dancefloor rippling with glittery gowns and slick suits, white smiles and jewellery; it seemed all of LA's movers and shakers were here. Glasses were being raised, laughter spiking, Limelight on everyone's lips. Despite all the hidden drama around Verity's story, Lara had to remember the launch of Alex's magazine was the reason everyone was here. Alex had taken a huge leap of faith, aligning the Globe with Tinsel Town's biggest industry, and it looked like it was paying off. It had been a long time since Lara had heard anybody talking about print media in such an excited way; people were actually standing at the bar reading it. She could see Alex in the far corner, deep in conversation with Hollywood leading man Sam Charles, and Lara felt a swell of pride. She left him to it, threading between the glitterati, enjoying the energy of the night, and beneath it all, Lara could just hear a familiar smoky voice coming through the speakers. Verity Jones singing 'Show Me How You Feel', the B-side from her debut 45. Lara had become something of an expert on the Laurel Canyon scene over the past couple of weeks. By tomorrow, she supposed, the rest of the world would be familiar with Verity Jones too, as the dazzling news of her new Scholarship spread. *Don't be a sore loser*, she thought with an rueful smile. Perhaps the story hadn't quite turned out how Lara had intended, but at least now people would remember Verity as Todd and Bobby and Martha remembered her: as a beautiful life force, as a mentor and a friend. And soon, hopefully, people would remember her for *that* song too. You couldn't ask for a better epitaph than that.

As she passed a corner booth, Lara caught sight of Natasha King, her head thrown back in laughter as Will Anders leant in with a wicked smile on his face. Natasha reacted by playfully pushing Will's shoulder. No wonder they were happy; Alex had handed the bridge expose back to them now Elise DuBois in the City Department of Works had been served with federal charges. They had a scoop – and they had chemistry, too. It reminded Lara of her relationship with Alex when they had been 'just friends', before they had finally got together. Smiling, Lara walked out onto the terrace. The night air was still warm and full of the scent of white jasmine.

Lara tipped her head back, gazing up at the dark blue sky, the stars indistinct against the wash of LA's streetlights, but they were up there all the same. Could she really live here? She wondered. Back in her student days, devouring books and essays by writers like Joan Didion, Simone de Beauvoir and, yes, Martha Riding, Lara had imagined herself following in their esteemed footsteps, dashing around the globe, mixing with artists, living in Paris or spending a year in Tangier. That was what writers did; they went interesting places, absorbed new ideas, they had adventures. *Perhaps I've become too comfortable*, she thought. What was stopping her? Why not take a leap as Alex had done?

'Hey, beautiful.'

She felt a warm kiss on her neck.

'That better be Alex Ford,' she smiled.

'I'm sorry to say, it is,' he murmured, nuzzling into her bare shoulder.

'Don't be sorry,' said Lara, turning to face him.

'Well, I'm sorry about Stephen Savage, anyway. I had no idea he was going to say any of that.'

Lara put a finger to his lips.

'It's fine,' she said. 'You were right, Alex, when you were talking about the mayor, how there are different ways to win. Tomorrow, everyone will be talking about the Limelight launch; I'd say that was a good result.'

Alex put both hands on her arms.

'No, I'll tell you what a good result is. Your story – however it came out in the end – has changed people's lives. If you hadn't been so curious and tenacious and…'

'…Bloody minded?'

Alex laughed. 'Yes, that too. Because of all that, hundreds of talented young people are getting a brand new creative future.'

'And what about our future, Alex?' she asked. He pulled her closer.

'My future is wherever you are, Lara Stone. I've done what I needed to: I've launched the magazine and turned the Globe's circulation around. My work here is done: I can come home to London.'

Lara shook her head.

'This is home, Alex. For now, at least. And your work here has only just begun.'

'But if you…'

'I'll be right here with you.'

A grin spread across Alex's face.

'Seriously?'

'Seriously. We'll get a house right on the beach -

Martha's already promised to use her contacts to find us something.'

'You'll really stay?'

'Why not?' she smiled. 'If the past few weeks have told me anything, it's that there are stories everywhere – and America is a big place.'

Alex kissed her again. 'So what now?'

Lara took him by the hand and led him back towards the party.

'Come on,' she smiled. 'Let's dance.'

Thanks for reading!

If you enjoyed The Malibu House, why not join Tasmina's VIP Book Club for news on releases, giveaways and events?

www.tasminaperry.com/joinbookclub

Have you read the rest of Tasmina Perry's Lara Stone mystery series?

The Yacht Party

What happens onboard, stays onboard…

Investigative reporter Lara Stone is heartbroken when her friend Sandrine is found dead, but Lara doesn't believe it was an accident. Sandrine's death seems linked to the murder of Jonathon Meyer, a secretive financier famous for hosting glittering networking parties on his Monte Carlo yacht Pandora.

What secrets are hidden onboard Meyer's yacht? What deals were brokered that were worth killing for? And can

Lara get to the truth before she herself becomes just another inconvenient guest at the party?

The Yacht Party takes you from London's high society to Paris, via Monaco and the Caribbean in this glamorous escapist mystery.

The next in the Lara Stone series:

The Last Supper

Murder is on the menu…

Viggo Widlund is the darling of the food world and his remote Swedish restaurant Kluven is the most exclusive place to eat in the world. Only accessible by one road, there is just one communal table for 12 lucky people.

When Investigative reporter Lara Stone snags a reservation, it promises to be a night to remember, but murder is on the menu. Viggo is found dead and everyone spending the weekend at the snowy retreat is a suspect. Can Lara untangle the lies and find the killer before she finds a knife in her own back?

…And the third Lara Stone mystery:

The Ivy

Benedon College, the elite New England university, has a new guest lecturer, investigative journalist Lara Stone.

For Lara, it's an opportunity to get away from it all, to meet some interesting academics and perhaps attend a campus ball or two.

But there is darkness beneath the glittering surface. The previous semester, a beautiful student died in mysterious circumstances and now a professor suspected of having an affair with the young woman has also been found dead.

Lara soon discovers that the tragic pair were hiding secrets, secrets that could expose a scandal. Secrets someone will kill for.

What readers are saying about the Lara Stone series:

'Lara Stone is like Dan Brown's Robert Langdon in high-heels.'

'Miss this sensational read at your peril.'

'I loved the first book featuring Lara and this one didn't disappoint.'

'A book to cancel plans for – I was completely gripped.'

www.tasminaperry.com

www.sunflowerandco.com

Printed in Dunstable, United Kingdom

65256818R00234